THE
GREAT GAME

Also by
Michael Kurland

Featuring Professor Moriarty

The Infernal Device and Others
(includes *The Infernal Device, The Paradol Paradox,*
and *Death by Gaslight*)

THE
GREAT GAME

A PROFESSOR MORIARTY NOVEL

Michael Kurland

ST. MARTIN'S MINOTAUR ≈ NEW YORK

www.minotaurbooks.com

Design by Lorelle Graffeo

Library of Congress Cataloging-in-Publication Data
Kurland, Michael.
    The great game : a Professor Moriarty novel / by Michael
Kurland.—1st ed.
        p. cm.
    ISBN 0-312-20891-X
    1. Moriarty, Professor (Fictitious character)—Fiction.
2. Scientists—Fiction. I. Title.

PS3561.U647 G7 2001
813'.54—dc21
                                                    2001019577

10   9   8   7   6   5   4   3   2

TO LINDA ROBERTSON

For more reasons than I have words to tell

PROLOGUE

. . . there is neither East nor West, Border, nor Breed, nor Birth,
When two strong men stand face to face, though they come from the ends of
earth!

—RUDYARD KIPLING

Mrs. Hudson, the landlady at 221B Baker Street, knocked on the sitting room door of her illustrious tenant. "Mr. Holmes," she called. "There's a gentleman to see you."

There was a scurrying sound from inside, and Sherlock Holmes opened the door a crack and peered through. "What sort of gentleman?"

"Here's the gentleman's card." Mrs. Hudson slid the pasteboard through the crack. Holmes reached for it with his long fingers, pulled it inside, and immediately closed the door.

Mrs. Hudson waited patiently outside the door. She heard Holmes cry, "Professor Moriarty!" through the door, and then again louder, "Professor Moriarty!" in a querulous voice, and then, "How amusing," and then silence. After a moment he called, "Mrs. Hudson?"

"Yes, Mr. Holmes?"

"Are you still there, Mrs. Hudson?"

"Yes, Mr. Holmes."

"Good, good. Show the gentleman up."

Professor James Moriarty was a tall, angular man with a face like a hawk and deep-set, dark eyes that missed little of what passed before them. When Mrs. Hudson told him to go on up, he

1

removed his black frock coat, placed it and his top hat on the coat stand by the door, and stalked up the stairs. The door to Holmes's sitting room was ajar. He looked at it thoughtfully for a moment and then pushed it open. The room inside appeared to be empty. "I'm here, Holmes," he said without attempting to enter.

Moriarty's calling card, crumpled into a ball, was thrown over the door into the hall, and then Holmes appeared from behind the door clad in a red silk dressing gown, a half-smoked cigarette in his left hand and an iron poker in his right. "None of your tricks now, Professor," he jeered. "I'm ready for you!"

Moriarty pursed his lips. "Is this why you sent for me, Holmes?" he asked. "For more of your puerile accusations and infantile behavior? Really! I was in the midst of replying to a letter from an American physicist named Michelson when your telegram arrived, and I put aside the correspondence to rush over here. Michelson has devised a novel way to measure the speed of light waves through the ether, but the ether doesn't seem to want to oblige. He requests my advice—you accuse me of tricks. Clearly I should have stayed at home and finished the letter."

"Of what possible use to anyone can it be to know the speed of light waves through the ether?" Holmes asked.

"The pursuit of knowledge requires no justification," Moriarty said.

"On the contrary," Holmes told him, pulling the door fully open. "The collection of useless facts is destructive of orderly and methodical thinking." He put the cigarette between his lips and inhaled deeply, then exhaled slowly so that the smoke wreathed his face. "I could not understand criminal behavior so well if I did not collect, sort, and analyze the minutia of past crimes and observe new crimes as they occur. If I allowed myself the luxury of studying, say, the flight of butterflies, or the spectra of light emanating from the sun, I might be invited to lecture at the Royal Academy, but I should be hard put to solve even the simplest crimes."

"Indeed?" Moriarty said. "It is my experience that the more one attempts to cram into one's mind, the more it will hold, and the more information one commands, the better the results of one's attempt at deductive reasoning."

Holmes raised one hand in the air as though stopping a cab. "What telegram?" he demanded. Moriarty's hand went to his jacket pocket, and Holmes raised the poker. "Careful, Professor!"

The professor pulled a folded telegram from his pocket and held it out in front of him. Holmes put his cigarette precariously on the edge of a bureau and grabbed for it. Moriarty examined Holmes's face critically. "You haven't shaved in a week, and your pupils are the size of shillings," he said. "You've been indulging in cocaine again, I fancy, judging by the wild gleam in your eyes and the upraised poker. Really, Holmes . . ."

Holmes retreated back into the study and lowered the poker. "I sent you no telegram!" he interrupted. "I would asseverate that you sent it to yourself, I wouldn't put it past you, except that I can see no gain for you in such an action. Someone is diddling us both. Surely the wording of the message, 'Come at once, stop. 221B Baker Street, stop.' should have alerted you to its spurious nature. Why, if for some unimaginable reason, I would send for you, would I not sign my name?"

Moriarty came into the sitting room and glanced around. "I thought perhaps you were saving the four pence. Perhaps the consulting detective business has fallen on hard times."

Holmes chuckled. "My last client was—let us say a member of one of the noblest families in the kingdom—and my fee was considerable. I am about to leave for—a certain country in Europe—to undertake a commission for the government. Have no fears for my financial resources. I take only those cases that interest me these days, and my recompense is generally excellent, save when I remit my fee altogether."

"Glad to hear that, Holmes," Moriarty said, crossing to a bookcase against the far wall and peering at the titles. "Perhaps if you are sufficiently occupied you will leave me alone. It would be a welcome novelty not to find you dogging my footsteps every time I pursue some innocent errand; not to hear your shrill accusations every time a sufficiently notorious crime is committed anywhere in England."

"Oh, in the world, Professor, in the world!" Holmes almost danced over to a high-back chair and dropped into it. "I have too high a regard for your iniquitous abilities to imagine that your activities are confined to this little island."

"Bah!" said Professor Moriarty.

A heavy, solid footfall on the stairs presaged the arrival of Holmes's friend and companion, Dr. Watson, who bustled into the room and threw off his coat, draping it over the arm of a chair. "Afternoon, Holmes," he said. "Sorry I'm late. Afternoon, Professor Moriarty. I see you're here already."

Holmes rose from his chair and pointed a slightly quavering finger at Watson. "You expected him?"

"Professor Moriarty?" Watson nodded and took a seat at the small table that served them for eating meals when it wasn't covered with Holmes's newspaper clippings waiting to be filed. "I sent him a telegram."

"You did what?" Controlling himself with a great effort, Holmes sat back down on the edge of his chair.

Moriarty laughed briefly. "There you have it," he said. "The unexplainable explained."

"Watson, sometimes you—" Holmes paused and took a deep breath. "Watson, old friend, I pride myself on my intellect, but I haven't a clue—not the slightest clue—what could have induced you to send a telegram to"—Holmes waved in Moriarty's general direction rather than saying his name—"and what you thought to gain from it."

"I thought to shock you out of your lethargy and drug-taking, if you must know, Holmes. I thought that perhaps the sight of Professor Moriarty in the flesh might have some effect." Watson turned to Moriarty. "He hasn't left this room for three weeks."

"Seventeen days, Watson," Holmes corrected him. "It was seventeen days ago that I came in after chasing the Hampstead Heath Strangler for two days and nights until he finally drowned himself in the Thames."

"I see," Moriarty told Watson. "And you thought that the very sight of me would send Holmes fleeing down the stairs?"

"No, no, nothing like that," Watson said.

Holmes studied them both for a moment, and then fell back in his chair and chuckled. "Oh, I fancy it was quite like that, Watson. Quite like that."

Watson looked embarrassed. "Well, old man," he said, "perhaps there was some element—I mean, you were going on about the professor and how he was plotting against you. And when you began looking behind the couch and up the chimney to see if he was concealed there—well, old man, I thought I'd better do something. Cocaine is an insidious drug, at the level you're taking it."

"So it is, Watson," Holmes agreed. "I came to the same conclusion. And so I've stopped taking it."

Watson sat on the couch and stared dubiously at his friend. "You have?"

"Indeed. About two hours ago. Now I intend to sleep for as long as nature allows me, and then indulge in a soak, and then prepare for our trip. I shall not touch the needle again until after our forthcoming adventure is over, if then. You have my word."

"Truly, Holmes?"

Holmes shook his head. "I told you, old friend, that I resort to drugs only to relieve the considerable ennui of existence. When I observe that the practice seems to be clouding my judgment, particularly in regard to my old nemesis Professor Moriarty—when I find myself peering under the bureau to see if he is lurking there—then it would seem to be time to stop."

"Wisdom indeed, if a long time coming," Moriarty commented. "You realize now that I am not the villain you have made me out to be?"

"Not at all, Professor," Holmes averred, "I merely realized that you would never fit under the bureau."

Moriarty raised an eyebrow. "You keep accusing me of committing the most heinous crimes, and you seem positively disappointed when you discover you are mistaken, Holmes. I freely admit—in the confines of this room—that some of my activities are not what this straitlaced society would consider proper, even that I have broken the laws of this country on occasion. But I am not the monstrous master criminal you make me out to be."

"If so," Holmes said, shaking a finger in Moriarty's general direction, "it is not for lack of trying."

"Bah!" Moriarty turned to Dr. Watson. "It is not merely the

cocaine," he said, "his brain is addled. Take care of him, Doctor."
He nodded to both of them and strode out of the room and down
the stairs.

Holmes shook his head. "A telegram to Professor Moriarty.
What an idea. Watson, sometimes you amaze me." He stood up. "I
shall sleep now, Watson."

"Good idea, Holmes."

ONE

PLAYING THE GAME

Ah Vienna, city of Dreams!
There's no place like Vienna!
—ROBERT MUSIL,
THE MAN WITHOUT QUALITIES

It was Tuesday the third of March, in the year 1891, the fifty-fourth year in the reign of Victoria Saxe-Coburg, queen of the United Kingdom of Britain and Ireland and empress of India, and the forty-third year in the reign of Franz Josef Habsburg-Lorraine, king of the dual monarchy of Austria and Hungary and emperor of the Austro-Hungarian Empire, that the incidents here recorded might properly be said to have begun. Although, as any reasoning person knows, beginnings are rooted deeply in the past, as endings resound into the future.

The Habsburg rulers traced their ancestry back to the ninth-century Count Werner of Habichtsburg, and their dynasty back to 1273, when Rudolf Habsburg was chosen emperor of Germany. Their dynastic fortunes put the Habsburgs on the throne of the Holy Roman Empire, which for a time covered much of Europe, including Spain and northern Italy. It had been reduced in size for the past century, and no longer claimed to be either holy or Roman; but now, as the Austro-Hungarian Empire, it still embraced Austria, Hungary, Bohemia, Moravia, Slovakia, Slovenia, Bosnia, Rumelia, Herzegovina, Carniola, Galacia, Silesia, Bukowina, Croatia, and bits and pieces of Poland and Rumania. But its size was no longer an indication of either strength or stability, and heirs to ancient dynasties do not necessarily make wise or competent rulers.

With the start of this closing decade of the nineteenth century an almost palpable feeling of imminent great change was in the air. The coming century promised continuing invention and exploration, and a renewed sense of novelty and innovation. These last years of the old century were already being called the *fin de siècle*—the end of the century—as though they were a time apart. There were those, as there are at the end of every century, who thought that it marked the coming end of the world: that a great cataclysm would wipe out the human race and all its works, or that the Christ was destined to reappear and walk among us and save the elect, and leave the rest of us to our predestined horrible fate. The years 1898 and 1903 were two favorite predictions for this event, as well as the change-of-century year itself; although there was considerable disagreement as to whether this would occur in 1900 or 1901.

For many people, particularly in the great cosmopolitan centers of Vienna, Paris, and London, the *fin de siècle* marked not the end of time, but the beginning of everything new. A new and creative spirit was already at work. New thoughts and ideas in fashion, in the arts, and in politics occupied those young enough to look forward to spending their lives in a new century and horrified those firmly entrenched in the age that Victoria had made her own.

Political change was as a tempest upon the land, and a score of political philosophies, some old and reborn, and some new and still only partly formed, fought for dominance in the minds of the intellectuals and the students and the hearts of the petite bourgeoisie and the poor. Some were materialistic, some authoritarian, some socialistic, some pacifistic—and some were nihilistic and violent.

In another time and place he was Charles Dupresque Murray Bredlon Summerdane, the younger son of the Duke of Albermar, with an income in his own right of some thirty thousand pounds a year. For the first decade of his adult life he had drifted, going where the tides and his appetites and interests took him. After Eton he had attended Oxford, the University of Göttingen, and the University of Bologna, and had studied what he felt like studying, coming away with a smattering of knowledge about this and that, and a talent for languages. Then for a while he had returned to his residence in Belgrave Square, taken up his membership in White's, Pitt's, the Diogenes, and other clubs where the men who rule Britain sip their whiskies-and-sodas and complain of the state of the world. He had done, as the rich and titled have felt privileged to do from time immemorial, very little. He had spent money on his own pleasures, but not nearly as much as he could have; his pleasures being restricted to collecting rare books on history and biography, singing and acting (incognito) in the chorus of several of Messrs. Gilbert and Sullivan's operettas, and occasional discreet trips to Paris for reasons of his own. For the last decade he had been on every list, in those places where they make up such lists, as one of the most eligible bachelors in London.

But for now, and for good and sufficient reason, he had put that life aside. He had grown a wide mustache and a small spade beard, and moved into two rooms on the top floor above a draper's shop at No. 62 Reichsratstrasse. They knew him there as Paul Donzhof, a struggling writer of pieces for the *Neue Freie Presse* and other intellectual journals, and a composer of avant-garde orchestral tone poems. "Paul" had occupied these lodgings in Vienna's bohemian Rathaus Quarter for almost a year. Since he arrived he had made many friends among the students and intellectuals, as well as a strange assortment of bohemian poets and playwrights, for he was known to be generous with the allowance of three hundred kronen his father, a Bavarian manufacturer of beer steins, sent him every month.

For the past six months "Paul" had been on intimate terms with a young lady named Giselle Schiff; just how intimate is their concern only. She lived conveniently near, in the apartment one floor below his own. A tall, lissome blonde of twenty-two, Giselle was an artist's model, and she was saving her kronen so that before the artists traded her in for a younger model she could open a store selling toys for small children. Even now when she was not modeling she made dolls with lovely porcelain faces, designing and sewing the filmy clothing for her miniature princesses herself. Paul suspected that "Giselle" was her own creation much as "Paul" was his; an artist's model who produced a French name did more posing than your common garden variety Ursula or Brunhilde. It apparently wasn't necessary to actually speak French, or even have a French accent; Giselle spoke a slightly sibilant, if charmingly lilting, Viennese German, into which she would occasionally toss a delightfully mispronounced French word, particularly when she was discussing either of her two passions: art and food.

Paul spent most days dressed in the casual garb of a bohemian artist, sitting in one or another of the various cafés and beer halls that were sprinkled about the city, surrounded by the notebooks in which he wrote his essays and his music. Each café, each beer hall, catered to a different clientele, and the circles intersected only slightly. Paul's acquaintances of one café did not associate with his friends from another. The Socialists, who squabbled daily at the Café Mozart on Opernstrasse, seldom even passed by the Café Figaro on Neustiftgasse, which the anarchists occupied like an invading army. The Kaiserreich Bierstube on Idarstrasse, where imperial civil servants stared dolefully into a mug or two before heading home, might have been in another world from the Baron Münchhausen Bierhalle around the corner on Prinz Rupert Platz, where the young officers attached to the Imperial General Staff strutted and preened.

On the nights when he did not stay home working, Paul dressed like a gentleman and escorted Giselle to the opera or the theater, or on occasion went alone to one of the clubs of questionable legality and dubious morality at which Austrian gentlemen, accompanied by women who were assuredly not their wives, went in for the more earthly pleasures.

This afternoon Paul was just completing a leisurely lunch at a table by the window in the Café Figaro when a short, hunchbacked man with a large nose, an oversized slouch hat, a dark brown raincoat of the overly-protective sort worn by carriage drivers, and a furtive air came in out of the chill drizzle that had settled over Vienna on Sunday and showed no signs of departing. The man shook himself off, unbuttoned his raincoat, and sidled over to Paul's table. "Good afternoon, Herr Donzhof," he murmured, sliding into the chair across from him.

Paul studied the apparition carefully for a minute. "Feodor— Herr Hessenkopf—is that you?"

"Please!" The man dropped his voice until he could barely be heard at all. "No names! And keep your voice down. They are always listening!"

"You used my name," Paul said mildly. "Why are you got up like Quasimodo? Are you trying for a part in the opera?"

"Opera?" Hessenkopf blinked. "Is there an opera of 'Notre Dame'?"

"Certainly," Paul said. "Why not?"

Hessenkopf thought it over for a moment and then shook his head. "I think you are joking," he said. "I am not for the opera. I am in disguise."

"A hump?"

"Why not a hump? It is one of the first principles of disguise: a disfigurement or abnormality will cause people to look away from you. Number One explained that to us, if you will remember."

"I think he meant an artfully created scar across the face, or something of that sort," Paul suggested.

"I do not know how to create such a scar," Quasimodo said.

"Ah!" Paul said. "That explains it."

"You should not talk. The way you dress—that brown wool pullover, which once surely belonged to a much larger man; that aged and now shapeless army greatcoat; that too-wide brown cap with its too-narrow bill—you can be identified from across the street." Hessenkopf signaled the waiter to bring him a cup of coffee. Paul also made a similar gesture in the waiter's direction.

"Yes," Paul said. "And so?"

Hessenkopf shrugged, afraid he had offended his acquaintance, the source of several unpaid loans. "Nothing—nothing."

"You confuse disguising your person, which you have not done very well, despite the hump, with disguising your intent," Paul told him. "When I sit here in my brown sweater and cap, with my greatcoat—which you neglected to mention is in a particularly notable shade of green—tossed negligently onto the empty chair beside me, people look and think, 'Oh, that's just Herr Donzhof, he's always here drinking coffee and writing in those notebooks of his.' I could be disposing of stolen gems, dealing in counterfeit ten-kronen notes, or plotting to assassinate some royal personage—"

"Hush!" Hessenkopf hissed, looking nervously about.

Paul laughed. "But when they see you, they say to themselves, 'Here's Herr Hessenkopf made up to go into the park and frighten little children. Perhaps we should follow him about and see what he's up to.' "

Hessenkopf leaned forward, his elbows on the table, his chin inches above the sugar bowl. "You are not so wise or so humorous as you believe," he said, his voice barely above a whisper. "Have you not heard the news?"

"You see? This is just what I was talking about," Paul told him. "Sit up and speak in a normal voice, you'll attract less attention. What news?"

Hessenkopf sat up, but he was not happy. He glanced nervously around the room, and seemed unable to speak. In a few seconds he had slid so far down in his chair that his head was barely above the table.

Paul sighed and shook his head. "Never mind," he said. "What news?"

"We almost succeeded—" Hessenkopf stopped in midsentence and took two deep breaths. "A great tragedy has been narrowly averted," he began again. He nodded, pleased with himself at this new construction. He actually sat up slightly in his chair. "A great tragedy has been narrowly averted," he repeated. "Shortly before noon, it was. Archduke Franz Willem and Count Tisza had just left the Parliament together in a carriage with six—I think it was six—outriders from the Household Cavalry, when—somebody—threw a bomb at the carriage right there across from the Reichsrat. The bomb blew the right rear wheel off of the carriage, and the horses bolted. The postilion was thrown; I think he was killed. It took the coachman three blocks to stop the carriage, and I don't know how he managed it at all; the horses were truly and thoroughly startled and were leaving the area at a full gallop. As it turned out, neither the archduke nor the count were injured. The fool was too far away when he threw the bomb to place it properly."

"And what happened to the bomb-throwing fool?"

"The luck of the inept. Several of the cavalry guard galloped toward him, and the idiot was too frozen with fear to move. But someone standing next to him—some complete innocent—panicked and ran. So naturally the guard chased the other man down and took him away."

"You were there, I take it?"

"I was a distant but well-placed observer." Hessenkopf dropped his voice. "We may have missed our target, but the bomb will serve as yet another warning to the oppressors—and perhaps a wake-up to the oppressed."

"Yes," Paul said. "But we keep waking them up and waking them up, and still they are asleep. Perhaps the throwing of bombs and the shooting of guns is no more effective than the chirping of a cuckoo clock. Perhaps instead of endangering ourselves and murdering hapless postilions we should purchase cuckoo clocks and distribute them among the working classes. With little homilies tied to their little wooden beaks. 'Arise ye prisoners of class exploitation! Coo-coo! Coo-coo!' "

Hessenkopf stared at Paul. "Sometimes I wonder about you, Herr Donzhof," he said. "You are so always humorous. You take things so always lightly. Why, if the unconcern you manifest is your true state of feeling, are you indeed one of us?"

Paul slapped his thigh. "You've caught me!" he exclaimed. "I confess. I am actually Agent G of the *Kundschafts Stelle*. We secret police can always be spotted by our tendency to break out into raucous laughter at inappropriate moments."

"No, not that. You are not a police agent. But something . . ."

"Just what do you think I am, other than myself?" Paul inquired.

"I do not like to seem to accuse you of anything, Herr Donzhof," Quasimodo said, but there was something about the way he said it that suggested that he would have liked to have done just that. "It is probably nothing more than my imagination, seeing secret policemen and *agents provocateur* behind every door. Suspecting everybody. It is my nature."

The conversation paused while the waiter brought the coffees to the table. "Good afternoon, Herr Hessenkopf," the waiter said blandly, putting the cups and coffee presses down.

Paul broke out laughing as the waiter left. "You see," he said. "So much for the Quasimodo look."

"The waiter is my cousin," Hessenkopf said. "What I came over to tell you— there is to be a meeting tomorrow night."

"Ah!" Paul said. "Where?"

"The Werfel place."

"Ah! The temple of chocolate. The smell alone makes it worthwhile to attend."

"Ten o'clock. Sharp!"

"I shall be there."

Hessenkopf nodded and rose, taking his coffee and his hump off to a different table to share the joy of his existence with another soul.

After a time Paul got up, stuffed his notebooks into a well-worn leather briefcase, slid into his green greatcoat, tugged his cap firmly over his eyes, and left the Café Figaro. Moving at an unhurried pace, he headed off down the street.

A few moments later two men, one tall and lean with a thin, hawklike nose and the other solid, almost portly, with something of the bulldog about his appearance, rose from a back table and also left the café. When they reached the street the tall one murmured in English, "Wait in that shop doorway, Watson; see if you can follow our humpbacked friend when he leaves. I'll go after this one."

"As you say, Holmes," his companion replied. "Button your top buttons, please, and wrap that scarf securely about your neck. No point in getting a chill from this damn drizzle."

Holmes clapped his friend on the back. "Good old Watson," he said, tossing the knitted wool scarf around his neck. And with that he strode off in the direction that Paul had headed when he left.

As Paul moved away from the Café Figaro he began to walk faster. Shortly he was moving through the streets with the long stride of someone accustomed to walking great distances for pleasure. His path took him along Halzstrasse, and then through a series of narrow streets leading progressively deeper into the ancient Petruskirche District, a part of Vienna that the ordinary tourist never gets to see. He turned onto Sieglindstrasse, now well into an area where decent, law-abiding citizens would prefer not to meet anyone they knew.

There were women in various stages of dishabille sitting in many of the ground floor and first floor windows along the street, showing various parts of their bodies to interested passers-by. Many of them appeared to be girls in their teens. Men in black knit sweaters and black caps lounged in the doorways, eager to dash out into the rain and discuss the charms and prices of the merchandise or to offer other commodities to any potential customer. There was a time when the *filles de joie* whistled to attract their clientele, and the ponces accosted pedestrians to encourage them, but the police frowned on whistling and actively discouraged accosting, so the game went on in silence these days. The area was not particularly dangerous—at least not during daylight—the police were too efficient for that. But it was unsavory, and questions might be asked as to what commodity or service you were attempting to purchase in an area where women were only the most visible of the illicit attractions.

Paul turned onto Badengasse, a narrow cobblestone street, innocent of sidewalks, that had an almost timeless quality of decay and neglect. The two-story buildings with narrow storefronts that lined the street had looked ancient and decrepit when Vienna was first besieged by the Turks in 1529; they looked the same as Paul walked down the street now, and so they would look a century hence. The street ended at a fenced-off cement works where craftsmen mass-produced angels, nymphs, woodland creatures, and busts of famous men for the gardens of the bourgeoisie.

Paul paused at the door of a shop three houses from the street's end and looked around. If he noticed the tall man who had paused to tie his shoe at the entrance to the street, he gave no sign. The small, barred window to the right of the shop door displayed a teapot that might have been silver, a sackbut that was assuredly brass, and a violin case that might or might not contain a violin. Three brass balls no larger than olives set into the masonry above the window served as a device for the shop. A small sign tacked to the side of the door read: LEVI DAVOUD—MONEY LOANED ON OBJECTS OF WORTH.

Paul opened the shop door. The interior was lit by one oil lamp which swung from the ceiling. A counter with a barred window separated the clients of the establishment from the proprietor—or, in this case the proprietor's assistant: a small, swarthy lad with alert eyes who wore a dark brown caftan and looked as though he was attempting to grow a beard.

"Good afternoon, Joseph," Paul said cheerily, stamping his feet on the outer sill to dislodge the mud caked to his shoes before entering the shop and closing the door behind him. "Is the old man in?"

"It's hard to say, Herr Donzhof," the lad replied. "Sometimes he is, and sometimes he isn't. I'll go see."

Joseph retreated into the back of the shop leaving Paul to ponder over the array of items on the shelves behind the counter. Many were wrapped in brown paper and tied with string; anonymous bundles lying dormant, awaiting the return of their owners to redeem them and bring them back to life. But some were not wrapped, or were identifiable by their shape through the wrapping. Paul made out a set of carpenter's tools in a wooden box, a dressmaker's dummy, an artificial leg, a pair of lady's shoes with silver buckles, several table lamps, a brace of walking sticks, and an assortment of hats and caps. There were also, in the corner, a harp and a tuba.

"Ah, Herr Donzhof," the proprietor said, appearing in the back doorway and advancing toward the counter. Levi Davoud was a short, pear-shaped, elderly man with eyes deeply set in his round, wrinkled face, and a bulbous nose that seemed to ride on top of his carefully-trimmed white beard. Paul was accustomed to seeing the elderly moneylender in the shapeless gray housecoat he usually wore around the shop, but today he was dressed for the street, and a much finer street than the one outside his door. A gray silk four-in-hand scarf was tied precisely around his white wing collar and tucked neatly into a black Chesterfield overcoat, and he was carrying a pair of black kid gloves, an ebony cane, and a black silk top hat.

"Good afternoon, Herr Davoud," Paul said. "I commend you on a degree of elegance that I imagine is seldom seen within the sound of the Petruskirche bells. I assume that Petruskirche has bells, although come to think of it, I don't remember ever hearing them. Are you coming or going?"

"Oh, returning, I assure you, returning. I have just been about the tiresome business of having yet another young rapscallion twig of the nobility explain to me why he was willing to allow me to loan him a considerable sum of money." Davoud set the gloves, cane, and hat down and took his coat off; carefully fitting it onto a hanger, pulling out its shoulders and smoothing down the velvet collar before hanging it out of sight behind the back doorway. "Come," he said, opening the door in the counter, "come in the back and have with me a cup of black tea."

"Just the thing, Herr Davoud," Paul said, and followed the shopkeeper into a small room in the back. The lighting in this room came from an inverted V-shaped skylight with twelve panes of glass and a web of iron bars beneath to make sure nothing but the light came through.

"They were stolen," Davoud commented, settling into one of a pair of overstuffed armchairs. "Take off your coat and hat and hang them over there. Joseph, my boy, put the kettle on."

Paul did as he had been bidden and dropped into the other chair. "What was stolen?"

"The church bells. Sometime in the sixteenth century, I believe, they were stolen. It is my opinion that the church itself stole them, as the authorities were planning to take them and melt them down for cannon. The authorities at that moment had a great need for cannon. The Turkish army, I believe, was at the gates and behaving in an unfriendly manner."

"Ah!" Paul said.

The two sat in comfortable silence while Davoud busied himself filling and lighting a long, curved clay pipe. With a gesture he offered Paul some tobacco from an ornately carved wooden box, and Paul took a well-chewed brown pipe from his jacket pocket and filled it with the strong latakia mixture. "Thank you," he said. "Cigarettes for action, but a pipe for reflection."

"That's what I say myself," the old man replied.

"I know." Paul smiled. "I was quoting you."

"Ah!" The two men were puffing away contentedly when, a couple of minutes later, Joseph wheeled a tea tray to the space between the two chairs and filled two cups from a silver urn.

Davoud took the clay pipe from his mouth and put it aside. "I saw a woman—a lady, actually—smoking a cigarette earlier today," he said, taking his cup in both hands and breathing in the aroma of the fresh-brewed tea.

Paul looked at him inquiringly.

He nodded. "It was at the Hotel Metropol, where I went to meet the young nobleman who wished to permit me to advance him five thousand kronen. She sat in the lobby. A dainty young thing with her hair up in a bun—so—and a trim black lace bonnet with a satin ribbon and a black velvet half-cape over a hunter-green gown. Elegant, she was. And while I waited for the youth to appear, she lit one of those long Balkan cigarettes and puffed away at it."

"You have a better eye for women's clothing than most men," Paul commented.

"My wife, God rest her soul, was a dressmaker," Davoud explained.

"So, what happened?"

"The young branch of a noble bush finally showed up—"

"With the lady who smoked," Paul interrupted.

"Well, in the end nothing," Davoud said. "The manager and the desk clerk and a couple of other hotel employees gathered in a clutch to discuss the matter in horrified tones, but I heard the name 'Princess Someone-or-Other' mentioned a couple of times, which I gathered referred to the young lady in question, and in the end it was evidently decided that royalty trumps manners, so they retreated. Eventually she put the cigarette out. Now tell me, Herr Donzhof, what can I do for you today?"

"A cup of tea," Paul said, "a little conversation."

"And perhaps a discreet name or two from my list of distinguished clients?"

"If any new ones have come your way . . ."

Davoud pointed a long, arthritic finger across the tea tray at Paul. "I wonder about you," he said.

"I thought you might," Paul said.

"You are not what you seem."

"You are the second person to tell me that today," Paul said. "Is my nose growing longer? Is there no hope that I'll become a real boy?"

Davoud shrugged a tiny shrug. "I am not suggesting that you lie, that would be pointless. Of course you lie. We all lie. Complete honesty would quickly become unbearable. What you do is"—he searched for a word—"more interesting. You allow those you deal with to assume things about you—unspoken things—that they believe they have discovered on their own. But these things, I believe, are not so."

Paul leaned back in his chair, his eyes wide. "Really?" he drawled. "What sort of things?"

Davoud patted the air with his hand in a calming gesture. "Do not be alarmed. I have no desire to give you away. Besides, I would have no idea to whom to give you or what they would want with you. I have not discovered who you are, merely who you are not."

"Do go on!"

Davoud laced his hands together over his belly and rested his chin on his thumbs. "What I know about you is little," he said contemplatively. "You are a good conversationalist, highly intelligent, well-educated, *gemütlich*, and generally agreeable."

"How can I deny any of it?" Paul asked, smiling.

"You are also of the upper class, a fact which you do your best to disguise, but which comes through in your air of natural superiority and your complete ease in dealing with servants. I have noticed that only born aristocrats treat servants completely naturally; either as equals, as children, or as furniture according to their nature. The middle classes treat their servants with arrogance or suspicion." He peered at Paul, who remained silent.

"Also your German, while excellent, is not native. There is something indefinably foreign that lingers about it. Most people would not notice, I grant you, but the accent is nonetheless there."

"I went to school in Italy and England," Paul offered.

"Perhaps. Now let us look at our—what shall I say?—business relationship. You approached me last May—"

"Was it that long ago?"

"I keep a diary. May twelfth of last year it was. You were interested in the names of my clients—"

"The politically or socially important, I believe I said."

"You did. And military officers of staff rank and above."

"Indeed."

"And you declined to tell me what you intended to do with the information, but you did assure me that my name would never be disclosed."

"Just so."

"I thought you were some sort of high-class criminal."

"Is that so? You never told me."

"It would have been impolite."

"Ah! But what would I—if I were a crook—want with the names of people who need your services? They would obviously have little to steal, having pledged everything of value to you."

"But if you were a clever crook, and even at the time I could see you were clever, you might wish to use some distressed member of upper-class society as entrée into the houses of the rich. Once there—"

"How clever of me," Paul commented.

"But you didn't," Davoud continued.

"Ah!"

"Or then again you might offer to advance large sums of money to some of these wastrels against their future inheritance. And then, after a discreet length of time, a carefully arranged fatal accident to the relative with the money would bring a nice profit to you."

"Why Herr Davoud, you have a criminal mind!"

"I do, I confess it. I came up with a total of, I believe it was, twelve different schemes that you might have been engaged in. And I find that, as far as I can tell, you are pursuing none of them." Davoud wiggled an accusatory finger at Paul. "And you led me to believe, in oh-so-subtle ways, that you, also, have the mind of a criminal."

"A criminal?"

"I discovered that you were letting it be known among certain groups of our, ah, more adventurous citizens, that you were in actuality an agent of a British master criminal known as Professor Moriarty."

"I never made that claim," Paul protested. "Someone—I think it was a jeweler named Berkmann—made that assumption, and I admit that I did not disabuse him of the notion."

"A master jewel thief named Berkmann, yes. The professor Moriarty had provided him with assistance once or twice, and he is

convinced that the professor has a vast criminal network throughout Europe."

"Well I assure you that I never heard of this Professor Moriarty
until Berkmann mentioned him. But then, well, if being his agent
would simplify my life, then I would become his agent."

"So again you found the truth, whatever that might be, less
than useful. Is that so?"

Paul leaned back in his chair and sipped his tea. "Let us go over
this in a reasonable manner," he said. "I somehow caused you to
believe that I was a criminal. And now you have concluded that I'm
not. And you are shocked to discover that I'm an honest man."

"I would be at least mildly surprised to discover that anyone
was a completely honest man," Davoud said. "It's merely that the
manner of your dishonesty eludes me at the moment." He moved
his hand in a patting motion, as though he were soothing an invisible cat. "I mean nothing disrespectful."

"How do you know that I am not engaged in any of your imaginary nefarious schemes?" Paul asked.

"I keep a close eye on several of my, ah, clients," Davoud said.
"With one gentleman the eye is that of his valet, and one cannot get
much closer than that. Had you been so engaged, I would have
heard."

"Ah!" Paul said. "Tell me, if you feared that I was some sort of
master criminal, why did you supply me with the names? Surely not
for the few kronen that I offered?"

Davoud shrugged. "Frankly, I was interested to discover what
you planned to do. You have so far managed to scrape an acquaintance with several of the 'names,' but with little result that I can
see. You spoke to Graf von Pinow at the opera bar—"

"A performance of *Nabucco*," Paul remembered. "With the
libretto translated into German. Verdi's music should not be sung
in German. It turns the most romantic of melodies into the barking
of large dogs."

"And Colonel Kretl, you sat across from him at baccarat—"

"Oh, yes. At the Club Montmartre. Why the Viennese think
that vice must have a French name is beyond me. German vice is
perfectly acceptable. It's more orderly and well-behaved."

"So with each of these gentlemen you have a meeting, two

meetings, casual—nothing of any value discussed, I believe. And then, that's it. Nothing! So of what use to you is any of this?"

Paul considered for a moment, and then he drank some tea and considered some more. "Is it of great interest to you," he asked Davoud, "what happens to your clients?"

"Pah!" Davoud grimaced. "These people, these aristocrats, these men gentled by noble birth; they would just as soon walk over you as walk around you. At least the ones that I deal with are of that sort, although I am aware that there are others—yourself, for example, if I am right about your upbringing. These young highly born gentlemen can hardly hide their dislike of me, even when they're trying to borrow money. They smile and nod and it's, 'Good evening, Herr Davoud, how good of you to come by.' And then I leave and it's, 'That fat old Jew will have his pound of flesh. His kind loves nothing but money!' As though it were I who was pledging ancient family heirlooms to pay gambling debts!"

"You're not fat," Paul said.

"Strangely enough, neither am I a Hebrew," Davoud told him. "They all assume that because I'm a moneylender, I must be Jewish."

"And you're not?"

"Look at me. Am I wearing a skull cap?"

"Sometimes you wear a little knitted cap."

"It keeps my head warm. It covers a spot where my hair, for some unaccountable reason, seems to be getting thin. But I do not wear it all the time. A Jew, I believe, must keep his head covered all the time."

"That is so," Paul agreed.

"Actually my family comes from eastern Persia," Davoud told Paul. "I am a Persian by heritage and a Zoroastrian by religion." He refilled Paul's tea cup and then his own. "Not that I am a particularly religious man. I do not, if it comes to that, care what they call me, but their arrogance and hypocrisy does not endear them to me."

" 'I count religion but a childish toy,' " Paul quoted, " 'And hold there is no sin but ignorance.' "

Davoud thought it over for a second. "Yes," he agreed. "That's very good."

"Christopher Marlowe said it first," Paul said. "An English playwright."

Davoud nodded. "I know of him," he said.

"You wish to know what use I'm making of the names you pass on to me?" Paul asked. "I arrange to make the acquaintance of some of them. In return for supplying them with sums of money, I attempt to induce them to supply me with what I am most interested in—information."

"Ah!" Davoud said. "Information. I see."

"Do you disapprove?"

He thought it over. "Not necessarily. How do you go about doing this? One can't just walk up to a stranger and say, 'I understand you need money. Tell me a secret.' "

"Not quite so, ah, bold," Paul said. "I might approach my subject at the opera, or at the racetrack and talk to him briefly about this and that. And then I will get up and say, 'My patron understands that you are in need. Please don't be insulted, but he asked me to give you this.' And then I will hand him an envelope and walk away."

"And in the envelope?"

"A sum of money, the amount depending on who the person is and what his needs are. It is a delicate decision; too small a sum might insult the subject, too great a sum might frighten him."

"Your patron?"

Paul smiled. "I am too modest to take the credit for myself. Besides, having an invisible patron adds an air of mystery."

"Aren't you afraid that your, um, subject will throw the money in your face or, perhaps, call the police?"

"That's why I rapidly walk away. I don't want to be standing there smirking at them when they open the envelope. I don't want to have to answer any questions, and I don't want the subject to have to make an instant decision. Let him have time to think it over, to feel the weight of the money in his wallet."

Davoud slowly and methodically cracked the knuckles of his right hand with his left, while staring into his cup of tea. "Perhaps we should not discuss this any further," he concluded.

"Perhaps not," Paul agreed.

"There are some things better left unsaid."

"That is so."

Davoud shifted his gaze to Paul's face. "If you require any assistance in the future, you have but to ask," he said. "But try not to be too specific."

DOORWAY TO DEATH

Our revels now are ended . . .
—WILLIAM SHAKESPEARE

A blanket of fog had settled over London on Monday the ninth of March and seemed reluctant to leave. By Wednesday morning it had spread its tendrils into every cranny of the great city. It thickened through the course of the dank, chill day until now, in early evening, objects faded into invisibility at any greater distance than an outstretched arm. Pedestrians felt their way along the streets, finding familiar fence railings and building doorways to guide them. Carriage drivers depended on their horses' senses to take them along familiar routes. And the horses, being cautious beasts, would not venture into the unfamiliar. The lamp lighters had to climb two steps up the lamp poles and peer at the lights through the faceted glass to assure themselves that the gas mantles had lit and were burning.

A short, thin, angular man made his way slowly, cautiously, almost delicately along the east side of Russell Square. Despite the hour—it was barely 5:00 P.M.—the man wore a black tailcoat over an overly starched white shirt with a stiff collar surrounded by a black bow tie, and he clutched a top hat in his left hand as he walked. His dress suit, although not yet threadbare, showed signs of wear, and gave an impression of necessity rather than of elegance; as though the garb were a professional requisite. His appearance was not dignified enough to be a butler or a waiter, but he might perhaps have

25

been a teacher at a boy's school where such dress was still common. Not in England, of course; there was something definitely un-English about the man. Perhaps it was the lines of uncertainty and repression that shaped his face and posture; perhaps the vaguely incorrect style of the garment: the lapels a trifle too narrow, the bow tie a trifle too wide, the hat a trifle too short and its brim a trifle too thick.

Halfway down the street the thin man reached the front steps of 64 Russell Square and, after peering closely at the brass address plate, ascended the steps and pulled at the bell pull. After a few moments the door swung open and a tall, solid man filled the doorway. Although he was attired in the impeccable garb of the proper English butler, there was, in the bulk of the man's muscles and the twist of his nose, a suggestion that he had perhaps once had a different profession. After looking his visitor carefully up and down for a moment, he said, "Sir? Can I help you?" in a deep, rasping voice that made the words as much a challenge as a question.

The thin man nodded and pursed his thin lips. "Good day," he said, essaying a smile; but it was a weak sort of smile, as though he were out of practice. "I believe that this would be the residence of Herr Professor James Moriarty. Am I in that assumption correct?"

"You are," the butler agreed.

"Good, good," the thin man said, nodding some more. "I have come a long way to speak with the Herr Professor. He is, I trust, in?" He reached into his waistcoat pocket and extended a calling card to the butler.

"One moment, sir," the butler said, taking the card between two white-gloved fingers. "I shall enquire."

The thin man raised an explanatory finger. "Tell the professor that it is in regard to one of his agents in Vienna. The young man is in danger. Great danger."

"Yes, sir. One moment, sir." The butler closed the door gently but firmly in the thin man's face. It would have been more polite to invite the caller in, to have him wait in a sitting room. But there were those who might wish to see Professor Moriarty who would not be permitted past the front door without a constant escort, and others who would not, under any conditions, be permitted past the front door.

Professor James Moriarty, Ph.D., F.R.A.S., sat at the large oak desk in his ground floor office, the two front windows closed and curtains drawn to keep out the fog. A coal fire burning in the small fireplace across the room kept away the damp and chill of the day. The professor's attention was focused on the winter issue of *Die Zeitschrift für Fortgeschrittene Theoretische Astrophysik*. As the clock on the wall softly chimed four times, Mr. Maws, the onetime bare-knuckle heavyweight champion of Kent now serving as the professor's butler and gatekeeper, entered and stood silently by the desk, waiting for the professor to look up. It was a few moments before Moriarty inserted a paper slip at the page and closed the journal. He removed his pince-nez glasses and turned his gaze to the bust of Galileo on the cabinet to his right. "Those German theorists," he said. "They're infatuated with causation and yet they pay so little attention to materiality. One would think they would have some interest in what *is* before hounding off on a hunt for where it came from."

"Yes, Professor," Mr. Maws responded. "Someone to see you." He held out the thin man's calling card.

Taking the card by the edge, Moriarty replaced his pince-nez glasses and peered down at it as though it were an interesting, but as yet unclassified, insect. It read:

KARL FRIEDRICH MARIE STASSENKOPP, LITT. D.

Moriarty rubbed the card between his fingers. "Foreign card stock," he said. "Probably French or Hungarian."

"Yes, sir, quite possibly. The gentleman said to tell you that it was in regard to one of your agents in Vienna. That he is in danger."

"Really? How curious." Moriarty looked up at Mr. Maws. "What does the gentleman look like?"

Mr. Maws flexed his thumbs thoughtfully. "A foreigner. Not a toff. Straight enough, I'd say. He looks as if he doesn't enjoy eating—or much else, if I'm any judge," he appraised.

"Ah!" Moriarty said. "An aesthete or a worrier? Well, we'll see. Show the gentleman in."

Mr. Maws nodded and left the room. Seconds later he returned.

"The gent ain't worrying anymore," he announced in a carefully impassive voice. "He's dead!"

Moriarty raised an eyebrow. "Well!" he said. He rounded his desk and strode into the hall. Karl Friedrich Marie Stassenkopp, Litt. D. was lying on his back inside the entranceway, his feet bent to one side, his eyes staring sightlessly upward at the gaslight in the hall. He looked surprised. A pool of blood was growing under his shoulders, and a smeared line of blood led out the closed front door.

"I see you brought him inside," Moriarty said, indicating the bloody trail.

"I pulled him inside so I could close the door," Mr. Maws explained. "I didn't want people noticing the poor gentleman until you decided what to do. Besides, I didn't think you'd be wanting to stand in the doorway with whoever killed him still out there."

"Ah! Sound logic." Moriarty felt for a pulse in the man's neck and bent over, his head next to the man's face, to listen for sounds of breathing. After a few seconds he raised his head. "You're right," he said. "Dead. Now, as to what caused his sudden demise—" He gingerly rolled the man over.

Two inches below Karl Friedrich's shoulder blades, to the left of the spine, a thick, black-feathered shaft could be made out protruding slightly from the bloody hole it had made entering the body. The fabric of the suit jacket had been twisted and pulled into the wound along with the projectile.

"Well I'm damned!" Mr. Maws exclaimed. "A bleedin' arrow!"

Moriarty carefully loosened the cloth around the shaft and examined the wound. "Actually it's a crossbow bolt," he told Mr. Maws. "Practically silent, and very deadly. It must have pierced the heart, killing him instantly. Hence the comparatively limited loss of blood." He laid the body down and stood up. "Interesting," he said.

THE FAT MAN

Adventures are to the adventurous
—Benjamin Disraeli

The fat man and his three companions boarded the *Rete Mediter-ranea* first-class carriage at the Monza station. The train had just braked to a stop with a great letting of steam from the aging engine, when Benjamin Barnett caught a glimpse of them through his compartment window.

The fat man was perched precariously on an upended black portmanteau from which he gesticulated to the others. He wore a wide-brimmed gray felt hat and a white suit, a red handkerchief flopped with bohemian abandon from his jacket pocket. His companions, who were paying close attention to his every word and gesture, were a small, round-faced clergyman with thick, circular-lensed eyeglasses, carrying a straw suitcase; a dark youth with big feet and dull eyes, wearing a mud-yellow and brown checked suit at least one size too small for his lanky frame; and a woman of inde-terminate age and odd, birdlike movements, clothed in black from the top of her veil to the soles of her patent-leather high-button shoes. Her only impediment was a covered birdcage about the size of a breadbox.

Barnett, a stocky, brown-haired expatriate American in his late thirties, watched the quartet with interest. They seemed to him a strangely assorted group. "Italy once again shows us her diversity," he told his wife, who was sitting across from him. "What do you make of those four?"

Cecily Barnett looked up from the red-backed Baedeker guidebook of Northern Italy and peered out the window just as the *treni diretti* came to a shuddering stop. She was a slender, blond, self-contained, gently beautiful woman some five years younger than her husband. Her eyes, the lines of her mouth, and the way she bore herself told of determination and, for those who could read the most subtle indications, of an unresolved sadness that she carried with her.

"Actually they are quite interesting," she said, after examining the group for a minute as they gathered their baggage and prepared to board the train. "The stout gentleman would seem to be an artist of some sort. One of those gay bohemians currently infesting Paris and Vienna. Or, at least, so he would have the world think. The youth is a sporting type of little intellect. The priest—the clerical raiment hides many possibilities. The woman is something of an enigma. She is dressed like a widow, but has no wedding ring on her finger. She carries a birdcage that is so devoid of independent motion that one suspects that it does not contain a bird."

"You have a consummate eye for detail," Barnett said. "Why do you say 'He would have us think so?' You have begun to suspect everyone you see of being other than he seems."

Cecily turned to look at him, and he realized he had said the wrong thing. "Not everyone," she replied sharply. She folded her hands neatly in her lap and stared straight ahead; a look that Barnett knew masked extreme annoyance. "And it's not a question of suspicion. I am merely relating my observations and deductions. If you don't want my opinion, why do you ask me?"

"I was merely making conversation," Barnett replied, trying not to sound defensive. "And I do value your opinion. I'm so sorry if you feel otherwise. You are an extremely perceptive person. Even Professor Moriarty has said so. But I thought I was pointing out some interesting native fauna, not another mystery. I admit I think you've been overwrought lately." He reached out to pat her hand, but she drew it back sharply into the folds of her green traveling-cloak.

"I believe, as I told you, that we've been watched since we left

London," Cecily said coldly. Whether the studied lack of emotion in her voice masked anger or fear, or both, Barnett couldn't tell. "This is the result of my observations and deductions, which you usually are willing to credit with being fairly accurate. I am no Professor Moriarty, perhaps, but I do seem to have the knack for that sort of thing. The professor himself, you will remember, has valued my opinion on occasion. But just because you can't think of any reason why anyone should be watching us, you give no credence to what I say and think that, because I have not been well of late, I'm either incompetent or insane. That would certainly tend to make one overwrought."

"I don't think you're insane," Barnett protested. "I merely think that, in this instance, you're mistaken."

"You wouldn't think so if I were a man," Cecily said, and turned pointedly back to her book.

That, Barnett thought, was an unfair remark. He repressed the urge to call it "female logic," since he had a feeling that would do more harm than good, and he didn't want to start any more of a fight than they were already in. There is a time for discussion and a time for letting it lie, he thought, leaning back in his seat. He had the virtuous feeling of one who knows he is in the right, but allows another the last word.

Barnett had tried in various ways to check on the people Cecily believed were watching them, but it's hard to tell whether someone on the same train or staying at the same hotel is really there just to keep watch on you. None of Cecily's objects of suspicion skulked about peering at them from behind lampposts. And it was an unlikely series of people—an old man with piercing blue eyes at the Majestic in Paris; a little, bulldog-faced man on the train to Rome; a handsome, aristocratic-looking woman who struck up a conversation with Barnett at the Hotel Excelsior in Rome—that Cecily suspected of being in league to keep an eye on the Barnett family. Barnett admitted to himself that he would have found it easier to believe if he could think of any reason why anyone would find them interesting enough to want to follow them about.

The *Capostazione*, the master of this Italian railway station, bedecked in a uniform that would not look out of place on the leader of a circus orchestra, appeared on the platform to give the departure signal, and the train heaved itself back into motion. As it gathered speed, the fat man and his companions tramped down the corridor and distributed themselves among the nearly empty first-class compartments. Barnett saw the fat man pass by and peer through the glass in the compartment door at them; he was closely followed by the woman in black. Judging by the sounds, they settled in the next two compartments. The clergyman and the youth passed not at all; they must have chosen earlier compartments.

That, Barnett reflected, was odd. They had certainly known each other on the platform, and here they were settling in different compartments. He was about to mention it to Cecily, but he decided that, in her present mood, she would think he was humoring her.

It was now Tuesday the tenth of March, 1891. Benjamin and Cecily Barnett were indulging in an off-season tour of Europe that had already lasted for six weeks and would probably last for as many more. Cecily was recuperating from a late-term miscarriage, her second in two years, which had debilitated her mentally and physically. Their only companion, a midget-of-all-work named "Mummer" Tolliver, was ahead of them with the bulk of their baggage, supervising its installation in the *pensione* on Lake Como that was their next destination.

This long overdue vacation was the first either of them had taken that was not combined with a business trip of some sort. Even their two-week honeymoon in Paris had been used to set up a French bureau for the American News Service, Barnett's cable news bureau based in London, which supplied European news to American newspapers. Cecily Barnett had once worked for her husband, but she was now the editor of *Hogbine's Illustrated Weekly*, one of the most successful magazines of the Hogbine group.

"I am assured by the conductor," Barnett said after a couple of minutes' silence, "that the train's *carrozza ristorante* will be opened for dinner after the train leaves Monza. Would you care to join me?" Barnett used the Italian phrase for "dining car" in a self-conscious attempt to end his spat with Cecily; she was always amused by the way he pronounced any foreign words. But sometimes the best-laid plans do not work.

"If you're not afraid I'll make a scene," Cecily said. "Perhaps waving my arms about and accusing the conductor of spying on us. I wouldn't want to make a scene."

Barnett sighed. "I'll trust to your discretion," he said.

They went back to the *carrozza ristorante* to eat thin slices of pounded veal and green peppers, thick slices of crusty bread, and a massive salad with olives and anchovies, and drink a fruity red wine. The trains of the *Rete Mediterranea* were in a period of genteel decay, with neglected twenty-year-old cars pulled by patched-together twenty-year-old engines. A trip that might take five hours on a rapid train elsewhere in Europe could take up to twenty hours on the *treni diretti*. Or thrice that, if it was unfortunate enough to break down. Traveling in Italy, even first class, was an adventure. But the food was good.

The train was entering that part of northern Italy between Lakes Como and Lecco called the *Brianza*, and the view out the dining room window was of terraced hillsides covered with naked grapevines ready to begin their summer's growth. In the distance were a scattering of cottages, sporadic freshly plowed plots of brown earth, and patches of somber woods. An occasional walled villa with its complex of outbuildings would suddenly spring into sight and then disappear into the mist.

The fat man trotted up from the rear of the train and entered the dining car almost immediately after Benjamin and Cecily sat down. He lumbered by them, selecting a table three down and across the aisle. Barnett watched with amusement as he gingerly pushed and prodded at the wooden chair seat before lowering his bulk onto it and intently studying the bill-of-fare. About ten minutes or so later the dark adolescent also appeared from the aft end of the train, and, after a few whispered words with the fat man, crossed the dining car and exited the front.

"Curious," Cecily said. "Two of your four friends seem to have been holding a convention in the rear of the train."

"Perhaps they have acquaintances among the third-class passengers," Barnett suggested. "Or perhaps they were seeing to their baggage. The baggage car is at the rear."

"Perhaps," Cecily agreed, coldly.

"Listen, Dove, I don't want to fight with you. Honestly I don't," Barnett said, dropping his voice to a whisper. "But you surely wouldn't want me to say I agree with you when I don't. Would you?"

"If you knew how many times I had done just that for you," Cecily told him, "you would hesitate to ask. It seems that there is one law for the Medes, and another for the Persians." She pushed her plate of veal aside and stood up. "I am no longer hungry. I will meet you back in our compartment."

Barnett also stood, out of automatic politeness to his angry wife. There are times when anything you can do is wrong, and this, Barnett perceived, was one of them. Whether he exhorted Cecily to stay, returned with her to the compartment, or let her go by herself, she would not be pleased.

The cursed unreasonableness of women! Here he was, a reasonable man, behaving in a reasonable manner, being put constantly, and unfairly, in the wrong by his wife, who was usually the most rational, sensible of God's creatures. It was infuriating!

"I must apologize for this interruption." An oily, slightly shrill voice sounded in Barnett's ears as he stood there.

"You are, perhaps, the Barnetts? Mister and Mrs. Is that so?"

"Why?" Barnett asked, turning. It was the fat man, risen from his seat and hovering unctuously by Barnett's side. This was too much. Had the man been eavesdropping? Even so, what on earth could he want? Whatever it might be, Barnett was in no mood to deal with it.

"I do really apologize for this unseemly interruption," the fat man said. For a second his lips formed into a smile, which promptly disappeared. "The *conduttore* mentioned to me of your presence on this train. I was overjoyed at the coincidence. A fortuitous happening, surely, you will admit."

"Will I?" Barnett was conscious of the three of them frozen there by the fat man's rudeness; Cecily poised for flight, and he undecided whether or not to follow, and the fat man talking. And talking. And talking.

"But yes." The fat man paused, one hand on his cheek, and grimaced as though just stricken with a horrible possibility. "You are, are you not, the Barnetts of the American News Service?"

"That's correct," Barnett said, grudgingly. How could this man possibly know that? And why should he care? Perhaps there was, after all, something to Cecily's apprehension. On the other hand, if the man wanted to do anything besides merely speaking to them, he didn't have to follow them around until they were in the *carrozza ristorante* to do it.

"Good. Good," the fat man said. "It is as I thought. You will pardon the intrusion, but, with the most honorable of intentions, I must seize this moment to speak with you. It is a matter of some urgency and some—delicacy." He whipped a hand into his jacket pocket, and it came out again clutching a white pasteboard. "My card, if you would be so good."

Barnett took the card, glanced at it, and passed it to Cecily. Gottfried Kasper, it said in firm but delicate brown lettering, *scrittore e giornalista*, Milano.

"What can we do for you, Signor Kasper?" Cecily asked the fat man sweetly. "Please, sit down."

Barnett looked at her in amazement. "Yes," he said, choking back a comment, "please do." Cecily surely must have some reason for asking the fat man to sit—unless it was merely to show Barnett that she would prefer anyone's company to his right now. Or perhaps, since she suspected the fat man of some sort of chicanery, she was going to try to prove it. Barnett sincerely hoped that she was not planning to do any such thing.

"You are most kind," the fat man said, as he lowered himself gingerly into a chair on the aisle while Benjamin and Cecily regained their seats. He looked relieved, but perhaps that was just at being able to sit again. Hauling his bulk around, particularly on a moving train, Barnett thought, must be a constant battle.

"So you are a journalist, eh?" Barnett said. "Looking for work?"

"No, no!" Kasper held up one chubby hand in protest, as though to ward off the very suggestion. "Of course, if there were any way in which I could be of service to the great American News Service . . . You have, perhaps, read my series on the aesthetic differences among the capitals of the European monarchies? It had a brief European vogue about a year ago, and was translated into many languages."

"I don't believe so," Barnett said.

"What was it called?" Cecily asked.

" 'An Aesthetic Analysis of the *Fin-de-Siècle* Styles and Manners of the Capitals of the European Monarchies.' It was well-received, if I may be permitted to say so myself. It evoked quite a bit of comment at the time. But it has not, as of yet, had the honor of receiving an English translation."

"Catchy title," Barnett commented.

Kasper turned and looked at him suspiciously for a moment, but decided to ignore whatever he saw there. "Do you think your American public would have any interest in an article of that nature?" he asked. "It is a heavily researched article and finds many similarities of thought among the more important European capitals."

"Send a copy to my London office," Barnett told him, "and I'll be glad to look at it. And now—"

"Ah, yes. Thank you for your attention. But that, of course, is not why I am imposing my presence on you, despite our lack of any sort of proper introduction. Oh, no, no!"

"It's not?" Barnett found the man's protestations, accompanied with a lot of chubby hand waving, to be simultaneously irritating and amusing.

"Not at all, Mr. Barnett, far from it. It is I who have an offer to make to you."

"You do? What sort of offer?"

"In this matter I represent the *Staatlicher Überblicken*, a monthly journal of conservative opinion published in the city of Zurich."

"I have heard of it," Barnett said, "although I don't read German. My wife does." He turned to Cecily.

"I know the magazine," Cecily said. "Tell me, Signor Kasper, what have you to do with it, or it with us?"

"I shall explain. You may know, then, that the *Staatlicher Überblicken* publishes a profile every month of an important, but little known figure of these closing years of the nineteenth century. Those individuals who have accomplishments which are of value to European civilization, but which have gone relatively unnoticed, are the subjects of these profiles." The fat man turned from Benjamin to Cecily and back, as though waiting for a reaction, and surprised that it was not there.

"Yes?" Barnett said. He glanced at Cecily, who gave an imperceptible shrug.

Kasper leaned forward and placed his palms on the table. "Mr. Barnett, you are a friend of the great criminologist and consulting detective, Mr. Sherlock Holmes, is this not so?"

"I am certainly an acquaintance of Mr. Holmes," Barnett replied, repressing a strong desire to laugh at the question. "I doubt whether he would consider me his friend."

Kasper shrugged. "An acquaintance, and a journalist. You are certainly the man we want. There is, as you must know, much curiosity and interest in the life and the professional abilities of Mr. Holmes. Several European police agencies are adopting his techniques for their own detective bureaus." He paused and took a wheezy breath, and then another. "Mr. Barnett, I would like to commission you to write, for the *Staatlicher Überblicken*, a profile of Mr. Sherlock Holmes."

Barnett stared at the fat man, speechless. There was hardly a less appropriate journalist in the world than himself to write such a piece. But how was the fat man to know of the enmity that existed between Sherlock Holmes and Barnett's friend and mentor Professor Moriarty? "Well," he said after a moment, "that is certainly an interesting suggestion. But I am not really the man for the task. I have hardly any time to do any writing at all anymore. And, although I have worked with him on several occasions, I'm hardly what would be described as a friend. Why don't you ask his associate, Dr. Watson, who has been recording various cases of his for the past few years?" Barnett couldn't escape the nagging feeling that there was something wrong with all this—the fat man, the meeting, the offer, and all—but he couldn't figure out just what it could be, or should be.

"The good doctor is not suitable to our needs," the fat man said. "He is not of the true journalistic tradition—the probing question, the in-depth answer, the letting of the chips to fall where they may."

The small, round-faced clergyman who had boarded the train with Kasper entered the dining car from the front, his black robes swishing about as he scurried up the aisle. *"Signor Kasper,"* he called in a low, intense, breathy voice, *"Desidero parlare con Lei, per piacere."*

"English, please, Father Ugarti," Kasper said. "Pause for a moment. Allow me to introduce Mr. and Mrs. Barnett. This is Father Ugarti, a man of the cloth."

Father Ugarti nodded, bobbing his head up and down rapidly and peering at them through his round, thick spectacles. His face creased into a large smile that showed many brown, discolored teeth. "It is pleasurable to be making of your acquaintance," he said. "You are an English couple on your honeymoon, perhaps? Traveling through our romantic mountains and lakes. You should find our countryside most interesting. Most interesting." He turned to Kasper. "I hate to seem impolite to your charming friends, but I must, after all, speak with you for a moment."

Kasper struggled to his feet. "I will be a moment, only," he told the Barnetts. "Then we can finish our so-interesting discussion." The fat journalist and the small clergyman went off to the rear of the car and consulted earnestly together.

"This is very strange," Barnett whispered to Cecily when the other two had left the table.

"How odd that you should think so," Cecily replied, smiling sweetly at him.

"What do you suppose it's all about?"

"I imagine we shall find out soon enough, but be on your guard. That priest is not a priest; and that fat man is no journalist."

"I believe you," Barnett said. "But I wish I could figure out what they're after."

Cecily patted his hand. "I think they seek something we do not have."

Before she had a chance to explain, Kasper returned to the table and Father Ugarti left the way he had come.

"A minor matter of liturgical interest only," Kasper told them, "but I most humbly apologize for the interruption. Now, let us return to the matter at hand. An extensive article by you concerning the habits, manners, and abilities of Mr. Holmes would be welcome. I think something of his history, also, should be included. Where he went to school; how he developed these marvelous deductive powers for which he has become so justly noted; his relationship with Professor Moriarty—"

"His what?"

"His relationship with Professor James Moriarty, author of *The Dynamics of an Asteroid*, and a well-regarded monograph on the binomial theorum. Surely his association with such a distinguished scientist must have had some impact on Mr. Holmes's own theories and techniques."

"I couldn't say," Barnett replied.

"Come now, it is well known that you, yourself, are an associate of Professor Moriarty."

"I have the honor to be his friend," Barnett replied, "but I know nothing of his work. I am not a scientist." He stood up. "I regret to have wasted your time, Signor Kasper, but I am afraid I cannot take a commission from the *Staatlicher Überblicken* at this time."

Kasper pushed himself to his feet. "On the contrary," he said, "if that is the case, then it is I who have wasted your time. I wish you good day." He nodded to Cecily and stalked firmly off down the aisle.

"Of all the nerve," Barnett muttered. "I am impressed with that man's gall!"

"I am impressed with his information," Cecily said. "It's not exactly public knowledge that Mr. Holmes ever had anything to do with Professor Moriarty, or that you are an associate of the professor or know Mr. Holmes. Dr. Watson never mentions it in any of his case histories."

"That's true," Barnett admitted. "Holmes once asked Watson, in my presence, not to mention the professor until Holmes had apprehended him for some major crime. Which is a good example of the state of their 'relationship.' And, as that has never happened—"

Cecily stood up. "I'm tired," she said. "Let's return to the compartment."

"Are you still mad at me?" Barnett asked.

"No. I'm no longer angry. Do you grant me that there was something odd about the confrontation we just had?"

"How could I deny it?" Barnett said.

They went back to their compartment and settled down, Cecily to her Baedeker and Benjamin to staring out the window at the passing hillsides. After a while Cecily put down the book and began rummaging through her traveling bag.

"It is a puzzle," Barnett said after a while. "I wish Professor Moriarty were here. He enjoys puzzles."

"Benjamin!"

"What is it, Dove?"

Cecily put the bag on the seat beside her and took a deep breath. "Somebody has gone through my traveling bag."

"Gone through? You mean searched?"

"Yes. Somebody has been pawing about my personal belongings." She shuddered. "It makes my skin crawl to think of it."

"Is anything missing?"

"No. I don't think so."

"But you're sure?"

"I can tell. The bag has been rearranged. I am sure." She got up and pulled the large leather portmanteau from the shelf.

Benjamin caught her and the bag as she staggered back with it. "Here," he said, "let me." They put the bag on the opposite seat and opened it together, undoing the straps and unlocking the small brass lock with a key which Barnett kept in his watch-pocket.

"What do you think?" Barnett asked.

"That red scarf has been refolded. Your two light sweaters are out of line. Someone has been through this bag also. Very carefully, but undoubtedly."

"But why? Nothing seems to be missing. Is anything missing from this bag?"

"No. Your gold cufflinks and studs are still here. My bracelets and earrings are still here. They're not particularly valuable, but they are certainly portable. Whoever searched our belongings thinks it more important that we remain unaware of it than that he makes a profit. If I weren't, as you keep telling me, excessively orderly and organized, we never would have noticed."

"That Kasper fellow!" Barnett said.

"My belief also," Cecily told him. "It was obvious from his second sentence that he was one of the group following us."

"His second sentence?"

"Certainly. He said that the *conduttore* told him who we are. The conductor of this train has no idea who we are. The ticket was booked by the hotel, and they got our name wrong."

"That's right," Barnett said.

"Kasper was just keeping us out of the way, so that his companions could search our belongings."

"Say," Barnett remembered, "he and that adolescent came into the dining car from the rear of the train. I'll bet they were in the baggage van. It must have disappointed them to discover that our luggage was sent on ahead."

Cecily closed the portmanteau and fastened the straps. "I feel degraded," she said. "I must have all my clothing laundered before I wear any of it again."

"I believe it has something to do with Holmes or Professor Moriarty," Barnett said.

"Well I hope that, whoever they are and whatever they want, that they're done with us," Cecily said. "I don't want this to go on and ruin our vacation."

"We won't let it!" Barnett said stoutly.

"Well it already is!" Cecily said, and burst into tears. "First these people are following us all over, and then you won't believe me when I tell you about it, and then they come into our very own railway carriage and paw through our personal belongings. I'm sorry, Benjamin, but I am very upset."

Barnett pulled a clean pocket-handkerchief from his jacket and passed it to his wife. "There, there," he said, taking her in his arms. "Mustn't be upset, really you mustn't. We won't let anything else happen to spoil our vacation. I've learned my lesson. From now on I shall listen abjectly to anything you say."

"Not abjectly, my love," Cecily said, wrapping her arms around his neck, "but carefully and honestly. I am usually right, you know."

"Yes, dear," Barnett said.

FOUR
THE FREEDOM LEAGUE

One man, with a dream, at pleasure,
Shall go forth and conquer a crown;
And three with a new song's measure
Can trample a kingdom down
— ARTHUR WILLIAM EDGAR
O'SHAUGHNESSY

The Vienna cell of the *Geheime Verein für Freiheit*, the Secret Freedom League, met in the box cellar of the Werfel Chocolate manufactory in the Mariahilf District of Vienna. A dank, cold, windowless room separate from the main cellar, it held a table, a few chairs, a row of cupboards along one wall, and an assortment of abandoned packing crates. What light there was came from the glare of a single-mantle gas fixture emerging from the ceiling, and the glow of a couple of ancient oil lamps suspended from hooks in the brick walls. Neither Herr Werfel, nor any of the management of the chocolate manufactory knew of the use to which their box cellar was being put.

The members of the League professed anarchism and practiced terror. Their weapons were the bomb, the pistol, the ice pick, and the lives of their members. They seemed to be well financed, although how or by whom was known only to their leaders. The Vienna cell numbered between twelve and twenty-two men, depending on the phases of the moon, the vagaries of conscience, and the diligence of the *Kundschafts Stelle*—the Austrian counterintelligence bureau.

Fourteen men were present at tonight's meeting; among them a pair with the thick-necked, broken-nosed look of professional toughs who would not be out of place at a daily police lineup; a trio with the furtive look of unsuccessful sneak-thieves; and a well-dressed young man with a bowler hat and the detached air of a gentleman of leisure, or a successful pickpocket. Most of the rest looked like—and for the most part were—university students who divided their time between attending lectures on the economic consequences of the great upheavals of 1849 and plotting upheavals of their own.

The cell leader was known as "Number One" at meetings. Outside, as Paul Donzhof had discovered with a bit of discreet research, he was Dietrich Loomer, called "the Ferret" by his acquaintances. He was a gaunt, sallow, notably short, totally bald man with no eyebrows who habitually wore a black cloak made of a material usually reserved for horse blankets and a black, wide-brim hat pulled close over his eyes. This gave him a furtive look which made one instinctively put him down as a sneak thief or a police spy. He had been both. His formative years had been spent in a horse regiment of the Austrian Army, where he had risen to the rank of corporal before being kicked out for irregularities of a highly personal and unmentionable nature.

Paul, known as "Number Thirty-seven" to his fellow anarchists, was assigned to guard-duty for this meeting. His job was to stand outside the door and give warning if danger, in the form of the police or a Werfel employee, approached.

After a little while he was joined by Feodor Hessenkopf, who paused to smoke a cigarette before joining the meeting. They kept the door open a crack, so they could hear what was going on inside. Hessenkopf had forgone the humpback and was now dressed as a railroad conductor. Perhaps, Paul thought looking at him, the little man truly *was* a railroad conductor. The gray uniform showed the proper sort of wear that suggested that it was not a costume. Hessenkopf was to be called "Number Eleven" while at meetings; members were under strict orders to address each other only by their numbers and they were not encouraged to know each other outside, although most of them frequented the Café Figaro and could easily be identified by any of the waiters.

For the first half hour the members heard the reading of a new anarchist manifesto called *The Coming Revolution*, which had just arrived from Paris. It was supposedly written by the anarchist Brakinsky from his jail cell shortly before his execution for murdering three policemen.

A young man named Mandl with a vibrant voice and a sense of pathos stood under the gas mantle in the center of the meeting room and read from the pamphlet. " 'The day is coming when the landlords and the bourgeoisie shall no longer snatch the bread from the mouths of the children of the workers,' " he read fiercely. And, further on: " 'They would have you fight for your country, like a lamb fighting for its shearing pen, or a swine fighting for its abattoir. You are enslaved by fetters of the great lie called patriotism; they are invisible but they hold more surely than iron chains!' "

While Mandl throbbed on, the Ferret slunk outside, saw Hessenkopf, screeched, "My god! That uniform!" and immediately grabbed Hessenkopf and pulled him around the corner of the building. Paul could hear the muffled voice of the Ferret evidently bawling out Hessenkopf, but he couldn't make out what was being said. He thought of sneaking over to listen, but decided it wouldn't be wise. In a minute the Ferret came back, paused to glare at Paul, and went on to the meeting room. Hessenkopf did not return.

After Mandl had finished and sat down, the group ardently discussed the manifesto. What their argument lacked in logic it made up for in fervor, which increased as the discussion hopped from member to member. They spoke of man's inhumanity to man, and touched on man's inhumanity to woman and child. They dissected the inherent contradictions in the capitalist system that must surely cause its downfall. They reviewed the inherent evils of monarchy and agreed bitterly that kings would never voluntarily vacate their thrones.

These things, they agreed, made it necessary to agitate the masses, who were too mired in their own misery ever to agitate themselves. Strong measures must be taken to make the lumpen proletariat aware of its own helplessness, of the need for change. Eggs must be broken so that the omelet of social justice might be achieved.

Then on to the business of the night. Paul was called into the meeting room, where the entire group once again renewed their anarchic vows, raising their right hands and swearing never to

44

reveal the secrets of the organization, under pain of death. They swore to obey the orders of their leaders, which Paul found particularly amusing for an organization of anarchists, but he did not smile. Then the new members were taken aside and taught the elements of the anarchists' cipher, which was not a cipher but a book code based on the Lutheran Bible. Then they all went around the room, shaking hands with each other, replying "Anarchy and revolution!" to each murmured salutation of "Justice and equality!"

Number One smiled, not an attractive sight. "With this renewal of our vows we once again pledge to fight to liberate the slaves from their masters, the working men from their bosses, the governed from the evil hand of government," he said. "I trust you will prove to be brave and resourceful." He turned and pointed to Paul. "Number Thirty-seven, there is a message that must be delivered." He pulled a large envelope from an inner pocket of his jacket and appeared to consider for a moment before saying, "In the name of the League I entrust you with this letter."

Paul took the envelope. Number One handed him a slip of paper. "Here's the address. Memorize it and destroy the paper. Deliver it as soon as possible, and only to the person named."

"Now?"

"Yes, now. Tonight. You're not afraid of the dark, are you?"

Paul grinned. Was that sarcasm or solicitude? No matter. He stared at the paper for a moment and then handed it back to Number One. "You destroy the paper. I'll go."

Paul left the cellar, climbed up the half flight of stairs to the alley entrance, and paused to think. The address was across town, and there was a cab rank at the corner of Bosestrasse, a few blocks away, but a good long walk would be just the thing to clear his head. He paused to button his coat up to the neck and then strode off down the street.

Inside the cellar room Number One nodded at the man in the gentleman's disguise, and he and one of the sneak-thief trio left and fell in behind Paul. They kept at least a block away and alternated which was closest, changing hats and manner of walking every few blocks so that Paul would not notice he was being followed.

* * *

Number One gathered the remaining league members around him and said, "you will all leave here shortly, but one will stay behind. One of you will undertake an important action for us, one that has been planned for some time. One simple act which will prove our seriousness, and strike a blow for our cause. Since I'm sure you would all be eager to volunteer, just gather around the table and we'll draw straws."

They gathered and each of them pulled a straw from the bunch in Number One's fist. Member Number Five drew the short straw. The Ferret had arranged that Member Number Five would draw the short straw, but he was clever with his hands and nobody had noticed. The others congratulated Number Five and filed out of the damp cellar until only he and Number One were left.

Number Five was Carl Webel, a twenty-two-year-old art student, who felt that there was something drastically wrong with society; a feeling not uncommon to twenty-two-year-old art students. He had been led to believe that the poor needed to be shaken out of their complacency in order to rise up and establish a classless society, and that only random acts of violence on their behalf could do the shaking. He wanted desperately to be one of the shakers.

Number One went to a cupboard in a corner of the cellar and removed the heavy padlock. Inside were two packages, a bulky one wrapped in layers of oilcloth, and a small, rectangular one wrapped in brown paper. He removed them both and returned to the table. With the air of a man disclosing a religious artifact, he unwrapped the oilcloth, revealing an aging Shugard Seuss revolver. "Here it is, Number Five," he said, passing the heavy weapon across the table. "You think, perhaps, you can handle it?"

Webel took a deep breath and hefted the revolver, willing his hand not to shake. "I just point and pull the trigger, right?" he asked, assuming the sort of bravado he thought was required of him. "I can do that, Number One."

"You open the weapon like this," the Ferret said, demonstrating, "and you put the bullets in thusly. And then you snap it closed like this. You see?"

"Simple," Webel assured him.

"Even so, practice it."

"Of course."

"Very good. You keep it concealed until the last second. You pull back the hammer thusly as you draw the weapon from your pocket. The Shugard Seuss is double action, but it has a very heavy trigger pull, which is liable to throw off your aim, unless it is cocked first. When it has been cocked, a feather touch is sufficient to fire it. You'd better practice shooting it with no bullets in it."

"I shall."

"Take the time to aim carefully. At a distance of no more than five meters you cannot miss. Any further than that, and it becomes problematical. Then you casually walk away, escaping in the confusion. Everything will be arranged for your escape. Make sure your pockets are empty, and destroy anything you have at home that might connect you with us in case anything goes wrong."

"I intend to be much closer than five meters!" the art student said fiercely. "For the Cause! For Freedom and Social Justice! For the Dignity of Man!"

The Ferret smiled, displaying two rows of crooked, yellowed teeth and repeated the litany. "For the Cause! For Freedom and Social Justice! For the Dignity of Man!" He slapped Webel on the back. "There remains some more preparation to be done. I will meet you at noon tomorrow at your rooms with final instructions." Webel nodded, and the Ferret handed him six well-greased cartridges from the paper-wrapped box and watched him leave. Three minutes later the Ferret extinguished the oil lamp and left himself, carefully locking the small door behind him.

As the Ferret's footsteps faded away outside, there was a stirring from inside one of the small packing crates. The end popped off, and a man's feet appeared. Slowly the rest of the man emerged from the crate, a tall, lean man with a large, hawklike nose and piercing eyes. He stood and dusted himself off, then stretched and twisted his body in an effort to relieve the cramped tension that four hours crouching in a small box had given to his muscles.

"So," the man said, softly, "the game is afoot!" He let himself out the door with a key that was a duplicate of the one the Ferret had used, and then carefully locked the door behind him.

FIVE

LAKE COMO

There is a time, we know not when,
A point we know not where,
That marks the destiny of men,
For glory or despair.

           —JOSEPH ADDISON ALEXANDER

The Villa Endorra stretched precariously along a steep hillside out-side of Bellagio, overlooking Lake Como. Above and behind it a thick stand of pine forest cut off the view of all but the surrounding mountains, providing, as the joyously random English of the Ital-ian guidebook put it, "a splendiferous emotion of isolation among the beatitudes of Italian harmonies without the necessitude of dis-commoding the tourist with the inconvenience of veritably being isolate."

Before and below the villa, a hundred feet down a vine-clut-tered, rocky hillside, the blue waters of the lake reflected dappled April sunlight off its choppy surface; the azure near the shore quickly deepening to a somber dark blue as the bottom fell away to uncharted depths.

Benjamin Barnett ended his morning run at the lakeside of the villa and, panting heavily, leaned over the rail that separated the path from the hill to watch a trim white sloop beating across the lake. As he watched, it made a final tack that would bring it alongside the pier below. The blue-jacketed man at the boat's helm handled the wheel and sails with an agility and grace that spoke of years of practice.

"What are you watching, my love?" Cecily came across the

garden and joined him at the rail. "Has a monster of the deeps suddenly surfaced?"

"It's that white sailboat," Barnett explained, putting his arm around her waist. The week they had been at the villa had been good for her, he thought. The pain was disappearing from her face. The spring air, the beautiful countryside, and even the continuing mystery of who was interested in them, and why, seemed to take her mind off the recent past, and the dreadful miscarriage that had so debilitated her.

"Oh." Cecily sounded disappointed. "I was so hoping for a monster of the deeps." She leaned over the rail and, shading her hazel eyes from the morning sun, peered down at the lake. "It certainly is a trim-looking craft. Is craft the right word? Boat people get so annoyed when you use the wrong word."

"Notice how she's being handled," Barnett said. "Yon gentleman in the blue jacket is doing the job of three men and making it look simple. I find it hard not to instantly dislike such a man."

Cecily slipped her arm through his. "You cannot do everything well," she said. "And those things you do well, you do very well indeed. I never knew you had a secret desire to be a master mariner."

"Nor did I until I watched the performance of our friend below."

A woman in a white dress emerged from the sloop's cabin, unfurled a red-trimmed parasol, and stood watching unconcernedly as the small yacht neared the dock.

"A very pretty picture," Cecily said. "I believe I shall ask that German fellow, Herr Lindner to capture it in oil for us. At least we could find out whether the man really can paint or not. Come have breakfast."

Barnett put his arm around Cecily's waist. "I see that you're convinced that Lindner is not really an artist," he said. "I shall have Tolliver check him out today."

Cecily shook her head. "I never said he wasn't an artist. He may very well be an artist, although I doubt it judging by his checkered jacket. I merely said he didn't come here to paint. I think he's spying on us."

"Why do you suppose he's watching us?" Barnett asked.

"I don't know," Cecily said. "Why did those men on the train search our baggage?"

"You've got me there," Barnett said. It was still as big a mystery as when it had happened. The fat man and his friends had disappeared by the time Barnett got the conductor to search the train, probably by jumping off as it chugged up a hill or slowed for a curve. The Italian police were informed at the next station, but they were no help; the descriptions of the villains fit no known criminals. *"Banditti,"* suggested the captain of police who had taken their statement, shrugging.

"But then why was nothing stolen?" Cecily had asked sensibly.

The captain of police had merely shrugged again. Who can tell what the *banditti* will do?

And now a German painter had arrived at the villa-turned-pensione, and Cecily was convinced that he was a fraud. Barnett was resolved to pay serious attention to his wife's convictions. But if she was right, the questions multiplied. Why would anybody have any reason to watch them? Who could be responsible for this seemingly endless supply of watchers? What was their objective? Did they intend to do anything beyond simply watch? Were they aware that they had been detected? Barnett rather doubted that, since he was barely aware of it himself. And, finally, what should he and Cecily—and the mummer—do about it? Time, Barnett decided, would tell.

The blue-blazered gentleman at the wheel of the sloop dropped the sail at the last second and spun the wheel, nosing the craft gently up to the dock. Two men who had been waiting on the dock stepped out of the shadow and helped him tie off the boat fore and aft before he leapt onto the dock and helped the lady step ashore. It was hard to make out details from this distance, but it looked to Barnett as though one of the men was remonstrating with the boatsman. He took it patiently for a moment, and then spoke sharply to the man, who appeared to step back respectfully. The boatsman held his arm out for the lady, and the two of them strolled ashore.

"What do you suppose that was about?" Barnett wondered aloud.

"Pirates," Cecily suggested promptly. "Arguing over the booty."

"Ah!" Barnett said. "And the lady?"

"Take your choice," Cecily told him. "She's either the pirate queen, or the booty in question."

"Obviously," Barnett agreed. "How silly of me not to have guessed immediately."

"Shall we breakfast?"

"Good idea. Let me get out of these flannels and into something decent, and I'll join you in the breakfast room. I shall drown my jealousy in an egg, or possibly an entire omelette."

Half an hour later Barnett and Cecily made their way to a corner table in the large parlor that Frau Schimmer, the Swiss concierge of this Italian villa, used as a breakfast room. For her English guests, Frau Schimmer believed in what she called "the English Breakfast," which consisted of slices of every meat or cheese about the kitchen that could be sliced, with platters of fried eggs. It had taken work for Barnett to convince Frau Schimmer that he would, really, prefer one of her delicious omelettes.

The only other guests in the breakfast room when they entered were a honeymooning couple in their early twenties from Rome who called themselves Pronzini, and spent most of their time in their room, and Herr Lindner, the German painter. Lindner, a skinny, balding man with heavy, dark eyebrows and a black toothbrush mustache, rose and bowed mechanically to Benjamin and Cecily as they crossed the room, and then went back to reading the Zurich newspaper and eating his *pfannkuchen*. The honeymooners merely looked up, nodded, and giggled, and returned to eating rolls, drinking coffee, and gazing into each other's eyes.

Benjamin and Cecily sat and told the serving girl what they wanted, and began going through the mail that "Mummer" Tolliver had passed on to them as they came downstairs. Barnett went through his letters quickly, and then settled down to his omelette and the latest issue of *The Illustrated World News*. Fifteen minutes later he tossed it aside with more than necessary violence. "Really," he said, "this is insufferable!"

Cecily put aside a long letter from her employer, and looked up from her buttered egg at her husband. "I particularly love you when you're angry," she told him. "You sound so English when you're angry. One can hardly believe that you grew up in Brooklyn, U.S.A."

Barnett looked across the breakfast table at his wife, and felt the anger and the pain dissolve, to be replaced by a feeling of quiet joy. "Married all these years," he observed, "And I still find myself rather fond of you. How do you explain that?"

"It passeth understanding," Cecily told him. "Now, what has raised your bile so much that you've lost that trace of American accent that women find so irresistible?"

Barnett passed the newspaper to her and tapped one of the columns. "Here," he said. "Read this!"

Consulting Detective Aids Crown
DETAILS REVEALED IN ARTICLE.

In an article shortly to be published in the *Strand* magazine under the title of "The Adventure of the Beryl Coronet," Dr. John H. Watson has revealed the details of another extraordinary case of his friend and companion, the consulting detective, Mr. Sherlock Holmes of 221B Baker Street, London.

The case involved a matter of great importance to Her Majesty's government concerning a most difficult problem requiring the most delicate handling due to the high social standing of the persons involved. Mr. Holmes succeeded where the police failed in retrieving and preserving a state treasure— the aforementioned beryl coronet—and apprehending those involved in its disappearance.

Although the identities of several of the persons involved in the case have been altered to preserve their anonymity, it is clear that the case involved royal personages and persons in high government positions. The beryl coronet is part of the state regalia of a royal duke, and has been a state treasure for more than three centuries.

Dr. Watson and Mr. Holmes are at present abroad enjoying a no-doubt well-deserved vacation, and could not be reached for comment.

"Of all the unmitigated—," Barnett began.

"Quiet, dear, and let me read it." Cecily perused the item silently, and then pushed the magazine aside and returned to her egg.

"Well?" Barnett demanded.

"I don't quite see the reason for your irate response," Cecily told him calmly.

"Mr. Holmes began his 'investigations' by accusing Professor Moriarty of arranging the theft of the coronet," Barnett told her, punctuating his words by tapping his ring finger on the table. "He hung around outside the professor's house in a puerile disguise, dressed as some sort of common loafer, and accosted everyone who approached the door. The professor was finally forced to find the coronet himself to get Holmes to go away—a fact which I'm sure Dr. Watson's version of the events will not include."

Cecily reached over and cupped her husband's hand in hers to stop the table-tapping. "Could it not be that your fondness for Professor Moriarty and your, let us say, cool feelings toward Mr. Holmes have caused you to overstate the case just a bit?" she asked.

Barnett's frown slowly dissolved into a smile at the touch of her hand. "Well," he said, "perhaps just a bit."

Benjamin and Cecily had met while Benjamin was working for Professor James Moriarty, who was perhaps best described as a scientist who dabbled in crime, and was admittedly one of the most brilliant men in Britain. Barnett had founded the American News Service as an information gathering agency for the professor, and Cecily had answered an advertisement for the position of office manager.

A little over four years ago Barnett had quit the professor's service to marry the woman he had come to love, taking Moriarty's blessings and the American News Service with him.

Barnett chuckled at his memories. "The professor used to

describe himself as the world's first consulting criminal," he told Cecily. "Moriarty planned ingenious crimes, for a fee. He said it was to support his scientific research, but I fancy he enjoyed the challenge. It was his way of tweaking the nose of a society that he found stupid, intolerant, stodgy, and dull. Looking back on my time as his associate, I certainly cannot condone his actions, but they kept life interesting."

"Mr. Holmes has called Professor Moriarty the 'Napoleon of crime,' " Cecily said.

"I myself have heard Holmes say that," Barnett admitted. "My belief is that, for all of Holmes's genius in solving crimes, he could never catch the professor. And this so upset and unnerved him that he blamed Moriarty for every crime that happened within a hundred miles of London. But he was known to call upon Moriarty himself when he was out of his depth in a problem."

Barnett finished his breakfast silently, deep in memories of the years he had spent with Professor Moriarty. Cecily, a truly wise woman, did not disturb him, but read her magazine and ate her buttered egg. Curiously the article she was reading, an illustrated study of Abdul Hamid, the sultan of Turkey, brought back memories of the time she had first met Benjamin. It was shortly after Moriarty had helped him escape from a Turkish prison, where he was being held for a murder he did not commit. She had thought him awfully proper and straitlaced then, for a newspaperman, and had been mildly shocked as, gradually, she came to realize that Barnett was Professor Moriarty's trusted right hand, and that the stern, fatherly professor was probably the most brilliant criminal mind of the nineteenth century.

Cecily closed the magazine and allowed the young waitress who hovered about their table to pour her a cup of coffee. She watched as Frau Schimmer escorted a couple into the breakfast room, brushing aside their apologies for being so late, and seated them at a table directly across from the Barnetts. Judging by their dress, it was the couple they had last seen docking a sailboat. And, now that she saw him at a reasonable distance, Cecily recognized the man. "Look," she said softly to Barnett. "The mystery is solved."

Barnett looked over at the table Cecily indicated. "Aha!" he said, acknowledging the nod of the newly seated gentleman. "It's our friend Signor Buleforte. And the lovely lady must be his wife. I didn't know he was a master mariner, along with his other talents."

Ariste Buleforte had been at the villa for the past two days, awaiting the arrival of his wife. He had met Cecily and Benjamin over the bridge table the night of his arrival. He was well traveled, a pleasant conversationalist, and a keen bridge player.

Deciding that a mere nod was insufficient greeting, Signor Buleforte rose and bowed to Benjamin and Cecily. "A pleasure to see you this morning," he said in his precise English. "Allow me to present to you my wife, Diane Buleforte. My dear, these are the Barnetts; that English couple I mentioned to you. They are avid bridge players."

Barnett rose in turn and bowed slightly over Signora Buleforte's hand. "Delighted," he said, deciding not to dispute Buleforte's belief that he was English. "We watched you arrive on the sloop a little while ago. It made a charming picture. You are an excellent sailor, Signor Buleforte."

"Please," Buleforte said. "Ariste. I insist. Ariste and Diane. And we will call you Benjamin and Cecily." He said it as though he were conveying a special favor on them instead of being slightly rude. But somehow, when he said it, it was charming.

Benjamin found deep within his soul a touch of jealousy at this man whose mastery of the social graces was so smooth that he could smilingly ignore them. Barnett was sure that if he walked up to some comparative stranger and said, "Ho Mr. Smith—let me just call you 'George' from now on," the stranger would reply "not on your life," and stalk off. But if Buleforte did it, George would feel grateful and hand him a cigar. There was something about the man. Barnett did feel grateful, even as he was annoyed at himself for doing so.

"Ariste, then," Barnett agreed. "And is your lovely wife as avid a bridge player as you are? If so, perhaps we could get in a couple of rubbers after dinner."

"What could be nicer than a bit of mental stimulation after a day's physical stimulation?" Ariste Buleforte asked. "A morning of tennis, an afternoon dip in the lake, and an evening's auction bridge. Surely no prince could spend a better day. Or princess, either. What do you say to that, my princess?"

"It will be most relaxing," Diane Buleforte replied, smiling a winsome smile. "Mr. and Mrs. Barnett—Benjamin and Cecily—would perhaps like to join us for tennis. We could perhaps play doubles."

And so they did.

Herr Lindner left the breakfast room while the Barnetts and the Bulefortes were discussing their future. Thoughtfully, as though considering a matter of the greatest importance, he made his way up to his room. Once inside, he locked the door and opened wide his window, which faced out upon the lake. The last of the haze had lifted, burned off by the late morning sun, and there on the lake, as far out as he could see, was a black dot that, with the aid of a pair of binoculars that he kept on the window ledge, resolved itself into a small boat with its single sail furled. Lindner was gratified by the sight, but it was not with the eye of an artist that he regarded it.

He went to the bottom drawer of his bureau and withdrew from it an elaborate apparatus of brass and wood, folded about itself into a compact mass. Slowly and methodically, still deep in thought, Lindner unfolded the parts and fastened them together, until the apparatus was revealed as a portable heliograph sitting on a short, sturdy tripod.

Whistling tunelessly as he worked, Lindner set the device up on the far left-hand corner of the window sill, where it would best catch the direct rays of the sun. Then he carefully aimed its mirror so it would send flashes of sunlight to the distant boat.

Now, for a moment, Lindner paused and stared thoughtfully at a fading print of *Beauty Unveiled* on the wall next to the wardrobe. Then he opened his portmanteau and drew out a sheet of foolscap. Laboriously, using a thick leaded artist's pencil, he composed his message: *"Der Herr Barnett und seine frau . . ."*

He carefully left a space between each line as he wrote it. He could have made the message shorter, leaving out the articles and the honorifics and such, but he had a strong distaste for the telegraphic style. When the whole was done, he went back and, with the aid of a thin length of brass and ivory that looked like a six-inch slide rule, but was scribed with letters instead of numbers, wrote an encrypted version of the message in the space between the lines.

Without haste, as the sun rose to its zenith in the noon skies, Lindner clicked out his recognition signal and waited for the boat's reply—just the merest brief sparkle of the Morse letters DK to assure him that he had the right target. Then, slowly and methodically, he tapped out his message to the waiting boat. When he had finished, and sent the final "SSS" that indicated "end of message," the boat raised its triangular sail and went on its way.

Lindner packed up the heliograph and put it away, and turned to his paints and easel. Perhaps, today, he would attempt a landscape on the rear lawn. He rather fancied himself as an artist.

CHARLES BREDLON SUMMERDANE

All'meine Pulse schlagen, und das Herz wallt ungestüm . . .
(How every pulse is flying, and my heart beats loud and fast . . .)
—FRIEDRICH KIND,
FROM THE LIBRETTO TO *DER FREISCHÜTZ*

On Thursday evening Paul took Giselle to the opera. It was her first chance to wear the new pink dress that she had just picked up from her dressmaker's. It was from a design that she had created herself, cutting and pinning it on one of her dolls until it looked just the way she wanted. Frau Ardbaum, the dressmaker, had realized the miniature in full, with the skirt flounced just so, and the bodice tightened just so. Giselle looked like a princess, lovely and pure, with just a hint of—well, no need to go into what there was just a hint of.

Paul had purchased tickets for aisle seats in the sixth row of the orchestra, feeling vaguely guilty, as though he were spending his food money for the month, as he did so. So well was he into his new bohemian persona that he had to remind himself that, as Charles Bredlon Summerdane, he could have bought out the entire orchestra every show and still dined well.

"I love this place," Giselle told Paul as they approached their seats. "Just think, we just walked up the Imperial Staircase. The emperor himself uses that staircase."

"As does everyone else," Paul pointed out, but Giselle didn't care.

The opera that evening was *Der Freischütz*, by Carl Maria von Weber, based on a German ghost story about magic and shooting, and the "Black Huntsman," who would give a hunter six perfect shots in return for his soul. It had a handsome hero and a lovely heroine and an evil villain and an occasional glimpse of the devil himself; who could ask for more?

Giselle clutched Paul's hand through the performance and was enthralled by the music and the magic. "You may take me to the opera any time," she murmured to him during the a scene change in the first act.

"I shall take you to the opera many times," he told her.

"But it is very expensive!"

Paul laughed. "I have a friend who can afford it."

Giselle raised his hand to her lips and kissed his knuckle. "I do love opera," she told him. "I come here on occasion and get a standing room ticket. That is very cheap, but not as enjoyable as it could be; the opera police are very strict."

"The opera police?" Paul looked quizzically at her.

"Oh, yes. Those who stand must do so behind that railing," she pointed to the side at the rear, "and there are men with little opera patches on their coats who watch you to make sure you don't sneak in to take a seat, or even sit on the steps."

"For the whole three or four hours?" Paul asked.

"Even so. They are very firm."

"And they are not swayed by your beauty or the piteous glances that I'm sure you give them? They must be strict indeed."

At the second intermission Paul took Giselle back for a cold chocolate at the refreshment stand. He found a chair for her and then excused himself. "There is someone I must speak to for a minute," he explained.

Paul worked his way through the press of well-dressed people to where the man he had selected as the next subject to be approached was standing with his daughter. The man, a portly, balding gentleman with thick graying eyebrows over close-set eyes, a toothbrush mustache, and bristly beard that almost concealed a receding chin, was Hermann Loge, a middle-level official in the Foreign Ministry. His daughter, who appeared to be about seventeen, wore an expensive, fashionable gown in a shade of green that made her white skin look motley and diseased, cut so that it emphasized her thick waist and undeveloped bust. Her hair was coiffed to look as though it concealed a dinner plate carefully balanced on her head.

Hermann was in need of money. Keeping a wife and two mistresses on a minor minister's salary was a constant juggling act, and Hermann was beginning to lose control of the balls. Or so Paul had been told by Levi Davoud. Paul paused to look Hermann over. He looked weak and indecisive, not like the sort of man who would cultivate a wife and two mistresses. But perhaps many of us lead secret lives that would astound even our closest friends.

Paul approached his quarry and pulled a sealed envelope from an inside pocket. "Herr Loge?" he asked softly.

Loge swiveled to face Paul. "Yes?"

"My patron sympathizes with your need," Paul said, "and he asked me to give you this." He thrust the envelope into Loge's hand and turned around.

"Wait!"

Paul paused.

"Is this all?"

Paul turned back to Loge. The man had ripped open the envelope and was riffling through the bills inside. Obviously he could add up sums of money very quickly. There was five hundred kronen in the envelope. What did this high-living bureaucrat expect, and, come to think of it, why did he expect it?

"All?"

"There is, what, five hundred kronen in here. I was promised a thousand!" The words came sharply, but in an undertone that did not carry above the noise of the surrounding crowd. No one, as far as Paul could tell, turned to look at them to see what he was talking about.

Paul thought fast. "The rest will come later," he said.

"Well, it better." Loge took a folded paper from his pocket and handed it to Paul. "Here. Although what you want this for is beyond me. When do I get the other five hundred?"

"Soon," Paul promised. "Soon!" He thrust the paper into his pocket and stalked off as though he knew what this was all about.

For the rest of the opera Paul's thoughts dwelled on the paper.

What was it that serendipity had tossed his way, information concerning some minor intrigue, or possibly a state secret that would change the course of European affairs for a generation? It took an effort of will for him not to unfold the paper on his lap and try to read it in the light reflected from the stage.

Paul couldn't shake off the feeling that someone was watching him from somewhere in the dark seats behind him. But, if so, nobody did anything about it, and, as far as he could tell, nobody displayed the slightest interest in him or Giselle when they left the opera house and boarded one of the carriages pulled up along the curb to go home.

The night was clear and chill. Paul wrapped the carriage blanket around the two of them and stared up at the sky. He pointed out the constellation of Orion, the great hunter, chasing the Great Bear through the spring sky. "There's one of the problems we all face as we go through life," he told her, "determining whether we are the hunter or the bear."

Giselle examined his profile in the light of the street lamps. "Sometimes," she said, "I don't understand you."

"Sometimes," he agreed, "I don't either."

It was after two in the morning when Giselle left his top-floor flat and wafted down the one flight to her own so that she could wake up in her own bed surrounded by the assumption of morality. Paul carefully double-locked his door, made sure that the curtains on his sitting room window were fully closed, lit the gas ring on his side table, prepared himself a cup of thick black coffee with an excess of sugar, and relaxed. He sank into his easy chair, allowed the persona of Paul Donzhof, Bavarian bohemian, to drain away and permitted himself to become again, if ever so briefly, Charles Bredlon Summerdane, younger son of a duke, English spy. The only way he knew to play the part he had to play all day every day was to become the person he was playing. He had not made it too difficult for himself; Paul Donzhof was in many ways Charles Summerdane, or what Summerdane would have been had he been born into a middle-class German family. But it was still a welcome respite to think in English, and to think those things that Paul Donzhof kept locked away in the recesses of his mind.

It was Charles Summerdane who went to his closet and pulled the folded-up paper from the breast pocket of his evening jacket. He spread it open on the table in front of him. It was a numbered list of seven items that made no apparent sense to him:

1. 24 AND 26 APRIL
2. THAT WEDNESDAY
3. UNKNOWN
4. ENGLAND, FRANCE, GERMANY, AND RUSSIA
5. UNKNOWN
6. 3RD AND 4TH OUT OF 6
7. YES

Summerdane studied it for a while and the longer he looked at it, the less he knew. A glance at the calendar told him that the 24th and 25th of April fell on a Friday and Saturday. And so? But it must mean something, perhaps something important. Well, he'd look at it again. For now he had other work to do.

Summerdane assembled the notes gathered from observations, discussions, and reports of his compatriots over the past fortnight, added to them with some insightful comments and observations of his own, and condensed them into one continuous message:

> Greetings from Vienna. Austrian general staff has received reports on range and accuracy of new French 12cm short-recoil field piece. Suggests spy in place in French Army high command.
>
> Two battleships in drydock in Pola. The Kronprinz Erzherzog Rudolph for repair and refitting and the Tegetthoff for complete reconstruction.
>
> I am now member 37 of the GVF. Last night I delivered envelope to man named Brommel at 578 Brandtstrasse. Was followed there by GVFers. Don't know whether I am suspected, or it was standard procedure. An assassination attempt is being planned, possibly more than one. Also something big in progress. Do not know what, we apprentice anarchists are told only what we need to know. But hints from several sources indicate major outrage is due soon.

> GS tells me the Interior Ministry believes Russian agents
> increasing activity in Hungary and Serbia . . .

The report went on for another page and a half. He ended it with the note:

> I have just come into possession of a list that might be important but at present tells me nothing. I shall continue to stare at it from time to time to see if its meaning suddenly leaps out at me.

When he was done, he put the pen back in its holder, capped the inkwell in his small writing desk, and carefully checked over what he had written. It said what he wished to say; it was comparatively tersely written; it would have to do. He spent the next two hours encrypting the report with his own specially devised cipher: page after page of a specially composed "Paul Donzhof" tone poem for chamber orchestra, written with thick black pencil on pre-lined paper. The musical score he created was playable—not enjoyable, but playable; and that would suffice. Then he carefully burned all his notes and the plain text message in the room's small fireplace and went to sleep.

Late the next morning, when most of the citizens of workaday Vienna were done skittering about on their way to their employment, Herr Paul Donzhof hailed a passing fiacre and took Fraulein Giselle Schiff to the Café Prinz Eugene for breakfast.

"I do so enjoy being out with you," Giselle said as they settled at an outdoor table to the right of the entrance, one that would get more of the March sun and less of the March breeze. She looked up at him with a wide smile on her full red lips and her head arced just so. "We are such an attractive couple, passersby cannot help but stop and admire."

"Well," Paul said, "half of us is, anyway. You must have practiced in front of a mirror to look so artless."

"For hours," she agreed. "Klimt is painting me as Mary Magdalene with just this look."

"Ah!" Paul said. "In that case your wonderful innocent look might become quite well known. Klimt's work has been described as 'degenerate' by the *Neues Wiener Tagblatt*, which might draw a large audience to his next show." He intercepted a passing waiter and demanded two coffees and the pastry tray.

"What do they mean, these critics, when they say 'degenerate'?" Giselle asked.

Paul considered. "It depends on just whom the 'they' is," he told her. "The word has come into vogue, and different groups are using it to mean just what they choose it to mean, neither more nor less, as Humpty Dumpty once said."

"Who is this Humpty Dumpty?"

"A childhood friend, never mind about him."

Two waiters descended on them, one with their coffee and the second wheeling a heavily laden pastry cart. After due deliberation they made their selections: a Linzer *törtchen* for Giselle and a *mohn strudel* for him.

"This is, perhaps, degenerate, is it not?" Giselle suggested. "Pastry for breakfast?"

"Decadent at least, if not fully degenerate," Paul agreed. "But then breaking one's fast at"—he twisted around to peer at the clock on the wall inside the café and then twisted back—"almost eleven, would be considered in itself degenerate enough by the respectable burgers of Vienna. Early rising is synonymous with morality and industry."

Giselle used her knife and fork to cut a tiny sliver from her *törtchen* and convey it to her mouth. "And what else is degenerate, my sweet?"

"I know that voice." Paul said. "You're wondering now many degenerate acts we can accomplish before you sneak out of my room tonight."

"No such thing!" Giselle stated, contriving to look shocked.

Paul laughed. "All right. Let's see," he said, "there's the church's definition of degenerate: Whenever you hear a priest fulminating against degenerate behavior, you can be pretty sure he's talking about s-e-x. Then there's the Italian Doctor Cesare Lombroso, who thinks that criminals are degenerates, and he can pick them out by the shape of their nose and the angle of their earlobes. The police have a problem with his theories, as they've had little luck identifying criminals by their earlobes, and besides the police's definition of 'degenerate' usually involves blatant homosexuality. If the homosexuality isn't blatant, then the person involved is spoken of in hushed tones as an 'invert.' "

"This is something I do not understand, homosexuality."

"You wouldn't," Paul said. "Any man who doesn't look at you with great interest is beyond your understanding."

"Well, I am interesting to look at, am I not?" Giselle asked, arching her back slightly and smiling her most innocent smile at him.

"You certainly am," Paul agreed. He continued his linguistic excursion: "There's the pseudo-Darwinian theory of degeneration, based on a misunderstanding of the theory of natural selection, which holds that some races of humans or animals or plants—although they don't seem very interested in plants—are reversing their evolutionary rise to higher forms and degenerating back into lower forms. Lombroso's notions are an offshoot of this sort of thinking."

"And this is not so?" Giselle asked.

"Evolution does not have a direction," Paul explained. "Wherever it gets to is where it was going."

"So."

"And then there's the inventive pan-Germanic idea of the degenerate: anyone or anything that is not German, particularly if it is Czech, Hungarian, or Jewish."

Giselle thoughtfully cut herself another sliver of *törtchen*. "Sometimes you surprise me with these things that you know," she said.

"I believe that mankind can best be studied by its follies," Paul told her.

"Which is why I study you," she said. "You are a folly all to yourself."

Paul laughed. "And you are my folly," he told her. "I am mad about you."

Giselle nodded. "Yes," she said. "And I am sane about you." She put her hand on top of his and squeezed gently. "We will discuss this. And now I had better go. I am posing for Klapmann today. I am a water nymph, and it takes me half an hour to properly arrange the construction of papier-mâché and gauze that he thinks is appropriate costume for a water-nymph." She stood up. "And what are you planning to do today?"

Paul considered for a moment. "I plan to wander about the city disconsolately searching for truth and beauty, knowing I will find neither until I see you this evening."

Giselle smiled down at him. "Keep that thought," she said, kissing him on the forehead. "I'll be home around four, but I want to work on my dolls for a few hours. You may take me out to dinner."

"Thank you, you are so kind," Paul said. "I kiss your hand." And he did so, following the old Viennese custom with perhaps a shade more ardor than was absolutely correct.

"You certainly do!" Giselle agreed. And she walked off down Verdegasse toward Klapmann's studio a few blocks away. There was, perhaps, a shade more sway in her walk than there would have been if she hadn't known that Paul was watching.

Charles Summerdane looked out through Paul's eyes and wondered how Giselle would react when he proposed marriage to her; when he confided to her that he was actually an English gentleman. The fact that he was immensely rich, he knew, would not bother her in the least. He would have to give up the great game, but perhaps it was time he stopped playing games, even for the good of the Empire. There were other ways he could be useful. Besides, he was already pushing his luck. There were signs that some of Paul's associates were getting suspicious of the perhaps-too-carefree composer. Paul was half convinced that the young man in the fur-trimmed greatcoat who had entered the café shortly after they had was the same young man he had seen loitering across the street from their apartment building when they had come out this morning.

Not for the first time he found he was glad that he was the younger son of a duke. If he were heir to the title and estates, it would be impossible to consider marrying a Viennese artist's model. The crowd, as the aristocracy called themselves for some reason, would never allow it. Even as it was it would be difficult.

He could, of course, marry someone else and keep his artist's model discreetly in a flat in London. But he didn't want to marry someone else. And Giselle would not easily consent to being kept in a flat in London. Well, he would marry her—if she'd have him—and the crowd could just make what they would of it. If they became too oppressive, he and Giselle could just buy a house in Paris. Perhaps they should do that anyway. Giselle would love living in Paris.

Paul sighed and sipped at his coffee. A few minutes later he rose and entered the café, and headed straight back toward the lavatory. When he left he paused at an empty table to tie his shoe. "I think I'm being followed," he said in an undertone to a placid-looking, balding gentleman one table over, who seemed totally absorbed in the morning edition of the *Neue Freie Presse* and his half-eaten napoleon. "You don't know me."

The man frowned slightly and kept reading. Paul dropped a thick white envelope containing his latest tone poem onto the chair next to him, shielding the action with his overcoat, and then returned to his table, threw a few coins on it, and headed off down the street.

SEVEN

CHANCE

Kingdoms are but cares,
State is devoid of stay;
Riches are ready snares,
And hasten to decay.
                                          —HENRY VI

Age, Barnett reflected, was creeping up on him. Or perhaps it was merely his sedentary habits. Four days of playing tennis with the Bulefortes was taking an unfamiliar toll on muscles he had forgotten he had. Two sets of tennis each day was proving to be much harder work than he remembered it being. And, despite the fact that he kept telling himself he would benefit from the exercise, it was not getting easier as the days passed. His calf muscles were complaining bitterly now that today's session was over. Other muscles, he was sure, would soon join in. He should either play more often or give it up entirely. He soaked himself in the bathtub for half an hour, until the water grew quite tepid, and then set about dressing for dinner.

Barnett found himself taking more care than usual over assembling the right evening costume. The new dinner jacket that he had been saving for Paris. And the gold links and studs with the opal insets that Cecily had given him for his last birthday. He rejected three collars before finding one that seemed to have the necessary pristine whiteness.

Cecily was closeted in her room with Bettina, a young round-faced domestic that the hotel had sent up to act as her lady's maid, and Barnett felt odd about entering until her toilette was completed lest he should see her partially clad with a third person in the room.

Being alone with one's wife was one thing; and how one chose to dress or not to dress was then one's own business. But, with even a maid present, seeing one's wife *déshabillé* was just not done. Wasn't it amazing, Barnett reflected not for the first time, how the French had words for everything.

Barnett had no doubt that Cecily would emerge looking elegant. She always looked elegant. What he wanted was her reassurance that he looked, if not elegant, at least passable. Somehow the impending dinner with the Bulefortes made him want to look as close to elegant as he could manage. This was, for him, a most unfamiliar feeling. He peered into the glass and struggled with the ends of his bow tie.

The mummer trotted in and perched his tiny frame on the edge of the chaise longue. Dressed in a suit of wide, light brown cheeks and carrying a dark brown bowler, he looked like a cross between a racetrack tout and a bill collector. "Evening', Gov," he said. "My, don't you look swell."

"Thank's, Mummer," Barnett said, adjusting the points on his collar. "It's my swell disguise. I'm going into swell company this evening."

"I knows it. Who says I don't?" the mummer said, nodding sagely. "A big dinner with them Bulefortes what you been associatin' with."

"That's right," Barnett agreed. "Signor Buleforte has invited us to a private dinner before our evening of bridge. It's to be very spoff."

"Cook it himself, will he?" the mummer inquired.

"Of course not, Mummer. Don't be silly."

"There's somethin' off about them Bulefortes," the mummer said.

"What? What do you mean 'off'?"

"I don't know, Gov. They ain't what they seem, if you can see what I mean. They's got more servants than what they should, for one thing. I been hob-nobbin' with the population below the stairs 'cause of that other job you gave me. Only in this here establishment, they mostly resides up in the attic. And them Bulefortes got too many servants. And a couple of strange ones, too."

Barnett decided that his bow tie looked as good as it ever

would, and turned to face Tolliver. "You've got my interest, Mummer. How do you mean 'strange'?"

"It's hard to say. They ain't really servants, I guess is what it is. At least not the sort what I has come to recognize as of the servant type."

"That doesn't mean there's anything wrong with the Bulefortes," Barnett pointed out. "You're not really a servant, when it comes to that."

" 'At's the truth," the mummer admitted. "But then our provenance is not really of the most respectable, you and me, if you get my drift. We has a few old bones in our closet what might keep us off the honors list."

Barnett took this attack on his respectability calmly. From anyone else he would have been insulted, but from the mummer these hints of shared memories of unspeakable crimes were a sign of friendship and respect. "What function do you think these nonservants of the Bulefortes fulfill?" he asked.

"I don't rightly know. They looks like toughs to me."

"Toughs?"

"Yes. That's what I thinks. I heard them down in the pantry yammerin' away in some foreign tongue, of which I didn't understand a thrip. But the sense I gets out of it, if you know what I mean, was that they was toughs of some sort. Pro—you might say—fessional maulers and scrappers. They goes out in the scullery yard once a day and practices doing exercises simul—as it were—taneous, like. One of the serving girls told me that. She thinks they is bodyguards. She says they is annoyed with Signor Buleforte for not letting them stay right up next to 'im and 'is missus the whole time."

Some Cockneys omitted their H's, some added them at every opportunity, some reversed their usage; Tolliver wove them in and out of his sentences with a random artistry.

"Interesting," Barnett said. "What about that other business? You get anything on Lindner?"

" 'Course I did. Who says I didn't?"

"What'd you find out?"

"Well, he may be an artist, like he says, but he ain't been doing it very long. His easel and all his paints and brushes and stuff are pretty much brand new. And he's got a couple of pamphlets hidden away in his dresser drawer in his room on how to mix paints and set up a canvas, and like that. The kind of stuff you'd study if you were trying to convince everybody you was a artist. And besides, he's only got a small tube of zinc white. First thing you learn if you're really trying to paint anything is to get a big tube of zinc white. A great big tube. And he picked the wrong shades of blue and yellow. If he mixes them he'll get mud."

"Where did you learn so much about oil painting?" Barnett asked the little man.

"I used to do portraits at Brighton Beach. One shilling for an amazing likeness, done at breakneck speed in charcoal. Two and six for a formal portrait done somewhat slower in oil. I was quite popular. The customers got quite a kick out of seeing a small person standing on a wooden box and painting away at their likeness. I don't know nothing about art, you see, but I does know a bit about oil painting."

"You're priceless, Mummer," Barnett said.

The mummer looked pleased. "I got me price," he said. "And there's something else what you might find interesting about that Lindner cove—he's got himself an helio-stat."

"A what?"

"One of them devices what with you send messages by sunlight. A little wooden stand with a mirror, and a kind of scrunched-up telescope for aiming."

"How odd," Barnett said. "What can you see out his window?"

"Water," the mummer said. "You get a grand view of the lake."

"Thanks, Mummer," Barnett said. "We'll ponder that one for a while."

Cecily came through and stood, like a goddess in shimmering red, in the doorway. She nodded at the mummer and then turned to Barnett. "Dinner, my love," she said. "Shall we go down? We mustn't keep our host and hostess waiting."

"I was going to ask you how I look," Barnett told her, taking her arm, "but with you beside me, no one will glance at me anyway. Let us go."

Cecily smiled. "Now I remember why I married you," she said.

The dinner, served in a private room off the regular dining room, was delightful. The room held a small but ornate wicker table, just right for four, with matching chairs and sideboard. There was a large pair of French doors giving a fine view of the mountains on the far side of the lake. The sort of room, and sort of view, that encouraged pleasant dining. Ariste Buleforte played host, having arranged the entire meal beforehand with the chef of the pensione, who was delighted to show off what he could do given a free hand and a slight monetary consideration. Three waiters and a pair of busboys were kept busy running back and forth with assorted dishes.

In addition, Barnett noted the two muscular servants that the mummer had mentioned. There were two doors to the room, one to the main dining room, and one to a hall leading to the kitchen. One of these large men stood by each of the doors looking impassive and as unobtrusive as a very large man can look. They reminded Barnett of Gog and Magog, and he decided that the mummer was right, they must be bodyguards. He wondered what there was about either of the Bulefortes' bodies that required guarding. He would like to have asked Cecily what she thought, but there was no way to do so without the Bulefortes noticing.

Soon he gladly put aside all such thoughts to concentrate on the food and the company. There was a cold white fish in a tart lemony sauce, a puff pastry collage of the meat of various shellfish, a layered dish involving pork and eggplant that seemed curiously Middle Eastern except for the pork, and a roast game bird with greens. Then pounded slices of veal with mushrooms. And on the side, artichoke, sauteed spinach, and gnocchi. Three different wines accompanied the diverse foods.

After a certain point dinner became a sort of haze of good food, good wine, and fine conversation. Then the plates were cleared away to make room for dessert and coffee.

"I see your plot," Barnett told Buleforte, staring down at a cake and compote construction that he obviously couldn't take another bite of without bursting. It was incredibly good. Cautiously he took another bite. A short waiter with a large mustache busied himself sweeping crumbs from the table with a silver mounted brush.

"Which plot is that?" Ariste Buleforte asked, his face showing deep interest.

"You're attempting to have us so contented and befuddled with fine food that we are easy pickings at the bridge table this evening." Barnett waved a finger at Buleforte across the table. "Don't say you're not. There can be no other explanation."

"Ariste likes nothing better than good company, and enjoys entertaining," Diane Buleforte said. "We get so little chance for anything so intimate at home. And you have yet to prove, as you call it, 'easy pickings.' "

A tall waiter with a dour expression brought in four delicate blue glasses nesting in ornate silver cages and filled them from an even more ornate urn of espresso coffee.

"Easy pickings," Ariste mused. "A nice expression. It is this which I love about the English language; it is so permissive of idiomatic construction. Of course it is just this which makes it so difficult for the unwary; but once one develops the ear, it is greatly pleasurable."

"Your English is excellent," Cecily told him.

"You have been greatly complimented," Barnett said. "My wife has a fine ear for language. Her father is a world-famous linguist."

"Is that so?" Ariste turned to Cecily with a lively interest showing in his face. "And what can you tell from my speech?" he asked her.

Cecily considered for a moment. "You have a very interesting accent," she told him. "It might be a textbook case for the student."

"Ah!" Buleforte said. He turned to his wife. "You see, my dear, I am a textbook case."

"It is a question of what my father calls the 'overlays,' " Cecily explained. "Your native tongue is one of the Slavic group; I cannot tell which, unless I hear you speak it, of course. You spoke it interchangeably with French as a child. You learned English from someone who is perfectly fluent in it, but also not a native speaker."

"Your father must be very good," Buleforte said. "How can you tell all this?"

"The Slavic base shows up in your treatment of V's and W's, and a slight liquidity of the sibilants," Cecily explained. "In your case it takes a good ear to detect it. The French is evident in a certain emphasis about your vowel sounds."

"And the fact that my instructor in English was not himself a native speaker?"

"The very precision of your language and the paucity of idiom. No one whose native language is English speaks it quite that well. You were stressed on speech patterns by someone who was, himself, similarly stressed."

"And how, if I spoke both French and Rumelian—for I admit it, and the Slavic language in question is Rumelian—if I spoke both of these interchangeably as a lad; how can you tell which was the native language?"

"Simple deduction," Cecily explained. "Little Rumelian schoolboys learn French, but little Parisian schoolchildren do not learn Rumelian. Indeed, the French are almost as linguistically xenophobic as the British."

"Astonishing!" Ariste Buleforte exclaimed. "You do yourself an injustice when you call it a simple deduction. Indeed, it is the sort of logic that is obvious when one hears it, yet one would never think of it on one's own."

Cecily nodded. "One of the secrets of the trade," she said, smiling at the Bulefortes. "Although, as my father keeps telling me, the clever magician never reveals his secrets."

"And you," Diane Buleforte asked, "do you speak any other languages?"

"I do," Cecily said. "We traveled on the continent a lot when I was a little girl. Professionally, you know. My father was the director of a touring theatrical company, and acted in the troupe. My mother was the leading lady."

"Actors?" Diane Buleforte looked faintly startled. "My dear, how dreadful for you," she said, extending one dainty hand to pat Cecily sympathetically on the arm. "What an improper childhood."

Cecily laughed. "Not at all," she said. "Actually, it was quite wonderful, and almost unbearably proper. The one way it made me unfit for contemporary society was that I never learned that there are things women cannot do. As a result, I've always been able to do anything I set my mind to, and for that I will be everlastingly grateful. It came as quite a shock to me to realize, as I approached adulthood, that there were professions that most people, including other women, thought women incapable of learning and uninterested in practicing."

"But surely, my dear," Diane Buleforte said, "there are many things that women or, at least, ladies should not indulge in."

Ariste Buleforte pushed his chair back. "I never thought I should hear you admit that there was anything you could or should not do, my dear," he said to his wife.

"Oh," Diane Buleforte said. "But those things I wish to occupy myself with are all—" she waved a hand in the air, searching for the right phrase "—proper for a woman to do," she finished. "That is to say, I would never wish to do anything improper, so the question of whether I should or should not never arises."

"And if something you wished to do were to be regarded as improper by others?" Cecily inquired.

Diane Buleforte looked slightly shocked. "That would never happen," she said.

"Never?" Cecily persisted.

"Oh, come now," Ariste said, taking his wife's hand. "There are some in our, ah, circle, who would consider our merely being here to be improper."

Diane laughed.

Here? Barnett wondered. Italy, or Como, or the pensione, or this room?

"I suppose it is possible that some narrow-minded persons could consider some things I do, or might wish to do, to be slightly improper," Diane acknowledged, after a moment's thought. "But I refuse to allow myself or my actions to be limited by the prejudices of a few narrow-minded old ladies."

"I, also," Cecily said. "The one thing that your aristocratic background, and my growing up in the theater have given us in common. I will not conform my activities to the preconceived notions of the narrow-minded old ladies—of either sex!"

"Aristocratic?" Barnett asked.

"Oh, yes," Cecily said. "Judging by Signora Buleforte's accent, she is of the French nobility. It is quite unmistakable. A hundred years ago, during the Terror, she would have been in danger of la Guillotine every time she opened her mouth."

Diane Buleforte nodded, her eyes wide. "*Incroyable!*" she said. "Indeed, several of my ancestors were unlucky enough to be caught by the mob, and so lost their heads. But, my dear, several hundred years ago, surely, you yourself would be burned as a witch!"

Cecily smiled.

Ariste Buleforte leaned back in his chair and signaled to the waiters. "I thought it might be pleasant to conduct our bridge game in here this evening, rather than retiring to the perhaps overcrowded card room," he said. "I have spoken with Frau Schimmer, and she has graciously given her consent. The waiters will shortly be going off duty, but my men will take care of our needs."

"It sounds good to me," Barnett said, pushing back his chair and getting up. "But it might be nice to stretch our legs for a bit before settling down to the game."

"Perhaps a brief stroll in the garden?" Ariste suggested. "It will give the servitors time to clear the table and prepare it for gaming." He got up and went over to the French doors. "I don't believe it is too chilly out. Although the ladies, perhaps, would like their wraps? We will send one of the waiters to your rooms, if so."

"I don't think I'll need a wrap," Cecily said. "At any rate, I'm willing to make the experiment."

"I'm sure I shall be quite comfortable," Diane said, peering doubtfully through one of the panes of glass.

Ariste Buleforte opened the French doors and stepped outside. The slight breeze that came through the open doors was cool, but not uncomfortable. One of Buleforte's impassive servitors did his best to rush around the room without appearing to be rushing around the room to get through the French doors and out into the garden right behind his master.

Barnett took his wife's arm, and together they strolled into the garden. The sun was down, and a large lunar disk was just appearing over the distant mountains. "A lovely night," he said, "with a full moon rising in a cloudless sky."

"Indeed," Diane Buleforte said, coming up behind them. "It feels peaceful, and endless; if a bit chill."

"Where one puts aside the cares of state, eh?, and reflects on the essential oneness of the universe and all its creatures." Ariste Buleforte turned and smiled at them. "And we are all one, are we not? We creatures that swarm upon the earth? All one in the futility of our hopes, and the brief flicker that is our lives."

"Ariste!" Diane said.

"I apologize," Ariste said. "I did not mean that as maudlin as it, perhaps, sounded. Indeed, until the words came from my mouth, I thought they were going to be jolly. The stars have a strange influence upon man."

"Upon you, at any rate, my dear," Diane said, taking his arm.

A man stepped out from behind a tree about thirty feet away and yelled something at them in German. As Barnett turned to look, the man's arm swung forward and the object in it flew in an arc toward them. A red spark circled the object as it spun through the night sky.

"My God!" Ariste Buleforte yelled. "A bomb!"

Several things seemed to happen at once, in slow motion. Ariste Buleforte pulled his wife down onto the grass and fell on top of her. The huge servitor broke into a lumbering run toward the whirling speck of red light, but it was clear that he would never make it in time. He was on the left of the group, and the bomb was going to land on the far right. Right past where Barnett and Cecily were standing.

Without any conscious thought, Barnett shoved Cecily behind him, yelled, "Get down!" and took three running steps forward. He leapt into the air, his left hand raised to field the object, which smacked into his palm like a great hardball. His hand went numb, but he kept his hold on the massive iron globe.

Barnett came down, switched the object to his right hand, and with one motion hurled it as hard as he could back where it came from.

It arced through the air once again, the red spark spiraling toward the sky and arcing back to earth. And then, as it was almost at the end of its arc, the red spark disappeared.

For a moment that seemed to Barnett long enough to remember every detail of his life that he might have trouble explaining to the recording angel, nothing happened. Then the earth shook, and the sky turned red orange, and a great hand came and slammed across Barnett's chest, knocking him down.

EIGHT

DEATH IN VIENNA

Per Me Si Va Nella Città Dolente,
Per Me Si Va Nell' Eterno Dolore,
Per Me Si Va Tra La Perduta Gente . . .
Lasciate Ogni Speranza Voi Ch'entrate!
(This way to the city of sorrow,
this way to eternal misery,
this way to join the lost people . . .
abandon all hope, ye who enter here!)
— DANTE

It was approaching noon on Friday. Paulus Leopold Hohensuchen, duke of Mecklenburg Strelitz, and his delicate and ethereal new bride the Princess Annamarie of Falkynburg, were on their way to make a formal call upon their imperial cousin, Franz Joseph, king of the dual monarchy and hereditary emperor of Austria-Hungary. Their for-state-visits-only gilded carriage, pulled by six finely matched grays, sandwiched between an honor guard of eight Household Cavalry officers in glittering uniforms, left the wide gates of their small Schloss on the Eugenegasse and proceeded to the wide and lovely Ringstrasse to make a formal circuit of Vienna's imposing circle of splendid municipal buildings before pulling in through the for-state-visits gate of the Hofburg.

The people of Vienna were used to such spectacle as a gilded coach escorted by eight of their splendid Household Guards, all in gold and red and high-plumed busbies. But the people of Vienna loved spectacle, and everyone on the street paused to watch as the lovely procession passed, and turned to tell his neighbor just who it was, and just what the relationship of Archduke Leopold was to their much beloved Emperor Franz Joseph.

By the monument to Maria Theresa, where the carriage would turn into the Hofgarten, a small platform had been erected and a cluster of people stood in front of it watching a puppet show in progress on the tiny stage. To one side, a small group of bureau-crats had paused on their way to lunch to watch the show, and they now turned toward the street as the carriage approached. Behind them waited a large Shugard Seuss revolver, stuck in the waistband of the student Carl Webel.

Carl wore an all-enveloping green greatcoat several sizes too large for him and a wide brown cap that had been stuffed with newspapers in the sweatband to make it fit. These had been sup-plied by Number One, who insisted that he wear them. Why this was important in the great scheme of things Carl did not know, but the first thing taught to a young anarchist when he swears on the blood of his parents never to divulge the secrets of the Secret Free-dom League is to obey orders. Carl pulled the cap down, turned up the collar on the green greatcoat, and peered through his wire-rimmed spectacles. The Ferret had wanted him to remove the spec-tacles but he had assured the Ferret that, if he was actually expected to hit anything, that was impossible. The Ferret had grudgingly agreed.

The procession was just coming into sight around the curve of the Ringstrasse, unmistakable in its horse guard, state carriage, horse guard configuration. The remaining cluster of people watch-ing the puppets turned and drifted over to line the street as the car-riage approached. Carl Webel nervously unwrapped the scarf from around his neck and unbuttoned the green greatcoat. "Desperate times require desperate measures," he muttered; a litany he had learned from the Ferret, and one he firmly believed he believed.

His right hand reached for the revolver and clasped its bulbous grip firmly. As the leading pair of horse guards clattered toward him, he pulled the pistol from his waistband and held it ready, under the greatcoat and over his heart.

The horse guard rounded the corner. Webel tensed himself, ready to step out of the shadow, insert himself between a portly, red-faced man and his stocky, grossly over-mustached companion, and fire the revolver into the carriage as it came abreast of him. He tried to decide between "Death to the tyrant!" and "So perishes a vile oppressor of the people!" as the most impressive thing to yell as he fired.

The moment of truth arrived. Webel brought the Shugard Seuss from under his coat and put his thumb on the hammer. The approaching carriage came into amazingly clear focus, while everything else around him retreated into a fog. His feet seemed to have glued themselves to the ground, and become impossibly heavy to move. With one last deep breath he pulled himself free and ran forward toward the carriage and, yelling "Death to the people! Death to the people!" fired the heavy revolver repeatedly through the beautifully lacquered Mecklenburg Strelitz ducal arms on the carriage door.

The coachman whipped the horses forward, following his instructions to get away from any such event as quickly as possible. The horse guards wheeled around and headed off in at least three different directions, searching for the cause of the gunfire. Webel turned and ran back through the crowd, which seemed to part before him. One man clutched at Webel's greatcoat in an effort to stop him but Webel, in a blood-fury of exhilaration and fear, brought the Shugard Seuss revolver down sharply on the man's head and kept running.

Somewhere behind him there was a sharp explosion. A bomb had been set off in the path of the carriage. Two of the four Household Guards who were pursuing Webel, wheeled and galloped off to counter this new, and more immediate threat, but the others came pounding on.

The Ferret appeared before him and grabbed him by the shoulder. "Lie down!" he ordered. "Now!"

Webel dropped. Several pairs of feet pushed and prodded him, and he rolled into an empty space that appeared before him. As a flap was lowered behind him he realized that he was under the platform holding the puppet show stage. Outside there was yelling and screaming and the sound of running feet and cantering horses, as the Household Guardsmen searched for their prey. Inside all was dark. Webel rolled over to get deeper into the space and something sticky brushed his cheek. He reached up and traced the stickiness to the shoulder of his coat, where the Ferret had grabbed him. Rolling back, he lifted the end of the tent flap slightly and looked at his hand. There was a slender smear of almost-dried blood. Blood! What had the Ferret been doing to get his hand stained with blood?

It was approaching six o'clock when Paul entered the lobby of his building. A large man sitting on the staircase looked up as he entered. "Herr Paul Donzhof?"

"Yes?"

The man produced a Mauser automatic from the folds of his overcoat and pointed it at Paul. "We are of the police. I am Inspector Harcev. Please raise your hands above your head. Make no motion toward your pockets or I shall shoot you."

"What?"

Paul heard a footstep behind him, and then suddenly he was embraced in a powerful bear hug from behind by one man while another rapidly and impersonally went through his pockets and prodded and squeezed every place on his body where he might have concealed a weapon. Then his hands were twisted behind his back and a pair of handcuffs were screwed onto his wrists. The whole procedure took less than thirty seconds.

Charles Summerdane stood mute and impassive at this display of overwhelming force, but his mind raced. Had the police discovered who he really was or what he was doing in Vienna? Had they stumbled upon the lesser truth that, as Paul Donzhof, he was a member of an anarchist group? He had thought that it was the uneasy anarchists who were following him about. Could it, instead, have been the police? Perhaps the *Kundschafts Stelle* had been watching him for the past few weeks, and was even now rounding up the other members of his group.

Summerdane decided that a general denial, just to set the tone, would be in order. He would adopt the attitude of a truly innocent man until he found out just what they believed him guilty of—and probably beyond.

"I don't understand what this is about," he said with as much dignity as he could manage with his hands manacled behind his back and two large men holding him by the shoulders. "Why are you treating me like a common criminal? Am I under arrest? I have done nothing."

"That is for the magistrate to decide," Inspector Harcev said. He gestured. "Bring him."

"Yes, Herr Inspector," one of his captors voiced. With one man grasping him by the elbow, the other prodding him in the back, and the inspector leading the way, they propelled Charles up the four flights of stairs to his landing.

The front door to his apartment had been broken in and was drooping crazily, hanging from its lower hinge. Several men in black suits were visible in the hallway inside the apartment, tramping about and examining everything there was to examine.

"Bring him!" the inspector repeated, heading into the apartment.

Summerdane was propelled into the apartment by somebody's hand pushing the flat of his back. He stumbled, but managed to catch himself before he fell. "Say!" he said. "That sort of thing isn't necessary."

Inspector Harcev stood by the door to the bedroom and gestured within. "And that, Herr Donzhof," he said, "was that necessary?"

Charles stood next to the inspector and looked into the bedroom. There, on the checkerboard brown-and-white goose-feather quilt that covered his bed, was a great pool of blood. Beside it, and partly over it, was the body of Giselle Schiff. She was in her white smock over a patterned shirtfront with puffy sleeves. Her stockinged feet were in red knitted slippers from Persia that Paul Donzhof had brought her for her last birthday. Her throat had been cut straight across in one deep slash by a very sharp blade, leaving a gaping red mouth of a wound. Her eyes stared sightlessly at the doorway where Charles was standing. Great splotches of blood were on the wall in the bedroom and leading out of the hallway, as though someone, his hands covered with blood, had staggered from the room, perhaps overwhelmed with what he had just done.

"Oh, God!" Charles said, and a white fog of pain suddenly swept over him, and he felt as though he had been kicked in the stomach and without any conscious thought he found that he was bent over and had begun throwing up everything he had eaten that day.

"Goddam!" Inspector Harcev muttered, hopping aside, "he's

retching over my shoe. Take him into the bathroom in the next apartment—they're not finished with this one yet—and clean him up when he stops vomiting. Then take him to the central police station and put him in a holding cell. We'll bring him before an examining magistrate in the morning."

INCOGNITO

In the four parts of the earth are many that are able to write learned books, many that are able to lead armies, and many also that are able to govern kingdoms and empires; but few there be that can keep a hotel.

—OMAR KAYYAM

A great roaring sounded in Barnett's ears, and three white blobs appeared in the blackness that had been his vision and faded away again. The roaring increased until it filled his whole mind and being, and several eternities passed, but then ever so slowly it died away to a dull, flat buzz. The blobs reappeared, filling his vision, and then receded some and came into focus, and they were heads. One of them belonged to Cecily. Behind her was a window and a ceiling. Barnett realized that he was lying down.

What had happened? The last thing he remembered was walking on the grass with Cecily and the Bulefortes. And then—Oh, yes, a red spark came spiraling through the air. A red—he remembered! He had caught the infernal device that had been heaved at them and thrown it back. And then—nothing. How long had he been lying here, he wondered. Had the bomb gone off? How were the Bulefortes? He tried to sit up, but it seemed that his muscles couldn't remember how.

He peered up at Cecily and the other two heads. "I think you're beautiful and wonderful," he told Cecily, "and whatever happened to me, I'm so glad you're all right."

Cecily seemed to be staring down at him and smiling encouragingly, but her expression did not change, and she didn't reply. Oh, of course, his words had been thought but not spoken, they had not come out. He must try again.

He tried to take a deep breath, but couldn't manage, so he settled for a shallow one. He concentrated on working his mouth and vocal cords. "Hello!" he croaked.

"You're awake!" Cecily said, reaching over and putting a hand on his forehead. He realized that she was sitting on a chair by the bed.

"What am I doing here?" he asked. The words sounded unnaturally loud, and his head began to ache. One of the heads disappeared from view, and he heard a door closing.

"Hello, my love," Cecily said.

"Well, that is a change," a new voice said. "Most usually the first question is 'Where am I?' but you have jumped right over that one." A genial-looking stout man with a great walrus mustache peered down at him over Cecily's shoulder.

"This is Dr. Silbermann," Cecily explained. "From Vienna. Luckily he is a guest at the pensione, as the closest regular doctor is in Como."

"Not that I am an irregular doctor, you understand," Silbermann insisted, "but merely a doctor on vacation."

"I remember," Barnett said. "I have seen you in the dining room, doctor. How am I?"

"Very lucky is how you are, young man," Dr. Silbermann said. "By all rights you should have had, at the very least, a concussion. But the probability of that seems to be diminishing. And the flying shards of the infernal device have bypassed you completely, except for a comparatively minor slice taken from your thigh."

His thigh? Barnett felt down beneath the pristine white bedclothes and encountered a mass of bandages that seemed to begin at his waist and go down as far as he could feel. He tried to sit up to explore the extent of his bandaging, but he was pushed firmly back down by Dr. Silbermann.

"Not quite yet, young man," Silbermann said. "The possibility of concussion is not as of yet quite eliminated, and I wish you to lie very still until such time as it is."

"When will that be?" Barnett asked.

"When, after some time, you have shown no signs of having a concussion," Dr. Silbermann told him. "In medicine, as in logic, it is always more difficult to establish a negative. But we shall see what we shall see. Hold the light for me, please, Mrs. Barnett." The doctor rolled a sheet of paper into a tube and peered through it into Barnett's left eye, and then his right. "You may have a mild headache," he told Barnett. "That is to be expected. If, however, it gets severe, please notify me at once."

Barnett tried to nod, and discovered that it hurt his head. But not, he decided, severely. He grinned weakly and turned to Cecily. "How are you?" he asked.

She smiled. "Unharmed. You hurled that horrible thing away and saved us all."

Barnett thought about that for a minute. "It is seldom," he said, "that a man can appear a hero in the eyes of his wife. I will not say that it was worth it—but that is a consideration. Where am I? I don't know this room, but it doesn't look like a hospital. And what time is it? And how are the Bulefortes?"

"You are in one of the downstairs bedrooms at the villa," Cecily said, sitting on the edge of the bed. "It was thought unwise to attempt to move you upstairs while we were still uncertain about the extent of your injuries. It is about eleven o'clock in the morning. You slept through one entire day. And the Bulefortes are fine. Diane got a cut on her knee when Ariste pushed her down, but she is not complaining. Klempt, their bodyguard, lost a piece of his nose."

"It was sliced cleanly off," Dr. Silbermann said with the enthusiasm of the professional, indicating the area removed with the two fingers of his right hand, "and presents no further danger to his health, although it will do little for his appearance. I understand the Swedish astronomer Tycho Brahe wore a silver nose for most of his life, his own having been cut off in a duel. The only danger Klempt now faces is infection, and the cartilage in the nose, with such a slight blood supply, is not prone to become infected."

Barnett turned to Cecily. "Then he was, indeed, a bodyguard," he said.

"Evidently not a very efficient one," Dr. Silbermann said. "It's no thanks to him that the body is still around."

"The only fatality," Cecily said, "was the bomb-thrower himself. And he will not be sorely missed."

"Who was he?" Barnett asked. "What happened to him?"

"No one knows who he was," Cecily said. "He was carrying no identification."

"A man in his mid twenties," Dr. Silbermann said, "In good health, well nourished, Caucasian, Nordic-type; weight about seventy kilos. Blue eyes, blond hair, cut short, sparse body hair, uncircumcised—beg pardon, Madam—scars from what must have been a severe childhood injury to his right knee, but he seems to have maintained the mobility of the joint. Death caused by rapid exsanguination caused by a fragment of the bomb which severed his carotid artery."

"Ex—," Barnett began.

"He bled to death. It couldn't have taken more than a minute or two, and he was already unconscious from another fragment of the bomb connecting with his temple."

"You threw the bomb right back at him, you know," Cecily said.

"I didn't have time to think about it," Barnett said. "It was like fielding an infield fly. Who would ever have thought that the habits built up by playing baseball in Central Park would one day save my life? But I'm sorry he's dead."

"In that case I'm very glad you played so much of that peculiar American sport," Cecily said. "And don't feel sorry for the bomb-thrower. You did to him what he was trying to do to us." She leaned forward and kissed him on the forehead.

"I'm only sorry because, were he alive, he might be able to tell us what he was doing, or rather, why he was doing it. Which among us is a target for a mad bomber?"

"That is the question," Cecily agreed. "At first I was inclined to think that the people following us about might have instigated this. But if they wanted to kill us, they could have done it easily on the train, so why wait until we got here?"

"And what do you think now?" Barnett asked. "You've had more time to think about it than I have. Although I think I dreamed about it. At least I dreamed about explosions, and a bright maelstrom that was sucking me in, trying to take me somewhere I didn't want to go. And, somehow, I couldn't fight it, I just had to go along."

"How horrible!" Cecily said.

"The unconscious mind sends us strange signals," Dr. Silbermann said. "Some of my colleagues are attempting to interpret them, even now. The emotional content of a dream is an indicator of its meaning. But in this case—a dream of horror in response to an event of horror—it is to be expected, no?"

"At the same time it seemed strangely peaceful," Barnett said. "I don't remember ever arriving anywhere. I guess the dream just sort of faded out." He reached a hand out for Cecily. "What opinions have you arrived at regarding our bomber?"

"Not so much an opinion as a feeling, based on a little information," Cecily said. "And I'd rather not go into it until I know a little bit more than I do now."

Barnett looked speculatively at his wife for a second, and then said, "Fair enough. I think I'll go along with your feelings from now on."

There was a knock on the door, and Frau Schimmer and a serving-girl entered with a pair of trays. "Breakfast for the invalid," Frau Schimmer announced cheerfully.

And, with the word "breakfast," there came to Barnett the realization of a substantial hunger. "You must bear with me now, Doctor," he said, pushing himself to a sitting position. "Because I intend to eat breakfast. And if I don't sit up, I shall get it all over myself, and possibly choke."

The girl put her tray down at the foot of the bed while Cecily and Frau Schimmer propped Barnett up with pillows. "Eat, eat," Frau Schimmer said. "Good food is the best medicine. A delicate omelette, slightly undercooked as befits the situation; *brötchen*, marmalade, hot cocoa. And a tray for you, also, Signora Barnett. To eat along with your so-brave husband."

"You haven't eaten yet?" Barnett asked.

"She has not yet left your side, the signora," Frau Schimmer said. "I do not believe she has slept."

"I napped a little," Cecily said. "It's not important. Let's eat breakfast."

Dr. Silbermann examined Barnett's breakfast tray and pronounced it suitable fare for an injured man. "But do not stuff yourself," he warned. "Eat lightly for a day or so, my boy."

Frau Schimmer looked disapprovingly at the doctor for giving advice that went so strongly against everything in which she believed. They left the room together, and her voice could be heard in the hall explaining to Dr. Silbermann the health benefits of copious amounts of good food.

Benjamin and Cecily ate in silence. There was, for now, nothing to say that needed words. After a few minutes Barnett's hunger deserted him completely and he pushed the tray further down the bed and sipped his hot chocolate, staring discontentedly at the half-eaten omelette on his plate. He felt that he was letting Frau Schimmer down, but he could eat no more.

There was a knock at the door, and the Bulefortes came in. "Ah! You are awake!" Ariste Buleforte came over to the foot of the bed. "We would have been in to see you earlier, but we were told you were still sleeping. But finally Diane said we must look in on you anyway, and so we are here. How are you feeling?"

"Tolerably well," Barnett said. "Suffering no pain at the moment except for a slight headache."

"Thank the good Lord," Diane Buleforte said. "We were so worried about you. It would have been unforgivable if you had suffered serious hurt."

"Two policemen have arrived by *vapore* from Como," Ariste said. "They are engaged in looking at the, um, deceased, now. But they will want to question us shortly. I apologize for the inconvenience."

"Don't take it so personally," Barnett said. "It's not your fault."

"Ah, but I'm afraid it is. It was, after all, either me or my wife, or more probably both of us, that this insane person was trying to assassinate. That he used a bomb capable of removing us all was merely a sign of his exuberance."

"Now hold it," Barnett said. "Don't be so all-fired eager to take the credit. We don't know who the man was after. It might have been Cecily and myself, after all. Strange people have been following us around since we left for this trip, and going through our belongings."

"Is that so?" Buleforte asked. "Why?"

"We don't know. At first I didn't notice them myself, but Cecily did. As you have seen, she is very observant. It wasn't until after our baggage was mysteriously searched on the train to Como that I would believe her."

Buleforte shook his head. "You are trying to make me feel good," he said. "Less culpable. It is I who am responsible—not through anything I have done, but merely through my position. It was not fair of me to subject you to such danger. Although, I will say in justification, I believed we were safe, here; that our presence was unknown."

Barnett leaned back into the coolness of the pillows behind his head and found that they cushioned the throbbing of his headache. "Come now, sir," he said. "I admit you have me intrigued. What is it about your very presence that brings danger?"

Cecily took the two breakfast trays from the bed and placed them on a side table. "I'm afraid it is the climate of the times," she said, sitting back down beside Benjamin. "Royalty is considered fair game by the disruptive elements of our society. It matters not what royalty, whether good or bad, kind or cruel, progressive or repressive."

"Royalty?" Benjamin asked, looking in astonishment from his wife to Ariste Buleforte; who was looking with almost as great astonishment at Cecily.

"You know?" Buleforte asked.

"I suspected," Cecily replied. "I did not know until late last night, after the incident."

"I apologize for the deception," Buleforte said.

"I, also," said his wife. "It was distasteful to me. But if we had traveled as who we are, we would have moved about as a small army. How did you find out, Cecily dear?"

"Signore Buleforte's accent told me what part of the world you were from, and Frau Schimmer loaned me an *Almanach de Gotha* to peruse yesterday while I was sitting here."

"What are we talking about?" Barnett asked, sounding a little peeved.

"Benjamin, my love, let me introduce our bridge partners for the past week by their proper names and styles," Cecily said. "Ariste George Alexander Buleforte Juchtenberg, Crown Prince of Rumelia and Duke of Lichtenberg; and his wife, the Princess Diane Maria Melisa d'Ardiss Juchtenberg, eldest daughter of le Compte d'Ardiss."

"Actually I am the sister of the current count," Diane said. "My father died about two years ago."

"I'm sorry," Cecily said. "It must have been an old edition of the *Almanach*."

"Well!" Barnett said. He looked at the quondam Bulefortes and back at his wife. "Well!" he repeated. "Who would have guessed?"

"One person too many, obviously," the Crown Prince of Rumelia said.

"Well—Your Highness—what are you doing here? I mean, this is a perfectly nice pensione, but I thought royalty only stayed at the more exclusive watering places, 'hobbing and nobbing with their fellow bigwigs,' as a city editor I knew on the *New York World* liked to put it."

"Please, not 'Your Highness,' " Buleforte said. "At least for the remainder of the time we are here, let us remain 'Ariste' and 'Diane,' if you don't mind. This may be our last chance at such informality—perhaps forever."

"Ariste does not much enjoy the company of his fellow royals and nobles," Diane told them. "He finds them boring."

"For the most part," Ariste agreed. "They sparkle, they go to much trouble to sparkle, but they do not shine. It is as your Shakespeare put it: 'Some are born great, some achieve greatness, and others have greatness thrust upon them.' When you are born great you find that you have inherited a position that you neither respect nor desire. Because, I suppose, you have done nothing to earn it. Or, at least, that is how I feel. Others believe that being *hochgeboren* is a sign of God's favor, which must be convenient for them."

"You feel unworthy of being a prince?" Barnett asked.

"Not at all," the prince said. "Do not misunderstand me. I feel just as worthy as anybody else. I think it is not a matter of worth, but of luck. What I feel, if I must define it, is blessedly lucky at having been born great; for I do not know whether I could have achieved greatness. And without greatness—without the social position I was born to—I could not have, among other things, met and married the Lady Diane d'Ardiss. And without her I would be much less than I am."

"Silly man," Princess Diane said, smiling the indulgent smile that women give their silly husbands. "I would have married you if you were the son of a miller."

"So!" Ariste said. "And I believe you, my love. But you would not have met me had I been the son of a miller, so it would never have come to the test."

Barnett wondered what was so ignoble about being a miller, but he did not ask. "I'm afraid your incognito will not do you any good here any longer," he said. "After all, someone has just thrown a bomb at you; presumably he knew who you are."

"That's true," Ariste acknowledged. "An interesting question, is it not? How did the forces of darkness discover, with such apparent ease, our presence at the Villa Endorra?"

"Does no one know where you are, Your Highness?" Cecily asked.

"Come! Please, I insist," Ariste said. "For the duration of our stay here we will have none of this 'highness' verbiage. When you come to visit us at Weisserschloss, I'm afraid the formalities will be in place. But not here."

"And you will come visit us," Princess Diane said. "So that we may thank you adequately. Besides, Ariste has no one to play bridge with back home. We think they're all afraid to win; a trait that you two have decidedly not shown."

"As far as knowing that we are here," Ariste said, "very few people know that. Outside of those I travel with, only my mother, my chief minister, and Frau Schimmer knew. Most incognito is a joke, you know. Your prince of Wales traveled to Paris as the Baron something-or-other; but everyone he came in contact with was warned as to who he really was. The Tsar goes incognito, but never as anything less than a duke, and only among those who already know who he is. It is merely so that a layer of formality can be done away with by pretending that the tsar is not present.

"My incognito, on the other hand, is honest. First of all, I really enjoy traveling simply and without adornment; and without the score of retainers that would be necessary for the least sort of official visit. So does the princess."

"The first time Ariste suggested it," Diane said, "I confess that I thought he was out of his mind. But he was insistent. And he was right. If you travel with your household, the only thing you really change is the climate. You get to see nothing of the people, or their customs, or their problems. You know nothing of those who depend upon you."

Prince Ariste nodded. "There is a story that when the last tsar traveled through Russia the army went ahead and made sure that the houses were freshly painted in the towns he passed through. And if the people of the town were too poor to paint all the houses, then they made sure that the houses on the street through which the tsar passed were painted. And if the people were too poor to paint the houses along the street, then they made sure that at least the fronts of the houses were painted. The tsar lived his entire life without ever seeing a dirty house."

"So you do this at least partly to keep in touch with what's going on among the common people?" Cecily asked.

"Yes," Prince Ariste said, and then he shook his head. "But there is something going on throughout Europe that the common people know no more about than the aristocracy. There is a great conspiracy afoot to kill off the important people. Not merely the royals or the nobles, but ministers, police officials, politicians of any and all political stripes, land owners, factory owners, newspaper publishers and editors. It seems as if anyone who has his head sticking up above the crowd is liable to have it lopped off at the neck by unseen hands."

Barnett nodded. "I have noticed the tendency, Your—Ariste. I think it's a wave of the sort of general madness that sometimes sweeps across populations. The Children's Crusade, witchcraft, tulip mania; such insanities come along and then disappear. Now it's assassinations. Small, unconnected groups, each feeding off the actions of the others as reported in the press. Some think of themselves as socialist or anarchist, some reactionary, some are barely aware of the motive that impels them into violence."

"I would like to think that," Ariste agreed. "A cluster of unconnected groups, all acting out of a common madness but not a common cause. It would make it, indeed, merely a horrible passing fad. But I'm afraid that there is some intelligence at work here. That all these murders are somehow connected. This is the third— no, the fourth—time they have tried to kill me, you know."

"No, I didn't," Barnett said.

"How silly of me. Of course you didn't. How could you have? Well, it is. This is why I have developed such an interest in the subject. But, until today, I thought our incognito was safe. For four years Diane and I have traveled forth as the Bulefortes; to Florence, to Venice, to Rome; and each time ending up here at the Villa Endorra for a week or two. It was our treasured vacation. And now we will be unable to do it anymore. It is not safe for any of the other guests of the hotel to have us here. Diane and I will have to go to one of those well-guarded spas of the aristocracy along the Riviera."

"You really believe that all these assassinations are part of one conspiracy?" Barnett asked.

"When someone is trying to kill you, Mr. Barnett," the prince said, "you put a lot of thought into whom and why. The whoms, in my case, have been several different people, entirely unrelated, part of no common conspiracy that Section Seven of the Imperial Commissariat, which is charged with the safety of we minor princelings, could uncover. Now I find it strange that four different people who do not know either me or each other should each independently decide to attempt to kill me. I am, after all, not an important monarch. Indeed, I am largely a figurehead, since most of the administrative authority of Rumelia has long since been relegated to the Imperial Ministers of the Austro-Hungarian Empire. I am a vassal of the emperor more surely than any of my subjects, who, after all, are all free to move if they wish."

"You picture a vast conspiracy," Barnett said. "What would anyone have to gain from such a scheme?"

"That," Prince Ariste admitted, "is the question."

MORIARTY

The condition upon which God hath given liberty to man is eternal vigilance;
which condition if he break, servitude is at once the consequence of his crime and
the punishment of his guilt.

— JOHN PHILPOT CURRAN

His Grace Peter George Albon Summerdane, the seventh duke of Albermar, hung his frock coat on the bentwood coatrack by the far wall and lowered himself into one of the sturdy Georgian chairs surrounding the small dining table. He waved Professor Moriarty into the opposite seat. "Please accept my apologies for having sent for you in this unorthodox manner," he said. "I did not think it would be advisable for me to be seen consulting you."

They were in a small, well-appointed dining room off the kitchen in the Diogenes Club, a ground-floor room that could be reached by coming down a flight of stairs from the butler's pantry, or by passing into a narrow alley off Compton's Court and entering an exterior side door which led to a corridor that bypassed the kitchen. His Grace had come the former route and Moriarty the latter. One of the duke's men stood outside the dining room door to assure that they would not be disturbed.

"I take no offense," Professor Moriarty said, pulling off his gloves and draping his black Chesterfield overcoat over a chair. He settled into the chair opposite the duke and stared at him over the golden owl head that surmounted his ebony walking stick. "It is evident that it is a matter demanding the utmost tact and secrecy upon which you wish to consult me, a matter possibly involving something extra-legal, or at least beyond the scope of Her Majesty's government. My assumption is that you wish to engage me to conduct a mission for you in some foreign land, possibly Austria. I should warn you that I will probably turn down your offer, although I am certainly prepared to listen."

Albermar raised an eyebrow, for him an expression of great surprise. "How in God's name did you know all of that?" he asked. "I told no one."

"I surmised it," Moriarty said. "The process of ratiocination involved was fairly simple."

Albermar pursed his lips for a moment and shook his head slightly. "Explicate it for me."

"A man identifying himself as your private secretary called at my house to arrange this meeting," Moriarty said. "Although you are secretary of state for Foreign Affairs in Her Majesty's present government, you sent your private secretary rather than a factotum from the Foreign Office. Further, although you certainly have access to government conveyance, and certainly have carriages available from your own household, your secretary arrived in a hansom cab. Obviously the sight of an official brougham or a carriage with Your Grace's ducal arms on the door would have defeated your intentions. What am I to conclude but that you wish our discussion to be, let us say, confidential. Then, to strengthen this conclusion, your secretary informs me that we are to meet in the Diogenes Club, one of the most private clubs in London and a favorite of senior level government employees. I believe that Mycroft Holmes is a member here."

The duke smiled. "Yes," he said. "An interesting and talented man. A man who sometimes seems to think that he *is* Her Majesty's government. And, on occasion, is almost correct in that assumption. His brother, also has on occasion been of use to us."

"So I have heard," Moriarty said dryly. He paused for a second and then continued, "And not only do you arrange our meeting in this most exclusive club, but in a private dining room within that club obviously only used for the most clandestine of appointments." He gestured toward the door. "And the man you have outside the door is in your service, not that of Her Majesty's government, judging by his attire."

"Yes, that is so."

"And the means of ingress you suggested for me was certainly designed to reduce the possibility that my presence would become known. So, as you would not chance being seen entering my house or even chance my being seen entering your club, I conclude that this is a personal matter that does not concern the government, or rather, one that you would have the government kept out of. And since my reputation is one of facilitating crime—"

"I have heard you referred to as 'the Napoleon of crime,' " the duke interrupted.

"Yes," Moriarty replied dryly. "I, myself have heard that. From the Javert of busybodies."

"Mr. Sherlock Holmes is incorrect, then, in his supposition?"

"My morality is my own business," Moriarty said. "Suffice it to say that I have never been convicted of any crime, and any public statement accusing me of any sort of criminal activity would be actionable."

"These days private morality is increasingly of public concern," Albermar commented.

"Only for public personages," Moriarty said. "I am not, and have no intention of becoming, a public personage."

"Sometimes it happens whether we will or no," Albermar said. "But I am neglecting my manners. The coffee urn on the sideboard is full. May I offer you a cup?"

"Thank you," Moriarty said.

The duke of Albermar poured two cups of coffee, diluted them with cream and sugar, and passed one over to Moriarty. "Another sign of my need for complete secrecy," he observed wryly. "It has been some time since I poured my own coffee." He settled back in his chair and cupped the coffee in his hands. "And how did you conclude that my mission for you concerns a foreign land, possibly Austria?"

"Surely on this island," Moriarty said, "as a peer of the realm and high official in Her Majesty's government, you possess the resources, or can command the allegiance of such forces, as you might require for any conceivable contingency."

The duke nodded. "True," he said. "But might not I be calling upon you as, ahem, one of those resources? You have performed signal services for Her Majesty in the past, including once saving her life, I believe."

Moriarty nodded acknowledgment. "Because, with other resources available, you would not be calling on me. Despite the fact that none dare call me a criminal to my face, the epithet 'Napoleon of crime' is not entirely unknown in the reaches of government. If any relationship between us became known it would reflect unfavorably on you and might hurt your political career. I'm not saying you wouldn't call on me if the need were great enough, but surely you would try other avenues first."

"How do you know I haven't?"

Moriarty shrugged. "I fancy I would have heard. Therefore my assumption that, as I am reputed to have an extensive network of—ah—associates throughout the continent, you wish me to deal with some foreign matter that, for some reason, you cannot put to the staff of your own department to handle. Another reason for my assumption that, whatever the problem is, it is personal and not governmental."

The duke was silent for some time. And then he asked, "and Austria?"

"I may have overreached myself there," Moriarty admitted. "It could be a mere coincidence that a week ago a man was murdered in my doorway, and that his last words were that my agents in Vienna were in great danger."

The duke of Albermar stood up suddenly, pushing himself to his feet with his palms on the arms of his chair. "Great danger, you say? Great danger? Come now, that's very curious. And did you ascertain whether this was true?"

"I was unable to," Moriarty said. "You see, I have no agents in Vienna, or anywhere else in Europe for that matter. I have a few employees here in England and an artificer in Aberdeen that could be described as my 'agent' if one were to speak loosely, but that is all. It has been my experience that a man who relies on the intelligent cooperation of others in the furtherance of his goals is doomed to failure two times out of three. For that reason I have few permanent alliances, but a large number of people in various professions and walks of life with whom I share useful information. I have no 'gang.' Contrary to Mr. Holmes's opinion, I do not sit at the center of a vast web of informants, and control every criminal activity from here to Sebastopol."

"But surely—your reputation—"

"Perhaps I find it useful to have it believed that my resources are greater than they actually are. I admit that I do not discourage such stories, but that does not make them true."

The duke slumped back in his chair and stared bleakly across the table. "Ah!" he said, "I was rather hoping that they were true; that you had a vast and resourceful network of associates throughout Europe, especially in Austria."

"I never thought to hear myself apologizing for not being the Napoleon of crime," Moriarty said, "but I'm sorry I have to disappoint Your Grace."

Albermar shook his head. "I don't know—I'm not sure what to do next," he said.

"If your trouble, whatever it is, is situated in Austria, surely for a man of your position in the government, the Secret Service could be of some aid," Moriarty said.

The duke smiled wryly. "Now you have reached to the heart of the problem," he said. "Except for the India Bureau, the 'Secret Service' is largely a myth today; the creation of certain sensational writers of that class of literature that I believe is known as the 'penny dreadful.' Three centuries ago, during the reign of Queen Elizabeth, agents of Her Majesty's secretary of state, Sir Francis Walsingham, were able to thwart the plans of Philip of Spain and considerably weaken the force sent against England even before the Armada set sail. But that was three centuries ago. Today foreign intelligence is mostly gathered by perusing foreign newspapers. Some of our ambassadors are quite capable, but others consider it more important to dress for dinner than to understand the workings of the government to which they are accredited."

"So?" Moriarty said.

"So, since Her Majesty's government will not pay for the professional intelligence service it requires, it relies upon amateur help."

Moriarty raised an eyebrow, but said nothing.

"Truly," His Grace said. "Young men from some of our best families are spending their leisure time prowling about the major European forts disguised as butterfly hunters and drawing plans of their gun emplacements and such. Junior army and naval officers are using their leave time to take small sailboats into estuaries along the North Sea and note shipbuilding activities. Other young men of independent means are eschewing the London season in favor of living abroad under assumed identities and gathering information on hostile activities that might affect the British government or increase the chances of war."

"It is astonishing the way the young will seek to amuse themselves," Moriarty commented.

"Indeed," Albermar agreed. "They call it 'the Great Game,' this clandestine battle of wits between Britain's amateur spies and the espionage and counter-espionage services of Europe's great powers."

Moriarty nodded thoughtfully. "It does not seem in this stolid and tranquil world we live in that the chances of a European war are very high," he said.

Albermar stared across the table at Moriarty, but he was seeing a private vision. After a moment his eyes focused again on the man in front of him. "Oh," he said, "there will be a war. We may be able to put it off for a while, perhaps even for a decade or two; but there will be a war. Under the facade of tranquility there is a crumbling edifice. The European balance is too precarious, the rivalries are too intense, the hatreds are too strong. The French are too intransigent, the Austrian Empire is too weak, and the Kaiser is too belligerent for the status quo to last much longer. And there are forces at work that seem determined to spur all of Europe into war."

"And the British?" Moriarty asked.

"The British are determined to remain detached from European affairs, and so they—we—will not get involved until it's too late," Albermar said. "That's why we have no effective Secret Service; why we're unofficially sending untrained boys to do the work of skilled men."

Moriarty took a deep breath. "What you say does not come as a complete surprise to me," he said. "But were I to concern myself with the inanities of men, I would have no time left for my serious pursuits."

"Which are?" the duke asked.

"If I were to say, 'the greater mysteries,' you would take me for a theologist or perhaps an occultist," Moriarty said. "But I am neither. I refer to the mysteries of science that have only begun to be answered. In some cases the questions themselves have only recently been formulated. How are we here? Why are we here? What causes the sun to burn, and why hasn't it long since gone out? How vast is the universe and how came it into being? These are just a few of the things that we do not know, I could continue indefinitely. But we are on the verge of knowledge. We now have some hints of where to look for some of the answers."

"We differ in our perception of serious pursuits," the duke said, reaching into his vest pocket and pulling out a cigar. "I concern myself with the affairs of men. I believe the universe will take care of itself, as it has so far."

"These men whom you concern yourself with are, as Darwin has shown, descended, or ascended if you prefer, from ape-like creatures that lived tens of thousands of years ago. Our closest relatives are the chimpanzees and gorillas. And the universe cares about our comings and goings as much as it does those of the monkeys that scamper about Gibraltar, no more and no less."

The duke smiled a tolerant smile. "I dare say," he said. He stared at his cigar for a moment and then thrust it back into this pocket. "Who is to say which of our views of the universe is correct? Perhaps they both are."

"Yes," Moriarty acknowledged. "You could well be right. It may be a slight difference in temperament that concerns you with people and me with distant stars. Unfortunately, from my point of view, I lack the sort of private resources necessary to finance my research, and so the world of men occupies much of my time. I solve other people's problems to give me the leisure to peer into the depths of space. I have developed a kite which I can use to loft scientific instruments and keep them in place for days at a time, given a steady wind."

"A kite?"

"Yes. The devices are not merely children's toys. They have been used in the American Civil War and the Franco-Prussian War of 1870 for intelligence gathering, by lofting them above enemy positions and taking photographs of what lies below. I have developed a new kite, based on an ancient Malay design, that can carry heavy weights to extreme heights. I wish to loft a series of them with special cameras of my design, and take pictures of what lies above. I have been using tethered balloons, but kites are cheaper and more durable."

"Very interesting," the duke said.

"No doubt. But I must finance my kite-flying and my other scientific interests by taking on problems of a more mundane nature. Only last month—no, excuse me, two months ago now—I cleared up a little question of inheritance for a member of the Swedish nobility, and shortly before that I was able to locate a silver mine in the American state of Colorado that had been lost for a quarter of a century, based on a crudely drawn map and the deathbed utterances of a crazed prospector. The problems were not without interest, and my fees for those undertakings will finance six months of kite flying, as well as the construction of a twenty-six-inch reflecting telescope of my own design at my private observatory on Crimpton Moor."

Albermar took an oversized white handkerchief from his breast pocket and used it to mop the back of his neck. "I'm afraid my problem is not so easily solved," he said. "I'm not sure what I expected—hoped—you would be able to accomplish, even were you the Napoleon of crime with a vast network of your minions at your disposal."

"What, exactly, is your problem?" Moriarty asked. "I have been of assistance to others in the past who thought their dilemmas insoluble, perhaps I can suggest something that would be of some use. Come now, clearly you have to confide in someone."

The duke stared at the table in front of him for a minute. "One of these men who is doing the work of England in a foreign land has fallen into serious trouble," he said. "Under his assumed name of Paul Donzhof he has been arrested in Vienna and will probably—certainly—be charged with two murders and an attempted murder, along with sundry other offences. The Austrians do not as yet know who he really is. To say it would result in strained relations between our two countries if his true identity became known is an understatement. He is, undoubtedly, innocent of the charges against him, but I can't give you many of the details because, for obvious reasons, our people there can't take too great an interest in the case."

Moriarty folded his hands over the golden owl handle of his cane and rested his chin on his hands. "Unfortunate," he said.

"Yes."

"Who is he supposed to have killed?"

"He is accused with assassinating the duke of Mecklenburg Strelitz and seriously wounding his wife, the Princess Annamarie of Falkynburg, by firing a pistol into their carriage. After which, according to the charge, he went back to his apartment building and murdered a woman who lives in the flat below his own."

"And you assume that, as an agent of the British government, no matter how unofficial, he is incapable of murder?"

"Why would he assassinate the duke? He is a secret agent, a gatherer of information, not an anarchist. He may be essentially self-appointed, but he has been reliable, perceptive, and of great value to Her Majesty's government. Why would he murder some girl in his apartment building?"

"Perhaps he had a personal grudge against the duke. Perhaps there was a personal relationship between him and the young lady."

"He did not know the duke. As to the girl, well, I don't know what his relationship was with her, but I cannot imagine him killing her. I know the boy too well."

"You do?"

His Grace Peter George Albon Summerdane, the seventh duke of Albermar, took a deep breath. "Yes. Very well indeed. He is my son."

"Ah!" Moriarty nodded.

"My younger son. Charles Bredlon Summerdane."

Moriarty examined a wall sconce thoughtfully for a minute. "I understand," he said. "An interesting dilemma."

"You could say so," the duke agreed.

"This has the potential for becoming a grave embarrassment to you and to Her Majesty's government should his identity become known. And it will surely become known if you attempt to aid the lad in any way."

"A fair statement of the facts," Summerdane acknowledged. "And yet—he is my son, and I love him dearly. I must do something."

"What?"

Summerdane shrugged and then dropped his hands to the table. "That's the problem. Unfortunately, I have no idea."

"So one of the three most powerful men in the British Empire—I believe that's a fair assessment—is reduced to impotence while his son is about to be put on trial for murder in a foreign land."

Summerdane rose. "I don't know why I am burdening you with this," he said. "As it seems you cannot help me, I should probably say no more."

Professor Moriarty watched silently as Summerdane donned his frock coat and pulled on his gloves. Then, seeming to come to a decision, he made an abrupt gesture toward the chair the duke had occupied. "Please, Your Grace, be seated," he said. "I will endeavor to solve your problem, provided we can come to an understanding of just what your problem actually is, and I am allowed a free hand. If you will supply the few things I will need it will save time, and I will leave immediately for Vienna."

Summerdane stared down at Moriarty for a moment and then dropped back into his chair. "You speak German?" he asked.

"I speak many languages, but I am particularly fluent in German. I was at the University of Heidelberg for four years."

"You matriculated there?"

"I taught mathematics there."

The duke took a deep breath. "What will you need?" he asked. "And what are your terms?"

ELEVEN

INNOCENCE BY ASSOCIATION

I know you: solitary griefs,
Desolate passions, aching hours.
—LIONEL PIGOT JOHNSON

Periodically through history waves of madness sweep across what we like to refer to as the civilized world. In the year 1213, thirty thousand little children, chanting "O Lord Jesus, restore thy cross to us!" marched to death or enslavement in a juvenile crusade. In the sixteenth and seventeenth centuries tens of thousands of poor innocents were tortured and burned alive as witches across Europe and the Americas. In the latter half of the seventeenth century a passion for murder by slow poison spread from country to country, mostly among upper-class women, and thousands of unwanted husbands, fathers, and assorted relatives are known to have died at the hands of those they most trusted. The number of unguessed-at murders was probably many times higher. Each of these madnesses ran its course in time and disappeared as an organized activity.

"There are many other examples," Barnett said. "There was the tulip mania in Holland, when a single tulip bulb of a particularly desirable shape or color might be sold for enough to buy a house—and quite a nice house, too."

"Nobody was killed in that one," Cecily said.

It was late afternoon, four days after the explosion. They sat in the smaller drawing room of the Villa Endorra, Barnett and Cecily and the Prince and Princess of Rumelia, who were leaving the next morning for more aristocratic and better-guarded accommodations on the *Cote d'Azur*. With a perhaps inescapable curiosity they were discussing the recently defunct bomber and his place in the epidemic of assassinations that had been plaguing Europe for the past few years.

"You think, perhaps, that it's merely that we live in such a time of madness that Diane and I, not to speak of our more exalted relations, must go about in fear of our lives?" The prince shook his head sadly. "After a thousand years, all of Europe—poof!—decides it has enough of royalty? No, my friend. If the people do not like their rulers they rise up against them—as happened in 1789 and again in 1848—they do not skulk in doorways and stab them with ice picks, or leap out of crowds and throw infernal devices into their carriages."

"The nihilists do," Cecily observed.

"Ah, yes," Ariste agreed. "Those Russian emigrés with their strange political beliefs. My imperial cousin Nicholas has created quite a problem for himself with his vacillating between concessions and repressions. The people are emboldened by his concessions and then maddened by his repressions." Ariste shrugged. "But for those of us west of the Carpathians, the solution assuredly lies elsewhere."

"Those historical manias that you were speaking of, Benjamin," Diane asked, "is it that they just sprang into being from nothingness? I find that difficult to imagine."

Barnett leaned back as comfortably as his securely bandaged left leg and torso would allow, and spent a minute in thought, trying to remember his European history. He had graduated from New York City's Columbia University with a degree in history, a fact which he had seldom admitted to his colleagues at the *New York World* in his days as a reporter. American newsmen prided themselves on a combination of ready wit and invincible ignorance.

"The times were right for them, of course," Benjamin said. "Whatever that may mean. As I remember, the Children's Crusade was instigated by two phony monks who went about preaching that some verse of the New Testament or other showed that Christian children would take back the holy lands from the Saracen invader."

"Fancy that!" Princess Diane said. "Religious hysterics, no doubt?"

"My recollection is that they planned to take the children east and sell them into slavery."

"The witch hunts were similarly inspired by greed every bit as much as by religious zeal," Prince Ariste said. "There were professional 'witch smellers' who went from town to town rooting out the supposed disciples of the Devil for a fee. They did very well at it, too. One of my ancestors had the pleasure of arresting and trying one of those rogues when he went too far. Accused the local bishop of dancing naked at a witches' Sabbath."

"Silly man," Cecily commented. "Must have lost his head."

"Indeed," Ariste agreed. "At the neck."

Diane, who was perched on a light green chaise longue, pulled her knees up, smoothed her skirt, and wrapped her arms around her limbs. "Tell us about the poisoners," she asked Barnett.

"They were encouraged by a secret clique of mysterious women who traveled about in the guise, usually, of fortune-tellers," Barnett told her. "The, ah, subjects would go to have their fortunes told and discuss their most intimate problems over cups of tea. If the problems involved a relative, particularly one whose passing would enrich the subject, a delicate and subtle solution might be offered. The poisons the women supplied became known as 'inheritance powders.' "

"You see," Ariste said. "In each of these cases there actually was a unifying factor: someone stood to gain."

"I guess that's so," Barnett admitted. "But if there is one in the current madness, it eludes me. And I think that there has to be a predisposition for such madness before the germ can take hold."

"You think, perhaps, it happens by infusion, like some strange epidemic?" Ariste asked. "Perhaps the idea of assassination is 'in the air.' Perhaps the people could be vaccinated against it as they are for the pox."

"Well, whyever these horrible people are doing it," Cecily said, taking Diane's hand, "please be careful."

"I promise, my dear," Princess Diane said with a wistful smile.

"Although our safety is rather in the hands of others, I do what I can to assure that those hands are competent."

"We leave tomorrow for Monaco to visit our royal cousin Prince Albert," Ariste said. "In ten days we shall be back at Weisserschloss, our royal residence at Spass. It has over two hundred very drafty rooms, several of which we would insist upon putting at your disposal would you care to join us for a week or two."

"We go from here to Austria," Barnett said. "And from there back to Paris, and then to London. I think Spass is in a fairly direct line from Innsbruck to Paris, isn't it?"

"Direct enough for us, my love," Cecily said, laughing. "If the American News Service can do without you for an extra week, I'm sure Mr. Hogbine can do without me. Besides, think how jealous he will be. He received an invitation to one of the queen's afternoon teas once, about ten years ago, and he hasn't ceased speaking of it since."

"Good!" Prince Ariste said. "Then it's settled. A week of bridge evenings. How delightful!"

"Perhaps they won't wish to play bridge every evening," Princess Diane suggested.

Ariste looked hurt. "Not want to play—"

"Of course we will," Cecily said. "Diane, how could you be so cruel?"

"It's a wife's job," she replied, patting her husband fondly on the arm. "Well, as long as you understand what we have planned for you in the way of entertainment, we shall look forward to seeing you in three weeks."

"One second," Ariste said, reaching behind him. "I have a gift of a rather utilitarian nature for Benjamin." He brought forth a slender walking stick of a dark wood, with a silver handle in the shape of a duck's head, and passed it to Barnett. "Dr. Silbermann says that your wound will probably continue to trouble you for another few weeks, so I thought you might find this useful. It is not thick, but I assure you that it will bear your weight. The handle is in the shape of the Juchtenberg drake, our family's device, and the full arms are emblazoned on the back. I trust you will not find that an impediment to its use."

Barnett took the stick and hefted it in his hand. It was the prince's own walking stick, he realized. "I thank you, Ariste," he said. "Using it will give me both support and pleasure."

"It is capable of offering another sort of support also," Prince Ariste said, "one which I trust you will never need." He reached over and pushed the drake's head, right beneath the embossed Juchtenberg coat of arms. There was a soft click, and the shaft of the stick separated from the handle and slid down, revealing the razor-sharp rapier blade within.

"Well!" Barnett said. "A handy-dandy little device, indeed." He felt at the blade gingerly with his thumb, and examined the mechanism. "The walking stick is so small in diameter that one would hardly suspect that a blade could be concealed within."

"There are artisans at Spass to equal the finest in Berlin or London," Prince Ariste said. "Particularly von Yucht for small arms and Shostak for fowling-pieces. This cane is a von Yucht."

"Also glassware, my dear," Princess Diane told Cecily. "And linens. For those of us who already have quite enough fowling-pieces."

Prince Ariste shook his head sadly. "She doesn't mind eating the bird once it's on the table," he said, "but she has no interest at all in how it came to be there."

"That is so," Diane agreed, nodding. "To the butcher should be left the butchering, say I."

Frau Schimmer appeared in the doorway and knocked on the door frame before entering. She carried a silver tray on which rested a squat, dusty bottle and five wide-mouth stemmed glasses with lacy silver trim on bowl and stem. "*Gnadig Furst und gnadige Furstin,*" she said, "Signor and Signora Barnett; I wish you to share with me a final schnapps before you leave my establishment." She wiped the dust off the bottle and carefully and gently pried out the cork. "There are but six of these bottles left in the cellar. When they are gone—" she shrugged. "But how can they be used better than by toasting good friends?" She poured an inch of the dark amber liquid in each glass.

"Cognac?" Ariste asked as she handed the glasses around.

"It is the Grande Champagne Cognac d'Epeursé," Frau Schimmer explained, running her hand lightly over the bottle, as though she expected it to purr.

Barnett looked at his glass doubtfully. It would be impolite to mention that he preferred beer.

"My god!" Ariste said. "After all these years? That it should still exist—that it should still be drinkable—that I should find it here—it is too much. No disrespect meant, dear Frau Schimmer, but this is absolutely incredible!"

Frau Schimmer beamed. "It is perhaps the last six bottles left in the world. They were in the cellar when I acquired the villa. Left here, no doubt, by some fleeing aristocrat during the time of the Terror."

Prince Ariste turned to the others. "Drink it gently," he said. "This is the cognac of kings. From the time of Louis the thirteenth, who was known as Louis the Just, to the time of Louis the sixteenth, who lost his head, the kings of France drank d'Epeursé cognac. And even they had to save it for special occasions, there was so little of it produced."

"Well!" Barnett looked at his glass with new respect. "Marie Antoinette," he said. "Anne of Austria. Madame du Pompadore. The Sun King."

"And perhaps, when Louis the fourteenth entertained Voltaire, he broke out the d'Epeursé—or perhaps not," Prince Ariste commented. "After all, what sort of palate could be expected of a philosopher?"

Princess Diane smiled. "A toast?" she suggested.

Prince Ariste raised his glass. "To—" he thought for a moment. "To friendship," he said finally. "For, as the Hebrew sage Solomon said, 'A faithful friend is a strong defense, and he that hath found such a one hath found a treasure.'"

Barnett felt a warm glow of pleasure. Such a sentiment from such a man was almost worth getting blown up to receive. "To friendship," he repeated, and the three ladies echoed the words in the same breath.

"Let us toast our good-byes with the cognac of vanished royalty," Prince Ariste said. "Let us pledge to remain faithful even though the world changes, and be reminded by this noble liquor that it does, indeed, change."

"It is my husband's great tragedy that, having been born a prince, he couldn't become a philosopher," Princess Diane said.

"But I think that's all to the good. He is a very happy prince, but he would be a very sad philosopher. Whenever he speaks of the habits, the entertainments, or the fate of the human race, he gets very serious and makes me cry."

Prince Ariste turned to stare at his wife in astonishment. "Why I never realized," he said. "I promise never to be serious again."

Early the next morning, after a farewell breakfast, Benjamin and Cecily stood at the front door of the villa with Frau Schimmer and a gaggle of the villa's employees and watched the Buleforte-Juchtenbergs ride off in a post-chaise, with a brace of armed outriders to assure that the tranquility of the northern Italian countryside was preserved.

"I hope they're all right," Cecily said, as the carriage wheeled out of the gravel driveway and off down the road.

"I do too," Barnett said soberly. He stood there staring at the receding dust cloud while the others retreated indoors from the brisk morning air. And then, suddenly, he broke out laughing. "He's a prince and she's a princess, and they live in a big white chateau on a hill—with two hundred rooms—and we're wondering if they're all right."

Cecily drew her wool shawl around her shoulders and shook her head. "To be living in fear—"

"They should be safe enough," Barnett said. "They'll be well protected from now on. If anyone is still targeting them, he'll have his work cut out."

"Would you trade places with them?" Cecily asked.

Barnett considered. "No," he said, "but not through fear. I enjoy my work, and would not choose to give it up, not even to live in a large white chateau and have people tug at their forelocks as I drove past. Why the poor man can't even find a decent game of bridge!"

Mummer Tolliver, a great green scarf wrapped around his neck, slipped out the front door and came over to join them. " 'E's left, you know," he said, stamping his patent-leather shoes on the gravel.

"Who?"

"That German fellow. Lindner. Late last night 'e took off in a dog-cart what come up for 'im. Bags and baggage, parcels and paints. All gone."

"Interesting." Barnett said.

"Either he was not watching us, or he has done watching us," Cecily commented. "I wonder which."

" 'E were watching you," the mummer said.

"How do you know?"

"I knows," the mummer said. "I, in my turn, were watching 'im. You told me to watch 'im, and watch 'im I did. Who says I didn't?"

"Very good, Mummer," Cecily said. "You have again shown that intelligence and perspicacity upon which we have grown to depend. Let us go back inside and discuss this."

They returned to the sitting room of their suite. "Well, Mummer," Barnett said, settling onto one side of the well-worn faded blue chintz couch that took up most of one side of the room. "Let's have it."

"When you was downstairs last afternoon, socializing with them Bulefortes," the mummer explained, perching himself on the edge of a hardback chair so that his feet stayed on the ground, "I set myself to keep a steady glom on this Lindner. Being as 'ow you hadn't relieved me of the responsibility, if you see what I mean."

"You were watching him?"

"Not 'im, exactly. I was more like watching the door to 'is room. After ascertaining, you might say, that 'e was indeed in residence. 'Ere's 'ow it goes. I takes up my station in a convenient broom closet what was only a bit down the hall, settles comfortable-like on a pile o' dirty sheets and towels, and waits; peering through the keyhole whenever I 'ears a noise. I don't expect nothing in particular, you understands, I are merely doing my job. So, after about a half-hour, that's when 'e comes out, and I sees where 'e goes." The mummer paused for emphasis.

"Mummer, you have a compelling narrative style," Cecily said. "Please continue."

"Straight, 'e goes, up to your door—that is, the door to your room, if you see what I mean, and 'e knocks on 'er. Then 'e knocks again. But you're not 'ome, o'course."

"Of course," Barnett agreed. "He was just making sure that we were still downstairs."

"You've got it," the mummer said approvingly. "Then the bloke takes a key from 'is waistcoat pocket, unlocks your door bold as brass, and strolls in."

"Leaving you in the hall," Barnett said. "What a shame. It would be interesting to know what he was interested in among our belongings."

" 'E were not interested in your belongings rightly at all," the mummer said. " 'E were interested in your communications, you might say."

"How's that?"

"Tell us all," Cecily said. "This is most interesting."

"Well, as soon as Lindner goes through the door to the sitting room, I leaves my closet and enters the suite through the other door, the one to Mrs. Barnett's dressing room, which, you will recollect, uses the same key. Then I sneaks up to the connecting door, which is ajar, and, laying myself flat on the carpet, peers around the edge of the door to watch what 'e is doing in the sitting room."

"Very good!" Cecily said approvingly.

"What 'e is doing is going methodical-like through all the papers on the writing-desk and in your portmanteau. 'E looks carefully through the lot o' them, being extra-careful not to disturb their arrangement as 'e does so. 'E takes a writing pad out of 'is pocket and jots down a couple of notes as to the contents of these 'ere papers. Then 'e leaves the premises."

"What papers?" Barnett asked.

"A fair question," the mummer said. "I don't know what papers, as I didn't 'ave no chance to peruse them myself. But it was that very pile o' documents right there," and he pointed across the room to the writing desk.

Barnett went over to examine the small stack of papers on the desk. "It's our travel documents and such," he said. "Our tickets for the *vapore* tomorrow, the telegram confirming our reservations at the Jaegerhof in Innsbruck for the day after tomorrow. The reply to my telegram to the Paris office. Nothing worth the trouble of peering at, I would think."

"I guess his needs are different than ours," Cecily said. "Clearly he needed to know where we are going."

"But why?" Barnett asked.

"After 'e leaves this 'ere room," the mummer continued, " 'e goes back to 'is own room. By now I is very curious about what this gent is doing so I determines to find out."

"The secret police lost a fine agent when you decided to become a pickpocket, Mummer," Barnett commented.

"It wasn't my choice," the mummer said. "It was my father. 'E felt that a chap should have a trade that 'e can fall back on, 'e did."

"So what happened?" Cecily demanded. "Did you get into the room?"

"O' course I did," the mummer said. "Who says I didn't?"

"Go on," Barnett said.

Tolliver took a butcher-paper package from his jacket pocket and unwrapped a length of baguette stuffed with butter and Swiss cheese. "If you don't mind me eating and talking," he said, tucking his handkerchief under his chin and taking a bite.

"There's some bottled water on the dresser," Cecily said, getting up. "I'll get you a glass."

Mummer nodded his thanks, took another bite, and went on, "Well, after 'e's been in 'is room for a while, with me hiding in the hall closet as before, 'e comes out with a towel round his neck, so I figgers 'e's going to the bathroom down the hall. So I takes the opportunity to sniggle myself into 'is room."

"Sniggle?" Cecily asked.

"Well, 'snick' if you prefer. So I snicks into 'is room and finds myself a place of concealment."

"Perched atop the clothes-press, no doubt," Cecily said. "Disguised as an old leather suitcase."

The mummer smiled patiently at her. "The ladies will have their bit o' fun," he said.

Cecily looked abashed. "Sorry, Mummer," she said.

"No need," he told her. "Fun's fun, after all." The mummer smiled broadly to show that he could take a joke and tapped the side of his nose significantly. Barnett wondered what that was supposed to signify, but he decided not to ask.

"After looking around for a place of concealment," the mummer went on, "I slides myself under the bed, which may not be original but is adequate for the purpose, and I waits to see what occurs. Shortly 'e returns from 'is ablutions and changes 'is clothes. Then 'e sits on the bed, and 'e sits and sits. 'E's reading over some notes and talking to 'imself, but I can't make heads nor tails out of it, cause 'e's doing 'is muttering in German, in which language I is very poor. The professor 'as taught me a bit of it, so I can understand some of the singing in *Tristan und Isolde*, and a few other of Wagner's operas, of which I am inordinately fond. But not enough to follow Herr Lindner's muttering."

"You like Wagnerian opera?" Barnett asked, trying not to sound surprised.

The mummer nodded. "Very jolly," he explained.

"Yes," Barnett agreed, "that's how I'd describe them."

The mummer took another bite of baguette. "After a while 'e takes that helio-stat of 'is out of the drawer and puts it together by the window. And then for a while 'e's clicking away sending a message to someone out on the lake. And then 'e's peering into the telescope and scribbling into 'is notebook, by which I figure 'e's getting a answer." Mummer took another bite of baguette. "And then 'e says a couple of impolite words of a religious nature, and starts scurrying around the room and throwing everything into suitcases. And in a short order after that, 'e 'as vacated the room and is on 'is way."

"Sounds like whoever was on the other end of that helio-stat gave him his marching orders," Barnett commented.

"I was thinking some such thing myself."

"Let's hope he keeps marching," Cecily said. "And marching and marching. Let's hope they're done with us, whoever they are."

"Let us hope so, but let's keep a watchful eye on the surroundings nonetheless," Barnett said.

"That's what I've been saying all this time," Cecily reminded him.

"So you have," Barnett agreed.

* * *

Four days later the Barnetts left the Villa Endorra, taking a *vapore*, one of the little paddle-wheel steamboats that traveled the length of Lake Como, to Gravedona, at the north end of the lake, where they would get a train for Switzerland.

It was, according to Benjamin's pocket-watch, just ten minutes past ten in the morning when the green-and-white *Monte Bollettone* huffed into sight around the curve of the lake shore. It was twenty-five past ten when the tubby sternwheeler pulled alongside the dock and two burly boatmen hopped onto the dock and tied it off.

"Two and a half hours late, by the most liberal interpretation," Barnett said, snapping the gold lid of his watch shut and stuffing it back into his waistcoat pocket.

Cecily, who had been sitting on one of their steamer trunks, closed her parasol and allowed Benjamin to help her down. "The most liberal *British* interpretation, dear," she said. "You forget, we are in Italy."

"I'm not likely to forget that," Benjamin replied. "These people have no sense of time. None at all!"

"We are not in a hurry," Cecily reminded him. "Our train doesn't leave Gravedona until tomorrow morning, so we have all day to go a little over thirty kilometers. Even an Italian steamboat ought to be able to do that."

"Let us hope," Barnett said, and watched as four sailors staggered up the gangway with their two steamer trunks, six suitcases, and assorted smaller pieces of luggage.

The captain of the *Monte Bollettone,* resplendent in a light blue uniform laced with enough gold braid to ransom a king and a couple of dukes, leaned out from his second-story perch and yelled something at them through his silver speaking-trumpet. Whatever it was did not carry over the chug of the idling steam engine, and so, with an annoyed grimace at their shrugs of incomprehension, he pointed several times at them and then at the deck of his ship.

"I think we are to get on board," Cecily suggested.

"In a hurry now, is he?" Barnett asked. "Come along, my dear." He shifted his cane to his left hand and held out his arm for Cecily, escorting her at a deliberate pace up the gangway. He still walked with a slight limp, and his wound still troubled him slightly when he stood for any length of time, making Prince Ariste's gift a most useful addition to his wardrobe.

After supervising the loading of the last of the suitcases, the mummer skipped on deck, tipped his cap to Benjamin and Cecily and disappeared somewhere below.

There were two classes of *vapore* travel: *primo* and *inferiore*; which meant "first" and "everyone else." The difference seemed to be mainly the price of the ticket. A first-class passage was about five times the price of the other, and allowed the Barnetts to sit in wooden seats toward the front of the boat, which were identical to the *inferiore* wooden seats in the rear of the boat. They did have the advantage of being further away from the chuffing of the engine and the churning of the wheel. And, of course, sitting forward of the cabins (which could be made available to the *primo* passenger by paying a few additional lire to the purser) gave one an unimpeded view of the lake.

Lake Como and its surrounds were eye-fillingly beautiful. The eye went from the deep blue of the lake to the ever-varying shoreline of cliffs and beaches, rocky promontories and idle inlets; to the vineyards and villas and small towns above; and beyond that to the white-capped mountains which seemed to surround the lake protectively, and thence the impossibly blue sky. "They seem to have a much better sky here than we do in England," Barnett commented to Cecily as they sat holding hands and watching the passing scenery. "I must commend the government."

The two classes were separated by a white fence stretched across the deck and guarded by a stern-faced sailor. There were about twenty *inferiore*, a wild assortment of men, women, children, babes-in-arms, chickens, and at least one goat. The Barnetts had but three fellow travelers with them in *primo*: a solemn but well-fed prelate of advancing years who sat several seats down from them and was troubled, Barnett decided, by either distressing spiritual matters or indigestion, and a man and woman traveling together, sitting on a small bench to the side, who made a most distinctive couple. The man was a stocky, middle-aged aristocratic-looking gentleman of medium height, with a carefully clipped spade beard. His air of self-possessed authority was heightened by the small, twelve-pointed gold star, emblematic of some noble order, pinned to the lapel of his impeccably tailored gray suit. His companion was a strikingly beautiful woman in her early thirties dressed in an elegantly simple blue frock and gray traveling-cloak. She had an expression of quick intelligence, and was studying a paperbound manuscript which Barnett noted was a musical score of some sort.

"Yes, she is quite attractive," Cecily whispered, closing the *Baedeker* guide to Austria she was reading and leaning over to him.

"I, ah, was just wondering where they acquired those cushions they're sitting on," Barnett said.

"Of course you were," Cecily agreed. "I believe that if we wave a few coins at the deck steward, he'll bring us a couple."

"Of course. Good idea." Barnett gestured to the white-coated steward, who came promptly over.

"*Signore?*" The steward gave a little bow and waited expectantly.

"Cushions," Barnett explained, reaching into his pocket and bringing out some change. "We would like a couple of cushions for the bench, *per favore.*"

"*Signore?*" the steward repeated.

Barnett turned helplessly to Cecily, who smiled sweetly and went back to reading her guidebook.

"Cushions," Barnett repeated firmly. He pointed to the red, stuffed objects his neighbors were sitting on. "Cushions!"

The steward smiled, shook his head, and shrugged his shoulders. He would clearly, his manner indicated, love to earn even the few *centesimi* that the *signore* was waving at him, but unless the *signore* could figure out how to communicate, they were doomed to never complete the transaction.

"What's the matter," Barnett whispered to Cecily, who remained immersed in her Baedeker, "forget all your Italian?"

The lady in blue leaned over toward Barnett. "If you will permit me," she said, and waved a finger at the steward. "*Inserviente!*" she called. "*Il signore*"—and she relayed Barnett's request to the suddenly obsequious steward. Her voice had a throaty, musical quality that was pleasant in English and truly magical sounding in Italian.

"*Ah!*" The steward nodded happily when she paused. "*Desidera i cuscini!*" and, giving Barnett a glance which clearly said, "Well, why didn't the *signore* say that in the first place," he grabbed a few copper coins from Barnett's hand and stalked off.

"Thank you," Barnett said, rising and trying to find the correct European approximation between a nod and a bow. "Thank you very much, *Signora*. But you're not Italian, are you? You sound English."

"How very perceptive," Cecily said under her breath.

"That's right," the lady in blue told him. "I was pleased to be of service to a pair of distressed countrymen." With a gracious smile, she turned back to her manuscript.

Cecily looked up from her book. "That's strange," she said.

"What?" Barnett asked. "And why wouldn't you help me with the steward?"

Cecily patted him on the knee. "I'm sorry, dear," she said. "Call it a whim. But it worked out nicely, didn't it? You got to speak to the nice lady who calls herself English."

"You mean she's not?"

"No more than you are, my dear. But it's probably of no significance. I've noticed that you allow yourself to be called English on occasion, to save bother and explanation."

"I hope you don't think I was, ah, interested in speaking with her," Barnett whispered.

"Of course you were," Cecily whispered back. "Look at her. You wouldn't be a man if you weren't. I hope *you* don't think I was jealous."

Barnett grinned. "Of course you were. You wouldn't be a woman if you weren't. But you must know that I care only for you, my dearest love. Just looking at you makes me absurdly happy. I could never seriously look at anyone else. Not for an instant!"

Cecily squeezed his hand. "Do you mean that?"

"Of course I do."

"I'm so glad."

The steward reappeared with a pair of red cushions under one arm and gestured flamboyantly with the other hand, obviously having given up attempting to communicate. They stood up, and the steward tied the cushions to their chairs. Barnett rewarded him with another couple of *centesimi*, and they sat back down. "A fundamental improvement, don't you think?" Barnett asked, bouncing up and down on his cushion a few times.

"Some fundaments are more in need of it than others," Cecily commented.

While Cecily read her Austrian *Baedeker* and made notes in the margin next to what interested her, Barnett went down to check on the mummer and their luggage collection. The luggage was fine, and the mummer professed a preference for remaining among the *inferiore*. "You learn a lot about the native ways of doing things from sittin' amongst them," he said.

"As you will, Mummer," Barnett said, and he returned to his cushioned seat and settled down to watch the passing shoreline, a mosaic of laurel-covered cliffs breaking away suddenly to carefully tended vineyards along gentler slopes. He pointed out an occasional particularly scenic villa or church to Cecily as they passed, and she occasionally queried him as to how strongly he felt about Mozart's birthplace, or how long he thought they should devote to the Kunsthistorisches Museum in Vienna.

The priest had dropped into an uneasy doze, punctuated by periods of snoring and an occasional muttered word in no known language. The distinguished-looking gentleman and his beautiful lady friend had produced a traveling chess board and were bent over it in concentration. The man, Barnett decided, had the look of someone who does not believe that anything is "only a game," while the lady was treating it as an interesting diversion, and would pause to regard some bit of passing scenery. They were interrupted periodically by a servant, up from the rear deck, who would stand at respectful attention while receiving information or instructions from his master, then return whence he came.

The chess game ended and the spade-bearded man got up and folded the board, looking rather smug, from which Barnett deduced that he had won. He had the look of a man who seldom lost, and would not do it well.

He suddenly turned to Barnett, who looked away hastily so he wouldn't seem to be staring. "I beg your pardon," the gentleman said, "if I might intrude for a second—" He clicked his heels sharply together and bowed.

"Excuse me?" Barnett turned to look at him.

"No, it is I who must be excused for this undue familiarity," the man insisted. "But if I may be so bold . . . This lady and I are about to indulge in a bottle of quite bearable white wine; a fine restorative on a warm day such as this. If I may be permitted to suggest that you and your lady share it with us, I would be quite honored." He spoke English with a broad German accent.

"Well—thank you," Barnett said, after a glance at Cecily, who had pursed her lips thoughtfully, but did not look disapproving.

"Good!" the man said. "It is true, is it not, that what would be undue familiarity in most circumstances becomes normal intercourse on a ship or a train journey. Among people of the same class, of course."

"Oh, of course," Barnett agreed, standing up. "Allow me to introduce myself. I am Benjamin Barnett, and this is my wife, Mrs. Cecily Barnett."

The man went through the heel-clicking routine again. "A privilege," he said. "And I, myself, am Graf Sigfried Karl Maria von Linsz. My companion is Miss Jenny Vernet, the well-known operatic contralto."

Miss Vernet laughed. "It is the sopranos who are well known," she said. "We contraltos are merely tolerated." She lifted a gloved hand for Barnett to shake. "It is actually on my account, Mr. and Mrs. Barnett, that Count von Linsz has braved the rules of etiquette and thrust himself forward, so to speak. And it is pure selfishness on my part. I merely wished to speak my native language for a while."

"Quite understandable," Cecily said. "You are English?"

"American, actually. I grew up in Boston. I came to London with my mother when I was fourteen."

The count raised a hand. "First the wine, and then the conversation!"

Von Linsz's minion appeared almost instantly from the rear deck, carrying a small wooden box and a stoneware sleeve holding a bottle of wine. He slid the bottle out of the sleeve and deftly uncorked it. From the box he produced a stem glass, poured a taste of wine into it, and passed it to the count, who tasted it and pronounced it good. Then he produced three more glasses and poured the wine.

"Thank you, Trapp," Count von Linsz said, handing the glasses around. "That will be all."

Trapp closed the box, slid the bottle back into its stoneware sleeve, snapped off a bow, and departed as quickly as he had arrived.

The count raised his glass. "To a pleasant journey," he proposed.

They all touched glasses and sipped the wine. It was light, fruity, fairly dry, and agreeably cool. "You must have a supply of ice," Barnett commented, "to keep the wine at such a drinkable temperature as mid-day approaches."

"Not at all," von Linsz explained. "The secret lies in the porous stoneware sleeve into which the bottle is inserted. The sleeve is kept moist, and evaporation cools it and the bottle."

"How clever," Cecily said.

Jenny Vernet looked at them over her glass. "Graf von Linsz is a very clever man," she said.

Von Linsz glanced sharply at her and then turned his attention back to the Barnetts. "And what do you do, Herr Barnett?" he asked, balancing his glass precariously on the armrest of his chair.

"I'm a newspaper man," Barnett replied.

"A journalist? That must be very interesting work."

"At times."

"Surely a peripatetic profession, Mr. Barnett," Jenny Vernet said. "Tell me, Mrs. Barnett, how do you feel about having a husband who keeps such erratic hours?"

"My hours are also fairly erratic," Cecily told her. "But Mr. Barnett and I manage to be together as much, I imagine, as most couples."

"We share the same disability," Barnett explained. "My wife is editor of a monthly magazine. For the magazine's schedule to be kept, sometimes the schedules of its employees must be sacrificed."

Graf von Linsz shifted his gaze to Cecily. "So you also work," he said. "How—quaint."

"Are you one of those men who believes that a woman's place is in the home, Count von Linsz?" Cecily enquired sweetly.

"*Küche, Kirche, und Kinder,*" the count pronounced. " 'Kitchen, church, and children.' In Germany no woman of quality would consider working."

"Perhaps more women than you know would consider leading lives more fruitful than the bearing of children, if there were not such firm social strictures against it," Cecily said.

Jenny Vernet laughed, a musical sound that cut through the gathering tension. "There are certain misunderstandings here," she said. "Perhaps I should point out that the count doesn't believe in *anyone* working. But he realizes that anyone so unfortunate as to be born without an inheritance of fifty thousand acres in, around, and including the town of Uhmstein, might be forced to consider accepting remuneration for what he does."

"It is so," the count agreed. "The army and politics are the only fit occupations for a man."

"And, despite his talk of '*Küche, Kirche, und Kinder,*' no woman in his family has seen the inside of a kitchen for five generations," Jenny added. "Of that I am sure."

"The expression," von Linsz explained, "is symbolic, only. It indicates the strong Germanic belief in the importance of women."

"Indeed," Cecily murmured.

"Truly, for what can be more important than the raising up of children? The future of the race is in the hands of the mothers of the race. This I strongly believe."

Barnett decided that he'd better change the subject. After her miscarriages, Cecily didn't need to hear a paean to the glories of motherhood. "I assume then, Graf," he said, "that you are well on your way to becoming either a general or a prime minister."

"You are right," the count said. "I have trod both paths. I was an officer in His Majesty's Seventeenth Regiment of Uhlans, until invalided out. Then I was in the Reichstag for two terms until I tired of pretending to make laws. Some people make a career of this pretense, but I found it soul deadening. I thought I could influence the course of events, but soon found that talking accomplished nothing but tiring the jaw."

"Human affairs are not so easily influenced," Cecily offered.

"Ah, but they *are*, madam," von Linsz told her firmly. "But the legislature is not the place to do it. A group of men—powerful men—working together for a common goal, are capable of influencing the affairs of the entire world. Look at the influence a comparative handful of Europeans—British, French, even Belgians and Portuguese, have had in Asia and Africa."

"The influence of breach-loading weapons and rapid-fire cannon over spears and bows and arrows," Barnett commented.

"Yes, even so. It is always the mighty who rule, it is a law of nature. The handle is to our grasp; if we do not take it, we have only ourselves to blame!" His hand went out convulsively at this image of his, and he grasped firmly at his imaginary handle.

Von Linsz's eyes gleamed, and his face had a queer rigidity for a second. And then this fleeting reaction was replaced by a broad smile. "But we must not speak of politics or other inanities on a beautiful day like this. We must enjoy the surroundings, the weather, the company. Tell me, Mr. Barnett, what is it like, the life of a journalist?"

They chatted for the next hour or so, while the paddle boat churned its way up the lake. It was shortly after one when the boat pulled up to the dock at Rezzonico, a picturesque ancient lakeside resort town.

"Ah!" Graf von Linsz got up and stretched. "Time for lunch. There is a very good inn here, from which one can peer up at three-hundred-year-old castle."

"Have we time?" Barnett asked.

"Officially, an hour and a half. Which, of course, means at least two hours. Come. Please. I will tell the captain to watch for us before he casts off. First-class passengers are valued by the company. Join us for lunch. It will be my pleasure."

"Why not?" Barnett said.

"We would be pleased," Cecily said.

The count led the way up the hill to the Trattoria da Cesare, where they gathered around a table under an ancient oak and settled down to enjoy a memorable lunch.

The more memorable because they had not yet finished when they heard the boat whistle sounding. "The boat's getting ready to pull out," Barnett said, rising. "We'd better head down to the dock."

"There is no need," Graf von Linsz told him, calmly sipping his glass of espresso.

"What do you mean?"

"Because you are not going anywhere just yet. Certainly not back on the boat."

"You may have pull with the captain," Barnett said, "but not enough to have him hold the boat waiting for us."

"Oh, he won't wait," von Linsz said. "Not for a minute." He took a revolver out of his waistband and pointed it at Barnett. "But you will."

"Oh, dear," Cecily said.

Barnett's impulse was to dive at the gun, and he might have done it, stupid as he realized it would be, if Cecily were not there. So he sat still. "What is it that you want?" he asked.

"Your master, if I may call him that, Professor Moriarty, interests us. We would very much like to know what his plans are."

"He isn't my 'master' and I have no idea."

Graf von Linsz smiled. "But how can I take your word for that? No, we must look into this more thoroughly. We await my carriage. Then you and your most lovely wife are going to accompany me to a small property I own nearby. There we shall talk."

Cecily turned to Jenny Vernet, who was sitting at the far side of the table, her hands demurely in her lap, watching the proceedings with interest. "Aren't you going to do anything about this, Miss Vernet?" she demanded.

Jenny Vernet shrugged. "I don't know what you think I can do," she said. "After all, he has the gun."

STONE WALLS

Hell hath no limits nor is circumscrib'd
In one self place; for where we are is Hell,
And where Hell is, there must we ever be:
And to be short, when all the world dissolves,
And every creature shall be purified,
All places shall be Hell that is not Heaven.
—CHRISTOPHER MARLOWE, *DOCTOR FAUSTUS*

The Vienna branch of the Austrian criminal police prided itself on being thorough, methodical, and up-to-date. Their criminal investigation department was headed by Dr. Hanns Gross, who had written the book on modern crime investigation (*Handbuch für Untertsuchungsrichter als System der Kriminalistik*—A Handbook for the Examining Magistrate Regarding a System of Criminalistics, 1883). Their system for processing not-yet-convicted prisoners and detainees (the distinction between the two was purely bureaucratic) combined the latest methods in identification and record-keeping with the most modern techniques in criminal psychology.

The morning after his arrest, Paul Donzhof, in handcuffs and shackles, was brought before an examining magistrate. A document containing the charges against him was handed to the magistrate, who silently read it. Paul asked if he could see it or have it read aloud, and was ignored. The magistrate peered at Paul over the tops of his tortoise-shell glasses, shook his head sadly, and signed the order for Paul's indefinite detention while the case against him was being assembled. Paul was then transported to Heinzhof Prison, where he spent the night in a transit cell next to the guard room.

The next morning he was taken to the Prisoner Identification

Section, where he had his photograph taken, full-face and profile, against a measured background grid; his head clamped into place so it would be precisely as far from the camera as all the other photographed heads. Then a technician in a white smock used a pair of giant calipers to take his anthropometric measurements; a means of criminal identification that had come into use by police departments all over Europe since it was devised by Alphonse Bertillon of the Paris Prefecture of Police a decade earlier.

The technician measured his height, the length of his outstretched arms, the length of his left foot, the lengths of several fingers on his left hand, the length of the left forearm, and several different measurements of his head. The photograph was affixed to an identification card, with the Bertillon numbers printed below. The information on the card was supposed to allow positive identification of Paul Donzhof from among thousands of others, should the need ever arise. The card was assigned a file number, filed, and cross-indexed by name, race, class of crime, and several of the Bertillon measurements. His modus operandi, peculiarities of dress or speech, and known criminal associates would be added by the records sergeant of the detective division as they were determined.

When the Identification Section was done with him, Paul was divested of all his clothing, which was put in a sack and tagged with his name and prison number. The sack was taken away to the Examination Section where the clothing, and especially the shoes, would be minutely examined under a microscope for traces of blood or other incriminating debris. Paul was then taken to a shower room, instructed to scrub himself well with a cake of dark-brown strong-smelling soap, and issued a prison-gray canvas pullover tunic and drawstring trousers. Then he was shut into a small cell on the first tier. All very businesslike and impersonal.

That was a week ago. Since then he had seen but four people: the guard who took him to the interrogation room on three separate mornings, the man who asked him questions, the barber who shaved him and trimmed his mustache and beard daily, and the trusty who came around to pick up his slop bucket every morning. His food trays were pushed through a slot in the iron door twice a day, and he never glimpsed more than a hand of whoever did the pushing. Once he had been taken to the weekly police line-up, designed to acquaint the local detectives with the current crop of malefactors. But since the light was in his eyes, and all the detectives were masked so the criminals couldn't return the favor and identify them, he didn't really see anyone on that brief excursion.

His interrogator was a stocky man with wire-framed glasses and a stubby black goatee who asked him questions without looking at him and wrote the answers on a thick-lined pad. The questions so far had been routine: name, age, place of residence, previous place of residence, occupation, nationality, parents' names and residence, schools attended, military service record, names of friends, teachers, schoolmates, and the like. He was asked about his relationship with the deceased Giselle Schiff, but the manner of her death or his supposed involvement in it was not discussed. He was also asked about his knowledge of or any supposed relationship with the duke of Mecklenburg Strelitz, but the reason for the question was not forthcoming. He had heard on the street that the duke had been assassinated that day, but why the police should link him with the event he had no idea, and at this point they were not telling. Just what crimes he was accused—or at least suspected—of, was a question that his interrogator refused to answer. When he asked on what charges he was being held, the interrogator smiled at him through irregular teeth, with a smile that was devoid of humor, and said, "You will be informed, Herr Donzhof." When he tried pointing out that he had been in a café at the time Giselle must have been murdered, and that surely someone there would remember him, the interrogator looked at him and said, "We'll get to that in due time, Herr Donzhof." When he asked what was known about the murder of Giselle, the interrogator replied, "That is not your concern, Herr Donzhof." He did not ask anything about the defunct duke, and no information on that subject was offered.

Paul knew how the system was supposed to work. Another up-to-date idea of the Austrian police, it had been described to him by several of the anarchists who had been arrested for this or that over the past few years. Based on the ideas of German psychiatrist Richard Krafft-Ebing, it was a reversal of what had been standard procedure. Instead of questioning him for hours endlessly, with occasional physical encouragements added to induce a certain amount of pain and a desire to talk, the new method was to isolate him and let him dwell on the enormity of his crimes until the desire to confess became overwhelming. Some prisoners had been known to confess endlessly and to anything and everything after a few weeks of this, just to have somebody listen to them; and the problem became to sort out the true confession from the made-up stories. Others were more stubborn, and for them the old methods were still available. Still others, an unfortunate few, went completely insane after a few weeks of isolation; a sure sign, the police felt, that they had been guilty of *something*.

For Paul the isolation was a blessing. The sudden seemingly random act of a baleful universe that had taken Giselle had left him numb. He felt as though every light were too bright and every sound too loud to bear, and the act of moving from place to place and answering simple questions took all his willpower and attention. He didn't have the energy to think of the charges against him, to speculate on what the authorities might know or think they know of his activities, or to worry about whether they knew or suspected his real identity. For the first few days after Giselle's death and his arrest he could not have discussed his activities in any coherent way, nor could he have told them his whereabouts at a given moment or his reasons for going to any particular place at whatever time.

It seemed to him that whatever significance his life might have had was now gone, dissipated with the death of his love. At first the emotion had been more elemental than that: he had felt as though some great invisible being was slowly and continuously punching him in the gut. Then, some days later—he wasn't sure how many— he was once more able to breathe without pain, but he didn't know why he was being allowed that useless privilege when Giselle was dead and the rest of his life was destined to be a pointless void.

There was little outward sign of Paul's inner angst. British public schoolboys are taught a degree of stoicism that would have impressed Zeno, and not even as Paul Donzhof could Charles Dupresque Murray Bredlon Summerdane allow the depth of his grief to show. This had prompted his interrogator to write in his notes, "Shows no emotion over death of woman who is believed to have been his paramour." Of course, had he wept copiously and continuously the interrogator would have written, "Appears overly emotional over death of woman who is believed to have been his paramour."

THE CLAIRVOYANT

Si j'avais les mains pleines de vérités, je me garderais de les ouvrir.
(If my hands were filled with truths, I should be careful not to open them.)
—BERNARD LE BOVIER DE FONTENELLE

It was on Tuesday, April 14, that the world-renowned mystic Count Alexandre Sandarel, Doctor, Psychic and Clairvoyant, Counselor and Advisor to Royalty on Three Continents, arrived in Vienna with his entourage and took a suite of rooms at the Adler: entrance hall, breakfast room, sitting room, three bedrooms, and a large balcony overlooking the Ringstrasse. There was also a pantry and a small room for his valet. His other three servants were installed in the servants' quarters on the top floor of the hotel.

On Thursday he and his assistant and confidant Madame Madeleine Verlaine went to the office of the Ministry of the Interior to register as resident visitors to His Imperial Majesty's realm, a formality required of any foreigner who planned to stay for longer than three weeks. The wave of assassinations and other outrages which was sweeping Europe had made the authorities of many nations suspicious of the foreigners among them.

Count Sandarel and Madame Verlaine arrived at the offices shortly after noon and filled in brief forms with their names, local addresses, and planned length of stay, which they gave, along with their passports, to the clerk at the counter. After two hours of patiently waiting on a bench that might have originally been constructed as a torture device for the Grand Inquisitor, they were directed past the desks of the examination clerks and to the office of an imperial examiner.

The examiner was a short, stout man with thick glasses and mutton-chop whiskers and a carefully cultivated air of doubting everything you might say minutes before you say it. The walls of his office were decorated with the record of his accomplishments, such as they were. Framed letters from high officials and photographs of him shaking hands with various members of the nobility were behind him; plaques and commendations and graduation certificates on the wall to his left. On the opposite wall were three oil paintings of dubious merit which Sandarel peered at through his monocle with interest before settling into one of the two chairs before the desk. Two were landscapes; one of rather uninteresting pasture land with livestock, and one of a meadow that seemed to slant up at an alarming angle, surrounded by snow-covered Alps; the third was an interior of a more than usually petit bourgeois parlor unnaturally filled with glassware. Madame Verlaine casually looked over the diplomas and certificates while the examiner ostentatiously studied the folder before him. When he looked up and coughed, she slid gracefully into the other chair.

The Imperial Examiner thoughtfully tapped the pair of pristine British passports on his desk with his forefinger and then looked up. "You are Count Alexandre Sandarel?"

"That is so. I choose not to use the title."

"And you are Frau Madeleine Verlaine."

"Even so."

"This is your married name?"

"It is."

"Your husband?"

"Is defunct. He died three years ago while traveling in a balloon."

"A balloon?"

"Yes. Well, actually the basket below the balloon. The ropes parted, you see. The balloon went up, and the basket and my husband came down. It was most unfortunate."

"I see. You and the count are traveling together?"

Madame Verlaine nodded. "I am in his employ."

"We travel together," Sandarel affirmed. "Along with our servants. They will be along to register shortly."

The examiner sniffed. "You have not been abroad before?" he asked.

"On the contrary, our previous passports were so full of stamps and visas that we had to request new ones." Sandarel's voice was deep and sonorous, compelling interest if not instant belief.

The examiner looked up at the tall, bearded man with the piercing eyes who sat before him. "Our records do not show anyone of your name ever entering Austria before."

"My loss," Sandarel said humbly.

"You speak German very well."

"Yes. Also French, Spanish, Italian, English, and Russian."

" 'Count' is not a usual British title," the examiner reflected.

"It is French. It dates back to the *ancien régime*. My ancestors fled to England during the Revolution and, having no fondness for any of the Napoleons or Louis's who came after, remained there."

"Then it is not an active title?"

"Extremely passive," Sandarel agreed.

"Ah-hem." The examiner turned the page. "And the purpose of your visit? Do you intend to work while you reside here?"

Sandarel raised an eyebrow. "Work? My dear man, really. Work?"

The examiner looked at Sandarel severely through his thick-lensed glasses. "We have heard that you intend to give what you call 'readings' while you are here. Is this not so?"

"Quite possibly. I teach, I demonstrate the higher arts, I give readings. It is a gift, this psychic ability that I have, that I share freely. I do not charge."

"You accept offerings?"

"If they are freely given, yes. To further my work. Not to do so would be an insult to those I have helped."

The examiner turned to the petite, slender woman sitting beside Sandarel. He didn't know much about women's apparel, but he could tell that the frock she was wearing was fashionable and expensive. The hat that was perched daintily on her head, with the net half-veil covering her eyes—his wife had admired one a lot like that in a shop window last week and it was a hundred and twenty kronen. Over a week's salary! The woman would be quite attractive, he thought, if she put on a little weight. To his eyes she looked almost emaciated and positively unhealthy. Like most Viennese, he liked his women pleasingly plump. "And you, Madame Verlaine, do you also accept gifts for your services?"

She smiled sweetly at him. "Why Herr Examiner," she said, "what would your wife think?"

The examiner stared stolidly at her, but his ears turned red. "Never mind that," he said. "You know what I mean. Do you also give readings, and do you accept gratuities in return?"

"I assist Alexandre Sandarel in his activities," Madame Verlaine explained. "And I never accept money for my services—whatever they might be."

"Ah-hem," the examiner said. He turned to Sandarel. "You know that fortune-telling is against the law here in Austria?"

Sandarel nodded. "And a good thing, too. Those people prey on the troubled and the weak-minded."

"What you do is not fortune-telling?"

"No."

Sandarel did not expand on his answer, and the examiner seemed at a loss as to what to ask next. Finally he took a book from his desk and riffled through it. "Here it is," he said. "Imperial statute three-three-seven-point-two-seven, paragraph four, 'Vagabonds on the Public Highway, Gypsies, Sneak-thieves, Fortune-tellers, Astrologers, Peddlers, and Persons of Disrepute. These shall be classified as vagrants and caused to move on or be imprisoned for a term to be decided by the examining magistrate, not to exceed two years.' "

"Yes?" Sandarel said.

"A fortune-teller is defined as one who, eh, 'through the use of cards, dice, crystal balls, or other devices, or the reading of palms or the soles of feet professes to be able to foretell the course of future events."

"The soles of feet?" Madame Verlaine smiled. "How amusing."

"Do you understand what I just read to you?"

"And," Sandarel told him, leaning forward, "so much more. Your statute would protect the subjects of His Imperial Majesty from charlatans."

"Even so," the examiner agreed, smiling a tight smile.

"I am not a charlatan."

The Imperial Examiner leaned back in his chair, his hands laced together and placed on the waistcoat covering his ample stomach. "But how are we to know that?"

"A fair question." Sandarel stared across the desk at the examiner. "I will demonstrate for you the higher arts of which I speak. They enable the practitioner to access knowledge not available to those unpracticed in the mantic disciplines. But they are not magical. They can be taught to the willing disciple." Sandarel paused and gestured across the desk. "Let us consider you as a subject. We have not met before, and you will grant that you are not secretly in my employ."

"Most assuredly not!"

"And I had no way of knowing which examiner would see us."

"That is so."

Count Sandarel held his left hand to his forehead and probed the empty air before him with his right. "Your name is Alfred Vogelmass."

"Come now," Vogelmass said. "One of the clerks must have told you my name."

"Nonsense," Count Sandarel said. "It's on that brass plaque on your desk."

"Oh," Vogelmass said. "So it is."

"And you thought I'd done something remarkable. But have patience, perhaps I shall." He mad a gesture with his right hand as though he were squeezing a juicy peach. Then he flicked the imaginary juice about the room. "You've been in your job for some years—"

"That is obvious! You—"

"But you do not like your job. You have been passed over for promotion several times, unjustly, you feel—" Sandarel's hand squeezed a few more peaches "—and you are right. You took this job in the civil service originally for the security it offers and at the instigation of others—family perhaps."

Vogelmass nodded despite himself.

"But you've always thought that your true talent lies in some other field—something artistic. Music? No, I don't think so. Drawing, perhaps."

"Painting," Vogelmass said softly.

Count Sandarel went on as though he had not heard. "Had you pursued your career as an artist, you would have achieved great recognition. But even within the Imperial Service there are opportunities to which you aspire. There is another job that you feel you are suited for, and that you would like to move up to. It is more suited to your intelligence and your abilities, both of which are under-utilized in your current position. I cannot tell you whether you will get it—that would be fortune-telling—but I can say that you need more preparation, or perhaps a better way to show those in authority that you have made the preparation, in order to have a chance. And if you can do that, there is a good likelihood that you will be rewarded."

"Rewarded? But how can I—"

"That I cannot say. Something to do with befriending someone unexpected. Who that may be, I don't know." Count Sandarel sank back in his chair. "I am fatigued. Madame, would you continue?"

Madame Verlaine rose and stared unblinkingly across the desk, not at the examiner but at a point over his left shoulder. "Two children," she said. "Girls. Angela and Rosalie. Lovely young creatures. I believe you married late. Yes. Your wife's name is Marie. A beautiful woman much younger than you, but she loves you deeply. And you her. You will have another child."

Vogelmass twisted around to look at the wall behind him to see what Madame Verlaine was looking at. There was nothing but green wall where her gaze was fixed.

"There is a great service you can do the emperor," Madame Verlaine continued. "What it is I cannot see, but it will be made clear to you."

"The emperor!" Vogelmass instinctively reached up to take his hat off. But then realizing he wasn't wearing a hat, he merely patted his head.

Madame Verlaine sat down. "Your aura is light blue," she told Vogelmass. "The pains you are suffering will soon go away."

Imperial Inspector Vogelmass was speechless. When one is told that one's abilities are undervalued, that one could have achieved great things as an artist, that one's young wife is deeply in love with one—a question that had been troubling him—and that one will soon have an opportunity to do a great service for the emperor; one would be ungrateful not to accept these assertions for the powerful insights that they so obviously were.

And so Count Sandarel and Madame Verlaine left the offices of the Ministry of the Interior with their passes stamped for an indefinite stay, subject to renewal in six months. As they boarded a passing fiacre for the trip back to their hotel Count Sandarel leaned toward Madame Verlaine and murmured in her ear, "A balloon?"

"And why not a balloon?" she murmured back.

FOURTEEN

SLIGHT OF MIND

The superior man is distressed by the limitation of his ability; he is not distressed by the fact that men do not recognize the ability he has.

—CONFUCIUS

Count Sandarel paced the floor of Madame Verlaine's bedroom, his hands behind his back. "You feel confident?" he asked.

"Reasonably," Madame Verlaine told him, looking up from her dressing table. "I work at it whenever I have the chance, to build up my speed."

"Good. We'll work at it together when we have private moments," Sandarel told her. "If we need to use it, we won't have time to prepare."

"I know." She turned to look at him. "Try me."

"All right. I'm going out into the audience. You're blindfolded. Close your eyes."

Madame Verlaine closed her eyes. "I am ready to receive your thoughts," she said.

"Everyone please refrain from talking or making any unnecessary noise," Sandarel said. Although he kept his voice soft, it now had the strong timbre of someone addressing a large audience. "You, sir, you have something for me?"

"A pocket watch," Madame Verlaine said softly.

"May I look at it?"

"A silver pocket watch."

"May I hold it, please?"

"A gold pocket watch with an inscription."

"Something more, sir?"

"Initials."

"Very interesting, very attractive, splendid."

"L—C—M."

"Madame Verlaine, what am I holding?"

She pressed her hand to her forehead dramatically, and spoke with a deep intensity. "Please hold it still. I see something round, but not too large. Something with great meaning to the owner. I sense wheels and gears. It is a watch—a pocket watch. The case is gold."

"Is that all?"

"No, I sense that there are some initials engraved on the case. First an L, and then an M. No, wait—something separates them—a C! The initials are L—C—M."

"Is that right sir?"

Madame Verlaine opened her eyes. "It damn well better be!"

Sandarel's valet knocked and entered the room, handing Sandarel a calling card. "I have put him in the sitting room, sir," he said. A gentleman."

"Thank you, Brom." Sandarel read the card and looked up at Madame Verlaine. "Peter Chennery?"

She shrugged.

"He's from the British embassy. I'll go see what he wants."

"I'll follow in a minute," she told him.

Sandarel opened the sitting room door and nodded to the sandy-haired young man in striped pants and morning coat within. The gentleman rose and bowed slightly, his mild blue eyes examining the man before him with some interest. "Prof—ah—Count Sandarel?"

"You may speak freely here," Sandarel said in English. "All the servants in the suite are my people."

"Ah, yes," the man replied. "You are actually Professor James Moriarty?"

"I am."

"I am Peter Chennery, first secretary to the ambassador of the British embassy here in Vienna."

"So I see by your card."

"Yes, well. Er. We've been instructed by Whitehall—by the minister himself actually—rather unusual instructions, I must say—to give you any aid you require. And the memorandum stressed 'any aid,' apparently no matter how unusual or, ah—"

Moriarty smiled slightly. "Illegal?" he suggested.

"Well it didn't exactly say that, not in so many words, but the suggestion was there," Chennery affirmed. "We were also warned not to give away your *nom emprunté*, or perhaps *nom de guerre* would be a better term, all things considered. The ambassador and I are frightfully curious as to what's going on, but the memorandum said we were not to ask." Chennery paused and looked expectant, and then continued, "So I guess I won't ask. Lord Sandown—he's the ambassador, don't you know, sent me along to see if there's anything we can do for you now."

"Yes," Moriarty said, "I believe there is. May I offer you some tea or coffee?"

"Thank you. Coffee, I think."

Moriarty rang for the maid. "Coffee and some of those small cakes, I think, Eleanor. And ask Madame Verlaine to join us." He turned to Chennery. "First, and most important, how many people know of the communication in question?"

"Just myself and the ambassador. Oh, and the code clerk, of course."

"Very good." Moriarty nodded approvingly. "Most people would have forgotten the code clerk." He raised a finger. "The first thing I require of you is, no one else is to know of this. If anything I ask of you requires assistance from any other person, they are not to know the true reason for the request."

Chennery nodded. "Our people are trained to do their jobs without asking questions," he said. "Although usually *we* know why."

"You will eventually," Moriarty assured him. "If this comes off as it should, you will be informed. If it doesn't come off, well, all of Europe will know about it, and you and your ambassador will be very glad that you are not directly involved."

"A question, if you don't mind," Chennery said. "Is there not a *real* Count Sandarel?"

Moriarty nodded. "There is. I have appropriated his identity as being more useful for the present purpose than my own."

There was a light rap at the door, and Madame Verlaine came in. Moriarty introduced her to Chennery and she smiled and crossed the room, extending her hand.

The first secretary gazed at her face perhaps a bit longer than was polite, then took her hand and kissed it, lingering over the kiss a shade longer than absolutely necessary, and then bowed. "A real pleasure, Madame," he said.

"Ah yes, the hand-kiss," she said. "I've heard how ubiquitous it is here in Vienna."

"More than merely a custom," Chennery told her, "it is an art. It conveys subtleties of meaning that are not available in polite conversation."

"I'll keep that in mind," Madame Verlaine assured him.

With an effort, Chennery turned his attention back to Moriarty. "And where is the real Count Sandarel?"

"In South America, I understand."

"He won't come back at an—ah—embarrassing moment?"

"He had the lack of foresight to predict the death of the current president of Peru. He is being held by the Peruvian authorities while they ascertain that he is not involved with any group planning to make that event come about."

"He always had a tendency to be a bit brash," Madame Verlaine commented. "Sometimes it furthers one's career; sometimes it gets one thrown in prison for a year or two."

"And you can do these, ah, fantastic things that are claimed of Alexandre Sandarel?" Chennery asked Moriarty. "Reading minds, predicting events, and the like?"

Moriarty smiled slightly. "I taught him," he said. "He was a not-very-successful stage magician working under the name of the Great Goldstone when he came to me for advice on another matter. In the process of solving that, I also suggested this new career and taught him some techniques he could use. The methods of stage magicians have always intrigued me as being useful in controlling people's behavior in specific ways."

"You mean like Mesmerism and hypnotism? I always thought they were bunk."

"They aren't pure bunkum, although some of their practition-
ers are masters of bunkum, but that's not what I'm referring to. I
had in mind methods using visual misdirection, misleading state-
ments, and deliberate misperceptions."

"I'm not sure what you mean."

Moriarty thought for a second and said, "I'll give you a brief
and unimpressive demonstration." He took a silver coin from his
pocket. "Now I'm going to place this in one hand," he said, "and
leave the other empty." He turned away from Chennery for a second and then turned back with both hands made into fists and held
in front of him. "Now, whichever hand you pick," he said, "I will
have the coin. Remember—you may select freely either hand, and
yet I will still have the coin."

"I'm to pick one hand?" Chennery asked.

"That's the idea," Moriarty said, patiently holding his fists in
front of him.

"All right." He stared at the two fists. "I'll take this—no this
one!" He pointed to Moriarty's right hand.

"You're sure?"

"I suppose I am."

"No supposing allowed," Moriarty said, raising his right hand
slightly. "This is the hand you have freely selected?"

Chennery nodded. "Yes, it is."

"And yet you could have chosen the other hand. This hand"—
he opened the chosen right hand—"contains nothing. As I told
you," Moriarty opened his left hand, "I still have the coin."

Chennery considered for a moment. "I see," he said finally.
"But, after all, it was a fifty-fifty proposition."

"Yes," Moriarty admitted. "But I had to win, whichever hand
you chose."

"Oh," Chennery said. "Some sort of slight-of-hand, was it?"

"Not at all, I merely took advantage of the fact that, although I
presume you listened closely to what I said, you didn't know in
advance what represented 'winning' this particular game."

"What do you mean?"

"What I told you was that, whichever hand you chose, I would
have the coin. It sounds positive, but actually it's a rather ambigu-
ous statement. Had you picked my left hand, the one actually con-

taining the coin, I might have said, 'See how my magical abilities forced you to pick the hand which had the coin,' and you would have thought that was the way the trick was supposed to go."

"Oh," Chennery said, but he didn't look convinced.

"A wonder explained is a wonder no more," Moriarty said. "Back to the matter at hand. Madame Verlaine is my associate, and any instructions from her are to be treated as though they came directly from me. That's one of the reasons I wanted you to meet her. If any other messages arrive purporting to come from me or Madame Verlaine, you are to ignore them unless the messenger recites the phrase—well now," he turned to Madame Verlaine, "what phrase should we use as our password?"

Madame Verlaine shrugged her slender shoulders.

"Can you suggest something?" Moriarty asked Chennery. "Something that will stick in your mind?"

Chennery paused and stared out the window. " 'The moving finger writes'?" he suggested.

"Ah, yes," Moriarty said. " 'And having writ, moves on.' Very good. Easy to remember and not apt to come out by accident."

"I hope it is not prophetic," Madame Verlaine said, and continued the quote: " 'Nor all thy piety nor wit shall lure it back to cancel half a line, Nor all thy tears wash out a word of it.' "

"There is truth in Omar," Moriarty commented, "but not always a cheerful truth."

The maid entered with a large tray bearing a coffee pot, pastries, and the necessary china and silver and set it on the sideboard. "Thank you, Eleanor," Madame Verlaine told her. "We'll serve ourselves."

Peter Chennery sat in one of the high-back chairs with a cup of coffee and a plate of pastry on the table to his left and regarded the two sitting across from him. Professor Moriarty he had heard about, but the stories were conflicting. He had looked the professor up in the embassy's small reference library and discovered that James Moriarty, Sc.D., FRAS, had lectured in mathematics at the Victoria University of Manchester in the 1870s and was the author of several monographs on astronomical subjects that were highly regarded by the few who could understand them. He was also, by some at Scotland Yard, believed to be a master criminal who was responsible for every major unsolved crime since the Great Bank Robbery of 1866. On the other hand there was the fact that, according to a confidential report he had foiled a plot to assassinate Queen Victoria some years before, and when asked what reward he would like had replied, "to be left alone," or words to that effect.

Of Madame Madeleine Verlaine he had discovered nothing except the strong possibility that that was not her real name. Not sharing the Viennese preference for chubby women, he found her exceedingly beautiful.

Of the usual gossip that followed even the most secret assignments there was none, except a word from the courier that this particular note, which he handed to the ambassador himself, was to be taken exceedingly seriously and kept exceedingly secret. The courier's warning was reinforced when the communication was found to be in the diplomatic service's most secure code; one to be reserved for matters of national importance. It was a puzzle, but one thing was sure: the ambassador had turned it over to him to handle, and if the handle slipped from his grasp, he would be spending the remainder of his time in the Foreign Service stamping passport applications in the closest approach to Hell that the foreign minister could devise.

"What I require at the moment," Moriarty told him, "is a house or apartment with some particular qualifications."

Chennery took out a small, leather-covered pocket notebook.

"No notes!" Moriarty said firmly. "If you have trouble remembering the list, I'll teach you a mnemonic system that works well and is not difficult to learn."

Chennery put the notebook away. "Sorry," he said. "I think I can remember what I need to remember. What sort of house or flat?"

"Good. First, it should be occupied by someone you trust completely, but who is not known to be connected to the embassy."

"Why not an empty house?"

"Because if a house or apartment is known to be empty, it might create undue interest if someone is seen entering it."

"Ah!"

"If the tenant is known to be a woman," Madame Verlaine offered, "it might cause talk if men were seen to be entering it."

"A point," Moriarty admitted.

"Have your guests dress like servants," Chennery offered. "Servants are, after all, merely servants, and tend to be invisible except to other servants."

"Excellent," Moriarty said. "Even so, if it is an apartment, it should be in a building without a doorman or concierge. Located somewhere within a half-hour carriage ride from let's say, the Burgplatz. Also it would be convenient if it had more than one entrance, possibly on different streets."

Chennery nodded. "It probably will have to be a flat of some sort if you want it in the city," he said. "Is there anything else?"

"Yes. Have it well stocked with food."

"Yes. I see. Of course." Chennery nodded.

"I think that's all for now. Deliver the keys, and of course the address, to me here tomorrow. Please inform the tenant of the apartment that some complete strangers are liable to show up at any time, and make sure that he or she understands that he is not to say anything to anyone about this."

"Tomorrow? Yes, I guess we can do it by tomorrow."

Brom, the valet, knocked and entered. "Excuse me, Count Sandarel, but Mr. Tolliver would like to speak with you."

"Tolliver?"

"He is in the breakfast room, sir."

Moriarty stood. "Very good. I'll be back in a minute, Mr. Chennery, please enjoy your coffee."

Chennery put his coffee cup down and stood up. "Actually, I'd best be leaving if I'm to locate an appropriate flat for you."

"That's so. I expect to hear from you tomorrow. You are doing well."

Madame Verlaine accompanied Chennery to the front door. " 'You are doing well,' " she said to him. "That is high praise from the professor."

"Is it?" Chennery asked. "Will I see you again?"

"No doubt," she told him. "But keep your mind on your work—for now."

Moriarty went into the breakfast room, to find Mummer Tolliver sitting on a chair and two cushions and eating pastry. Moriarty took a chair across the table from him and considered for a minute while the mummer ate. "Barnett and his wife are here in Vienna," he ventured finally.

"Near enough as makes no difference," the mummer affirmed.

"They're in some sort of trouble."

The mummer sat cross-legged on his cushion and looked admiringly at the professor. "Now 'ow'd you know that?" he demanded. "They've been grabbed by some madman as calls himself Graf von Linsz. Graf—that's 'count' in German."

"Is it? And just what do you mean, 'grabbed'?"

"We gets off this paddle-wheeler on the Como Lake at a little town called Rezzonico and the graf, what has befriended the mister and missus beforehand, takes them to a inn for lunch. Then he hustles them into a carriage and drives off."

"Ignoring you?"

"I wasn't present for the fun and games, I hears about it later when I goes up to the inn to see why they hasn't come back to the boat."

Madeleine came into the room while the mummer was talking and quietly took a chair next to the professor.

"I heard all the details from this serving girl at the inn," the mummer explained. "They was speaking English, which it happens is her native language, her having been raised in Surrey before her mom married an Italian stone mason and moved to Como with him. The graf, he says that he's taking them to this house what's nearby, and they gallops off in this carriage. So I asks around, with the help of Vicky—that's this serving girl—'cause my Italian is not of the best, and I finds out that the house in question is about eight kay away, which is less than eight miles 'cause a kay is not nearly as much as a mile. So I foots it over to the house and gives it a dekko."

"A dekko?" Madeleine asked.

"A glom, a pry, a look-see. Hello, Molly."

"Madeleine, at the moment."

"Madeleine, it is. An high-class name for an high-class lady. You still on the dip?"

"Picking pockets is only one of my skills now," Molly-Madeleine told him, "thanks to the professor."

"You always were something special," the mummer said admiringly.

"Go on with your story," Moriarty interrupted.

"Right. So, as I says, I looks the place over to see what I can figure out."

"And what did you figure out?"

Mummer blew his nose into the napkin and folded it up into a little ball and shoved it in his jacket pocket. "Well, this place is just a fancy big house. But he's got guards wandering around the grounds, so I has to wait until night before I can get close."

"Guards," Moriarty said. "That's interesting."

"I thought so. So I covers myself with mud, of which there's a plentiful supply by the creek, so I won't shine in the moonlight, and I waits until it's as dark as it's going to get, then I slips myself over the wall and to the house. There was one window on the first floor which I thought might be interesting, 'cause it's the only one which has bars on it. I mean, none of the ground floor windows has bars but this one on the first floor does. So I climbs up to the first floor and perches outside the bars, where there's like a little ledge which I could just fit my feet on."

"Being small sometimes has advantages," Moriarty remarked.

"Who says it don't?"

"Was your surmise right?" Madeleine asked. "Were the Barnetts in that room?"

"They was."

"Could you speak with them?"

"I could. I went 'Hist, hist!' a couple of times and attracted them over to the window. They was much surprised to see me. According to what Barnett told me, the graf grabbed them and was keeping them prisoner on account of you."

"Me?" Moriarty adjusted the monocle that had replaced his pince-nez as part of his Count Sandarel persona and stared at the mummer.

"That's right. You had disappeared from your usual haunts, it seems, and the graf and his people were most anxious to discover what had happened to you and where you had got to. They had got it through their heads that Mr. Barnett was your confidant and must surely know what you was doing and where and why."

"Where the Barnetts being—ah—mistreated?"

"Not so's you'd notice. Not at that time, anyway. Although what they have in mind for them here in Vienna, I'm not so easy about."

"Ah yes, Vienna. They were brought to Vienna?"

"They was. The very next day."

"And you followed?"

"I did."

Madeleine leaned forward. "That must have been quite an adventure," she said.

"It weren't no piece of cake, but I managed," the mummer said, looking pleased that someone had noticed that he'd done something of note.

"How did you manage it?" she asked.

"Barnett told me that the graf was planning to move them, but he didn't know where to, so I hid up the road a bit where they couldn't see me from the house and jumped on the back of the carriage when it went by. The graf had a private train waiting for him at the railroad station: an engine and three coaches. I rode under the last car part of the way—there's a sort of shelf under there you can clamber up onto it if you're not too big, which you'll observe is what I'm not."

"Small but clever," Madeleine complimented him.

"Go on," Moriarty said.

"Well, at the first stop, which was in the middle of some mountains what were very impressive, I sniggles myself aboard the last coach, which was filled with boxes and baggage, and conceals myself in a convenient corner. I eats and drinks and performs other necessities catch-as-catch-can for the next couple of days, while the train mostly goes but on occasion stops for maybe a few minutes or maybe a few hours."

"Those specials have to stop to allow regularly scheduled trains the right of way," Moriarty commented. "Also, of course fuel and water."

"Like that," the mummer agreed. "Then two days later we nips into a siding and I sees the Barnetts being removed into a horse cart. At first I am concerned because there is no convenient way for me to conceal myself in or around a horse cart, but then I sees that we are at a private siding, and the horse cart is merely taking the Barnetts up the hill to this here castle what is at the top."

"And then?"

"And then I figures that I can't get them out of there by myself, so I send's you a telegram back to Russell Square to ask for advice and reinforcements. And I gets a telegram back saying as how you're already in Vienna. So here I is."

"So you are. You've done very well," the professor said.

"Just a combination of skill and my enviable small stature," the mummer replied, looking pleased.

"This is very interesting," Moriarty said. "I have to think it over." He stood up. "I'm going to take a brisk walk. I find it stimulates the mental processes. If either of you would like to accompany me—"

"I ain't nohow done eating yet," the mummer said. "And then perhaps I'll sleep a bit."

"I've tried keeping up with you when you're on one of your brisk walks," Madeleine said. "I'll find something else to keep myself occupied."

"As you will," the professor said.

FIFTEEN

THE CONSULTING DETECTIVE

Also spielen wir Theater
Spielen unsre eignen Stücke
Frühgereift und zart und traurig
Die Komödie unsrer Seele
(Thus we play theater/Play our own scenes—
Premature and tender and sad / The comedy of our soul)
—HUGO VON HOFMANNSTHAL

His Excellency Herzog (Duke) Rudolf Karl Sigfried von Seligsmann, duke of Hrazpach and Bellenberg, colonel-general of the Second Regiment of Hussars of the Imperial Guard, chairman of the Internal Security Council—a small, most secret group which answered only to His Imperial Majesty Franz Josef—plumped his solid muscular body into a hardback chair and stared across the table at the tall Englishman. With his wide, thick white mustache, the effect was of a pair of sharp blue eyes staring over a uniformed hedge. "Well?" he demanded. "You've had over a month. What have you discovered?"

Sherlock Holmes returned his gaze unblinkingly. "Much," he said. "I do not have the whole pattern yet, but the threads are in my hand."

It was six in the evening and they were meeting in a small office on the third floor of the massive Baroque Hofburgtheater, the great showplace building on the Ringstrasse where the comings and goings of any number of random citizens would be relatively unremarkable and hopefully unobserved.

"The Council meets tomorrow with His Imperial Majesty," Herzog von Seligsmann said. "I cannot give them 'threads.' "

"I warned you that the investigation would take some time when your man visited me in London," Holmes said.

"True," the duke agreed, "but events are overtaking us. The heads of state of several of the great powers are meeting here in a little over two weeks to discuss, among other things, what to do about this continuing wave of outrages, and we are to offer them a plan. What sort of plan can we hope to offer them without a clear idea of who—and what—we are facing? Can it be coincidence that so many different groups have sprung into existence with but one goal—the destruction of government and authority throughout Europe? Do they all spring from common soil? Is it the disillusion of the middle classes, or this wave of nationalism that we've been seeing, or the teachings of these radical philosophers like Kant, Marx, and Wittgenstein that have energized the university students? Is it a secret plot of the Jewish Socialists? These are but a few of the questions we must consider. What we have asked of you is to follow just one of these groups and discern for us its roots, its goals, and how it recruits its members. And, most important, how and from whom it gets its information."

Holmes sat back in his chair and stared steadily at von Seligsmann. "The conditions you have imposed on me make it more difficult than usual, and this sort of investigation is difficult enough to begin with."

"What conditions?" asked the duke.

"Your man told me that you—or perhaps I should say the council—suspected that someone high up in the government was an agent for a foreign power."

"That wasn't a 'condition,' " von Seligsmann said, "that was the reason that we chose to hire you—an outsider—in the first place."

"Nonetheless, since you didn't know what official or what foreign power, I must conduct my investigation not only without any assistance from the government, but in the difficult position of having to avoid allowing the police, or any authorities, to know what I was doing."

"My understanding was that you commonly disdain police assistance in any of your cases," the duke said.

"I prefer to avoid the bungling interference of most Scotland Yard detectives," Holmes admitted, "but I work with their tacit acceptance, if not their approval. The Yard men know that I do not seek publicity for myself, but pass the credit on to them."

Von Seligsmann put his wide-brimmed kepi on the table in front of him and lined it up carefully with the table edge, as though preparing it for inspection. "And yet, with all the passing of credit, I have heard much of you and your exploits," he commented dryly.

"Some of my cases have been chronicled by my friend and colleague Dr. Watson," Holmes acknowledged. "I try to get him to record only those cases which best illustrate the process of deduction which leads to the solution, as this might be of some use to other criminalists—a term I believe was invented by your own Dr. Gross, whose work I have the most respect for—but Dr. Watson claims that the public is interested only in the more sensational or romantic aspects of my cases. In any event, in almost all of my cases I have allowed Scotland Yard or the local police to receive the credit, although in some few of them Dr. Watson may later have revealed my participation in the investigation."

"Ah, yes, the Dr. Watson, whom you have brought along as your assistant, although he of German understands not a word."

" 'Kind hearts are more than coronets,' " Holmes offered.

"How's that?"

"Tennyson," Holmes explained, "an English poet. I find Watson's loyalty and good English grit to be more valuable than any command of language. Besides, he does understand German fairly well, he just dislikes speaking it for fear of sounding ridiculous."

"It is then, ridiculous, the German language?" the duke drew himself up, but Holmes waved a placating hand.

"No, no," he said firmly. "It is just that Watson is aware that his pronunciation of the language is not very, ah, German. His ear hears what his mouth cannot speak."

"Ah!" the duke relaxed in his seat. "And you—you have no fear of sounding ridiculous yourself?"

"I?" Holmes looked quizzically at the duke. The thought had obviously never entered his mind.

"Your German is actually quite good," von Seligsmann assured him. "The accent is Prussian, yes?"

"I suppose," Holmes said. "I took lessons from an inspector of the Berlin Police, who was staying in London to study the methods of Scotland Yard. He ended up studying my methods, and I studied his language. It was a fair exchange." Holmes took a cigarette from a silver cigarette case and lit it with a wax match. "I decided it was necessary to learn German if I was to study the history of crime. Such interesting crimes have been committed in Germany. And Austria too, of course."

"I see," the duke said, not sure whether to be pleased or insulted. "Well, what have you discovered regarding this present matter? Outline for me these threads of which you speak. Perhaps I can help you discern the pattern."

Holmes stared into the column of blue smoke rising from the tip of his cigarette and considered. "There are many separate groups that meet here in Vienna whose avowed goal is, in one way or another, to 'set Europe ablaze.' That, I think, was the phrase used by that anarchist Brakinsky who was guillotined in France last month for blowing up three policemen."

"There is certainly much unrest," the duke agreed.

"The Serbian group—'Free Serbia' they call themselves—meets in the back room of a private lending library at thirty-one Stumpergasse in the Mariahilf District."

"What do they talk about?"

"I don't speak Serbian. Find me someone trustworthy who speaks Serbian and we'll find out."

"I know no one trustworthy who speaks Serbian," the duke said. "What else?"

"An anarchist group—it calls itself the 'Secret Freedom League'—meets in the box cellar of the Werfel Chocolate factory, which is also in Mariahilf. Your police must know about that one; they arrested one of the members for the assassination of the duke of Mecklenburg Strelitz a few weeks ago."

"Yes, and . . . ?" The duke sounded unimpressed.

" 'Poland Must Be Free' meets in various parks around Vienna. They play football and plot assassinations. Then there are the militant socialists, who mingle with their less militant brothers at the Café Mozart on Opernstrasse. They drink coffee and eat strudel at the tables in front and plan revolutions in the small rooms in the back."

"So?"

"I am now a member of the Thule Society," Holmes told him, "which believes, or professes to believe, that the true German is descended from a pre-Christian 'Aryan People,' and that they are a superior race, destined to rule over the inferior peoples. They are not as yet very large, but they number among their members middle-level bureaucrats, police officials, and officers of staff rank in the Austrian Army. Their symbol is the *hakenkreuz*, which they consider a runic symbol of great power. They are enamored of the runic alphabet and various secret signs."

"The *hakenkreuz*?"

"In India they call it the 'swastika,' and it is a symbol of well-being, probably derived from an early sign for the sun. It is a cross with each of the four ends turned to the right." Holmes sketched it on the table with his finger.

The duke shook his head and drummed his fingers on the table. "I do not like to tell you how to do your job," he said, "but it is clear to me that you are casting about in too many directions at the same time. How can you hope to discover anything useful if you spend your time running back and forth between these various unrelated groups? And, for that matter, why these groups? There are probably a hundred—a thousand—groups of varying degrees of secrecy and of antagonism to the government of the dual monarchy."

"Yes," Holmes agreed. "Groups of men with grievances seem to spring up like mushrooms in the dual monarchy; indeed all over Europe. It has become fashionable to blame the government—whichever government one lives under—for one's own inadequacies. And you employed me to discover why and how some of these people seem to have knowledge of the secret plans of your government."

"That is so. Not only great secrets, but small and seemingly insignificant ones. A minister leaves his office and goes to visit a church he has not been to for half a year, by a road that his carriage has not taken over before, and there is a bomb-thrower waiting for him a block away from the church. Archduke Ferdinand goes to inspect a new battleship, and the launch he is to take from the pier blows up when he should have been aboard. Had he not stopped to speak to a group of schoolgirls and sign their books, he would have been killed."

"It seems as if the contemplated movements of important officials must be regarded as a great secret at this time," Holmes commented.

"Yes. That is so."

"What of these other 'great secrets'?"

The duke was silent for a minute. Then he shrugged. "An example I can tell you," he said, "involves Plan B of the Imperial General Staff."

"Plan B?"

"It is the plan for general mobilization in case of—certain contingencies—that might lead to war. In an empire of this size a general mobilization is immensely complex. Troops must be called to staging areas, trains must be scheduled or re-routed, ammunition must be taken from depots to advance storage areas, appropriate clothing must be issued, food and supplies must be moved from here to there; thousands of details must be planned for in advance. There are only seven—I believe it's seven—copies of the full plan; a book which is many hundreds of pages thick. They are for the general staff only. Lesser commanders each have the appropriate portion of the plan to allow them to carry out their orders. They are kept in sealed envelopes secured in the safes of the commanders."

"And one of them is missing?"

"Nothing so simple," the duke said. "One of the master plans, kept in the safe of the office of the chief of the general staff may have been copied."

"Really? Copied?"

"Yes. When General Count von Speck removed it from the safe to look at—this would be about a month ago—he noticed that the pages seemed a little loose. It was inspected by the technical branch of the *Kundschafts Stelle*, our military intelligence section, and they discovered that it had been carefully unbound and rebound. They concluded that someone had probably taken it apart to photograph the pages."

"How interesting," Sherlock Holmes said. "The book would

have to be taken somewhere where a copying-camera could be set up and sufficient light supplied. But it would certainly be faster than copying such a document by hand. Have you determined who had access to the book?"

"As far as we can tell, nobody but the general himself could have removed the book from the safe."

"Come now, that is most satisfying," Holmes said, rubbing his hands together. "I assume that General count von Speck is himself above reproach?"

"You may take it from me that, although nobody but the general could have taken the book, he is not the one who copied it. And he claims—and we believe him—that he has not let the book out of his hands in any occasion when he had it out of the safe."

"Yes, of course," Holmes said. "And besides, if the general had done anything to the book himself, he would have hardly drawn attention to it afterward."

"So we thought," von Seligsmann said.

"I would like to take a look at the book," Holmes said.

"I'm afraid that is impossible," the duke told him.

"I am only interested in the spine and the pages, not the contents," Holmes assured the duke.

"Even so," the duke pointed out, "in order to show you the spine and the pages, you would undoubtedly catch glimpses of the writing, and that we cannot allow."

"Haven't you changed the plan?"

"It is not so simple as that. First of all, the plan was the best the general staff could devise, so any other plan would necessarily be inferior. Second, it would be foolhardy to put a new plan in place until we know how and by whom the old plan was taken."

"Ah!" Holmes said.

"And even if we wanted to change it, a plan for the complete mobilization of our forces takes many months to prepare. We are taking some steps to minimize the effect of the details of the plan being known. It would help if we knew just what foreign power it was that has the information."

"The problem is not without its interesting aspects," Holmes said. "I might have some suggestions for whoever is handling the case."

"I will pass the word," the duke told him. "Now about you and all these disparate groups you are investigating—"

"Ah! But you see, that's just it," Holmes said. "It would seem that the groups are not disparate. They are somehow interconnected."

Von Seligsmann screwed his monocle firmly into his right eye and stared across the table. "Interconnected?" he asked. "How?"

"An interesting question," Holmes allowed. "An even more interesting question would be, 'why?' "

"Explain," said the duke.

Holmes tapped the edge of his cigarette against the light blue glass bowl he was using as an ashtray. "I discovered this interconnection by following the leaders of each group about to see where they would lead me. In just about every case they eventually led me to another group. One man—a particularly loathsome individual called 'the Ferret'—is high up in three of these groups."

"You followed him?"

"Yes."

"Didn't he see you?"

"No. When I follow people they do not see me. They see an old bookseller, or an elderly prelate, or a street ruffian, or a tired bureaucrat wending his way home, or possibly a fiacre driver half asleep as his horse heads back to the stables; but they do not see me." The duke looked unconvinced, but Holmes went on.

"But, regardless of how I gathered the information, we must deal with the fact that the threat to set Europe aflame comes not from a thousand separate matches but from one coordinated fire. We must discover who is fueling the fire and what they expect to gain from the conflagration."

"You have as yet no notion?" the duke asked.

"It is destructive of the powers of deduction to hypothesize before you have all the facts. It causes you to favor your early hypothesis and ignore contrary evidence," Holmes told him. "I have a suspicion only; a direction to look in; a possibility to consider. But we must continue to look in all directions, to consider all possibilities, until we have eliminated all but the one that, by remaining, proves to be the truth."

"And what is your suspicion?"

"Very well," Holmes said. "A possibility only, as yet. There is a master criminal who calls himself Professor Moriarty who is capable of such deviltry. His headquarters are in London, but his tentacles stretch all over Europe. I have sent word to London to have him watched, and I am trying to locate the members of his criminal organization here in Vienna."

"Why, if you are right, would he be doing this?"

"For money, your excellency. Whatever Moriarty does, it is for money."

"Moriarty—Moriarty!" von Seligsmann tapped his finger on the table. "That name—"

"You have heard of him?"

Von Seligsmann leaned back and closed his eyes. "Professor James Moriarty?" he asked.

"That's the man."

"I have heard the name, and recently. He is the head, is he not, of the British Intelligence Service?"

"The British—" Holmes chuckled. "Wherever did you get that idea?"

"Aha!" the duke said, "but would you tell me if he were? You are, after all, British yourself. 'Rule Britannia,' and all that. 'This blessed plot, this earth, this realm, this England,' and all that. No, if you knew, you would not tell me."

"If I knew the name of the head of British Intelligence I would certainly not tell you," Holmes admitted. "But I will tell you freely and positively that it is not Professor James Moriarty."

"You are sure?"

"Positive."

"Then perhaps you can explain why this man, Paul Donzhof, who was arrested for the assassination of the duke of Mecklenburg Strelitz and the murder of some woman, is said to have been working for Professor James Moriarty, who is said to be the head of the British Intelligence Service?"

Holmes stubbed his cigarette out. "I am perfectly willing to believe that this Paul Donzhof is one of Moriarty's henchmen," he said. "But I think you'll find that Moriarty has nothing to do with Her Majesty's government. Indeed, Scotland Yard has been trying to arrest him for a decade now, with little success. The man is fiendishly clever, but he is a criminal, not a government agent."

"Aha! And would that not make a perfect—what do you say—cover—for the head of the British Secret Service?"

"I wouldn't think so," Holmes said. "Incidently, this Paul Donzhof is a member of one of the groups I'm surveying. It is fairly clear to me that he is innocent of the murder of Duke Paulus, although I have no knowledge of this other murder of which he is also accused. For some reason the leader of this group—this 'Ferret' that I spoke of—wanted Donzhof to be accused."

The duke shrugged. "That is not my concern," he said. "It is better for public confidence that we have someone locked up for the crime, is it not?"

"And perhaps hanged for it, whether or not he is guilty?"

Again the duke shrugged. "Perhaps."

"I see," Holmes said. He stood up. "I think I'd better get back to my task. But as I leave let me assure you once again that Professor James Moriarty does not serve the British government in any capacity whatsoever. As soon as I have something further to communicate to you, I will post a notice on the letter board at the Café Trieste, and we will meet back here."

The duke rose. "And I the same," he said. "This news you bring me, this amalgamation of underground groups, this is worrying. I don't know what it means."

"At the very least it means that these groups are not the spontaneous responses of dissatisfied minorities. The dissatisfactions are there, no doubt, and for that those in power must shoulder the blame. But these groups are the instruments of some person, or some circle, that is orchestrating them for reasons beyond our present understanding."

"Before you go," the duke said, "I have a suggestion. Well, possibly a request."

"Yes, your excellency?"

"When the heads of state meet, probably two weeks from

Thursday, I would like you to attend. Possibly to speak to the assemblage. They all know of you, certainly, and will be inclined to credit what you say."

"If you like," Holmes said. "Let us hope that I have substantially more information for them at that time."

SIXTEEN

A PERSON OF LITTLE IMPORTANCE

Life is mostly froth and bubble,
Two things stand like stone,
Kindness in another's trouble,
Courage in your own.
— ADAM LINDSAY GORDON

The warder with the outsized belly and the bottle-brush mustache swung open the door to Paul Donzhof's cell. "Your sister's here to see you," he said. "Come on out."

Paul swung himself off his cot and slid his feet into the prison-issue slippers. "My sister?" He went to the door.

"That's right," the warder said, pushing Paul out into the corridor in front of him and slamming the cell door. "And a lovely little thing she is, too, to be saddled with a murderous lout of a brother like you. Walk ahead of me now."

"Watch how you talk about my sister," Paul said, wondering who on earth his "sister" could be. He'd better move—and talk—carefully until he found out just what this was about. Charles Bredlon Summerdane had a sister, Lady Patricia Templar, now the wife of an energetic young prelate destined someday to become an archbishop, or even, if he had his way, a saint. But Paul was sure that his alter ego's sister was not the lady waiting for him in the visitor's room.

It was only two days ago that Paul had been permitted to see his first visitor, an elderly gentleman named Karl Stetelmeyer, possessor of a red nose, an overly bushy white beard, an old leather briefcase stuffed to the point of bursting its straps, and a mild and intelligent disposition, who had declared himself to be Paul's attorney. "I accepted your case," he had told Paul, "because the presiding magistrate wants you to be well represented, and I have a reputation, well-founded may I say, as an excellent advocate. Also I am too old to be overly concerned about what this case might do to my reputation. So don't expect miracles. Assassinating a duke! Murdering your own lady friend! I have reviewed the evidence against you. Would you like to, perhaps, plead guilty?"

"No, thank you," Paul had told him.

"Oh, well, one can but hope." He had stood up. "I shall return soon and we'll talk and see what we can do."

"Wait!" Paul also rose. "The evidence against me—what is it?"

"Soon!" Stetelmeyer had promised.

And now Paul's "sister" had come to visit. Was this, perhaps, some ploy of Stetelmeyer's? No, the aging attorney didn't look as though he was accustomed to use ploys of any sort. Paul paused at the door to the visitors' room. Well, here he was, and he would find out in a second.

The visitors' room was a small, airless cubicle with stone walls and two iron doors, one for the prisoner and one for his guest. The only furniture was a thick wooden table on a massive central pillar in the middle of the room, and two small wooden benches, one on each side. A wooden panel under the table assured that the feet of the prisoner could not reach the feet of the visitor. A thick black line across the center of the table separated the prisoner's space from his visitor's space.

The warder brought Paul into the room and sat him on the bench. Then he crossed his arms, stood by the door and glowered at Paul while a second warder came in and fastened a leg iron around his left leg. A short length of chain connected the leg iron to a large metal bolt sunk into the stone floor.

"Don't get off the bench," the new warder told him. "Don't touch your visitor or even pass your hand over that black line. Don't pass anything to your visitor or accept anything from your visitor. Is that clear?"

"Yes," Paul said.

The second warder left, and Paul sat silently, facing the door opposite and waiting to see what his sister looked like. The door opened slowly, and a tall, slim girl shyly entered. Her face had the fresh, wind-blown complexion of a true girl of the Alps, her blond hair was done into a severe bun atop her head, and her gray traveling dress was of a modest cut. She could well be the daughter of a comfortably bourgeois Bavarian beer merchant, and Paul had never seen her before in his life.

"Brother Paul," she said, sliding onto the bench on her side of the table. She reached across the table to touch his hand, but jerked her hand back at the cough of the warder, who was standing by the door on the prisoners' side. "Father and Mother and little Heidi miss you horribly," she said. "Father told me before I left, 'Ursula,' he said, 'tell Paul how much your mother and I love him, and that we're sure that he could never be guilty of what they say he did. Tell him that.' And I'm sure, too, Paul."

So her name was Ursula. That helped. And little Heidi, by god, that was a nice touch. But who was she really, and what was she doing there, and how could he find out with a warder standing behind him listening to every word?

As though she were reading his mind, Ursula looked up at the warder and said sweetly but firmly, "Herr Schnegel, the warden, told me that I could have a little privacy to talk to my brother."

The warder stared at her stolidly for a few seconds, and then, without a word, retreated to the far side of the door and closed it behind him.

Ursula smiled at Paul. "There now," she said softly in English, "that's better."

A physical shock slapped at Paul's chest, and he could feel the pounding of his heart. Who was this woman? Why did she speak to him in English? If this was some sort of trick—If this girl, whoever she was, was working for the authorities—If his secret was known—

"Excuse me," he said in German, "what did you say?"

His panic must have shown on his face. "Dear me," she said, "that was truly thoughtless of me. I apologize. I didn't mean to startle you. I come from your father. I mean, your *father*, the duke of Albermar. I switched to English because the warder is certainly trying to overhear our mumbles, and if we're mumbling in a foreign language he won't be able to understand any of it. But he shouldn't be able to tell for sure that it isn't German if we keep our voices down."

Paul took three deep breaths. "How did you get the warder to leave the room?" he asked.

"Herr Schnegel, the warden, a very pompous man who is overly polite to women, thinks that it's his idea," Ursula explained. "I told him, all wide-eyed and innocent, that I was sure you hadn't done what you were accused of and that I wanted to get you to tell me all about it so that I could find out what really happened and clear your name. He became all avuncular and held my hand. He said that he'd like nothing better and that if you were innocent he would personally see that you were released from here as soon as possible. I said that I was sure that I could get you to tell me about it if I was left alone with you because we've never had any secrets from each other. He made me promise that I would tell him everything you said—for your own good, of course. And here we are."

"And here we are," Paul agreed.

"Keep your voice low."

"My father," Paul said, "he doesn't think that I—that I . . ."

"Of course not," Ursula told him.

"I can't figure out how all this happened—how I ended up as the primary suspect in the murder of my—of the girl I was going to—"

"And the assassination of the duke of Mecklenburg Strelitz."

"Yes, and that, too."

"Professor Moriarty has a theory."

Paul looked startled. "Professor Moriarty?"

"Keep your voice down. Do you know him?"

"Several of my sources here—what did my father tell you?"

"It was the professor who spoke with him. We know what you were doing here and why and the names of some of your associates."

"Several of my sources here are convinced that I am working for this Professor Moriarty, and that he is the head of a vast criminal conspiracy. And I wasn't even sure that there was a Professor

Moriarty, I thought he was some sort of local myth, like the Rhine Maidens or the Iron Man."

"He's real," Ursula said. "Professor Moriarty is the most brilliant man I have ever known, and many men have attempted to impress me with their brilliance. Although he's not the head of a vast criminal conspiracy unfortunately, since it might be useful if he were. Your father employed him to come and save you. And I am working with him."

"Who are you?"

"My real name is—well—you can think of me as Madeleine, but for the present you'd better call me Ursula. We do seem to have a profusion of names about all of this, don't we? My profession used to be gun moll in the swell mob, but the professor says I'm fit for better things, and he's teaching me."

"A gun moll?"

She laughed. "Sorry, I couldn't resist that. It's thieves' cant. A 'gun' is a pickpocket, a 'gun moll' is a lady pickpocket. The 'swell mob' is a group of pickpockets that dress like ladies and gentlemen and show up at events where the swells will be milling about; like the opera or a fancy ball, or the better sort of racetrack."

"You're a pickpocket?"

"I was. There are worse professions for a lady."

"I suppose there are," Paul said, sounding unconvinced.

"Besides we got to travel all over Europe, and we had to know how to fit in almost anywhere. It's an education, believe me."

"I do believe you. Which, I suppose, explains your German."

She shook her head. "I grew up in Alsace, so I speak fluent German and French. I didn't learn English until we moved to Ipswich when I was twelve. I think the rest of my history had better wait until we get you out of here."

"Fair enough. How are you and Professor Moriarty planning to accomplish that?"

"That is still an open question. We could either prove your innocence or break you out of this place. As long as we can do it without letting the Austrian authorities figure out whom you really are, we'll go with whichever works best."

Paul thought that over for a minute. "You said that Professor Moriarty had a theory," he said.

Madeleine nodded. "How much do you know about the murder of the duke of Mecklenburg Strelitz?"

"Almost nothing. He and his wife were riding in a coach and somebody shot at them. That's it."

"Yes. He was killed and she was wounded. The assassin was seen to be waving a Shugard Seuss revolver about, which, if you don't know, is a very distinctive weapon. He was wearing a green greatcoat and a brown cap. After the shooting he ran off through the crowd and disappeared."

"A green greatcoat," Paul said. "So."

"So indeed. When you were arrested you were wearing a green greatcoat and a brown cap. Also a Shugard Seuss revolver was found in your apartment."

Paul thought that over. "I think someone does not like me," he said. "I think perhaps I have not been as subtle as I believed I was being."

"Someone wanted you blamed for the assassination, that is clear," Madeleine agreed.

"But—" Paul swallowed. "But what of Giselle? Why would anyone want to kill her? How could anyone—"

"She had a key to your apartment, yes?"

"Yes. It was just to—"

"Never mind what it was just to; it is not your morality that we're concerned with here. Nor the girl's either. It is the professor's belief that someone went to your apartment to leave the Shugard Seuss, and possibly a few other pieces of incriminating evidence, and your lady friend had the bad luck to walk in on him."

"Then she was killed by accident," Paul said, his voice showing his anguish. "There was no reason for her death—it wasn't even part of the attempt to get at me." He buried his head in his hands.

"Sit up!" Madeleine said sharply. "We don't want to give the guard any reason to come in before his time."

"Yes." With an effort Paul sat up and dabbed at his eyes with the sleeve of his gray cotton pullover shirt. "I'm sorry."

"Don't be. Crying is a good thing sometimes. I would pass you a handkerchief, but it is forbidden."

"Yes," Paul said. "They make rules here just for the pleasure of making rules. Is there any more to the professor's theory? So Giselle was killed by accident. Does he have any idea of who did all the rest of this, and why it was done?" He essayed a weak smile. "I thought I was a likable fellow, but I must have done something to offend somebody; but what could it have been?"

"Professor Moriarty's conclusion is based on the fact that no one has yet come forward to denounce you as a British agent. Even those who believe you're a minion of the notorious Professor Moriarty don't know that you're not really Paul Donzhof."

"That seems to be so."

"Therefore it is for Paul Donzhof that this plot was hatched. But Paul Donzhof, you will excuse me, is a person of little importance."

"Yes, of course. Deliberately so."

"So, if they, whoever they are, wanted to get rid of you, why not just murder you?"

Paul smiled grimly. "I'm glad you weren't around to give them, whoever they are, advice."

"I'm sure they thought of that. But they didn't do it. Because they wanted to see you discredited more than they wanted you dead."

"Discredited? What do you mean?"

"According to your father, your last few reports said that you thought you were being watched—followed."

"Yes. I'm pretty sure. I couldn't find out who was doing it, but I suspect it was someone from the anarchist group that I joined."

"Professor Moriarty thinks that someone suspects that you are other than you seem, but they don't as yet know just what you are."

"I thought so myself," Paul agreed.

"So they, whoever they are, wish to discredit you. To assure themselves that whatever you might say will not be believed."

"But not to kill me? Why the kindness?"

"Professor Moriarty believes that you know something that might prove dangerous to someone, and your enemy doesn't know whether you have passed this information on or not."

"What information, and on to whom?"

Madeleine sat straight up on her bench, her hands folded demurely on her lap. "There's the question," she said. "But, whatever it is, if you have passed it on, killing you would emphasize its importance, while making you appear to be a mad assassin would cause your masters to doubt whatever you might have told them. Remember, they believe you to be a spy of little worth."

"But I know nothing of such value. I report on tendencies and gradual shifts in policy, and who is spying on whom. If it's the anarchists, I report that they go around bombing and shooting; but everybody knows that they go around bombing and shooting."

"It is possibly something you know that you don't know you know," Madeleine told him.

"I think I understand that," Paul said. "It's true that I have uncovered hints that some major disruptive act is being planned by the anarchists, and curiously by a couple of the other groups that I was gathering reports on. I don't know whether it's the same big event they're all talking about or several that are coincidentally all looming on the horizon. But I know nothing of what this event, or these events, might be. I was preparing to try to find out when this happened."

"It may well be something connected with that," Madeleine agreed.

"There is one thing—," Paul said.

"What?"

"I don't know if this is important, but it was peculiar. A man named Hermann Loge, a minor official in the Foreign Ministry, gave me a slip of paper at the opera a few days before—all this. It had a brief numbered list that made no sense to me written on it."

"He gave you a slip of paper?"

"Yes. He didn't know me at the time. I believe he mistook me for someone else."

"How so?"

"Well, I gave him an envelope containing a large sum of money, and apparently he expected someone he didn't know to do just that. He was annoyed at me because it wasn't as much as he expected—the money, that is."

Madeleine sat back in her chair and stared at Paul. "I believe I've entered Wonderland," she said, "although my name isn't Alice. You gave a complete stranger an envelope containing a large sum of money, but he was disappointed because he was expecting some other complete stranger to give him an even larger sum of money in return for a slip of paper containing a numbered list that made no sense?"

"Admirable," Paul said. "You have it."

"I'd better pass it on to the professor," she said. "Where is this list—and why were you giving this stranger an envelope full of money?"

Paul explained his method of recruiting unwitting agents for his amateur espionage ring. "The list is in my apartment, if the police don't have it," he said. "But I doubt if they've found it or considered it important. It's on my desk, folded like a small envelope, writing side in, and I put some stamps in it."

Madeleine clapped her hands. " 'The Purloined Letter!' " she said.

"Right," Paul admitted. "I borrowed the idea from Poe. Let's hope it still works."

"I imagine the professor will want to see if it's still there. Right now what he wants is for you to go over the last few weeks before you were arrested in your mind and tell me everything you can remember. Every little thing. Concentrate on events that, no matter how unimportant they might have seemed to you at the time, were out of the ordinary."

"Strange events? I can't recall any such."

"No, not strange, just out of the ordinary. For example, if the postman usually brings the morning mail at nine, but one morning he came at eight or at ten, that's not particularly strange, but it is out of the ordinary."

"The mail was left in a box downstairs," Paul said.

Madeleine sighed. "Let us start on the Sunday two weeks before you were arrested. Cast your mind back and see what you can remember."

Paul closed his eyes and concentrated for a moment and then opened them. "Are you going to write this down?" he asked.

"No need," she told him. "I never forget anything I hear or see. It's one of the reasons Professor Moriarty asked me to accompany him on this trip, he thought that might be useful. And so, at the moment, it is."

Paul closed his eyes and thought and pictured each day of those last two weeks as best he could. He told Madeleine about the meeting at the Chocolate Factory and seeing Herr Hessen Kopf in a conductor's uniform, and delivering the mysterious package and everything else he could think of. She stared at him and nodded occasionally. When he was done, she smiled. "Very good," she said.

"Was any of that useful?"

"I have no idea," she told him. "I will pass it on to the professor, and he will know. Now we'll have to get to work to get you out of here. Actually, that's our second task, but the other doesn't concern you."

"What is this other task, or shouldn't I ask?"

"Two people, a husband and wife, are being held prisoner in less official circumstances than you. Their position is at least as dire and much more precarious than your own. We know nothing of the group that is holding them, or their motives, except that they would seem to also share the belief that Professor Moriarty is some sort of master criminal, or the mastermind of the Secret Service."

"They have my best wishes, this husband and wife," Paul said. "It is not pleasant to be held by the state; it must be truly trying to be captives of some criminal group. The state is, at least, predictable."

"I will visit with you as much as possible," Madeleine told him, "but I cannot tell you just when. Does your cell window—I assume you have a window—face the street or the courtyard?"

"The street."

"Good. Then we can communicate with you if we need to."

"Of course there's a wide patch of concrete and then the prison wall between my window and the street, if you're thinking of throwing messages back and forth."

"Nothing like that. If we must communicate with you, the professor suggested a musical code."

"I used a musical code to send my reports," Paul offered.

"Yes, but this can't be written, it will have to be sung outside your window on Grossvogelstrasse. Your father told the professor that you have perfect pitch, is that so?"

"Yes."

"This will be simpler than the code you used," Madeleine told him. "Starting at middle C and going up, using two octaves of a twelve-tone scale—the professor assumed that you can differentiate that—"

"I can."

"Good. That gives us twenty-four notes. Messages will be in English. We'll just superimpose the alphabet on the notes going up, with i and j one note, and s for z. That gets us down to twenty-four letters."

"I think I understand."

"Yes, but can you follow it fast enough?"

"I should be able to memorize whatever tune—if we can call such a hash of notes a tune—you send, and then work it out."

"Well, let's give it a try," Madeleine said. She took a tuning fork out of her string purse and hit it gently against the edge of the table.

"A," Paul said.

"Right," Madeleine agreed. She tapped the fork again and then went through a series of vocal exercises that sounded vaguely like the sort of modern music that Paul Donzhof wrote.

"Almost melodic," Paul said.

"Yes, but what was the message?"

"Give me a minute," Paul said. He closed his eyes and hummed softly. " 'Courage and patience,' " he said.

"Very good," she said.

"Actually I made it out to be, 'courage and pasience,' " he told her, "but I made the correction."

"I was flat?"

"Just a bit, I fancy."

"Well," she said. "A perfect memory and perfect pitch are two different things. But I do the best I can."

"You do indeed," he assured her. "And you have cheered me

up immeasurably. You've done as well as my real sister might, and I thank you. Do you think Professor Moriarty can really get me out of here?"

"You may put your faith in the professor. This will not be the first time he has removed a man from prison. What he says he is going to do, he does. It's as simple as that." She stood up and knocked on the cell door. "Good-bye now, brother. Be of good cheer."

WEISSERSCHLOSS

Friends should be preferred to kings.
—Voltaire

For connoisseurs of the palaces, chateaux, and other residences of Europe's nobility, *Weisserschloss*, the royal chateau of the hereditary princes of Rumelia, was a visual feast. The Principality of Rumelia must not be confused with Eastern Rumelia, which was currently part of Bulgaria despite Serbian protestation and a brief war; or with Great Rumelia, the European slice of the old Turkish Empire, which was now subdivided into Albania, Macedonia, and Thrace.

The principality was made up of the Duchy of Lichtenberg, the counties of Parmetz, Yucht, and Constantine, and a vast bog known as the Great Eastern Marsh, and had been a satrap of the Holy Roman Empire, now the Austro-Hungarian Empire, for the past thousand years, give or take a century. It had been ruled by the Juchtenberg Dynasty since Karl the Bald had claimed the throne in 1164, ousting Heinrich the Skewer, who had the unpopular habit of impaling people he disliked three at a time on a specially constructed lance.

Weisserschloss sat on a hill overlooking the capital city of Spass, and boasted a formal garden that had first been laid out by Agricola Germanica sometime in the first century A.D., when he had briefly served as imperial governor of the area. The earliest royal residence had been a fortified castle: walls, keep, moat, drawbridge and all, which was first begun in the twelfth century and gradually added to until it collapsed during extensive structural alterations in the sixteenth century.

By the early seventeenth century it was clear that stone walls might a prison make, but they weren't much use against siege artillery, and Alfred III of Lichtenberg began construction of a royal chateau up against the outer wall of the ruined castle. Holy Roman Emperor Rudolf II, who liked the stag hunting in the nearby forest, offered to pay part of the cost if Alfred would make his new chateau big enough to hold the imperial hunting party, and thus the foundation stone for the two hundred-room *Weisserschloss* was laid. Shaped like a U facing the formal garden, with a broad circular driveway, a facade of white marble from the Neander Valley, and interior fittings carved, painted, embossed, and decorated by the finest craftsmen in Europe, it was indeed a chateau fit for an emperor's visits. Books had been written about the social history of the building, and who had supposedly crept along what secret corridor to enter which bedroom in the middle of the night; about the carvings and frescos in the grand hall and the collection of oil paintings scattered elsewhere about the building; and about the ghosts that were said to inhabit the drafty passages of the imperial wing.

Now, 280 years later, *Weisserschloss* was becoming something of a white elephant, requiring a staff of eighty just to stay even with the cleaning and repairs, not counting the personal staff of the prince and princess, which increased the number another eighty or so when they were in residence. But the income of Ariste Juchenberg, the current crown prince of Rumelia and duke of Lichtenberg, was up to the strain. His ancestors had acquired wisely, and his father and grandfather had conserved well.

Almost two weeks had passed since Paul Donzhof's sister had visited him in prison. It was a little after one in the afternoon when Moriarty, in his guise as Alexandre Sandarel, and his companion Madeleine Verlaine left the train at the *bahnhof* at Spass and threw their two small traveling bags into a fiacre waiting outside the station, its canvas top pulled up to protect the passengers from the slight but chilly drizzle. Moriarty helped Madeleine clamber onto the seat. "Take us to the *Weisserschloss*, driver," he told the skinny, wizened, red-nosed man hunched over in the driver's seat with a thick blanket wrapped around him.

The man turned around and touched the brim of his oversized leather hat. "Yessir! Which entrance?"

Moriarty climbed up and took his seat. "What are our choices?" he asked.

"Well, lessee now, there be the trade entrance, which I don't see as you'll be wanting, and the servants' entrance, ditto, and the imperial drive, which be used when the emperor be in residence, which he never has been, at least the current one. I do believe his grandfather used to come for the shooting on occasion. It be also used for visiting nobility, but the prince usually sends his own carriage for them." The driver paused for breath and wiped his face with an oversized handkerchief. "Then there be the private entrance and the public entrance and the visitors' entrance and the guest entrance. And there be the regimental entrance, for when the troops are paraded. And there be a couple or so of others, but I don't know nothing about them."

"We're here to request an audience with Prince Ariste," Moriarty told the driver.

"Ah!" the driver said, twisting even further around in his seat to get a better look at his passengers. "Audience day be Thursday, but you must put your name on the list on Tuesday. So, since this be Friday, I'll be taking you to the *Hotel Herzogin Theresa*, that being the hotel suitable for persons of your caliber."

Moriarty screwed his monocle into his right eye and stared up at the driver. "Let us assume that the prince will see us today," he said. "If that were so, which entrance would you suggest we arrive at?"

The driver refused to be responsible for assuming any such thing. "T'aint my place to be suggesting," he said, shaking his head as though he'd never heard such madness, "but I suppose if t'were me, I'd place myself at the private entrance. Unless I got you figured wrong and you be trying to sell something; then it's the trade entrance for you."

"Perhaps we should try the private entrance," Moriarty said, "and I'll restrain any impulse to engage in trade."

The driver looked at Moriarty curiously, but then turned to the front and snapped the reins. "Come, Kneidl," he said to his horse, "we take this crazy man and his beautiful friend to the *Weisserschloss.*"

Twenty minutes later Kneidl trotted down the wide driveway that formed a great U as it passed in front of the chateau, and stopped at a pair of doors about midway along the left-hand wing. Less elaborate than the Great Entrance they had passed, the gold-framed great oak doors still would have shamed many a cathedral. The doors opened as the carriage stopped and a footman emerged holding a large umbrella and stood respectfully by the carriage door shielding them with it as Moriarty climbed down and helped Madeleine down after him.

Moriarty took an embossed visiting card reading, "Alexandre Sandarel—London, Paris" from his sleeve and wrote "concerning Benjamin Barnett" on the back of it with his traveling pencil. He combined it with one which his companion produced from her small clutch purse, which read merely "Lady Madeleine Verlaine," and placed the pair of them on the small silver tray held by the footman. "We would like to see the prince," he said. "We have no appointment, but I believe His Highness will grant us an audience."

The footman nodded his head sharply twice. "Their High-nesses are out riding at the moment, but they will return soon. This way, please." He led them to a small waiting room to the left of the doors and disappeared within the building. Two pikemen guarded the hallway to the interior of the chateau. Moriarty noted that, while their ceremonial uniforms were two centuries out of date, their pikes were sharp.

Three-quarters of an hour later the footman returned for them. "Please leave your baggage here," he said, "and your stick, sir, and follow me." He escorted them to the door of a small drawing room somewhere in the interior of the vast building. It was guarded by two burly men in black uniforms, one of whom ran his hands over Moriarty's jacket and looked inside Madeleine's small purse before allowing them to enter. "Sorry, sir, ma'am," he said, "but the prince's life has been threatened, and we must take precautions."

A tall, handsome man in one of the many ornate cavalry uni-forms available to Austro-Hungarian nobility stood before a small elegant writing desk inside the room. By his side, seated in the carved wood chair that was companion to the writing desk, was a slender, blond woman with delicate features and intelligent eyes. She was dressed in a simple, full-skirted riding costume. A maid was just removing their raincoats and wide-brimmed hats from the room, testifying to the haste with which they had come to this meeting. "I am Prince Ariste," the man said, "and this is my wife, Princess Diane. I apologize for the unseemly precautions, but my guards insist upon it with strangers."

"Your Highnesses," Moriarty said, inclining his head slightly in what might have been mistaken for a bow. "We understand and we take no offense." Madeleine curtsied gracefully.

"We have come directly from our afternoon ride without taking the time to change," Prince Ariste said. "Anyone who invokes the name of the Barnetts will gain an immediate audience with us. But I trust that you have something to say that warrants our attention." He looked at Moriarty sharply. "You are Alexandre Sandarel. I believe I've heard the name. You're some sort of charlatan, are you not?"

Moriarty chuckled. "Alexandre Sandarel has been so described," he admitted. "I must say that I don't agree with the description."

"Perhaps the Barnetts sent him to us," Princess Diane suggested, looking up at her husband. "I hope he is amusing."

"Is that the case?" the prince asked. "Did the Barnetts send you to us? They're due to arrive here any day now, you know."

"I understand your English is excellent," Moriarty said, switching to that language. "Let us continue the conversation in English, as there will be less chance of our conversation being understood if we are overheard."

"You mistrust my servants?"

"In matters of importance I mistrust everybody. Those who are not venal are thoughtless. Can you vouch for all your servants, Your Highness?"

Prince Ariste thought it over for a second. "No," he said, "I suppose not. There are so many of them."

"English is an acceptable language," Princess Diane allowed. "Besides, I've been told that my accent is charming, in English."

"And so it is," Moriarty agreed.

"Now, about the Barnetts—"

"I believe that their arrival will be delayed," Moriarty said. "Benjamin Barnett and his wife Cecily have been kidnaped by a man who calls himself Graf Sigfried von Linsz and are being held in a twelfth-century castle on a large estate apparently owned by him near the town of Uhmstein outside of Vienna."

"Kidnaped!" The prince clutched at the back of the chair his wife was sitting in. "How do you know this, and why did you come to us? Have you notified the authorities?"

Moriarty shook his head. "There are reasons why that would be unwise."

"Unwise?" Princess Diane asked. "How can it be unwise to notify the police?"

"I will explain," Moriarty told her.

Prince Ariste reached down and took his wife's hand. "How am I to know this is the truth?" he demanded. "Do you claim to know this by some sort of clairvoyant trick? Do you expect some sort of reward?" The words rushed from his mouth as the ideas were formed.

Moriarty shook his head. "Although there is an Alexandre Sandarel, who does claim to some clairvoyant powers, I am not he. My name is Professor James Moriarty, and Benjamin Barnett was for years my close friend and confidant. I have borrowed Alexandre Sandarel's identity for the moment to make my work here easier. I came to you because I believe our interests coincide. I neither request nor expect a reward."

"Professor Moriarty." The prince paused in thought for a moment. "I have heard of you," he said. "Barnett mentioned you and called you a friend. But I have also heard—" his voice faded out, but then he resumed, "Why do you travel under a pseudonym? Is that not a sign of guile, an indication that you are not to be trusted?"

"If it isn't an indication of deceit when you do it, Your Highness," Moriarty said, smiling, "then why should it be when I do it?"

"A point!" Prince Ariste admitted. "How do you know of my friendship with the Barnetts and, as it seems you must, the events surrounding it?"

"Mummer Tolliver told me the story. He was traveling with the Barnetts as their servant."

"The midget? I remember him."

"The mummer is a midget in stature only," Madeleine interjected. "In courage and quickness of wit he is a giant."

"Indeed he is," the princess agreed. "Cecily—Mrs. Barnett—and I spoke of him."

"Why is he not here with you?" Prince Ariste asked. "How do I know whether I can believe what you tell me? It sounds like the beginning of a fantastic story. The Barnetts kidnaped? Held in a castle? Why? Who is this von Linsz and what does he want?"

"Reasonable questions," Moriarty agreed. "The mummer is at the castle I spoke of, watching and waiting. He has been there for the—what is it now?—seventeen days they have been captive, leaving only long enough to notify me of the events. I—well—how can I convince you that I speak the truth? I can think of no better way than telling you the whole story of what Miss Verlaine and I are doing here, a thousand miles away from my London abode, and why. May I sit?"

"Of course. Excuse my lack of hospitality." The prince waved Moriarty and Madeleine over to a divan that stretched across a corner of the room and settled himself in a high-backed wooden chair against the wall. He turned to one of the guards by the door. "A bottle of the St. Joseph *Goldwasser* and some glasses—see to it, Karl."

The big man nodded and disappeared into the hall. In a second he was back, obviously having passed the message along to a servitor. A guard's job, after all, is to guard.

"A light, fruity, white wine, locally produced," the prince said when the bottle and glasses appeared so quickly that they must have been waiting outside the door. "It seems suitable for the moment. Now—"

With occasional interruptions for sipping the wine, Moriarty told the prince and princess the entire story of why he had come to Vienna, and what he knew of the Barnett's ordeal, leaving out only the identity of "Paul's" father, which he was sworn not to reveal. He was not interrupted.

When he had completed the narrative he leaned back on the sofa and stared fixedly at the prince.

Ariste returned the stare for a moment, and then shook his

head. "Amazing!" he said. He turned to Madeleine. "And you, Lady Madeleine, do you verify this?"

Madeleine nodded. "The parts of it I know first-hand have been accurately recounted. As for the rest, I've worked with the professor before, and he's a square shooter. I've met Paul in prison, and he is an Englishman, and he has, as far as I can tell, been framed. But as to why—that's beyond me."

"So," the prince said, turning to Moriarty, "you have come here to aid an English spy, and you expect me to help you."

"No, Your Highness. I do not expect you to help me in freeing Paul. That is my concern. But Benjamin and Cecily Barnett are not involved in any sort of espionage, and you might feel that you owe them something. So I have come to you to give you a chance to repay that debt."

"And why do you not go to the police?"

"Because they are ill-equipped to deal with such a thing. An aristocrat kidnaping a foreign couple? Who would believe it? They would go to the door of the castle and ask politely whether the Barnetts were there. Graf von Linsz would say no. They would thank him, tip their hats, and go away. Because further, until I have proof otherwise, I believe the local police to be agents of this graf."

Prince Ariste turned to his wife, who was staring wide-eyed at Moriarty. "What do you think, my dear?"

"I think that Mr. Barnett and his dear wife have been kidnaped, and we must do something to help them!"

"We must? Of course we must!" Ariste turned back to Moriarty. "Is that the only reason you're here? You want our help?"

"I believe we can probably help each other," Moriarty told him. "And I'm afraid it will take both of us to help the Barnetts."

The prince stared at a picture on the wall across the room for a while. A mountain landscape, it powerfully evoked the brooding stillness before a coming storm. One could almost feel the increasing wind as the dark clouds skittered across the sky. "Why do you suppose the Barnetts were kidnaped?" he asked. "What could anyone want from them? They have little money."

"Perhaps, my dear, this is related to the attack on you at the Villa Endorra," Princess Diane suggested.

"I did not want to think that," Ariste replied. "The idea that, by saving my life, Barnett has put his own in danger is repugnant to me."

"That may not be the explanation," Moriarty offered.

"Then you think the two events are unrelated?"

"No, I believe that they are definitely related, but not as cause and effect. I believe that we have two strands of a larger tapestry that have come together in this way, at this time."

Prince Ariste stood up. "I wish to hear your ideas," he said, "and I fancy we'll be speaking for some time. So I suggest that we adjourn this discussion for a couple of hours. I am hot and sweaty, and need to wash and change clothes after our gallop, and I'm sure that my wife feels the same. And we should give you a chance to freshen up after your journey." He pulled a pocket watch from an inner pocket of his jacket. "It's almost three o'clock. I'll have a valet take you to rooms, where you can refresh yourselves."

Princess Diane nodded. "And a lady's maid," she said to Madeleine. "We'll have Bentley send a maid up to your room to assist you."

"Bentley?" Moriarty raised his eyebrow.

"The chief steward," Prince Ariste explained. "He's English. English butlers are the best, or so they say."

"Do they?" Moriarty asked. "How curious."

"We'll meet again at five in the map room," the prince said. "I'll send someone to show you the way. It's not horribly difficult to get lost in here. I still do myself, sometimes."

The prince nodded and Karl disappeared through a door. Shortly a large, stalwart young man in yellow velvet knee breeches and a red velvet coat appeared to show Moriarty and Madeleine to their rooms.

Moriarty was deposited in a small but well-appointed bedroom and Madeleine was taken one door further down the long hall. A minute later there was a knock at Moriarty's door and two maids entered; one carrying his traveling bag and owl-headed stick, which she placed by the bed, and the other bearing a basin and a pitcher of hot water, which she put on the dresser. "If there's anything you require, sir," the basin-carrying maid said, "the bell pull is to the right of the bed." And they left.

Moriarty hung up his jacket and pulled his shirt off. He washed the grime of travel off his face and hands, and then lay down on the bed and closed his eyes. He had always been able to fall instantly to sleep, and to wake up just as rapidly. It was an ability that had proved useful on more than one occasion.

Two hours later a man in the black uniform of the prince's guards showed Moriarty and a refreshed and glowing Madeleine through the maze of corridors to the map room. "You look different somehow," Moriarty commented to Madeleine in an undertone as they followed their guide. "You've changed your dress."

"It's a new dress," Madeleine told him, "sent down by the princess. Bella, the maid, did my hair and helped me touch up my makeup. It was wonderful! I now aspire to having a lady's maid of my very own."

"A worthy goal," Moriarty agreed.

"Now that they've had a chance to think over what you told them, do you suppose they're going to help us, or have us arrested?" Madeleine asked softly.

Moriarty smiled a grim smile. "We'll know in a few moments," he told her.

The map room was a large room on the second floor with windows overlooking a closed courtyard. It held several dozen massive cabinets full of, presumably, maps. An oversized table surrounded by chairs filled the middle of the room, perfect for spreading the maps out and studying them. "My great grandfather was a field marshal in the war against Napoleon," Prince Ariste explained. "He developed a great fondness for maps."

"I, myself, have always been fascinated by them," Moriarty admitted.

"Feel free to peruse the ones in these cabinets when you have the time," Ariste offered. "There are a set of French military maps here that were captured during the Italian Campaign, and we've always fancied that the writing scribbled all over them is in Napoleon's hand. Perhaps the secrets of his military genius are right there in that cabinet, if only someone could read his handwriting."

"A pleasant conceit," Moriarty offered. "But I fancy that his genius lay not so much in what he did, as in the way he did it. And that is probably not written down."

"Please sit down everyone," Princess Diane said, seating herself at the far end of the table. "We have excluded the servants and guards from this meeting, as you seem concerned about what they might overhear. There are refreshments on the sideboard under the window. I am anxious to hear about poor Benjamin and Cecily."

"I'm afraid that their abduction is more my responsibility than yours," Moriarty said, lowering himself into one of the chairs and laying his owl-headed stick along the table top in front of him. "What the Barnett's captors seem most interested in is my whereabouts and my intentions. Since they have knowledge of neither, I'm very much afraid that the only reason they're being kept alive is to use in negotiating with me, should our antagonists manage to locate me."

"How could you know that?" Prince Ariste asked.

"Every night Mummer Tolliver climbs the castle wall and perches outside the barred window to the room in which the Barnetts are being held. They exchange information."

"Isn't that very dangerous?" Princess Diane asked.

"Yes," Moriarty replied, "it is."

"What do these scoundrels want with you?" Prince Ariste asked.

"They seem to have the notion that I am the mastermind of a vast criminal conspiracy that has connections and branches all over Europe. At the same time they alternate that with the curious notion that I am the head of the British Secret Service, with espionage agents in every chancery ready to steal the plans of whatever-you-fancy and thwart the machinations of whoever these people are."

"How can they think that?" Princess Diane asked. "Are you either of those things?"

"I assure you, Your Highness, that I am not. And, at any rate, I could scarcely be both, even if I were one or the other."

"Then how could they get that idea?" Ariste asked.

"I can tell you that," Madeleine interjected. "Sherlock Holmes."

"The consulting detective?" Prince Ariste frowned. "I have heard of him. What about him?"

Moriarty was silent, perhaps gathering his thoughts. "Well," Madeleine said, stepping into the breach, "Mr. Holmes seems to have concluded some time ago that the professor is some sort of master criminal, and he tells this to anyone who will listen to him, and then swears them to secrecy so he can't be sued for slander."

"Is this so?" Ariste asked Moriarty.

The professor nodded. "Lady Madeleine exaggerates slightly, but only slightly, I'm afraid."

"And thus badly distorted stories of the doings of Professor Moriarty have become—what can I say?—legend, perhaps, throughout Britain and have slowly spread across Europe," Madeleine continued.

Princess Diane smiled at Madeleine. "You are a strong advocate for your friend," she said.

"He has been more than good to me," Madeleine told her. "He has shown me, and forced me to believe, that I could be—more than I was."

Princess Diane nodded slowly. "I see," she said.

"And these stories told about you have no truth to them?" Prince Ariste asked Moriarty.

The professor paused, considering what to say. "I cannot say that I have always obeyed the laws or scrupulously followed the morés of my little island," he said, "but I have no gang, and I most assuredly do not head the British Secret Service. Or, for that matter, any other secret service."

"Then how do you account for Mr. Holmes's accusations?"

"It is an obsession with him," Moriarty said. "Holmes cannot stand being wrong or, for that matter, being puzzled for long. When he is faced with a crime he cannot solve, he turns to his amanuensis Dr. Watson and exclaims, 'Aha! This is the work of that evil genius, Professor Moriarty. And occasionally he comes over to my house and accuses me of this or that. I believe he has developed what your Dr. Freud calls an 'idée fixe.' " Moriarty sighed. "I had the misfortune, you see, to know him as a youth."

"The poor man!" Princess Diane said.

"Indeed," Moriarty agreed.

"I believe I can understand the conflating of master criminal with master spy in the minds of those who believe the, ah, myth," Prince Ariste said. "After all, a spy is generally regarded as the lowest sort of criminal, a man who would betray his country."

"And yet spies who are working for their own country, living in a foreign land, speaking a language not their own, are as brave as any soldiers on the battlefield. If they are caught they face an ignominious death," Moriarty remarked. "Curiously, they receive little credit, even from their own side. Napoleon's master spy, Karl Schulmeister, devised the capture of an entire Austrian army. And yet Napoleon refused to allow Schulmeister any military honors. 'The only thing a spy deserves is pay,' Napoleon reputedly told him, 'not honor.' "

"And is it honor this young man, Paul, was seeking?" Prince Ariste asked. "If so, he sought it in a strange place."

Moriarty shook his head. "The young man calling himself Paul Donzhof requires neither money nor honor," he said. "He is one of a number of men who are trying to keep Britain informed of European and Asian affairs despite the British government's apparent lack of interest. They call their enterprise 'the Great Game,' and finance their own travels."

" 'The Great Game,' " Prince Ariste said. "The English make a game out of everything. They are very sporting."

"The English upper classes believe that the talented amateur is better than the professional," Moriarty said. "Morally, if not physically. But then they have no need to make a living."

"You sound like a socialist," Princess Diane said, looking at him curiously.

Madeleine laughed. "My friend here is disdainful of almost everybody," she said. "He believes that the human race is full of fools and scoundrels."

Moriarty waved a dismissive hand through the air. "Let me say rather that I have noticed that my fellow men are mostly fools, with a smattering of scoundrels, and I feel free to comment on it."

"Well!" Princess Diane said. "I hope you exclude us from that listing."

"Oh, I do," Moriarty assured her. "From what I have heard of you from the mummer, I have respect for both your intelligence and your intentions."

"And would you tell is if you didn't?" Prince Ariste asked.

"Actually, he would," Madeleine assured him. "The professor has managed to directly insult a duchess, a marquis, and at least one member of the British royal family, to my knowledge."

Moriarty grimaced. "Have we not something to discuss of more immediate importance than my character?" he asked.

"That is so. Tell me, how do you propose we go about freeing the Barnetts?" Prince Ariste asked.

"That shouldn't prove too difficult, if you can supply a few trustworthy men," Moriarty said. "But I'm afraid that's only part of the job."

"There is more? What else?"

"We have a riddle to solve." Moriarty said. Then he shook his head. "That is, I do. I should not, and I will not, ask you to do anything beyond helping me rescue our mutual friends."

Princess Diane leaned forward, her eyes bright. "Tell us," she said. "What is the riddle?"

Moriarty screwed his monocle into his eyes and looked at her sternly. "I should not have brought it up," he said. "My problem is frustrating and dangerous, and I should not involve you."

"Is it related to the Barnetts' abduction?"

"Almost certainly, but not directly."

"Ah!" the prince said. "Then please tell us the riddle, and let us judge how deeply we should involve ourselves in your problem."

"Very good, Your Highness; as you say," Moriarty said. "The riddle is composed of these items." He closed his eyes and recited:

"One, twenty-four and twenty-five April;

"two, that Wednesday;

"three, unknown;

"four, England, France, Germany, and Russia;

"five, unknown;

"six, third and fourth out of six;

"seven, yes."

Prince Ariste got up and went to the far wall, where there was a large blackboard. "Recite that again, would you?" he asked. Moriarty did, and the prince wrote the list down on the board. Then he stood back and stared at it. "A riddle indeed," he said. "What does it mean? Wait—that's the wrong question. Where does it come from and how does it relate to our current problem, is what I meant to say."

"One night at the opera Paul Donzhof was handed a slip of paper by mistake by a minor official of the Foreign Ministry. He told Lady Madeleine about it when she went to see him in prison, posing as his sister. We went to retrieve it from his apartment. It was where he had left it, cleverly concealed by being folded into an envelope and filled with postage stamps. That—" Moriarty pointed to the list on the blackboard, "is how it read."

"Why do you think it's important?" Prince Ariste asked.

"Donzhof paid five hundred kronen for the paper. That is, he handed the man five hundred kronen in an attempt to enlist him as a source of information. The man must have expected someone he didn't know to hand him money in exchange for the paper, so he handed Paul the paper. He complained to Paul that he had expected a thousand kronen."

"So it was worth a thousand kronen to someone," Prince Ariste said. "There are all sorts of reasons that might be so."

"I went to find the man from whom Paul had received it to ask him what it meant and whom he was expecting. His name was Hermann Loge. He was in the planning department of the Foreign Ministry. I was too late, he was dead. He had been murdered in his bedroom the week before. His throat had been slit while he slept. Nothing was stolen. He and his wife slept apart, and she claimed she had heard nothing. The two maids slept in the basement. The police are operating on the theory that either his wife or one of his two mistresses must have done it, and as of when I found this out they were still trying to discover which so they knew who to arrest."

"You think he was killed for his mistake?" Princess Diane asked.

"I do. And I believe that Paul was implicated in two murders because he received that piece of paper. Killing him might have drawn attention to it if he had passed it on, but making him appear to be a murderer and assassin would discredit him."

The prince stared at the blackboard. "Hard to believe there's anything evil, or even particularly meaningful, in these seven items. 'Twenty-four and twenty-five April.' That's Friday and Saturday a week from now, if it speaks of this year. 'Third and fourth out of six.' " The prince shrugged. "I give that one up."

"Some major outrage is being planned for sometime in the near future," Moriarty said. "That much Paul Donzhof was able to find out from his own sources. I believe this list relates to that. Could it be planned for next Saturday or Sunday? Then how could a minor official in the Foreign Ministry know the dates? Will it happen simultaneously in England, France, Germany, and Russia? If so why are we learning about it in Vienna? And just what would constitute a major outrage to this group of people who think nothing of bombing, shooting, and stabbing random government officials?"

"That's your riddle?"

"That's it."

"How do we go about solving it?"

"We?" Moriarty put his hands flat on the table and stared across at the prince. "Are you sure you want to involve yourself in this?"

"If some group is going to blow up the Parliament or assassinate the emperor, I think I should get involved," Prince Ariste said. "But I do think that at some appropriate time we should find some appropriate authority to tell. The empire does have some resources, and not all its officials are stupid or venal."

"Agreed," Moriarty said. "As soon as we have something to tell that might be believed, and we know who best to tell it to, we will do so."

"Now," Prince Ariste said, "what are we to do about the Barnetts' incarceration?"

Moriarty leaned back in his chair. "I've come to you because Mummer Tolliver tells me that von Linsz's castle and the grounds around it are well guarded and well patrolled. I have a tentative plan in mind, subject to looking over the area myself. But for it I need some trustworthy men. And, as I said earlier, I have no 'gang' to command. Do you have some men available that you can trust to do as you say?"

Ariste nodded. "I do. About six hundred. I am commander of a regiment of light infantry. Most of them are reservists, and it would take an official mobilization to call them up now. But the headquarters company is regular army, and their barracks is about a mile from here."

"Well," Moriarty said. "More than I'd hoped for, but welcome just the same. If you have some way to select, say, a dozen of them to volunteer for some extra-martial duty, we can rendezvous with the mummer and perfect the plan."

"I'll do that," Prince Ariste said. "And I'll order up a special train to get us to Vienna. You can tell us the plan on the way."

EIGHTEEN

YOUR AMERICAN COUSIN

All nature is but art unknown to thee;
All chance, direction which thou can'st not see;
All discord, harmony not understood;
All partial evil, universal good . . .
— ALEXANDER POPE

Sherlock Holmes and Dr. Watson had adjoining rooms on the second floor of the Hotel Leopold, a solidly built, modern edifice which took up one square block on the Schwarzenbergplatz, about as central a location as one could get in the spread-out city that was Fin de Siècle Vienna. It was shortly before dinner time Thursday evening, and Holmes sat at the small writing desk in his room jotting down the day's notes in the next empty page in his notebook. Through the connecting door he could hear Watson whistling "A Wandering Minstrel" from *The Mikado* as he dressed for dinner.

"Spent the afternoon concealed in the waiters' pantry at the Danube Café," Holmes wrote. "Could hear the conversation in the private back room clearly, but could not always tell who was speaking. Much discussion of the 'great event' that is to take place in the near future. There were at least three groups represented that one would not think were related, or even amicable, and that certainly would not be expected to make common cause. There must be—"

There was a soft, tentative knock at the hall door. Holmes put down his pen. "Yes?"

"*Entschuldigen sie bitte, Herr Holmes?*" It was a woman's voice.

Holmes switched to German. "Yes? One moment, please." He

went to the door and opened it. The woman in the hall looked to be in her forties, and was well, if plainly, dressed. "What can I do for you, madam?"

"You are Mr. Sherlock Holmes?"

"I am."

"Please, it must be that I am sure of that—if you would tell me; what is your landlady's name, in London?"

"Ah!" Holmes said. "Just so. Her name is Mrs. Hudson. What do you have for me?"

The woman took a step back. "You know already that I have something for you? Did someone tell you to expect me? I told no one!"

Holmes gave the woman what he probably thought was a reassuring smile. "I didn't mean to startle you," he said. "Surely it was obvious from your question that someone sent you to me. It could have been that you wished to consult me, but then the question of my identity wouldn't be so urgent. So I deduced that someone had given you something for me, and the lady wanted to be sure that I received it myself."

"And now you know, without my telling you, that it is a lady who employs me." She took a small brown envelope from her purse and handed it to Holmes. "Here you are, sir. Please don't deduce anything else about me, or I'll scream, I swear I will!"

Holmes laughed. "You have my word," he said, digging in his pocket and fishing out a coin. "Now perhaps a little something for your trouble—"

"No, no, thank you, sir. I have been adequately recompensed. It's been—an event—meeting you. You are everything she said you were!" And with that the woman curtsied and scurried off down the hall.

"It's true you know, Holmes," Watson said, adjusting his bow tie as he came through the connecting door. "What seems a trite and commonplace deduction to you can be quite startling to the observer. How did you know that the lady was carrying a message from another lady?"

"Ah, Watson, you could have deduced it yourself if you were

standing here observing the woman as I was," Holmes said, stepping back into his room and closing the door.

"So you have often said in similar situations in the past," Watson told him. "And yet I never seem able to grasp what you consider the obvious until you have explained it to me."

"You do yourself an injustice my dear Watson," Holmes said. "You have improved your deductive ability greatly since first we began lodging together. Once you started applying the diagnostic skills you learned in the practice of medicine to the greater world about you, your observation of detail increased considerably. True, you have not yet developed skill in detecting the minutia that make for the finer distinctions, and the inferences you draw from your observations lack a certain, let us say, courage; but there is hope for you, Watson, there is hope!"

"Thank you for that, Holmes," Watson said. "But I am content to let you do the inferring." He stopped fiddling with his tie and shrugged into his dinner jacket. "What was it about that lady that led you to deduce that she was carrying the message of another lady?"

"She had some straight pins stuck through the collar of her blouse and her left sleeves," Holmes explained. "And there was a smudge of french chalk on the heel of her right hand."

"Really, Holmes!" Watson managed to sound mystified and exasperated at the same time.

"Surely the inference is clear," Holmes told his companion. "The woman is a dressmaker. And the hour indicates that she has hurried over at the close of her business day to deliver this message, certainly as a favor to one of her clients."

Watson said, "Humph! Surely there are a dozen other possible explanations."

"Perhaps," Holmes admitted. "But the probabilities—and the lady's own response—would indicate that mine is the right one. Now, let's see what this envelope holds for us."

Holmes held the envelope up to the gaslight, sniffed it, and peered at it intensely for a minute. Then he shrugged. "Seems to be just an envelope," he said. "Local manufacture. Well, let us see who knows I'm here, and what she has to say for herself." He slit the envelope open carefully with the blade of his clasp-knife, and pulled the folded paper out gingerly with two fingers.

Watson peered over his shoulder. "What is it, Holmes?"

Holmes unfolded the paper and smoothed it out on his writing desk. "A letter," he said. "In English." He peered down at it. "Come now, this is most interesting."

"Really? What does it say?"

"The salutation is, 'Dearest Emma,' " Holmes said.

"Dearest *Emma?*" Watson chuckled. "There you have it, Holmes. The letter is not for you after all. The woman must have a purse full of envelopes, and she gave you the wrong one. Perhaps she'll return in the near future to exchange messages."

"I somehow don't think so," Holmes said. "There is at least one other explanation for that salutation." He adjusted the gaslight over his desk. "It continues:

> 'So finally I have gotten around to writing the letter I promised you those many months ago. How quickly time flies! This letter, I hope, finds you and your father in good health. Really I apologize for not writing sooner, but I have been having a horribly busy time meeting people, making friends, and traveling about here in Europe, and have been most remiss in my communications. You know, I must confess I have not written Mama or Edward, or anyone.' "

"Does it go on like that?" Watson asked.

"It does:

> 'Have found the most wonderful agent who promises to help me with my singing career over here. Everyone, I must say, has been more helpful than I could have expected. And so I have wandered from Italy to Austria with the most wonderful companions! There you have it, and I hope you can forgive me for my indolence and sloth. Please, please, give my love to all those I left behind and tell them, especially Edward, that I miss them and think of them every day. Especially Edward. And, of course, save some of that love for yourself! I expect to be here for some time, and a letter can

always reach me at Post Restante, Uhmstein, Austria (which, my dear, is just a hop and a skip from Vienna).' "

Holmes paused in his reading there, and Watson asked, "Is that all?"

"It's signed, 'your loving Jenny,' " Holmes told him. "Nothing on the back of the page. This is most curious."

"As I said, Holmes, it's obviously some mistake," Watson offered.

Holmes stared at the letter for a minute, and then put it down and picked up the envelope. He carefully pulled it apart along its gummed edges and examined the inside. "I had thought perhaps—but I find nothing here."

"Come," Watson said, "Let's go down to dinner. There's nothing to be found."

Holmes took up the letter again and folded it carefully along its original creases. "You think so, do you, Watson? You don't see anything strange about the letter? No alternate solution for its misdirected salutation suggests itself to you?"

"No, Holmes, I can't say that anything comes to mind except that the letter was not intended for you, and you're attaching too much importance to an innocent mistake of some kind."

"Ah, well, Watson, perhaps you're right," Holmes said, putting the letter in the inner pocket of his dinner jacket. "Let's go down to the dining room and consider the matter over a pair of veal chops and some of that thick bean soup. And then there's the question of dessert which will require careful thought." They left the room and headed down the hall. "But nonetheless it's a very curious letter."

"If you say so, Holmes."

After dinner they retired to the hotel's reading room, where Watson found a comparatively recent copy of *The Strand* magazine with which to amuse himself while Holmes once again produced the letter and stared at it. After a while Holmes lit his pipe and puffed on it, alternating between staring at the letter, and staring at the ceiling. This went on for about half an hour when, all at once

Holmes sprang to his feet and exclaimed, "Of course! How stupid of me!"

Watson looked up from his magazine to find Holmes fairly dancing with excitement. "Come, Watson!" he said, "I believe the game's afoot!"

After all the years Watson had spent as Sherlock Holmes's companion and amanuensis, he still couldn't suppress the thrill of excitement that went through him when he realized that Holmes had picked up the scent and was on his way to solving another mystery. "Where to, Holmes?" he asked.

"First back to our rooms," Holmes told him, "and then we shall see—we shall see!"

Back in the room Holmes closed the door and turned up the gas mantle. "We want light," he said, "and heat."

"What have you discovered, Holmes?"

"It's what I am about to discover," Holmes replied. "I had it all in front of me, and I wasted a good hour staring at it. Was it not Jonathan Swift who said, 'There's none so blind as they that won't see'? Ah, Watson, I have no excuse—I should have seen it right away!"

"Seen what, Holmes?"

"What should have been obvious from the beginning," Holmes told Watson. "First, what were the chances that the message, as you suggested, was not for me?"

"I would say that the fact that it was addressed to 'Emma' was a good sign of that," Watson protested.

"It would seem that way at first thought," Holmes agreed. "But surely reflection on the way that seamstress was so careful to ascertain my identity before turning over the envelope would suggest otherwise."

"Then why the 'Emma'?"

"Combine that with the envelope's delivery by a seamstress, and what does it suggest?"

Watson took a deep breath. "I don't know, Holmes, what does it suggest to you?"

"That the sender could not have it delivered in the usual way; through the post or by a courier. Therefore that she was afraid to be seen posting a letter to Sherlock Holmes. And why is it headed 'Dear Emma'? Surely because she was afraid to be seen *writing* a letter to Sherlock Holmes."

"I see," said Watson. "But why would anyone go to such lengths to send you such a letter? It does not convey anything of interest; at least, not to my eyes."

"Therefore the real meaning is concealed. That is the conclusion I reached before we went down to dinner. But concealed how? At first I thought of pinholes. An old trick of prisoners and lovers is to prick tiny pinholes above the letters to spell out the secret message." Holmes held the letter up to the light. "But, as you can see, there are no pinholes in this paper. Then I tried reading every third word, or fourth word, or fifth word; and for my troubles I got gibberish."

"And then, Holmes?"

"And then we went down to dinner."

Watson dropped heavily into the chair by the window. "Really, Holmes, you can be the most exasperating man."

Holmes chuckled. "Sorry, Watson. But it came to me after dinner that I was getting too complicated, and the answer was probably very simple. And I looked, and it was. You see the first thing I looked at, the simplest cipher of all, is the first letter of the first word in each sentence. Now look—" he handed the letter to Watson. "The first four letters derived that way are S-H-T-R. Utter nonsense. So I stopped. I should have gone on. The first nine letters spell out S-H-T-R-Y-H-E-A-T. Or, as it suddenly occurred to me, S. H.—Sherlock Holmes—try heat!"

"Try heat?"

"Yes, Watson. There are several liquids—lemon juice is one of them—that you can use to write on paper with, and the writing disappears when the liquid dries. But then, when the paper is heated up, the writing reappears. Like this!" Holmes grabbed the paper back and held it up to the side of the gas mantle, moving it back and forth so that it would heat evenly.

For a time nothing happened. And then, slowly, on the backside of the message, letters appeared, first very faintly and then deepening into a dark brown:

Sherlock,

I'm in trouble. Guest/prisoner of Graf Sigfried von Linsz at Schloss Uhm, the castle on his estate in Uhmstein. The Barnetts, friends of Prof. Moriarty, prisoners here also. Von Linsz thinks I'm on his side, but not sure enough to let me write. He is one of the ringleaders of the plot. Goal to take over Austria/ Europe. Fete for locals planned for next weekend. Come in disguise. Other leaders coming here then I think.

Your American Cousin Jenny

"Uhmstein?" Holmes said. "Where is Uhmstein?"

"Who is Jenny?"

"Jenny Vernet," Holmes explained. "She is an opera singer. Contralto. Quite good. Related to me on my mother's side. Grew up in the United States. She was born in San Francisco, where her father had made his fortune selling supplies to gold miners. When she was quite young the family moved back East to Boston, then on to London when she was in her teens."

"What is she doing in Europe? And, more to the point, what on earth is she doing writing you a secret message?" Watson asked. "How does she know you're here? How does she know about any plot?"

"I know no more than you do," Holmes told him. "But if I had to guess—Mycroft."

"Your brother? What does he have to do with it?"

Holmes shrugged. "He knows I'm here, and what I'm doing. If some new information came to his attention, he is quite capable of acting on his own initiative and sending someone to investigate."

"And sending a woman? Your cousin? Really, Holmes!"

"Mycroft has little patience for the customary distinctions between the sexes. He often employs women as his agents. He finds them more reliable, more quick-witted, and less prone to make careless errors. I am quoting him, I'm not sure I disagree."

"Well this relative of yours seems to be a plucky young woman," Watson said.

"She always had amazing courage and initiative," Holmes

agreed. "If she'd been born a male, she'd probably be an explorer or something equally as adventurous. As it is her singing gives her all the independence she craves and the ability to travel about the world."

"It sounds like her independence is a bit limited at the moment," Watson commented. "What shall we do, Holmes?"

"Pack!" Holmes said. "We're going to Uhmstein—wherever that may be."

NINETEEN

A CASTLE IN UHMSTEIN

One should not bewail the death of hope until it has been buried.
—ALMA SCHINDLER

Schloss Uhm, the castle on the von Linsz estate, was not large as castles go, but it was still impressive against the skyline. A triangular structure some eighty feet high, with a tower that went up another three stories in each corner, it had a crenellated outer wall ten feet thick and twenty-two feet high. It was one of a chain of fortresses built in the twelfth century by the Order of the Knights of Wotan to defend the Holy Roman Empire against invaders from the east. The east eventually stopped trying to invade, and the eighteenth century counts of Linsz enlarged the arrow-slits into windows, filled in the moat, and did what they could to convert their dank and drafty fortress into an elegant and graceful chateau. But, with the curtain wall surrounding it, and the high stone towers, it always looked more foreboding than inviting.

When Sigfried Karl Maria von Linsz inherited the title and estate in 1878, he put bars on the windows, re-installed the portcullis, and did what he could to restore Schloss Uhm to its primal state as a medieval fortress. It was the stony obstinance of the original that he admired. As a child, the graf had cultivated a secret belief that he was a reincarnation of the original Sigfried, king of the Nibelungers, chief of the god Wotan's hero race, hero of the German people. And surely King Sigfried should live in a castle.

Graf von Linsz trotted up the stone stairway in the castle he called home and stood aside while a burly man in the black leather uniform of his personal guard unlocked a heavy wooden door and pulled it open. He waved the guard aside and entered the room, stooping slightly to pass under the five-foot-three-inch high doorway. The room was a small one, furnished with a bed, a chair, a cupboard, a wash basin, a small, square table, and a small bookshelf holding a history of Hungary in Hungarian, a railroad timetable in German, and a dozen or so ancient hymnals in old church Slavonic. One tiny barred window high up on one wall admitted the room's only natural light, which was supplemented by an oil lamp on the table. Benjamin Barnett sat on the bed reading a two-week-old copy of the *London Times*, and Cecily was in the chair sewing a button on a blouse. They both looked up as von Linsz entered, but said nothing.

Von Linsz stood just inside the doorway and spread his arms expressively. "Ah, Mr. and Mrs. Barnett, I have come up to see how you are doing. What a fine domestic picture you make. I apologize for having neglected you recently, but I have been busy, quite busy. I do hope you forgive me."

Barnett put down his paper and glared up at the graf. "How long is this farce going to continue?" he demanded.

Von Linsz shrugged. "It is out of my hands now, I assure you," he said. "Certainly you see that we cannot let you go at the moment. There is no way that we could insure your silence about your, ah, visit to my home. And, while I'm confident that we could handle the situation, what with accusations and counter-accusations, right now we cannot afford the attention that would be directed toward us. You must not think harshly of us, we are doing the best we can in a difficult situation."

"Harshly!" Barnett carefully folded his newspaper and stood up to face von Linsz eye-to-eye. "You have kept us captive here for the past two weeks, with the nonsensical notion that we can tell you Professor Moriarty's plans, about which we know nothing, or the even more ridiculous assumption that we care about your plans, whatever they may be. You have questioned us together and separately, and learned nothing, since we have nothing to tell.

You've made us the victims of what can most kindly be described as a horrible mistake, and the best way to remedy it would be to let us go—now!"

Von Linsz shook his head sadly. "You must blame your Professor Moriarty for your situation, and not us," he said. "We, with good cause, believed you to be his agents. Indeed some of us are still not convinced that you are not. If so, you can see that it was in our interest to eliminate you. And we could have done it in a much, ah, harsher manner."

Cecily looked up from her sewing and favored the graf with a pitying smile. "I have noticed that every lawbreaker blames others for his own actions," she said. "It seems to be one of the common aspects of the criminal mind. 'If only he'd just given me the money I wouldn't have had to hit him over the head!' 'If only they'd told me what I want to know I wouldn't have had to kidnap them and hold them prisoner.' "

"Yes, yes," von Linsz said. "All that would be very convincing, if only your Professor Moriarty had not disappeared from sight something over a week ago."

"Disappeared?"

"Yes, disappeared." Von Linsz stalked further into the room. "Having been forewarned that he is the head of your Secret Service, and has a large band of agents among the criminal classes all over Europe, we have naturally been keeping an eye on him. We managed at the last minute to intercept one informant, a teacher of something-or-other who had discovered our suspicions regarding yet another agent. We were successful in preventing this teacher from speaking with Professor Moriarty at his home in London, but Moriarty is no longer there. He has eluded our watchers."

"Who is this 'us' you keep talking about?" Barnett asked. "So far we have seen only you."

"There is no reason why you should not know. I speak for the New Order of the Knights of Wotan," von Linsz said. "Our presence is not yet widely felt, but assuredly it soon will be."

"And it's this order that is so concerned with the movements of Professor Moriarty?"

"Well put," von Linsz agreed. "It is, indeed, his movements

that concern us. A week ago he left his house, and he has not returned. It is believed that he was on the evening paddle-steamer from Newhaven to Dieppe, but after that he vanished from sight. How do you explain that if he is not trying to thwart our plans?"

"He's gone on holiday," Barnett suggested.

"Bah!" von Linsz said. "He's gone on a holiday like you were on a holiday—artfully timed to get you to Vienna just at the right moment."

"The right moment for what?" Barnett asked, the exasperation showing in his voice. "As I've been telling you for two weeks now, we don't know what you're talking about!"

"It's no use dear," Cecily said. "You can't convince him that we don't have the information he wants. And besides, by now we do know too much about his—their—affairs for him to let us go. We may not know what his gang is planning, but we know *something* is going to happen, and that is too much knowledge."

Von Linsz bowed toward Cecily. "Very true, madam. Unfortunate, but true." He bent over and backed out of the room. "The Festival of St. Simon begins in two days," he said, pausing in the doorway. "Celebrating one of our greatest victories. The traditional festival is held in the meadow in front of the castle over this weekend, and we must prepare. I have much to do."

The mummer perched himself on a table by the window and carefully drew the roller blind down the last quarter-inch. "This Thursday," he said, "that is, the day after tomorrow, there is to be a great festival here. It's the anniversary of the battle of Uhm in, I think it were, 1164, in which the Turks were beat back for an inch or two. They give thanks to St. Simon, who must have had something to do with it, I suppose. The festival goes from Thursday to Saturday, and then the locals spend all day Sunday in church. Or so I've been told. The grounds in front of the castle are being set up now with tents and the like."

Moriarty nodded. "Fortuitous," he said. "I think we can use that to our advantage."

They were gathered at one end of Prince Ariste's private railroad parlor-car. The special train had arrived at the rail yard outside the town of Uhmstein late the night before, and the prince's four cars were now detached from the engine and sitting in a corner of the yard. The dozen volunteers that Prince Ariste had brought along from his regiment were outside their car, exercising. Even in civilian clothes, it was hard for them not to look like what they were: highly trained soldiers from an elite unit.

"What are we to do?" Prince Ariste asked.

Moriarty stood, his hands clasped behind his back, his head jutting forward like a great hawk. "For the moment our time is best spent in gathering information," he said. He looked at the mummer. "Just where is the window to the Barnett's cell?"

"It ain't rightly a 'cell,' " Tolliver said, "just a room up on the fourth level. But, with its big, heavy oak door and the bars on the one window, which is real high up, I suppose the result's the same. It's on the left-hand side, second window in. I can point it out to you."

"Could you take one of us up there tonight?"

Tolliver thought it over. "Not likely," he said finally, " 'less the one of you we're speaking of ain't much bigger than what I am. First he'd have to get through the grating where this 'ere stream comes through the outer wall. And I has trouble passing through the bars, minuscule as I am. Then he'd have to climb the wall of the castle proper, which I does by utilizing the vines which grow up the side of the wall. They hold my weight—seven stone about—but I don't think they'd hold much more. And they get mighty thin and sparse around the fourth floor, where the window is, so even I has to be a might careful and precise. It's a matter of stature, you see. The builders of this here castle didn't figure on being invaded by midgets."

"Then you must remain our emissary, Tolliver," the professor said. "Are the Barnetts in good spirits, would you say?"

"I think as how they'll be in much better spirits when I tells them you're here, and you're plotting to get them out."

"Then by all means, tell them that we're here, and that we're plotting to get them out," Moriarty said. He turned to the others. "I think perhaps Madame Verlaine and I should make our way to the meadow where the people are preparing for these festivities. It may be time for Alexandre Sandarel to demonstrate some of his mystical powers."

"And what should we do?" Prince Ariste asked.

"Perhaps you should send word to Schloss Uhm that you're here," Moriarty suggested. "Nobility speaks to nobility, I understand. You've stopped over to see the fete on your way to Vienna. With any luck von Linsz will invite you to join him. Then keep your eyes and ears open, and learn what you can."

Ariste nodded. "I will send a footman to tell Graf von Linsz that we're here, and invite him to come over and have a drink with us in my private railroad car. He will certainly suggest that we come to the castle instead, and I will do him the great favor of acquiescing. He is, after all, merely a count while I am a prince."

"And a very princely one you are, my dear," Princess Diane told him, patting him on the shoulder.

"And I can have my men go down and seek casual employment as roustabouts or day laborers," Ariste suggested. "Perhaps they, also, can contribute to our pool of information."

"Excellent!" Moriarty agreed. "Keep someone trustworthy here, in this car, to gather and pass on information. If you are invited to stay in the castle overnight, find some pretext to refuse and return to your sleeping car here."

"My medication," Princess Diane suggested. "I am in delicate health, you know."

"All this is in aid of getting Barnett and the missus out of their captive environment?" the mummer asked. "I ain't complaining, mind you, I'm just curious."

"The dual purpose of arranging to get them out and finding out just why they're being held in the first place," Moriarty said.

"I told you that Barnett says that they want to know about you, Professor," the mummer said, "what you're doing and where you're doing it and why."

"Yes," Moriarty said. "And I need to know just what misapprehensions these people have that causes them to be so curious about my movements; and it might not be a bad idea to get some idea of just who 'they' are and just what they're up to."

* * *

Sherlock Holmes and Dr. Watson arrived in Uhmstein on the 11:14 day train from Vienna and stood on the station platform, traveling bags in hand, and allowed the wave of humanity that had emerged from the train with them to wash on by them and out of the station. Holmes, following Jenny Vernet's suggestion that he "go in disguise," had acquired a sharply pointed beard and a trim mustache, as well as dark blue trousers, a gray jacket with sloped shoulders and cord trim, and a Tyrolean hat with a carefully curled brim. That, along with a measured stride and a manner of barking out orders to all around him as though he expected them to be unquestionably obeyed, marked him as a military officer in mufti.

Watson, who was encumbered by a face that mirrored the bluff honesty of the English gentleman, and a native inability to dissemble, was not disguised so much as rendered so obvious as to be unobtrusive. From the collar of his narrow-labeled tweed suit to the soles of his thick oxford walking shoes he was every inch the British tourist, *Baedeker* in hand, on a European tour.

"I suppose the first thing is to find the local inn and get a room," Watson suggested.

"We can try," Holmes said, "but I fancy the local inns are all filled with revelers and those who hope to revel. Every burgher with a spare bed, and every farmer who can tuck a straw mattress in the hay loft, is probably going to have guests tonight. We may find ourselves sleeping under the stars. Still, it won't be the first time, eh, Watson?"

"That's true, Holmes," Watson acknowledged.

"No, I think the first order of business is to discover the whereabouts of Miss Jenny Vernet and what sort of trouble she has gotten herself into. For that, of course, we must visit the local inn. As I believe I've mentioned to you from time to time in the past, my dear friend, pubs and inns are invariably the best source for local gossip. And perhaps we'll be in luck and the innkeeper will know of a spare couple of beds, even if he can't supply them himself. Come, Watson." And with that, shoulders back, chin high, stick held before him like a saber, Sherlock Holmes departed the train station and strode into Uhmstein.

BILLET READING

The universe we observe has precisely the properties we should expect if there is, at bottom, no design, no purpose, no evil, no good, nothing but blind, pitiless indifference.

—CHARLES DARWIN

For the past few days powerful men had been arriving at Schloss Uhm. The carriages that pulled up to the portcullis were large and ornate and smelled of fresh paint, and they were drawn by matched quartets of spirited horses. Some had the dust of the road thick on them, as they had come from a great distance. Several had canvas panels on the doors where coats of arms or other devices had been covered to keep them from the eyes of the hoi polloi. The men who arrived by train came in their own private cars, and were met by a closed carriage from the castle.

The appearance of these important men went largely unnoticed among the arrival of so many for the fete. This was, after all, the Festival of St. Simon, and rich as well as poor enjoyed a good festival. Friday had dawned bright and warm, with just enough breeze to make the crowd feel alert and truly festive. The meadow in front of the castle held over six score tents as well as entertainment areas and spaces for the vendors of St. Simon medals, Turkish warrior dolls, and other bright and shiny objects. Close to two thousand people were on hand this first day—and it wasn't even the weekend yet. This year's festival promised to be a good one. The mountebanks were clever, the jugglers and acrobats were agile, the food was tasty, the beer was thick, rich and foamy, the little St. Simon twists—a crescent-shaped pastry filled with whipped cream, made locally just for this festival—were a special treat.

In a tent toward the rear of the meadow a small group of people stood in rapt attention. They had never witnessed anything quite like this before. A small sign on the tent door read: DR. ALEXANDRE SANDAREL—ASK AND YOU SHALL BE TOLD. And the telling went on throughout the day. Professor Moriarty, in his guise as Doctor Alexandre Sandarel, wearing a black, fur-trimmed frock coat with wide lapels, that emphasized his height; his chest crossed with a red sash that emphasized his importance, stood on a platform in the middle of the tent gazing down at his audience with eyes that, as one onlooker put it, "seemed to burn into your very soul." On a tripod stand by his side was a brass brazier about a foot and a half across, holding a small heap of glowing coals.

Madeleine Verlaine, in a pearl-colored gown that emphasized what it was meant to emphasize, handed each member of the audience a piece of paper, a pencil, and a small white envelope as he or she entered. "If you have a question for the doctor," she whispered, "write it down and seal it in the envelope." Periodically she collected the envelopes and brought them up to Sandarel on a silver tray.

Sandarel took a sealed envelope from the tray and held it up. "The young gentleman by the door, in the brown leather coat," he said. "This is from you, I believe."

"And what was my question?" the youth by the door challenged.

Sandarel thrust the envelope into the brazier and it burst into flames. He studied the rising smoke intently. "Yours is the oldest of questions," he said. "You want to know if she loves you—although you put it in earthier terms."

One man in the audience chuckled, and looked around to see if anyone else had gotten the joke.

"The answer to your question," Sandarel continued, "is in two parts: the first is 'yes,' and the second is," and here he shook a finger at the man, "not a chance, and you should know better than to ask—not until you get married!"

Most of the audience laughed nervously, several of them merely looked shocked.

Sandarel picked up a new envelope and ran his fingers over its surface. "From a young lady," he said. "Her name is Susanna, I believe. Are you here, Susanna? I won't embarrass you."

An attractive blond girl of perhaps sixteen in an aubergine chemise with a large bow in back and an abundance of lace trim raised her hand shyly.

"Ah, there you are," Sandarel said. "Let us send your question into the sky, and see what answer we can pluck out of the space between this world and the next." He dropped the envelope into the fire and it burst brightly into flames and was quickly devoured. "There, it's gone," he said. "And now no one can ever know what you wrote. But nonetheless let's see if I can get an answer to your question." He put his hand to his forehead and stared at the rising smoke.

"You want to know where someone—we won't mention his name—is right now. But wait! That's not what you really desire to know. You desire to know whether he loves you, whether he is being faithful to you. And let me reassure you, the smoke says yes. He is thinking of you even now as I speak."

With that the girl burst into tears and fled the tent.

The audience murmured amongst themselves. They were impressed with what they were seeing, but weren't sure of what to make of it. One old man backed out of the tent, making the sign of the cross in the air with his right forefinger, but nobody else seemed inclined to follow him.

Sandarel retrieved another envelope and studied it briefly and then tossed it onto the flames. "I will not identify the writer of this note by name, nor will I look at him directly, for I don't want to embarrass him," he said, his deep voice resonating throughout the tent. "But I am now going to tell him more than he wanted to know." Sandarel's gaze swept the audience. "Put back what you took right now and confess all. Those you have wronged will forgive you. Make restitution for what you cannot return. You know in your heart that this is what you should—what you must—do. If you continue down the path on which you have started, you will find nothing but ruin and heartbreak."

A gasp ran through the crowd, and they all looked around to see if they could tell who the writer was and guess just what he had written.

Sandarel picked up the next envelope.

It was now three in the afternoon of Friday, 18 April 1891. Outside the gates of Schloss Uhm the Festival of St. Simon was doing its raucous best to outdo all previous festivals. At the same time, in a private dining room of the castle, guarded by a phalanx of Graf von Linsz's private guards distributed about the halls and corridors, the officers of the New Order of the Knights of Wotan held their yearly meeting; this one, they knew, would be the most important meeting they had held since the founding of the order a dozen years before.

There were twenty-six people gathered around the dark walnut dining room table. Nine were high ranking officers in the armies of either Austria or Germany. Seven were of the European aristocracy (there was an overlap here, four of the officers were of noble birth). Three were ordained priests. Six were bureaucrats or elected officials: three Austrian, two German, and one French. Five were what the popular press was beginning to describe as "captains of industry": two armaments manufacturers, one owner of coal mines and newspapers, one textile manufacturer, and one exploiter of labor in the far-off colonies of various European countries.

There were also two trusted waiters to see to the needs of the order, and, squeezed into the bottom cupboard of an ancient oak sideboard where she had been hiding for several hours before the meeting began, was an operatic contralto named Jenny Vernet.

The large, throne-like chair at the head of the table was occupied by "Der Alte," (the Old Man), Herzog Robert Franz Willem von und zu Agberg, one of the co-founders of the New Order of the Knights of Wotan, and the highest-born of the membership since the other co-founder, Prince Meinhess, was killed recently in an unfortunate accident while boar hunting in the Black Forest. Der Alte, now well into his eighties, was the final arbiter of the customs and procedures of the order. He did not overly concern himself with what the order actually did, except to nod his approval whenever it was called for, but he was stern about their adherence to the ancient rules of Teutonic knighthood while they were doing it.

Graf von Linsz, who sat on Der Alte's right hand, chaired the meeting, calling it to order and nodding at each member to give him permission to speak. Each member got up in turn, began speaking with a ritualistic, "May it please the order . . ." and then told what he had been doing "on the order's business" for the past year. And much of what was said did please the order, judging by the appreciative murmurs Jenny overheard from her hiding place.

Jenny Vernet's cramped and uncomfortable presence in the sideboard was an act born of frustration. For the past few weeks she had been trying to convince von Linsz, not that she was on his side because the count didn't really care whether a mere woman was on his side or not, but that she was not interested in men's politics—and that she considered all of his mysterious shenanigans, including the kidnaping of the Barnetts, some form of politics that concerned only men and didn't concern her. But all she'd managed to get out of him were hints and threats and vague references that something big was on its way.

But now, at last, as she lay concealed, she was learning something more than hints.

"Now on to the most important affair," she heard von Linsz say. His usually dry and raspy voice had an undertone of excitement she had rarely heard before. "The event for which we have planned takes place next week. Probably next Thursday. The principals, we are assured, will be arriving. England, France, Germany, and Russia. And, of course, Austria. Everything is in place. The capture, the threat, the killing. It cannot fail to have the desired effect."

"And who gets the blame?" a voice asked. Jenny thought it was the textile man, but she wasn't sure. "Has it been decided?"

"Of course. The people are picked, letters have been written."

"But who?"

"Serbian nationalists. Specifically a group called 'Free Serbia.' "

"Serbian nationalists," someone said musingly. "I like it! Austria will mobilize to send troops into Serbia, just to keep the peace, of course."

"And then Russia will mobilize," someone said. "The tsar will come to Serbia's aid."

"Even after—?"

"Those who want to blame Serbia, will blame the Serbian nationalists," the voice said. "Those who don't, will blame the Austrian Army for the aftermath. And Imperial Russia feels that it has blood ties with Serbia."

"Ah! Of course. And Germany will come in on the side of Austria. And France on the side of Russia."

"France and Russia are not allies," someone said.

"Yes, but after 1870, France will welcome any excuse to go to war with Germany."

"True."

Jenny felt the need to sneeze coming over her. She gritted her teeth and held her nose, and felt her eyes water, but she fought off the sneeze.

"We must be prepared to nudge, to whisper, to demand," one of them was saying.

"My newspapers are ready."

"Think of it!" It was von Linsz. "A general European war. Chaos and the destruction of governments." His voice rose. "And out of the ashes of this war shall rise a new order! Led by the Knights of Wotan, the German people shall take their rightful place in the world."

There was the scraping sound of chairs being pulled back, and then a voice rang out: "To Greater Germany!"

"Greater Germany!" came the response.

"Wotan!"

"Wotan!"

Jenny fought back her sneeze as the group filed out of the room. A silence descended, and she was about to crawl out of her hiding place, when she heard another door open.

"You heard?" It was von Linsz.

"I heard."

A new voice.

"You arrived with no trouble, Highness?"

"Trouble? Wha-what sort of troub-trouble?"

"If you were recognized—"

"Bah! A slight alteration of facial hair. They see only what they expect to see. They d-do not expect to see me, and therefore I am not here."

"You do me a great honor in coming, Most Highborn—"

"Hush! Not here, and not from you. The mistaken belief that one man is b-better than another because of his birth, or his position in society that was d-determined before he was born, is for soft-headed fools. We may make use of it, but we must not ourselves believe it. There are too many examples of empires that have crumbled because a wise and forceful ruler was followed by a dunce or a dimwit who happened to be his son."

"But, you yourself, Most—"

"As I say—I am able and I am highborn. I also have brown hair and a bad temper and a se-slight tendency to stammer. Which of these did my highborn parents pass on to me? Nothing that ten thousand lowborn children don't share. That is the reason why I, of all people, must constantly remind myself of the truth that ability does not necessarily follow birth."

"If you say so, Highness."

"Indeed, the accident of my birth put me in position where I could achieve what must be achieved, and the, I must call it, accident of my being b-born possessed of outstanding abilities of planning and leadership have enabled me to forge this union of impossible-to-be-united groups."

"Who do not even know that they are united," von Linsz interrupted.

"Even so. That was, you will admit, the masterstroke."

"It was. And you are the master."

Jenny sneezed.

There were hurried footsteps, and the cupboard door was pulled open. "What are you doing in there?" von Linsz barked.

Jenny looked up, her eyes blinking in the light. "Looking for a fish knife," she told him.

TWENTY-ONE

GOOD-BYE TO ALL THAT

> *Ah God, for a man with heart, head, hand,*
> *Like some of the simple great ones gone*
> *For ever and ever by,*
> *One still strong man in a blatant land,*
> *Whatever they call him, what care I,*
> *Aristocrat, democrat, autocrat—one*
> *Who can rule and dare not lie.*
> *And ah for a man to arise in me,*
> *That the man I am may cease to be!*
> —ALFRED, LORD TENNYSON

Swinging his stick aggressively in front of him, Holmes strode briskly down the street in the direction of Schloss Uhm, with Watson trotting behind. They bypassed the first inn they came to, a bright, well-scrubbed establishment that was so close to the train station that Holmes surmised it must cater to travelers, and went on. A quarter mile further they reached the *Albrecht in Himmel*, a fine, ancient whitewashed building with a slate roof and a wooden sign, freshly painted with the image of a chubby angel gazing down from a cloud. Holmes peered over the thick wooden half-door and decided that it had a local trade, and they went in. There they received permission to leave their traveling bags, stood the innkeeper to a drink, and learned that a blond woman named Fräulein Vernet had been seen staying at Schloss Uhm with Graf von Linsz for the past few weeks. Not merely seen, but heard, for the lady was an opera singer, and she had been prevailed upon to give a recital of Schubert's Lieder at the church hall. Her rendition of "Der Tod und das Mädchen" had been particularly memorable, said the innkeeper.

"I imagine," Holmes told him.

When they asked about a bed, the innkeeper shook his head. He knew of none available unless they wanted to share a great trundle bed with his nephews: "Great strapping lads, they are, and what with the festival they probably won't be getting to bed until midnight, perhaps later." Holmes and Watson decided to forgo the pleasure. They headed for the great meadow in front of the castle on which the various tents, booths, and festivities were strewn.

It was early evening and they had been wandering around the meadow for a couple of hours, when Watson caught up with Holmes and found him frozen into immobility, staring through the open door into one of the tents. He poked the great detective on the shoulder. "What is it, Holmes?"

"Look at that man on the platform," Holmes said, pointing with his stick, "do we know him?"

"Dr., ah, Alexandre Sandarel? That's what it says on his little sign. What is he, some sort of charlatan?" Watson peered into the tent. "No, Holmes, I can't say I recognize him. The beard looks familiar."

"I fancy that if you were to pull it, it would come off," Holmes remarked. "No, no, Watson, try to look beneath the beard."

Watson stared intently for a few seconds. "Sorry, Holmes, he means nothing to me."

"Ah, Watson," Holmes said with a sigh, "you see, but you do not observe. Or, in this case, hear. Does not his voice sound familiar to you?"

"Well, Holmes," Watson told him with a slight air of petulance, "you said nothing about *listening* to him." He stepped closer to the tent flap and cocked an ear.

"Imagine him speaking English instead of German," Holmes offered.

After a minute Watson nodded. "I say," he said. "I believe I have heard that voice before. Rich and full, resonant, dramatic, precise pronunciation. Could it have been on the music hall stage?"

"Sandarel," in the meantime, had noticed the two of them standing by the tent flap. He motioned for Madeleine to take his place on the stage, and went over to them. "Sherlock Holmes, I believe!" he said in English. "Dr. Watson! This is an unexpected— ah—meeting. But I am never surprised when you turn up, like the proverbial penny."

"Well I'll be dashed!" Watson exclaimed. "It's Professor Moriarty!"

Holmes pursed his lips thoughtfully. "Even before I saw you I should have known you would be here," he said. "She wrote that the Barnetts were prisoners here, so it should have come as no surprise that you had come after them. A leader, even a criminal leader, cannot afford to be disloyal to his troops."

"And yet so many are," Moriarty said. "Who?"

"Who?" Holmes frowned. "Who what?"

"Who told you the Barnetts were here?"

"Ah! A young lady named Jenny Vernet; an opera singer who is apparently another guest of that household. She does not seem to be an actual prisoner, since she has been seen in public, but how free her movements are is open to question. You are presumably here to effectuate the release of Mr. and Mrs. Barnett; whereas I have arrived here to ascertain the status of Miss Vernet and rescue her if need be. And if possible to discover just what is going on and why. Incidently, I've been standing here listening to your billet readings for awhile. I must say, Moriarty, the stage lost a fine performer when you chose to become a master criminal."

"The two professions are not unrelated," Moriarty said, choosing not to quibble with Holmes's characterization of him. "How did Miss Vernet get involved with this Graf von Linsz?"

"As to that, I cannot say," Holmes told him. "My knowledge of Miss Vernet's recent doings is very slight. I only found out she was being kept prisoner by a message she managed to slip out to me."

"In code, it was," Watson said, "and invisible to boot. Holmes did a masterful job. It was addressed to 'Emma,' whoever she might be, and yet Holmes deduced that it was indeed for him. Incredible!"

"Elementary," Holmes said, looking annoyed at the praise.

"How are you planning to deliver Miss Vernet?" Moriarty asked.

"At the moment, I have no idea. I assume she's staying at the castle, but it's a large structure, and I don't know where she is within it, or how to effect an entrance without being instantly seized. My inclination is to pound on the door and insist that she be

produced forthwith, but I feel that would be counterproductive."
Holmes thrust his walking stick into the ground and leaned on it. "I
must consider the fact that her status here may well be part of a
larger problem I'm working on, but as yet I have no proof of that."

Moriarty locked his hands behind his back and leaned forward.
"A larger problem?"

"Yes," Holmes said. "I confess that I was tempted to believe
that you might be a part of that problem, but your presence here, as
you are now—" Holmes waved his hand about to indicate the tent
and Madeleine within it, "—would indicate that I was mistaken. It
would seem that we have the same enemies."

"And therefore we should be friends?"

Holmes smiled grimly. "I wouldn't go that far."

"I didn't think you would," Moriarty assured him.

"I assume that the Barnetts are being held physically captive,
and that you have a plan for rescuing them. How are you going to
go about it?"

"I do. By air."

Watson's eyes opened wide. "I say, Professor, did you say 'By
air'?"

"Correct," Moriarty told Watson. He turned to Holmes.
"Where are you staying?"

"There seem to be no rooms available," Holmes told him. "But
a bit of the meadow that hasn't been trodden down by the passage
of many feet will suffice for the night."

"Give my assistant and myself a few minutes to close up here,"
Moriarty said, "and then you must come with us. This may indeed
be one of those rare times when we can help each other."

Holmes stared at him for a moment, and then nodded. "We'll
just pick up our bags at the inn on the way."

Ten minutes later Moriarty and Madeleine led Holmes and
Watson through the jumble of tents that filled the meadow toward
the siding where Prince Ariste's train was parked. It was early
evening and a chill wind had come up. Most of the revelers were
returning to their lodgings, and those left in the meadow were gathering around charcoal fires in small cast-iron braziers, warming
themselves and setting a variety of wursts, schnitzels, and chicken
parts to grill, along with potatoes and turnips. Many of the fires

had pots of various sizes on them, and the rich smell of stew was beginning to waft from under the lids.

Prince Ariste and his princess were awaiting them when they reached the car. Moriarty introduced them to Holmes and Watson, and Ariste looked curiously at them, and then back at Moriarty, but he said nothing. "I would not go so far as to say we have joined forces," Moriarty explained, "but we are here for similar purposes and for the time being we have a better chance of accomplishing our ends if we work together."

"I see," Ariste said. "And the ends of Mr. Holmes, what are they?"

"A young lady named Jenny Vernet," Holmes said. "It would seem that she is staying in that castle yonder, possibly against her will."

"What?" Princess Diane exclaimed. "Another kidnap victim? Has this von Linsz then become a madman, given to kidnaping people off the street like some robber baron of medieval times?"

"From what I've been able to discover I would say that this man and his friends have a very serious goal," Holmes said, "and I'm afraid that it is one that will make kidnaping seem like a minor peccadillo."

"Come," Moriarty said, "let us pool our information and reason together. Perhaps we can make sense out of this madness."

"No time! No time!" Prince Ariste announced suddenly. "I haven't had a chance to tell you, Professor, but you are to come with me to the castle tonight."

"Really?" Moriarty swivelled to face the prince. "Excuse me, Your Highness, but whatever for?"

Ariste leaned forward. "Alexandre Sandarel is to give a show for all the notables gathered at the castle." He nodded his head and smiled. "When Diane and I went there to share a bottle of champagne with the count—why is it that when they entertain royalty, so many people think in terms of bottles of champagne? There are other wines—it occurred to me to speak of the great and talented Alexandre Sandarel, who happened to be here in Uhmstein, and who would be a great addition to the evening's festivities, to which the princess and I had just been invited."

"Ah!" Moriarty said.

"Yes. Graf von Linsz seemed quite taken with the idea. I described you—Sandarel—as a mystic and clairvoyant of international reputation. He was impressed. I think the count is something of a believer. He asked whether you were a spiritualist. I told him that I believed that your companion—" Ariste gave a little half-bow in the direction of Madeleine Verlaine "—was an accomplished medium. You will forgive me, I hope, for making up your history like that."

"I forgive you," Madeleine said. She smiled and added, "As does Mim Ptwa Nim, the ancient Egyptian priestess who is my spirit guide."

"I think you've done very well, Your Highness," Moriarty said.

"I thought so myself. You'll have an opportunity to look over the interior of the castle. Perhaps you can locate the Barnetts, and this Miss Vernet also. Of course, it's you two who will have to convince them that you are all those things I claimed you were, but I have the utmost confidence in you."

"Vernet?" Princess Diane joined in suddenly. "This Jenny Vernet, is she an American opera singer?"

"She is," Holmes said. "Have you heard of her?"

"No, well, not exactly. It's just that I believe she was on the printed list of people who were to perform tonight, but her name was crossed off." She turned to her husband. "Don't you remember, Ariste? Von Linsz showed us this printed list of the evening's performers. Wasn't an American opera singer named Jenny Vernet among them, but her name had a heavy line through it?"

"It might well be, my dear," Ariste said. "I confess I didn't inspect the list too carefully."

"Well, I'm sure that was the name," Diane said.

"I don't know what to make of that," Sherlock Holmes said, rubbing his hands together. "Is she still here or has she left? Or has she been taken away? She wrote that she was under suspicion. Perhaps, somehow, the suspicions have been realized and she is in immediate danger."

"Or perhaps they've been resolved in her favor," Madeleine suggested, "but she has a sore throat."

"Well, if she is still there, we may well have a chance to speak with her—or at least you will, Professor Moriarty, when you're together backstage," Prince Ariste said. "I noticed that there was a stage at one end of the ballroom, so I assume there's a backstage area. And perhaps you can do some exploring and find out how to get to the room in which the Barnetts are being kept."

"I doubt whether they will allow us to wander about the corridors," Moriarty said, "but nonetheless this is a good idea, Your Highness. We might learn much of value." Moriarty nodded his head thoughtfully. "We might indeed. But it occurs to me that this evening will demand formal dress, and mine—ours—is back in our hotel suite in Vienna."

"No problem, Professor," Prince Ariste said. "My valet can fit you out in the proper attire."

"And I believe that I have an evening frock that will do wonders for you, my dear," Princess Diane said to Madeleine.

"Something very simple," Madeleine said.

"Of course. Come with me."

"Have you an artificer among your people here?" Moriarty asked the prince.

"An artificer?"

"Someone with the skills to build something if I draw him a plan."

"Our Herr Heerschmit should be the man you want," Prince Ariste said. "He travels with the special train just to fix things that need fixing and make things that need making."

"Sounds like the man I want," Moriarty said. "Where can I find him?"

"He should be in the last car."

"Very good. I'll return in a few minutes and we'll see what your valet can do for me." Moriarty nodded and exited the car.

TWENTY-TWO

MADAME MADELEINE VERLAINE

Strange, is it not? That of the myriads who
Before us pass'd the door of Darkness through,
Not one returns to tell us of the Road,
Which to discover we must travel too.
—EDWARD FITZGERALD

Everyone of any importance who had come to Uhmstein for the St. Simon's Day festival, or who resided within tens of kilometers around the town in any direction, was at a table in the grand ballroom of Schloss Uhm that evening, partaking of the light refreshments kept in constant supply by a squad of waiters and watching the entertainment provided by Graf von Linsz. In addition to his fellow members of the secretive Knights of Wotan, who sat at widely separated tables throughout the room and effected but a languid and casual interest in their surroundings, there were two mayors, a bishop, three priests, the commander of the local cavalry troop and most of his junior officers, six government officials including the tax collector, a dozen or so members of the local gentry, along with their wives and unmarried daughters, and a retired field marshal.

The ballroom was a long rectangle with French windows facing the castle's inner courtyard. It was a recent addition to the building, having been built out on what had been the parade ground for the castle troop. A balcony ran around the room, narrow for the most part but widening over the windows to provide seating for a small orchestra. There was an orchestra up there now, about a dozen men dressed in the court costume of a bygone era: blue pantaloons buckled at the knee above striped stockings and a blue and gold jacket with wide lapels and a double row of large gold buttons running down the front. They didn't look happy but they made music on demand, and few in the audience spent much time looking at them.

It was a little after eleven that evening when Alexandre Sandarel and Madeleine Verlaine walked out together on the small stage that was set into the far wall of the ballroom. Sandarel was tall and commanding in his evening dress, the cutaway jacket tailored with a certain Viennese flair that was at once cultured and effortless. Madame Verlaine was a regal beauty in a white dress with a full pleated skirt and a high lace collar.

The audience had just finished listening to a group of traditional Hungarian folk songs sung by Madame Flora Zaropichenski, an aging contralto who would never see two hundred pounds again, accompanied on the piano by her emaciated husband, and they were getting restless. Sandarel and his lovely assistant soon captured their attention.

"Good evening Your Grace, Your Highnesses, Your Excellencies, ladies and gentlemen. I am Doctor Alexandre Sandarel and I am here to demonstrate, with the aid of my charming and highly skilled associate Madame Madeleine Verlaine, some of the amazing powers and abilities of the human mind." He paused and looked around the room. "Few of us use our minds to anything even close to their full potential. The ancient Greeks used to think that the heart was the seat of intelligence, and the brain was merely an organ for cooling the blood. For some of us that may be true. But for the rest of us, the more we use and exercise our minds, the more we can do with them." Sandarel stepped forward to have a better view of his audience. "With training and practice we are all capable of feats of mental concentration and divination that would seem astounding to the uninformed. Let us start off with a slight test of memory. You sir"—he pointed at a gentleman near the front— "give me a three-place number if you will."

As he spoke, Madeleine wheeled out a large blackboard that had been liberated from a schoolroom in the castle.

"Me, sir?" The man thought for a second. "Two-ninety-six."

Madeleine wrote the number on the board.

"Very good sir, and—" pointing elsewhere "—if you'd do the same."

"Four-eleven."

Madeleine wrote that immediately after the first number.

"And you, madame?"

"Oh my, let's see now. Eight-sixty-three."

"And you, sir?"

"Three-zero-seven."

"Let's have three more. You sir?"

"Five-ninety-one."

"And for the last three?"

"Eight—no, six-four-nine."

"Very good. Thank you all. Madame Verlaine, do you have all that?"

"I do, Doctor Sandarel."

"Fine. Without looking back at the blackboard, I will now tell you fine ladies and gentlemen that the number—the entire number—is two hundred and ninety-six quadrillion, four hundred and eleven trillion, eight hundred and sixty-three billion, three hundred and seven million, five hundred and ninety-one thousand, six hundred and forty-nine. Is that right?"

Madeleine had been underlining the numbers as Sandarel called them off. "Exactly right," she said.

The audience was not sure what to make of this, but there was a slight smattering of applause.

"Now, Madame Verlaine, please step forward and face the audience."

"Yes, Doctor Sandarel." Madeleine stepped to the front of the stage.

"Do you remember the number?"

"Yes, Doctor Sandarel."

"Please recite it for us—backwards."

"Yes. The number, backwards, is," Madeleine paused for a second and closed her eyes. She slowly recited: "nine-four-six-one-nine-five-seven-zero-three-three-six-eight-one-one-four-six-nine-two. Is that right?"

"Exactly right!"

This time the applause was stronger. The audience was beginning to realize they were seeing something different.

"Now, Madame Verlaine, please take this pad and go out into the audience and have them create for you another long number. Take one digit from each person you speak to. Write the number down as it's created, but don't tell me what it is."

Madeleine left the stage and moved among the audience, pausing to hear a whispered number and write it down, keeping up a seemingly meaningless patter to fill the silence. "Perfect, monsieur," she murmured to the first man. "Take your time," she told the second. "Marvelous!" she encouraged the third, and so on for twelve different people. While she gathered the numbers, Sandarel had someone from the audience come up and twist a scarf around his head to blindfold him.

"Would all those who have given numbers to Madame Verlaine please stand up," Sandarel said, facing the audience. "The blindfold is to help me concentrate, and to assure you that Madame Verlaine is not passing me any sort of secret signals."

The people Madeleine had spoken to stood up, looking bemused. "We're ready, Doctor," Madeleine told him from the audience.

"Very good. Now, if you will concentrate on the numbers, Madame, I will try to read them from your mind and the minds of the ladies and gentlemen who gave them to you, in the order in which you received them." Sandarel looked sightlessly around the room. "Those of you who are standing, when you hear your number called, please take your seat. If you do not hear your number, if by some chance I get it wrong, please remain standing in mute testimony to my failure."

The audience chuckled.

Sandarel pressed his hand to his forehead. "Please concentrate, madame. Ah, good, I am getting something. It's fuzzy—try to make a clearer picture in your mind. Yes, yes, thank you; very good. The number is—" he paused and then spoke clearly, pausing before each number "—nine-one-three-one—no, that's a seven—four-six-eight-six-nine-five-six."

223

As he said each number, one of those standing sat down, until there was but one man left. Sandarel whipped his blindfold off and appeared to be surprised that there was still a man standing. He pointed at the man. "You're still standing," he declared. "Ah, yes—yours is the last number." He closed his eyes and his left hand searched the air in front of him for the number, his right hand remaining pointed dramatically at the man. "Two!" he said.

The man sat. The audience applauded. Sandarel bowed.

For the next ten minutes Sandarel did a series of miracles with birth dates—

"What date were you born, sir?"

"December third, eighteen forty-one."

"That was a Tuesday, sir."

"Damned me if it wasn't, sir!"

—and divining the names of cities and countries, and, while blindfolded, naming objects that Madeleine borrowed from audience members.

"Now," Sandarel said, coming to the edge of the platform, "if I can prevail upon the staff to lower the gas lights, except for the spotlight that is illuminating me now, we will use our remaining time to investigate the spirit world. I assure you that there is nothing to be afraid of, ladies, nothing will occur that the faintest heart among you cannot observe with complete safety. But please remain seated and be very quiet while this demonstration continues. Madame Verlaine, who is a noted medium, will be working through her spirit guide, and any interruption while she is in a trance might prove harmful to her health."

While the lights were lowered Sandarel gave the audience a brief history of spiritism. "Madame Verlaine has retired for a moment to compose herself for the seance," he told them. "As you know, there is some dispute as to just what it is that happens during a seance. The Spiritualists and the Theosophists believe that the spirits of the departed can talk to us, or even interact in a more physical manner, through the mediumship of certain special people. The Rosicrucians and others believe that the past and future have been revealed to those with the talent through the intercession of ethereal powers . . ."

While he held the audience captivated—or at least captive—

with his talk, Madeleine was in the cloak room going through the overcoats of the guests and committing every bit of writing, every scrap of paper, every document she found, to her eidetic memory. For her it was like taking a photograph: she could memorize the appearance of a page of text and then retrieve it later from her memory to actually read it. She found the little leather slipcases holding the owner's visiting cards in many of the coats, so she could bring forth at need the names of many of those present. The scraps of paper she came across were like scraps of their owner's memories: with a little careful weaving and some bold deduction, the information on them could be made to provide seemingly miraculous insights into their lives and frightening glimpses into their future.

Madeleine left the cloakroom and came around by a connecting hall to the green room behind the stage. To her left was the stage, where she could hear Moriarty holding forth on the history of spiritism and the meaning of everything. The character of Dr. Sandarel, omniscient, didactic, and compelling, was one that Moriarty slipped easily into. He was good for another five minutes of lecture before the audience even noticed that Madame Verlaine had not yet appeared. There was time to do a little investigating. To Madeleine's right were two closed doors. She opened the first one, and found a small room that must have been the dressing room for the musicians. A row of evening clothes were hung up on a rack along one wall, and the few unused remnants of the sixteenth-century court dress the musicians were now costumed in were strewn along a rack next to the other wall. Madeleine retreated from that room and went to the other door. She turned the handle and found it unyielding.

Reaching down the neck of her dress with two fingers, Madeleine pulled up a cleverly contrived lockpick, which had been hooked over a small chain around her neck. In a few seconds she had the door open and she entered the corridor in front of her, pulling the door closed behind. The wall sconces in the corridor were unlit, and the dark was absolute, unrelieved by any hint of light spilling under a door or through a window.

Madeleine moved slowly along the corridor her right hand feeling along the wall until she came to a door, which pushed reluctantly open after she twisted the handle. She struck a match. The room was full of shelves, and the shelves were stacked with a variety of small boxes, jars, canisters, and sacks, holding the sort of detritus that isn't immediately useful but shouldn't be thrown away. The match went out, and Madeleine backed out of the room and closed the door. A second room further down the corridor contained chairs without backs, tables without legs, and assorted other furniture in need of repair, the sort of detritus that any castle is liable to build up over the centuries. A third door—was locked.

With a lighted match in one hand and the lockpick in the other, Madeleine worked at the keyhole. Now time was drawing short, so of course this lock proved difficult. Inanimate objects can be strangely perverse. She blew out the match, took a deep breath, and closed her eyes, relaxing and letting her fingers do the work of clearing the wards the way the mummer had taught her. It seemed that the rooms along this corridor were used for storage, and she would learn little of interest in this locked room. But, as the professor often said, there is no such thing as useless information. She kept on working on the lock and an eternity passed, and then another. And then her fingers felt the sweet feel of the wards clearing, and the lock rotated, and the door was unlocked. It had taken perhaps forty seconds.

Madeleine pushed open the door and lit another match. In its flicker she could make out sacks of grain, or flour, or perhaps sand, stacked against the far wall. Well, what did she expect? She turned to leave and waved the match out. As the light fled she caught, or thought she caught, a flicker of motion in a corner of the room. She held her breath and silently took two steps to the right, so she wouldn't be where the person had last seen her, if it was a person and if he or she didn't wish her well. It probably wasn't a person, she reassured herself. What would a person be doing in this locked room? It was probably a rat. After a long moment of listening and hearing nothing, she crossed her fingers and struck another match.

It was no rat. It was a woman in a brown dress, lying curled up on the floor, her feet and hands tied with heavy rope and her mouth gagged with some kind of rough cloth gag. The woman twisted her head and blinked at the light.

Madeleine spotted a candle set firmly on one of the sacks of grain and she lit it quickly before her match went out. Dropping to her knees by the bound woman, she worked at loosening the gag. The knot did not want to come loose, but Madeleine was able to stretch the fabric just enough to force it out of the woman's mouth and down below her chin.

"Ahhh!" the woman gasped.

"Hush!" Madeleine whispered. "If they hear us, we are undone!

"What's happening?" The woman spoke hoarsely, her mouth stiff from the gag. "Who are you?"

"There's a gathering in the ballroom. I'm Madeleine Verlaine. Who are you? What are you doing here? How long have you been tied up like this?"

"My name is Jenny Vernet," the woman tried to say. It came out "hennee hernee." Her lips were raw from the coarse fabric of the gag, and her tongue refused to form itself properly to make sounds. "I've been tied up like this since early this afternoon."

"Jenny Vernet," Madeleine said. "I understand. Sherlock Holmes is outside, determined to rescue you. And it looks like you might need rescuing."

"Sherlock is here? Oh, thank god! They are going to kill me!" Jenny said. "Sometime late tonight. They were discussing the best way to kill me as though I wasn't there listening."

"Well!" Madeleine said. She thought quickly. "I guess we'd better get you out of here now. Do you think you can walk if I untie you?"

"I have no idea," Jenny said. "I don't think there's any feeling in my legs."

"Oh, dear," Madeleine said. She bent over and went to work on the ropes around Jenny's arms. "Usually I have a small blade with me, sewed into my belt," she said, her nimble fingers pulling on the knot. "But this isn't my dress." The knots were stiff but the ropes were just thick enough so that she could get a fairly good grip. She twisted and pulled, but the knot resisted. She dug in with her fingers and pulled harder. "Blast!"

Jenny twitched. "What is it?"

"I just broke a nail," Madeleine whispered.

"Oh. I'm sorry."

"Me too. Wait a second, I think I have it."

One end of the rope had budged slightly, enlarging the hole. She took the other end and pulled, and the first layer of the knot slid open. Now that it was started, the knot gave way quickly, and in a few seconds Jenny's hands were free. They both now started to work on the ropes around her legs. They were not as well or as tightly tied, and fell loose with a few seconds work.

"Oh, bless you," Jenny said, her hands going to the knot in the gag, which was now around her neck. "Now what?"

"Now I have to get back to the stage and amaze an audience," Madeleine told her. You'd better come with me and hide in the cloak room while we figure out what to do. The professor will think of something."

"The professor?"

"Professor Moriarty. You can trust him. He's here under the guise of Doctor Alexander Sandarel, mystic and clairvoyant. I am his assistant, the noted medium Madame Verlaine. Mind you, I only became a noted medium a few hours ago, but I've been practicing for a couple of weeks now." Madeleine stood up and extended her hand to Jenny. "You'd better try to stand. If you can't walk, I'll carry you the best I can. We'd better get going."

"Professor Moriarty." Jenny took Madeleine's hand and pulled herself up. "Von Linsz has spoken of him. Indeed, for some time he could speak of little else. He has imprisoned two of Moriarty's acquaintances for fear that they are spies of some sort."

"We know," Madeleine said. "That's why we're here. Can you walk?"

Jenny took a step. "Ow!" she said. "It feels like I'm walking on a bed of nails, like those fakirs or whoever in the east." She took another step. "But I can do it. Lead the way!"

"Here," Madeleine said, "take the candle." She pried the candle loose from its mooring on the sack and handed it to Jenny. They left the room together and Madeleine closed the door and fiddled with the handle. "Hold the candle over here," she said.

"What are you doing?" Jenny asked.

"Locking the door behind me," Madeleine told her. "It may confuse them for a few seconds, and we may need the seconds."

They went down the hallway and came out in the cloak room. "Sandarel" was still orating in the ballroom, and he didn't sound strained and the audience didn't sound restless. Bless the professor and his limitless powers of oratory. Madeleine locked the corridor hall behind her. "I have to go on stage," she said. "Through that door is the green room, but who can tell who'll wander into it in the next little while. In the other door is the dressing room for the musicians. They won't be coming down for a couple of hours yet. Perhaps you'd better wait in there until the professor can decide how best to get you away from here. There is a rack of men's evening wear that you can hide behind if anyone comes in, but I don't think anyone will until the musicians return. Will you be all right?"

"I'll have to be," Jenny said. She went over to the door. "You have a lot of faith in Professor Moriarty."

"I do," Madeleine agreed.

"Good. Then I shall also."

Jenny disappeared into the dressing room. Madeleine brushed off the front of her dress, which showed signs of kneeling in the dust, took several deep breaths and composed her face into a look of complete tranquility. Then she appeared at the side of the stage and walked slowly and serenely out to join Dr. Sandarel.

Sandarel paused in mid-sentence. "I see our lovely medium is ready to begin," he said, taking her hand and escorting her forward. "Thank you all for your patience in listening to my poor explication. Now, if the spirits are willing, Madame Verlaine will demonstrate the wonders that we have been discussing." A heavy wooden chair with a high back had been placed in the center of the stage. He sat her in it and she crossed her hands on her lap and closed her eyes. "I will now place Madame Verlaine into a light trance to make her more receptive to the spirits."

Sandarel leaned over Madeleine and made restful washing motions with his hands. "You've been a while," he whispered. "I was almost at the point of discussing ancient Chaldean astrology. You found something?"

"Someone," Madeleine replied under her breath. "Jenny Vernet was tied up in a back room. She says they were going to kill her tonight. We have to get her out of here. She's in the dressing room next to the green room."

"Ah!" Sandarel said. He stood up and faced the audience. "Madame Verlaine is awaiting the arrival of her spirit guide," he announced. "In a few seconds she will be ready for your questions. You do not have to ask them aloud, if you do not wish to. The spirits will assist Madame Verlaine in her answers." He turned back to Madeleine. "Are you ready, Madame?"

"I am ready," Madeleine answered in a low, measured voice.

"Have you located your spirit guide?"

"She is here."

"Will she speak through you?"

"She will."

Sandarel began to ask another question, but paused when Madame Verlaine's body twitched and her head twisted rapidly from side to side, and her eyes opened and glared out at the world.

"Hello," Sandarel said. "To whom am I speaking?"

Madeleine leaned back and her head turned, her motions jerky and surreal like a puppet controlled by a tipsy puppeteer. "In life I was called Mim Ptwa Nim," she said in a high, gravelly voice quite unlike her normal tones.

Several people in the audience gasped, the rest seemed to be holding their breath.

"I was a priestess of the Temple of Amon, under the supreme high priest Ankha Shat, during the reign of the illustrious and most high god-king Sebeknofru, ruler of the upper and lower kingdom."

"That's right, by god! A pharaoh of that name ruled in the twelfth dynasty," someone whispered. Whether there was an Egyptologist in the audience, or Prince Ariste was doing his bit to add to the effect, Moriarty couldn't tell.

"Have you a message for anyone here?" Sandarel asked.

"Yes, yes, yes," Mim Ptwa Nim shook her head up and down rapidly. "There are several spirits waiting to get through."

"Please speak."

Madeleine closed her eyes and reviewed what she had read in the cloakroom. "A spirit here wishes to communicate with a man named Beske," said the voice of Mim Ptwa Nim, "Herr Beske, are you here?"

A slim young man stood up toward the back of the room. "You can leave me out of this," he announced loudly. "I don't believe in the spirits."

"We know," Mim Ptwa Nim said. "Your father's name is Maximilian."

"How did you—"

"He died about two years ago."

"Yes."

"He has a message for you. He asks you to forgive him."

"What?"

"He asks you to forgive him. That is the message."

The young man sat down, looking startled.

"There is a message for someone named Olga Tartosky."

"I am she," cried a lady in the audience.

"You have a friend—a close friend—named Bert or Bart—"

"Yes. Bertram. Oh, has something happened to him? Tell me he is not dead."

Mim Ptwa Nim shook her head rapidly from side to side. "No, no. You have not seen him for a long while. He has been away."

"Yes, oh yes."

"He will soon return. Things will work out for you, although you will have some problems at first—"

While Mim Ptwa Nim continued speaking, Sandarel slowly and unobtrusively backed off stage. Once out of sight, he turned and went to the dressing room concealing Jenny Vernet. "Miss Vernet," he said softly, "are you here?"

Jenny stepped out from behind an overcoat on the rack. "Professor Moriarty?"

He nodded. "It is I. Our time is limited. I believe that I have a way to get you out of here. Take off your clothes."

"It's a pleasure to meet you, too," Jenny said, her hand reaching for the top button on her blouse. "All of them?"

"No. The outer layer should suffice, although I am no expert in female garments. The important things are your skirts and whatever it is that's emphasizing your bosom."

"My bosom," Jenny said tartly, "isn't emphasized."

Moriarty looked her over critically as the blouse came off. "Perhaps not," he said, "but you couldn't pass as a man with those underpinnings."

"As a man?" Jenny asked. "Oh, I see." She loosened her skirt and petticoat and stepped out of them, and then pulled her camisole over her head. "Then the inner layer will have to go too. Help me with the stays on this corset." She turned her back to Moriarty and he loosened the laces. She squeezed herself out of the confining undergarment and then slipped the camisole back on before turning around.

Moriarty ran his hand along the rack of evening clothes left behind by the musicians and pulled out a jacket. "Here, try this on."

"One second." Jenny ripped a long, wide strip from her petticoat, and held one end of it in front of her, at the spot on her camisole that was just between her breasts. "You pull this tight while I turn," she instructed the professor.

"Ah!" he said. "Very clever." He held the strip of cloth open and taut while she slowly turned and wrapped herself in it.

"There's a safety pin on the neck of my blouse," she said, holding the cloth strip tight around her. "Would you get it for me?"

Moriarty complied, and she pinned the cloth in place. "And voilà, I'm a boy!" she said. "Now what?"

"Only to those whose vision is dim are you a boy," Moriarty said. "But luckily the lights will be low. See if that jacket fits you while I find a shirtfront and collar in this pile of clothing."

Five minutes later Moriarty was straightening the white bow tie under the points on the high, stiff collar he had appropriated from the pile. "Now the shoes," he said, "and we have to do something about your hair."

"They're dark brown shoes," Jenny pointed out, "and the trousers are much too long, so the shoes won't show much."

"True," Moriarty admitted, "but they have an entirely different sound. But, as the musicians all seem to have worn their own shoes, we'll have to take our chances. Now the hair—"

"I can braid it and wrap it really quickly so it will fit under a hat," Jenny offered. "Or I can sort of put it down the back of the jacket."

"Let's try that," Moriarty said.

Jenny pulled her hair tight in back and twisted it and tucked it into the jacket. "What do you think?"

Moriarty examined her critically. "I think it will be dark, and we'll have to take a chance. Wait a second." He took a dark blue scarf from the shelf and wrapped it around her neck and over her shoulders. "There, that might do. Drape it casually in front. That's good."

He took her to the door of the room. "You'll need courage and fortitude," he told her, "but this should work. It's based on the sort of misdirection that magicians are fond of, and they make their living fooling people. There's a curtain right outside this door separating you from the stage. Conceal yourself behind the curtain. In a few moments I'm going to call for a committee from the audience to come on stage and inspect Madame Verlaine for an effect we have planned. When the committee leaves the stage, you join them as though you'd been there all the time, and walk back along the right side to a table about halfway down the room. A man and woman are sitting there. The man is handsome and elegant, the woman beautiful and regal. I believe her dress is light blue, but it may be too dark to tell. Sit down with them. I'll have the man put both hands on the table, palms up, so you'll know where to go. The man is Prince Ariste Juchtenberg and his wife is Princess Diane. I'll speak with them while Madeleine—Madame Verlaine—is being inspected. They'll get you out of here."

Jenny Vernet took several deep breaths and adjusted her lapels. "I hope this works," she said.

"It should," Moriarty assured her. "Come out with me now."

Moriarty took Jenny to just the right spot behind the curtain and then went on stage. Mim Ptwa Nim was just finishing telling an elderly lady that her defunct husband would not object to her remarrying. "He favors it," she purred.

"He won't be jealous?"

"Where he is there is no jealousy," Mim Ptwa Nim intoned, "only love."

"I hope you have found this exhibition of interest," Alexandre Sandarel said, approaching the audience. "We will conclude," he told them, "with a demonstration of the reality, and may I say the playfulness, of the spirits. For this I would like some gentlemen in the audience to come up and assist me. You will form a committee representing the rest of the audience to assure there is no fraud or trickery in what is about to happen." He peered out. "You, sir? And you? Come onstage, please. And you, sir. And, yes of course, you also. Anyone else? You, sir? Come on up."

Seven men answered the call for volunteers. Madeleine remained passively seated in her high-backed chair facing the audience, still apparently in a light trance. Sandarel produced one end of a thick rope, which trailed off to somewhere in the back of the stage. "Madame Verlaine?" he asked, approaching her.

"Yes?"

"Is your spirit guide still here?"

"She is no longer speaking through me," Madeleine said in a soft monotone that the audience strained to hear. "But I can still sense her presence."

"Will she move some objects for us?"

"She will try, but she needs absolute silence and privacy."

Sandarel turned to the audience. "If we are very quiet, we may be able to induce Mim Ptwa Nim, Madame Verlaine's spirit guide, to show us her presence by physically materializing and moving some objects that we will place near Madame Verlaine. We must place screens around her to insure her privacy. So, to prove that something psychical is indeed occurring, I have asked these gentle-man to come onstage and assist me in tying up Madame Verlaine." He turned to the cluster of gentlemen onstage. "If one of you would please examine this rope to make sure that it is, indeed, what it seems to be: a solid length of number seven rope, of the sort used by mountain climbers."

One of the men looked over the rope carefully, as though he had some idea of what a "number seven" rope should look like, and then four of the men watched while three of the men tied Madame Verlaine securely to the chair, with her hands fastened to the arms. Sandarel supervised the bondage, and the whole audience could hear him urging them to, "Tie her tighter! Right, pull up on that rope! Now wrap it around a couple of times for good measure!"

When the committee was finished tying and roping and loop-ing, it would not have occurred to anyone in the committee, or in the audience, that the knots were cleverly devised so that Madeleine could slip her hands out of the ropes at will. Of such secrets are most miracles made.

Four tall screens were produced, and Madame Verlaine was boxed inside of them, along with an empty cigar box, a small brass bell, a tambourine, a silver bracelet, a brass carriage horn, a corked bottle of wine and four wine glasses, a vase, and a bible; all of which were placed in a semicircle on the floor in front of her. The committee distributed itself around the screens.

For about two minutes nothing happened, and then the manifestations began. First the cigar box came flying over the screen in front, and then a loud honking began from within the screens. Then the honking stopped, and the carriage horn in turn was tossed over the front screen. For a long moment there was nothing further, until all at once the bell rang and rang and the tambourine clashed and appeared atop the screen, apparently held by a ghostly hand, while the bell kept ringing.

This kept up for a while until, with a shocking suddenness, all four screens were blown outward as by a great wind, and everything came to a shattering halt. There, right where she had been, Madame Verlaine still sat, bound to her chair. On her lap was a wooden tray which had not been there before, and on the tray were four glasses of wine. The uncorked bottle was by her feet, but there was no corkscrew in evidence.

The committee untied her, examining the ropes carefully as they did so. Then they knocked and prodded at the arms and back of the chair in which she sat. But the rope was real and the chair was solid; no hidden panels, no trap doors.

"Look," Doctor Sandarel said, pointing to the floor near the chair. The bible that had been placed on the floor now lay open. The silver bracelet lay on the right-hand page. "It is a message," he proclaimed. "Will one of you please pick up the bible and read what is encircled by the band of silver?"

One of the committee picked up the bible and read:

> " 'The words of the wise heard in quiet are better than the shouting of a ruler among fools. Wisdom is better than weapons of war, but one sinner destroys much good.

" 'Dead flies make the perfumer's ointment give off an evil odor; so a little folly outweighs wisdom and honor.' "

Sandarel nodded. "Ecclesiastes," he said. "Perhaps it is a message for someone here. I will not try to interpret it, but perhaps My Lord Bishop has some idea?" He peered out into the audience. "No? Well, so be it. You gentlemen of the committee may return to your seats now, and we thank you for your assistance."

The audience applauded, and the committee left the stage and returned to their seats. Jenny, in her borrowed suit of black, slipped out with the committee and sat at Prince Ariste's table, and no one seemed to notice that the committee had one more member leaving than it had coming.

Sandarel took Madeleine's hand, and together they came forward and bowed to the audience. "Thank you for your attention, ladies and gentlemen," Sandarel said. "We have enjoyed this chance to enlighten you as to some of the mysteries of the human mind. You have been a kind and generous audience and as attentive as we could hope for. We trust that you will take away from this evening's presentation more than you came with. I know that we will. This ends our presentation. May St. Simon smile upon all your endeavors."

They exited together, amid enthusiastic applause. "A very exhilarating experience," Madeleine whispered to Moriarty as they entered the green room. "One could come to enjoy the attention and the applause."

"Bah!" replied Moriarty. "Come, let us get away from here. We still have much to do."

TWENTY-THREE

RESCUE

Twinkle, twinkle, little bat!
How I wonder what you're at!
Up above the world you fly!
Like a teatray in the sky.
　　　　　　　　—LEWIS CARROLL

Sherlock Holmes looked incredulously at Moriarty. "A kite?"

"Just so. A large kite."

It was two in the morning. Madeleine and Jenny Vernet had gone to their well-earned sleep, leaving Moriarty, Holmes, Watson, and the prince and princess sitting around the table in Prince Ariste's railroad car drinking tea and discussing the impending rescue of the Barnetts. Professor Moriarty had a plan. Sherlock Holmes was not amused.

"A man-carrying kite?"

"It's been done before," the professor commented dryly.

"By whom?"

"By me. I have some experience using a kite of a modified Burmese design, constructed for me in London by Prince Tseng Li-chang. In addition to his usual trade of creating Chinese antiquities for the European market, the prince aids me in the construction of astronomical devices. We found that a tethered kite can be quite stable for long periods of time. Usually I loft special dry-plate cameras, or recording manometers and thermometers, but on occasion I have permitted a man to go up."

"It must be quite exciting," Princess Diane commented.

"So I believe," Moriarty said. "As the kites will bear the weight of only a very light person, I have never been able to make the experiment myself."

"Yes, but in the middle of the night?" the prince asked. "Isn't it considerably more dangerous in the dark?"

"Many of my experiments have been conducted in the middle of the night," Moriarty explained. "Most of them are designed to further my astronomical research, although a few have had other purposes. Some things cannot easily be accomplished in daylight."

Holmes gave the table a resounding slap. "Well, I'm damned!" he said. "The Tainsburn and Belaugh Mint robbery—that's how it was done!"

Everyone turned to look at him, and Holmes explained: "it was a year ago February, I believe. I was called in to investigate a robbery at the Tainsburn and Belaugh Mint, a private company that engraves and prints the currency of many small countries that don't possess the facilities for such precise and delicate work themselves. On this night four specially constructed trunks full of Maldavian currency had been prepared for shipping the following morning. Someone—some gang—broke in during the night and made off with all four trunks, taking currency to the value of about two million pounds."

"I remember that, Holmes," Watson said. "It was one of your few failures, I believe."

Holmes glared at Watson silently for a moment, and then went on: "You will also remember, old friend, that the Scotland Yard refused to act on my suggestion. I cannot affirm that the case would have been solved if they had, but as they did not, I take no responsibility for their failure."

Watson wrinkled his brow. "Your suggestion? Oh, yes, I remember. When Inspector Lestrade asked you what you thought of the robbery, you replied: 'I call your attention to the footsteps on the roof.'"

"Indeed." Holmes turned to the others. "You must understand that the building housing the mint is, of necessity, a fortress. Six stories high, and standing alone on its block. All the windows are barred and, at night, securely locked from the inside. The trunks were taken out through a side door which was kept secure by dropping steel bars into slots on the inside. There was no possible way to open it from the outside as it had neither handle nor key. Nonetheless it lay open the next morning and the trunks were gone. The night watchman was found trussed up on the floor of the manager's office. He claimed that he had been struck on the head from behind while he was making his rounds."

"The footsteps on the roof?" Princess Diane asked.

"I discovered the marks of some footsteps in the dust on the roof—marks that must have been made on the day of the robbery as there was a heavy rainfall the night before which would have removed them."

Princess Diane raised an enquiring hand. "Why was there dust on the roof, so soon after a heavy rain?"

"It's London, your highness. There is dust on everything within hours of its being cleaned. Some attribute it to the coal fires burning in every hearth."

"And Scotland Yard failed to act on your information?" Prince Ariste asked.

"Inspector Lestrade arrested the night watchman. He said the footsteps could have been made by anyone. I pointed out to him that they began abruptly in the middle of the roof, as though someone had dropped from the sky, and went straight to the roof door."

"That's right, Holmes," Watson averred. "I remember. Lestrade said that if you wanted to go crawling about on the roof looking for footsteps, that was all right with him, as long as you left him alone to do his job."

Holmes pointed his forefinger at Moriarty. "There was no way anyone could have climbed up to the roof," he said. "I thought of a balloon, remembering that you have a fondness for balloons, but a balloon couldn't be controlled that finely. Besides, a balloon large enough to carry a man would surely have been seen. But a kite! That never occurred to me."

"I remember Lestrade's remarks were particularly pointed when you said that you detected the hand of Professor Moriarty in the crime," Watson added. " 'When has there been a crime in which you didn't see the hand of Professor Moriarty?' he asked you. And perhaps with some justification."

"You and Lestrade do me an injustice, Watson," Holmes said, leaning back in his chair and tucking the interlaced fingers of his hands under his chin. "I don't see the hand of my friend the professor in every crime. Only in those which elude solution and show a degree of cunning way beyond that of the average criminal."

Moriarty chuckled a hard-edged chuckle. "Confess it, Holmes," he said, "whenever you walk down a country lane, you see my minions crouching beneath every bush."

The two men glared at each other. Prince Ariste raised his hand as though inserting a barrier between them. "As pleasant as these reminiscences must be for both of you," he said, "we do have something of rather pressing importance to discuss."

Moriarty nodded and turned away from Holmes. "I have spoken with Herr Heerschmit, your artificer," he told the prince, "and he has constructed the device according to my rough sketch. It is about eighteen feet long and twelve feet across. The body is sailcloth and the frame is, I believe, willow. I use bamboo, but Herr Heerschmit assures me that this is strong enough. He also obtained five hundred meters of half-centimeter line from the railroad supply shed. It will be more than strong enough."

"Are we going to go ahead tonight?" Prince Ariste asked.

"I see no advantage to waiting," Moriarty said,

Princess Diane put down her cup. "May I express a concern?" she asked.

"Of course," Moriarty told her. "What is it?"

"Will not the escape of Jenny Vernet alert those in the castle to our presence?" she asked. "I don't mean *our* presence specifically, since we assume they don't know who we are, but the presence of some force inimical to their goals. Might they not be expecting an attempt to rescue the Barnetts? If so, will even the advantage of approaching the castle from an unfamiliar direction be enough to offset the loss of surprise?"

Watson slapped his knee. "By gad, I hadn't thought of that," he said.

"That is possible," Moriarty admitted, "but I don't believe it's probable. Graf von Linsz cannot be sure how Miss Vernet managed to escape. Since she, apparently, went through two locked doors, he will be more inclined to blame those inside the castle than to look for an outside antagonist. He may well credit the mythical 'Moriarty' whom he seems to regard as his nemesis with being involved somehow, but he will assume that 'Moriarty' has subverted someone in his household."

"Let's hope you're right," Prince Ariste said. "What's the plan?"

"Very simple," Moriarty told him, sketching a triangle with rounded corners on the sheet of paper in front of him. "Here's the castle. This"—he made an X—"is the front, and here"—another X—"is the room in which the Barnetts are being held. It's two floors below the roof. We can't approach from the front because of all the people on the meadow tonight. The kite will be sailed from this side," he pointed, "as there seems to be a prevailing wind from the south."

"It's very gusty," Prince Ariste said. "Will we have any trouble keeping the kite up?"

"My experience is that winds tend to be gusty near the ground, but that at twenty or thirty feet up they are usually fairly steady," Moriarty told him.

"I say," Watson said. "How are you going to get the contraption in the air in the first place?"

"A good question," Moriarty said. "I had thought of pulling it with a steam engine, but the tracks are on the wrong side. Besides, the noise will wake people whom we would prefer to stay asleep."

"Yes?"

"So we'll use a horse. Or rather a man on horseback. We'll tie rags around the horse's hooves to muffle the sound."

"Can a horse do it?"

"Oh, yes; the weight is negligible."

"And then? When we have a man on the roof, then what?"

"Then he drops a length of fishing line to the ground over around on this side, where with any luck no one is watching, and a waiting man attaches a heavy rope that has been knotted every few feet to make it easier to climb, which he pulls up and fastens to— whatever. Then your volunteers climb up to the roof and enter the castle from above, which will be an entirely unexpected, and thus unguarded, direction."

"Will they know what to do?" Ariste asked.

"I shall instruct them beforehand, and accompany them," Moriarty said.

"Ah!" Ariste smiled. "And I shall join you."

"And I," Holmes added. "You and Madame Verlaine rescued my cousin—very quickly and adroitly, let me say. I shall contribute what I can to this effort."

"And I," Watson said. "After all, you might have need of a doctor."

"Gentlemen," Moriarty said, "I thank you all."

"Who is going to ride the kite?"

"The mummer has volunteered. He is even now working out the harness to tie man and craft together. He is, I believe, the only one light enough."

"I'm light enough," Princess Diane said.

Everyone turned to look at her, and she colored under their collective gaze. "I mean, if Mr. Tolliver is unable to go—sprains his ankle or something—I could do it. I'm quite athletic and I'm not afraid of heights. Not overly afraid, anyway."

Prince Ariste leaned over and kissed his wife on the cheek. "My love," he said. He turned to the others. "If my wife wishes to fly, and it becomes necessary, she will do an excellent job of it."

"Then you'd allow her to do this?" Watson asked.

"I won't encourage her," Ariste said, "but I wouldn't dare try to stop her."

"Thank you, my dear," Diane said.

Holmes leaned back in his chair. "Someday sky-carriages will be devised that will carry people through the air great distances in comfort and safety. Held up by balloons and propelled by small, powerful steam engines, they will bring the nations of the world closer together. Several inventors are working on such devices now, in France and Germany and the United States of America, and they show great promise."

Moriarty rose. "I'd better go back to the car where the volunteers sleep and awaken them. They will have an hour to prepare for the assault."

"I'll come with you," Prince Ariste said.

"Very good," Moriarty said. "I want each man armed with a

sock full of sand. It makes a silent and effective club which can render a man unconscious with one blow but should not inflict permanent damage. Two of the sturdiest men should carry axes. Also, in case I'm mistaken and we do have to fight our way out, I want as many of the men to be armed with pistols as can be trusted not to use them unless instructed."

"They are all well trained," Ariste told him. "They will all obey orders."

"Good," Moriarty said.

It was three thirty in the morning when a sleepless guard in Schloss Uhm might have heard the uncanny sound of a horse with muffled hooves trotting through the pitch-black night along the clearing on the west side of the castle. If any of them did, they did not respond.

"He's up!" Watson said enthusiastically, running along behind the horse and feeling the cord rising under his hand.

"Yes, he is." Moriarty took hold of the horse's bridle as the rider reined it to a stop. "Now we tie the line to the spool of rope and start letting it out slowly."

One of the men came up with the spool. While it was being spliced, Moriarty ran over to where Mummer Tolliver was hovering about twenty feet off the ground. The kite could just be made out as a great black triangle against the star field. "How are you doing, Mummer?" he called softly upward, forming his hands into a megaphone.

"Piece of cake!" the mummer called back down from where he was strapped to the giant kite. "Who says it ain't?"

"I'll have you on the roof in no time," Moriarty called. "Make sure the roof is under you before you drop off the kite. Can you see?"

The mummer had been wearing a hood for the hour before his flight to give his eyes the best chance to adjust to the dark. "Well enough," he called down.

"Take care of yourself."

"Don't worry about me!" the mummer called in a hoarse whisper. "Worry about them!" He waved, but the kite started pitching at the motion, so he quickly grabbed the hand-bar and stopped shifting his weight.

The four burly troopers delegated to handle the rope began paying it out, and the mummer rose slowly into the breeze. Moriarty went back and led them to the spot where he had computed the angle of the line, about 30 degrees from the horizontal in this wind, would put the kite right over Schloss Uhm's nearest parapet. "About four hundred feet of line—a hundred and thirty five meters, let's call it—should do it," he told them. "Are you keeping track?"

"Yes, sir," the sergeant in charge assured him. "We're letting it out one hand-span at a time, as best we can." He illustrated this by spreading his arms wide. "That's just the merest bit over a meter. Sometimes it gets away from us for a bit, but I'm making allowances for that."

"Splendid. Watch for the mummer's signal." Mummer had been provided with a small dark lantern: one with a shutter so that no light would come through until he opened it. When he was in position over the roof, he would flash the lantern open briefly and the men on the rope would tie it in place.

Meanwhile an eight-man team had put up a scaling ladder against the outer wall and was gathered around it, waiting for their signal to go over. They would then gather at the spot by the inner wall where the mummer was to drop the line.

The kite was out of sight of the ground almost immediately as it climbed skyward, pulling steadily against the rope. Moriarty used a bit of string with a lead fishing weight on the end and a card on which he had marked off the degrees in a semicircle to check the angle of the rope. Then he closed his eyes and worked the problem in his head. "A few steps back," he told the men. "About six feet— two meters—if you please."

At the end of the line, suspended from the diamond-shaped canvas body of the kite, Mummer Tolliver stared down into the darkness below him and practiced breathing slowly and steadily to slow the pounding of his heart. The mummer was not afraid of heights; not afraid of the machine he was clinging to by three leather straps; certainly not afraid of the possible coming battle with the forces of darkness. He, although he would not have admitted it under torture, was afraid of failing the professor. Moriarty was the one man in all the world who the mummer respected, because the professor was the only man who had ever demanded of the mummer all the quick intelligence and the collection of unexpected abilities he was capable of giving. And the mummer was proud of the fact that he had never failed the professor. Until—he believed—now. Moriarty had sent Tolliver to accompany Benjamin and Cecily Barnett on their European vacation so that he could watch over them and protect them from harm, even though they weren't aware of it, and no particular harm had been expected.

And now look. They were locked up in this Graf von Whosis's hulking stone castle, and Moriarty had to drop whatever important work he was doing just to come and get them out. All because the mummer hadn't paid proper attention to his job. And the professor—bless him—had never even mentioned it or cast a dirty glance in Tolliver's direction. But nonetheless he knew he had let the professor down, and he was determined to make up for it if he had to fight his way to the Barnetts' room all by his little self, and get them out.

He was over the parapet now, and could see down to the roof some ten feet below, although he couldn't make out any details. He unclipped the dark lantern from his belt and wiggled a blip of light to those at the other end of the line. They responded with a couple of jerks that indicated that they were tying the line off to something. Mummer prepared himself, loosing the straps that held him to the kite and dangling now from the bar by his hands. The kite gave a quiet dip, and the mummer let go of the bar, dropping to the roof and falling forward. He didn't go into a full circus roll, since he couldn't see what he might be rolling into, but fell onto his padded knees and forearms. The shock was greater than he had expected, and the mummer lay there for a moment, not sure whether he had been injured or not. The kite, freed of his weight, leapt away into the sky.

Tolliver decided that he had nothing worse than a bruised shoulder, but he stayed where he was for a few moments longer and listened. If there was, by any chance, a lookout on the roof, he would surely come running to find out what the noise had been. But there was no sound of footsteps—indeed, there was no sound of anything at all. Mummer got up, brushed himself off, and took a quick look around the roof, trying to figure out what the dark, lumpy shapes surrounding him were. There was a stovepipe; he had just missed landing on it by a couple of feet, which would have made a horrible racket and might have cut him badly. No use worrying about that: he might just as well have missed the roof entirely or fallen down an air shaft, if the castle had such a thing, in which case he'd be dead. And he wasn't, just a bruised shoulder. Time to get on with his job.

The mummer looked up and found Ursa Major, the constellation of the Great Bear, just where Professor Moriarty had shown him it would be, and he followed the pointer stars with his gaze and found the North Star. So there was North, and the edge of the roof he wanted must, then, be over *there*. He went cautiously to the edge and peered over the parapet. The prince's men should have made it over the outer wall by now, and be there below him. But if they were he couldn't tell, it was too dark. He blinked his lantern briefly and waited—and waited. Nothing. Was he at the wrong edge? No, wait a second, there it was! A quick blink in return right below him.

Tolliver unwrapped the fishing line from around his waist and dropped one end into the blackness below. When he felt two quick tugs, he pulled it back up and took the heavy rope that came up with it. Making a big loop at the end, he fastened it to a heavy iron railing that ran around the inside of the parapet.

The first man was up the rope about six minutes later, and they came up at one or two minute intervals after that until there were a dozen men on the roof.

"Good job, Tolliver!" It was the professor.

"Course it was," the mummer whispered back. "Who says it wasn't?"

"Now let's find the Barnett's room, and get them up here and get out of here."

"Do we have any idea of where the door to the roof is?" the prince asked in a low voice. "I can't see a thing."

"We can use a dark lantern to look around," the professor said. "Just keep it low so it can't be seen from below."

Holmes called, "Here's the door, over here!"

The group gathered around the door and several lights came on as they examined it. A solid wooden door set securely into a stone wall, it seemed to be locked and there was no handle evident from the outside.

"We have two axemen," the prince said. "They should be through the door in a few minutes."

"Wait a second," Moriarty said, moving his lantern slowly around the door frame and peering at the stone. "Aha! Perhaps—" He reached out and pulled at a length of string that seemed to be coming from a small hole in the rock wall.

There was a click, and the door opened about three inches, just enough for someone to get his fingers around the edge and pull it open the rest of the way.

"I have made a study of old doors," Moriarty said.

"Opening them without a key, you mean," Holmes commented.

"Perhaps so. At any rate, I have noticed that many ancient doors, even at guarded strongholds, open like old farmhouse doors: with an inner latch pulled by a string from the outside. When the owner wants to lock the door, he merely pulls in the string."

"And, luckily, sometimes they forget," Watson said.

"Or more likely, not expecting visitors from above, they don't bother," Moriarty said. "Shall we go in?"

"Leave two good men on the roof," Ariste instructed his sergeant. "The rest of you, come along!"

The small room they entered held a capped water faucet, a coiled canvas fire hose, a large wooden box that investigation showed held a military telescope and tripod, and a stairs leading down. "The room we want is two floors down," Moriarty whispered, "and," he pointed, "in that end of the building."

The stairs only went down one flight, terminating in a sort of guard room that was at the moment, thankfully, without guards. They went on, two of Prince Ariste's husky bodyguards taking the lead with Moriarty behind and Holmes at the end of the force marking each turning with a bit of chalk so they could find their way back out without getting lost. The light from one shielded candle now provided their only illumination, as it would draw less attention than a lensed lantern should anyone happen to see it as it passed by.

"Do you suppose we're in the living quarters?" Watson whispered to Moriarty, looking at the row of doors they were passing as they skulked down the corridor.

"If so it's probably the servants'," Moriarty replied. "This is the top floor, where servants go to sleep when they have completed their daily tasks."

A tight little staircase showed up around the next corner, too narrow for two people to pass each other without complex gymnastics. Cautiously, the troop headed downstairs.

"This should be the floor," Moriarty said when they'd gone down and around, twisting twice, to the next landing. "Now the room the Barnetts are in should be that way." He pointed toward the wall across the corridor.

"This corridor seems to go the wrong way," the prince said. "But it's too dark to see the end. Or, for that matter, the other end."

"Perhaps we should send a man down each way while we wait here, and see if either of them turns in the right direction," Holmes suggested.

"Perhaps," Moriarty agreed.

There was a sudden sharp cracking sound from off to the left. The candle bearer blew out the candle, as he had been told to if he heard any unexplained sounds. They stood silent in the dark, listening.

"It may have been the wind," someone suggested softly.

"No," Moriarty whispered. "Quiet!"

The mummer pulled at Moriarty's jacket. "I'll find out," he whispered in the professor's ear when Moriarty bent over. Then he was gone, silently moving down the corridor.

A rustling and thumping noise came from the left, how far away was impossible to tell. Then voices, men's voices and perhaps a woman, distant and muffled, as through thick walls.

"Well?" the prince demanded. "Do we avoid them or attack them?"

"Wait for the mummer," Moriarty told him softly.

A minute later the mummer was back. "It's them," he whispered to the professor. "They're moving the Barnetts to a dungeon in the cellar where they can't be got at. They're doing it in the middle of the night so the spy, whoever he is, won't know about it. That's all I heard."

"Good man," Moriarty said. "How many are there?"

"At least three, maybe more. They was screwing hand shackles onto the Barnetts when I retreated."

"Let's get them!" the prince said, excitement showing in his voice.

One of the prince's bodyguards turned and bowed slightly. "Your Highness will please stay behind us if there's an altercation," he said.

Ariste patted the hulking giant on the back. "Thank you, Ernst, but if there's to be a fight, I'll be in the thick of it."

"Let's go," Moriarty said, "but quietly. No lights! Leave three men here to guard our retreat."

Moriarty in the lead, the group went as rapidly as they could toward the source of the sounds, feeling their way along the wall. After turning a corner and reaching the end of a new corridor, they saw the flicker of light coming from a turn ahead of them. Moriarty, visible now as a shadow in the flickering light, raised his hand and the group stopped.

"All at once," Moriarty whispered. "Use your sandbags. As little noise as possible. Ready?"

They all nodded, which couldn't be seen in the dark, but Moriarty assumed their assent. Of course they were ready.

"Let us go!"

They rounded the corner at a run. Moriarty in front, flanked by the prince's two bodyguards. The others were bunched up behind, as close as the narrow corridor would allow. Ahead of them, at the end of the corridor, perhaps twenty feet away, five of the count's henchmen were trying to bundle Barnett and Cecily into a stairwell leading down into the depths of the castle.

"You are all under arrest!" Moriarty thundered. "Resistance is futile! Unhand those people and surrender!"

The men mouthed expletives unheard in polite company, and one of them made a dash for the stairwell. He was halfway down the flight of stairs when the prince's bodyguard that was nearest to the action reached the stairwell and launched himself off the landing and into the darkness, landing on the fleeing henchman's shoulders. They went down together in a tangle of arms and legs, and it wasn't clear which had ended up on top.

But there was no time to find out. Moriarty and his group had reached the cluster of men around the Barnetts and waded in, swinging their sand-filled hosiery. The villains pulled long truncheons from their belts and held them defensively in front of them, warding off the blows and striking back; except for one who was armed with a military saber, which he brandished wildly in the general direction of Moriarty and his men.

Then someone blew out the lantern.

"Back! Back! Don't let go of them!" someone on the other side yelled. "Back to the room."

"Forward carefully!" Prince Ariste called. "Make sure of whom you're hitting before you strike. But push forward!"

"Mummer!" Moriarty called. "Where are you? Have you still got your dark lantern? Now might be a good time to spread a little light about the area."

"My thought exactly, professor," the mummer called, and a wide spill of light suddenly appeared on the far side of the action, illuminating the villains from behind and throwing them into sharp relief. The mummer had crawled past the villains and was perched on a window ledge set into the far wall.

With the enemy highlighted in Mummer's lantern, they went down swiftly before the onslaught. Moriarty took on the saber slasher, parrying his blade neatly with his cane and jabbing him sharply in the neck. Holmes stepped inside the truncheon range of one of the men and used a precise baritsu move to disarm his opponant and pin him face-down on the floor.

In moments the fight was over, the enemy either unconscious or subdued. Prince Ariste's bodyguard appeared at the top of the stairs, hauling the senseless body of his target and tossed it down on the floor. Dr. Watson checked the breathing of the unconscious men and pronounced them fit. "They will have headaches," he declared, "and it will serve them right." He then went to tend to one of the prince's men who had received a slash in his arm from the wild waving of the saber.

Moriarty went over to the Barnetts and worked at unscrewing their restraints. He dropped the offending ironmongery on the floor and stepped back. "Mr. And Mrs. Barnett, I presume," he said with a little bow and flourish.

"Thank God you came!" Cecily said.

"It took you long enough!" Barnett groused, rubbing his wrists.

TWENTY-FOUR

THE BLOODY HANDPRINT

If once a man indulges himself in murder, very soon he comes to think little of robbing; and from robbing he comes next to drinking and Sabbath-breaking, and from that to incivility and procrastination.

—THOMAS DE QUINCEY

Two Englishmen to see you, sir."

"Really?" Moriarty looked up from his paper-strewn desk. "Who might they be?"

His valet held out the silver tray. "Their cards, sir."

Moriarty took the pasteboards. "Peter Chennery. The young man from the embassy. And—ah! The duke of Albermar." Rising thoughtfully, he took his watch from his waistcoat pocket and clicked it open. It was a little after ten in the morning. "Show them in, Brom."

Seconds later the duke of Albermar burst into the room, with Chennery trotting behind. "I shouldn't be here," the duke said. "I had to see you. What have you discovered? Can you save my son?"

Moriarty raised an eyebrow and glanced at Chennery. "Good afternoon, Your Grace," he said.

"Never mind that!" the duke said. "And never mind Chennery here, he knows all. Or as much as I know. I have not heard from you since you arrived in Vienna. Have you made any progress?"

"Sit down, your grace," Moriarty said, lowering himself into his own seat behind the desk.

"I'll stand," Albermar said. "I can't stay. I must prepare for a major conference that begins Thursday. Day after tomorrow. Diplomatists and heads of state from all over Europe. Damned important affair. Very hush-hush. Premier Joubert of France has arrived by special closed train. The kaiser himself is coming this evening from Germany in complete secrecy; and for the kaiser to do anything in complete secrecy is probably unprecedented. Grand Duke Feodor of Russia has already arrived. He is the personal representative of his brother, the Tsar. All of them, one might say, are slipping into Vienna to attend a most secret conference. I am to represent Her Majesty's government. We are endeavoring to draw up a plan to decide what's to be done with the Ottoman Empire, or what's left of it. The 'Sick Old Man of Europe,' that's what they're calling it. Are we to shore it up or dissect it and divide the spoils of our good deed? That's why I'm in Vienna. But how can I concentrate? I have to know what you've discovered, what you're doing, what the chances are of saving my son!"

"The Sick Old Man of Europe . . . a secret conference . . . fascinating!" Moriarty paused to jot something down on the notepad on his desk, and then turned back to the duke. "Oh, your son's chances are excellent. 'Paul Donzhof' will be out of prison before he comes to trial, one way or another. I have been looking into ways of, ah, whisking him from his lodgings in Heinzhof Prison without official sanction, and have devised three different methods, one of them unique, as far as I know. But I don't think it will come to that. I have also spoken with his attorney, in my guise as Alexandre Sandarel of course, and I believe I can get all the charges against him withdrawn in a very short time. Which is, perhaps, the best method of all."

Albermar dropped into the chair. "All the charges withdrawn?"

Moriarty nodded. "The police of all nations share a reluctance to admit that they are mistaken, but I think that in this instance we can convince them. The case against him is flimsy. It was contrived by people who wanted to see him arrested and charged, but either it did not matter to them whether or not he was actually convicted, or the unexpected murder of the girl frightened them away. Perhaps both. Nonetheless the mill of justice continues to grind, and he will end up inexorably beneath the wheels unless we make an effort to remove him."

"The unexpected murder of the girl, you say? You mean it was an accident?"

"I believe that it was deliberate but unplanned." Moriarty rose. "Later today I'm going over to the apartment your son maintained under the name of Paul Donzhof to inspect it for indications as to what actually took place. My, ah, acquaintance, Sherlock Holmes is joining me, as is Dr. Gross, the head of the Viennese Criminal Investigation Bureau. Holmes feels that the case of Paul Donzhof might well be related to some work he is doing for the Austrian government. Besides, at the moment he is in the uncomfortable position of owing me a favor; a position he intends to rectify as soon as possible. Dr. Gross is joining us because he has heard of the great Sherlock Holmes, and is eager to observe his techniques of criminal investigation. And it seems that the officials have some reservations of their own as to the young man's guilt, so it was easy to convince Dr. Gross to conduct this experiment. Holmes is actually quite good when he's not working from a preconceived fallacy."

"Do you think this will help?"

"It may well. The apartment has, I understand, been kept secure since the murder. In the meantime, Your Grace, let me introduce you to some other people who were victims of the same plot that enmeshed your son."

Moriarty went to the connecting door between his office and the sitting room and pulled it open. "Mr. And Mrs. Benjamin Barnett and Miss Jenny Vernet."

The duke crossed to the door and looked curiously through. The three of them had been sitting around a table drinking coffee. They rose when the door opened.

"The duke of Albermar," Moriarty introduced. "It is his son that we are endeavoring to release from prison."

Barnett bowed. "Your Grace," he said. The two women curtsied.

"Two nights ago Mr. and Mrs. Barnett were prisoners of a man whom we believe to be one of the leaders of the group involved," Moriarty told the duke. "Miss Vernet was under threat of immediate execution from the same group."

"Execution!" the duke looked startled. "What was her crime?"

"I was discovered hiding in a cupboard," Jenny told him. "They took offense."

Chennery, who had been standing meekly alongside the duke, stepped forward. "Excuse me," he said, his face turning slightly red, "but—Madame Verlaine—is she about?"

"Ah, yes," Moriarty said, "Madame Verlaine. At this moment, your Grace, she is visiting your son, the prison officials having the mistaken impression that she is his sister. She should be back shortly."

"Visiting Charles? I should like to speak with her, but I can't stay." He turned to Chennery. "Will you wait for the young lady and bring her to me when she arrives? You know my schedule."

Chennery nodded. "Yes," he said. "Yes, Your Grace. Yes, of course, Your Grace. I'll be delighted to do that."

The duke looked at him keenly for a moment and then turned back to Moriarty. "I have to leave," he said. "Please get word to me through the embassy as soon as you have anything to tell me. Sooner. As soon as you anticipate having anything to tell me. Please."

"Of course," Moriarty agreed.

The duke turned to the others. "Your stories must be fascinating. I must hear them. When I get back from the conference I will be staying at the embassy, probably incognito. You must all come have dinner with me. And my son, whom I trust will be back with me by then." He turned to Moriarty. "You see, I *trust*. I have never felt so helpless at controlling the course of events. I hope my trust is well placed. Well, *auf wiedersehen*, as they say. Until we meet again."

With that, the duke of Albermar clapped his on hat his head and left the room as briskly as he had entered it."

An hour later, his Inverness cloak buttoned and tucked firmly about him against the chill drizzle, Moriarty stood across the street from the building where Paul Donzhof had lived before the Viennese police provided him with the snug, secure housing he now enjoyed. A gray, square, solidly middle-class stone building, it looked incapable of harboring the sort of violence that had occurred there a month before.

An official carriage pulled up to the door as he watched, and

Sherlock Holmes emerged, accompanied by a round-faced man with mutton-chop whiskers and a wide mustache, who was carrying an oversized leather briefcase secured with two straps. Moriarty crossed the street to join them.

"Professor, ah, that is Dr. Sandarel," Holmes greeted him. "Allow me to present Dr. Hanns Gross, the director of criminal prosecutions for the City of Vienna."

"Dr. Gross," Moriarty said.

"Dr. Sandarel." Gross moved his briefcase to his left hand and shook Moriarty's hand.

"A pleasure to meet you, Doctor," Moriarty said. "I've read your book, of course. The *Handbuch für Untersuchungsrichter als System der Kriminalistik*. The *Examining Magistrate's Handbook—A System of Criminalistics*. It's the first intelligent treatment of criminal investigation I've seen."

"Thank you," Gross said. "Mr. Holmes has told me of your intense interest in criminals and their activities."

"I'm sure he has," Moriarty said, glancing at Holmes. "I'm quite certain he has."

"I'm preparing a new edition of the handbook," Gross said. "I've been reading some of the cases of Mr. Holmes, as recorded by his amanuensis, Dr. Watson, and I'm incorporating the techniques learned from those cases in the new edition. Anyone seriously interested in criminalistics would do well to study the cases of Sherlock Holmes."

"I am pleased that you think so," Holmes said.

"It is no less than the truth."

"Watson always dramatizes my cases for their sensational aspects," Holmes commented sadly, "while I would much prefer that the analytical processes involved were treated more fully."

"A clear enough view of the process of ratiocination you employ is suggested in Dr. Watson's stories to make them of great value to the student of crime-solving," Gross told him, shaking his right forefinger in the air for emphasis.

Holmes nodded, accepting the implied compliment as his due. He tapped the side of his nose with his forefinger. "Studying the career of Dr. Sandarel here would also greatly reward the serious student of crime," he said, nodding gravely at Moriarty.

Moriarty gazed at Holmes with an expression that was difficult to read. "You are too kind," he said.

"Really?" Gross beamed. "Always delighted to meet a colleague. What is your specialty, Dr. Sandarel?"

"The mind of the detective as well as that of the criminal," Moriarty told him. "And how persistence can transform itself into obsession, which then clouds the mind."

"Yes, yes," Dr. Gross agreed. "I, myself have described that in my writing. It is necessary to have a clear mind and not form a definite opinion of a case too soon. A preconceived opinion is clung to with tenacity until the investigator is forced to abandon it, by which time the best clues may well be lost—often beyond the possibility of recovery."

"Mr. Holmes himself has said something like that," Moriarty observed, "and I'm sure he tries to live up to it. Don't you, Mr. Holmes?"

A slight smile twitched about Holmes's lips, and then was lost. "Let us go upstairs," he said. "I am anxious to examine this crime scene."

"I, also," Dr. Gross said. "It is fortunate that the area has been kept pristine, as it was on the day of the murder; although I'm afraid the most significant clues may have degraded or even disappeared by now just through the passage of time. It has been almost a month since the crime."

"I fancy I might be able to discern something that the Viennese police overlooked," Holmes said, "despite the wait."

"The examining magistrate would like to bring this case to court," Dr. Gross explained. "But we're not satisfied with the present state of the evidence. So anything you can find pointing to the young man's guilt or, of course, his innocence, would be of value."

They entered the building and paused at the foot of the wide staircase. "Top floor?" Holmes asked.

"Of course," Dr. Gross said. "When have you known an examination that wasn't up the very highest flight of stairs? It's what keeps the police force in such good physical shape."

"Why don't you go over the known facts for us as we go upstairs?" Holmes asked.

"Very well," Dr. Gross agreed. "But I may have to rest at one or more of the landings to catch my breath. I'm not as young as I used to be."

"Few of us are," Moriarty observed.

"Very well." Dr. Gross started upstairs with a determined look on his face. "The Rathaus Bureau of the Vienna Criminal Police was notified at eleven forty-five on the morning of Friday the twentieth of March that an attempt would be made by anarchists on the lives of the duke and duchess of Mecklenburg Strelitz as their coach passed along the Ringstrasse that afternoon. Unfortunately, by the time the guard could be notified, the attempt had already been made."

"So," Moriarty said, "the police were notified before the attack."

"Yes, that is so."

"By whom?"

"Nobody seems to know. The point has been investigated, but as to how the warning was received by the bureau, there is no information. It was stated in the warning that the anarchist in question would be wearing a green greatcoat and a wide brown cap and carrying a Shugard Seuss revolver."

"How specific!" Holmes commented.

"Was it not Hafiz who said, 'a man who has but one greatcoat will be seen wearing it everywhere?' " Moriarty asked innocently.

Dr. Gross paused and looked back at them. "I take your point," he said. "A wise man planning to commit a crime would not inform even his comrades of the color of the coat he will be wearing. But, as we know, criminals are seldom wise, and the inability to plan ahead seems to be one of the hallmarks of the common criminal."

"Just so," Moriarty remarked. "The common criminal. But this is an uncommon crime, and I think therefore we can postulate an uncommon criminal."

Dr. Gross started up the stairs again. "Becoming more and more common, unfortunately," he threw back over his shoulder, "these political assassinations."

"True," Moriarty said. "And there is a common thread that connects them; but it is not the thread of ordinary crime."

"Anarchists!" Dr. Gross declared. "Fast-growing evil weeds that sprout from nowhere."

"Yes, but financed and organized how?"

"Not all insane people are dirt-poor," Dr. Gross said. "Some of the very richest, most high-born spend their lives trying to destroy the very institutions that have placed them where they are. It is, according to our Dr. Freud, a way of striking back at a father who mistreated or ignored them. Dr. Freud says it is all in the unconscious mind. He calls it an 'Oedipus Complex,' after the Greek myth."

"I think in this case it is, perhaps, more than that," Moriarty said. "I believe that these people have a horrible purpose that we have yet to discover."

"This is the landing," Dr. Gross said, putting his briefcase down and pausing to breathe heavily for a few moments. "That," he pointed, "is the door. The door opposite is the apartment of a captain of artillery who has been on maneuvers for the past four months. The cleaning lady who come in once a week to dust says there's no sign that anyone else has been inside."

Gross went over to the Donzhof door. "This lock," he said, hefting the large padlock that had been fastened to the door at shoulder height, "was affixed to the door the day of the crime by the examining officers. The sign-up sheet for the key, which is kept at police headquarters, shows that only three people have had access to the apartment since that day: the chief investigating officer and the examining magistrate both of whom came three days after the crime, and I myself came two days later."

"Good," Holmes said. "Perhaps all indications have not been irretrievably destroyed. But first, the rest of the story."

"Oh, yes." Dr. Gross pulled a large Meerschaum pipe from his jacket pocket and worked at filling it from an oilcloth sack of a rather sweet-smelling tobacco. "Latakia cured in cherry schnapps," he said at their look. "You have perhaps a pipe and you would like to try some? No? Well then: the Rathaus Bureau received a letter sent by messenger shortly after the shooting, it identified Paul Donzhof by name as the assassin, and gave his address. I have the letter here." He unstrapped his briefcase and pulled out a sheet of writing paper sandwiched for safekeeping between two sheets of stiff card stock.

Holmes took it and examined both sides. "You have the envelope?" he asked.

"Unfortunately the so-intelligent sergeant at the desk disposed of the envelope before he realized that someone might like to examine it." Gross put a match to the bowl of his pipe and puffed it into life.

"Brief and to the point," Holmes said, reading the message. "Typewritten on an elderly typewriter with a weak ribbon: 'The man in the green coat who shot at the carriage on the Ringstrasse earlier is Paul Donzhof. He lives in a top floor apartment at No. 62 Reichsratstrasse.' "

Holmes passed the paper on to Moriarty, who passed it back to Dr. Gross. "Notice the continued emphasis on the green coat," Moriarty commented.

"Indeed," Holmes agreed.

Dr. Gross put the letter away in his briefcase. "Someone wanted to be sure we could identify the young man," he said. "Perhaps because he is guilty."

"Or perhaps, as in a conjurer's trick, Donzhof was dangled in front of you to keep you from looking elsewhere," Moriarty suggested.

Dr. Gross looked thoughtful. "Perhaps, I'll grant you that. Perhaps." He opened the padlock and stepped aside so that Holmes could enter first. "I want to watch you work unimpeded," he told Holmes. "I'm sure I have much to learn."

Holmes glanced suspiciously at Dr. Gross, not entirely convinced that such humility from a police official wasn't a subtle form of sarcasm, but then he nodded and whipped out his pocket lens to examine the lock on the door before entering the apartment. "Please stay behind me," he said, "and keep away from the walls. Some of the most suggestive detritus comes from the walls and the area of the floor near the walls at a crime scene."

Holmes crept forward, hunched over like a bloodhound on the scent, sniffing his way down the hall, peering through the pocket lens, his eyes inches from the threadbare carpet before him. With exaggerated care not to actually touch the wall, Dr. Gross lit the wall mantles as he came to them and turned up the gas to give Holmes as much light as possible on this dull day. Moriarty stayed behind and let Holmes go over the rooms. This was Holmes's field and Holmes was, as Moriarty had occasion to know well, expert at it.

"I cannot convince the Austrian police of the importance of examining carefully the walls and floor, especially the floor, and assessing every mark and bit of debris with a powerful glass," Gross said. "They regard it as crawling about in the dust, and are reluctant to spoil the crease in their trousers."

"Provide them with full-length smocks to wear only while they are at the scene of the crime," Moriarty suggested. "This will also prevent them from inadvertently adding anything from their clothing to the scene."

"Also have them take their shoes off," Holmes added from the corner of the bedroom. "Debris tracked in on the shoes of the investigators cannot readily be distinguished from that brought in by the killer or the victim. This, I assume, is where the poor girl fell?" He indicated an area of the floor by the bed. "And then she was pulled up here, onto the quilt?"

"So we believe," Gross said.

Holmes prowled around the room. "You searched the girl's flat?" he asked.

Gross nodded. "No signs that anyone else had been in it. The door was unlocked, indicating that she expected to return momentarily."

"So she ran upstairs expecting to meet her boyfriend, and she met—death," Holmes said, gazing at the bloodstained quilt which was still on the bed.

"Why did she come up here? How did she know anyone was in the apartment?" Moriarty asked.

"If it was Paul Donzhof, she must have been expecting him," Gross offered.

"But he never got home until after five," Moriarty said.

Gross turned to look at him. "Now, how did you know that?" he asked.

Holmes laughed. "I'll bet Dr. Sandarel knows as much about this crime as you do," he told Dr. Gross. "There are crimes that take place in Britain that he knows more about than Scotland Yard. Much more."

"Really?" Dr. Gross inspected Moriarty with new interest. "That is indeed a compliment, coming from Mr. Sherlock Holmes. I didn't realize he felt that highly about you."

Moriarty grimaced. "I think I can fairly say that Mr. Holmes and I have a high respect for each other," he said. "Sometimes I feel that Mr. Holmes's respect for me is entirely too high. He gives me far too much credit."

"As the girl's flat was directly below this one," Dr. Gross suggested, "perhaps she heard footsteps through her ceiling."

"This is a well-made building," Moriarty said. "And there are rugs on the floor. It is doubtful whether she could hear anything short of violent activity."

Holmes was on his hands and knees, peering under the bed. "Come one of you," he said, standing up. "Help me move the bed over."

"You have found something?" Gross asked. "But our men must have looked under the bed."

"It may be nothing," Holmes said. "There is an indication that the bed has been moved. See—here on the rug. Also some fresh wood fragments on the floor here, by the side of the bed. I would like to see why."

The three of them moved the bed aside, carefully stepping around the pool of dried blood on the floor.

"Hah!" Holmes said. "See here!"

Four holes has been gouged in the floor under where the bed had been, looking as though something had been ripped roughly out of the wood. They formed a rectangle of about six by eight inches, each hole about half an inch wide. Chips and splinters of freshly disturbed wood lay near the holes.

"That's what the poor girl must have heard," Holmes said. "There was something—probably a strongbox—fastened to the floor here with four long wood screws. Someone pried it up. It must have made a considerable noise in the flat below."

"How could we have missed that?" Gross asked, the question directed mostly at himself.

"When your man peered under the bed, he wasn't looking for holes in the floor," Holmes said. "The girl must have come upstairs when she heard the noise, expecting to surprise her lover—I assume they were lovers—instead she surprised someone else."

"Can we be sure of that?" Dr. Gross asked.

"The strongbox must have been secured to the floor by screws inside the box. If Donzhof had wanted to remove it, he would surely have opened the box and unscrewed the screws."

"Perhaps he lost the key," Dr. Gross suggested.

"There is your test," Moriarty said. "Search his belongings for a strongbox key. If it isn't among them, ask him where it is. If he can produce it, he is innocent; if he can't, he may be guilty."

"I think we'll need more than that," Gross said.

"Did you find the knife?" Holmes asked.

"Yes," Dr. Gross said, carefully putting his briefcase on a bureau and opening it. "The killer cast it aside. I have it here." He untied a piece of rolled-up brown paper and produced a large, wicked-looking knife from within. "It is a Mittelman-Mohl forged steel knife with a fifteen-centimeter blade; the sort of knife that hunters carry with them. They are quite expensive. The edge has been honed until it's razor-sharp, so be careful."

Holmes picked up the knife by the blade guard and examined it, with Moriarty peering at it by his side. The blade and the leather grip were both coated with blood, except for a blotchy area on the grip where it had been held by the murderer. "It was kept in a sheath," Holmes declared.

"A leather sheath with a metal mouth," Moriarty agreed.

"Such a sheath comes with the knife when it is purchased," Dr. Gross agreed. "How did you know?"

"It's too large and sharp to be carried about in one's pocket, or stuck in the belt without a sheath," Holmes said. "And the small striations on the blade here show where it was slightly scraped by the metal when it was inserted and withdrawn from the sheath."

"Was such a sheath searched for?" Moriarty asked. "Did your officers make a search of all the dustbins in the area, of all the gratings and hedges and such places where something might have been discarded? It's probable that the killer, realizing that an empty sheath would be as incriminating as a bloody knife, if it was found on his person, would have thrown it aside as soon as possible."

"I don't believe such a search was made," Dr. Gross said thoughtfully. "I can see that our assumption that Herr Donzhof was the killer has unduly colored our investigation. It is a great lesson, and I will make note of it. I was not involved with the investigation at that time."

"The killer panicked," Moriarty commented. "He came up here to plant evidence against Donzhof, and the girl was an unexpected complication. If he had planned to kill her, he would have thought to put the sheath in the top drawer of Paul Donzhof's bureau to implicate him in this crime as well as in the assassination." He turned to Dr. Gross. "I assume you did find evidence directly implicating Paul Donzhof in the assassination?"

Dr. Gross nodded and again went to his briefcase. This time he took out an oilcloth-wrapped revolver and carefully unwrapped it. "Aside from the green overcoat which the young man was wearing when we apprehended him," he said, "there is this revolver, found on top of that wardrobe in the corner. It is a Shugard Seuss model sixteen. Several of the onlookers identified the weapon fired by the assassin as a Shugard Seuss, which, as you can see, with its bulbous grip and exaggerated trigger guard, has a very distinctive appearance. It was designed for army officers to carry, the idea being that if one ran out of bullets, one could club the enemy with the grip. It hasn't been issued for the past twenty years, but any old military man, at least in the Austrian Army, can recognize the Shugard Seuss at a glance."

Moriarty nodded. "Which might be exactly why it was chosen. A man possessing a green overcoat and a Shugard Seuss revolver assassinated the duke, so arrest a man possessing a green overcoat and a Shugard Seuss revolver. Where was it found?"

"On the top shelf of that wardrobe," Dr. Gross said, pointing to the massive Renaissance Revival-style rosewood clothes cabinet which loomed over the room from its place facing the foot of the bed. "It was right at the front, not even out of sight."

While Moriarty examined the revolver, Holmes whipped out

his glass and began going over the wardrobe slowly and carefully, from bottom to top. Several times he paused to pick up something with a pair of tweezers and put it in one of the small envelopes he carried with him. After a while he rose and went to the bedroom wall, where he used his glass to examine the bloody markings made by the killer's hand.

For several minutes while Holmes peered closely at the bloody markings on the wall, Moriarty and Dr. Gross stood mute, watching him. The only sound was the patter of rain hitting the window, and the occasional snapping of the hammer of the Shugard Seuss revolver as Moriarty examined it. There was a barely audible sigh of relief from Dr. Gross when Holmes turned and put his lens away. "My preliminary examination is over," Holmes said. "Of course I would like the time to go over this room, and the whole apartment, in greater detail. But for now I have reached a few elementary conclusions based on certain facts I have observed. Further investigation should enhance my findings, but this gives us a direction in which to go."

Dr. Gross moved his eyes from the bloody splotches on the wall to the totally innocuous-looking wardrobe and then to Sherlock Holmes. "Yes?" he asked, "and what are your findings?"

"Your murderer is a short man, no taller than five foot three," Holmes told him, "and an anarchist. He has almost certainly been in trouble with the law before, possibly for burglary or housebreaking, and is a confirmed scoundrel. He has been in this apartment at least once before the murder, probably when Donzhof was away. I believe I can name him now, but that would be speculation, which should not be indulged in during the course of a criminal investigation. At any rate, it is unnecessary, since I can tell you just where to look for him, and we can undoubtedly identify the murderer when he is apprehended."

"A short man who has been in trouble with the law?"

"Certainly short," Holmes said. "I cannot be sure about the trouble with the law, but it's probable."

Gross stared at him. "Then it was not Herr Donzhof who committed this crime?"

"Oh, no," Holmes said. "Paul Donzhof is innocent of the murder of this poor girl."

"You are certain?"

"Yes. Which would seem to indicate that he is also innocent of the assassination of the duke of Mecklenburg Strelitz and the wounding of the duchess, since the real murderer went to so much trouble to make us think Donzhof was guilty."

"That is but an assumption," Dr. Gross said. "Whatever the case with the murder of the girl—and I want you to explain your reasoning on that—Donzhof might still have been the assassin of the duke of Mecklenburg Strelitz."

"Not if this is the weapon you found in the wardrobe," Moriarty interrupted.

Dr. Gross turned. "Excuse me? What's that you say?"

"This cannot be the gun which was used to shoot the duke of Mecklenburg Strelitz," Moriarty said, holding it in his two hands before Dr. Gross like an offering.

"And why not?"

"Because in its present state, it is incapable of firing."

"What?" Dr. Gross grabbed the gun from Moriarty and looked it over suspiciously. "There are four fired cartridge cases in the cylinder," he said.

"Indeed," Moriarty agreed. "Put there to make you think the gun had been fired four times. But look—" he opened the cylinder. "The weapon fires when the hammer strikes a firing pin in the breech, which then strikes the back of the cartridge, setting off the primer."

"Yes," Dr. Gross agreed. "And?"

"Each of the four expended cartridges has a strike mark—an indentation on the back where the firing pin struck it. Do you see?"

"Yes, yes, of course. I'm quite familiar with strike marks. We are experimenting with a high-powered microscope to see whether the strike marks from different weapons differ enough to use for identification. This will be more useful with automatic pistols, of course, since they eject their spent cartridges, which are often found at the scene of the crime."

"Well, let us rotate the cartridges in their holes so the firing pin will strike in a new place." He twisted each of the four cartridges just a bit and closed the revolver.

"You want to compare the new markings with the old?" Dr. Gross asked. "We'd need a microscope to see the differences— if any."

Moriarty handed him the gun. "Fire the weapon two or three times," he said, "and let's take a look."

Dr. Gross took the gun and glared back and forth between Moriarty and Holmes for a moment. He had thought to learn some little investigative tricks from Sherlock Holmes, but had not expected to have the whole case solved while he watched. Particularly not by Holmes merely going over rooms that his investigators had already examined. And now it seemed that this Dr. Sandarel was going to embarrass him further. Then the momentary flash of anger left him and he shrugged. He was here to learn, and it seemed that he was about to learn more than he expected. So be it. He pointed the gun at the ceiling, and clicked the hammer four times. "There," he said, breaking the gun open. "Now let's see if there's any—well I'll be damned!"

Holmes, who had been an interested if silent observer to the proceedings, peered over Gross's shoulder. "Curious," he said.

"You see?" Moriarty said. "There are no new marks at all. The hammer strikes, but the firing pin is broken. This weapon, as I said, is incapable of firing."

Dr. Gross sighed and took the gun back. He wrapped it again and returned it to his briefcase. "I didn't truly expect for our whole case to be turned on its head in the space of a few minutes," he said, "but I suppose I should be grateful. Are we done here?"

"For right now," Holmes replied, "but I would like the chance to go through these rooms more thoroughly."

"Tomorrow," Gross said. "I'll send a criminal police investigator up with you. Perhaps he will learn something. Right now I need a beer. Let us retire to a local establishment, and you can explain to me how you saw all these things that I and my trained investigators missed. Is there anything else?"

"One small thing that perhaps you should arrange as soon as possible," Holmes said. "There will be a meeting of an anarchist society at ten tonight in the box cellar of the Werfel Chocolate Company in the Mariahilf District. Have your men surround the place and arrest everyone inside. One of them is assuredly the murderer of that poor girl, and perhaps one of them is the assassin. I can show you how to identify the murderer, and I believe I know who it will turn out to be. Identifying the assassin will take a bit longer."

"How are we to identify the murderer?"

"You have his bloody hand-print on the wall of the bedroom," Holmes told him. "Compare the print on the wall with the prints of the right hands of all those you pick up, and one of them will match."

"A hand-print? Is this a sure identification?"

Holmes nodded. "Sir Francis Galton the noted expert on heredity, is preparing a book to be called *Finger Prints*, which should be published early next year. In it he estimates the chances of any two sets of finger prints matching to be one in sixty-four million. I was of some small help to him in developing the system of classification that he suggests using."

"Within the next few decades the study of fingerprints is going to be of as much assistance in catching criminals as the police whistle," Moriarty said. "The prints of at least four fingers of the right hand are clear on one of the bloody hand-prints on the wall."

"Has this system been used with success anywhere in the world?" Dr. Gross asked.

"The United States," Holmes told him.

"Also China and Japan," Moriarty added. "But not Europe. The Austrian police have a chance to be the first police force in Europe to apprehend a murderer by his fingerprints."

"So be it!" Dr. Gross said. "We will proceed to the central police station and arrange the raid. The beers, and the rest of the explanation, will have to wait. But the explanation, when it comes, had better be a good one, or my superiors are going to bring back the cat-o'-nine-tails for our special benefit."

"Have no fear," Holmes said.

"You can rely on Mr. Sherlock Holmes," Moriarty said. "At times his insights can be quite uncanny."

TWENTY-FIVE

ENGLAND, FRANCE, GERMANY, AND RUSSIA

When small men make long shadows, the end of the day is near.
—CONFUCIUS

The massive neo-Gothic building on Prince Eugene Platz that housed the British Embassy in Vienna had been built right before Napoleon was chased off the field at Waterloo, when the ties between Great Britain and the Austro-Hungarian Empire had seemed eternal and imperative. It had been constructed for the ages, and little about it had changed in the intervening eight decades.

The second-floor conference room, in which the British ambassador and the duke of Albermar were meeting with Moriarty and his companions, was hung with ancient red velvet drapes trimmed with gold thread, and around its great oak table were massive oak chairs with red plush seats in which the material had worn thin through the years of supporting stern men of importance and weight. The room had the air of a wealthy old dowager who found it difficult to change her habits or her clothing acquired in an earlier age.

As soon as the assemblage had finished assembling, the ambassador had retired to his residence, a few words from the duke of Albermar convincing him that there were some things he didn't want to know. The duke sat at the head of the table, with Professor Moriarty facing him at the foot. Gathered around the sides were

Sherlock Holmes, Dr. Watson, Jenny Vernet, Madeleine Verlaine, and Benjamin and Cecily Barnett.

"I don't have much time," Albermar told Moriarty. "In two hours I must leave for the conference I spoke of. I'm taking you at your word that this is as important as you say it is, but you're going to have to fully convince me if you expect me to convince the others."

"I trust that we'll be able to do that, Your Grace," Moriarty told him.

"Good. But first, please, about my son. You say Charles is going to be released?

Moriarty nodded. "It will take a day or two. The authorities, whether British or Austrian, are always much more eager to incarcerate a man than they are to release him."

"I don't know how to thank you," Albermar began.

Moriarty shook his head. "If any thanks are due, they should go to my friend, Mr. Sherlock Holmes. His reading of the crime scene was magnificent."

"Elementary," Holmes said.

Moriarty turned and regarded his quondam nemesis thoughtfully. "Surely more than that. 'A short anarchist who has been in trouble with the law? Possibly for burglary or housebreaking?' I am surprised you didn't just name him."

Holmes smiled grimly. "Unless I am mistaken," he said, "he is called 'the Ferret.' His real name is Dietrich Loomer. He is supposedly the head of a local anarchist group that calls itself the 'Secret Freedom League,' although I believe that he himself receives orders from someone else."

Moriarty clapped his hands together. "I knew it!" he said. "You see, Holmes, we should team up more often."

"I don't think so," said Holmes.

Moriarty chuckled.

"How do you know this?" Lord Albermar asked.

"A Shugard Seuss revolver was found in Paul Donzhof's apartment. It's the same make and caliber of weapon as the one used in the assassination of the duke of Mecklenburg Strelitz," Holmes explained. "But, as Professor Moriarty established, it was not the actual weapon used in the crime. Therefore it had been placed there to incriminate Donzhof. The gun was found on the top shelf of a wardrobe in the bedroom. When I examined the wardrobe I found a small clot of dirt on the bottom of the door frame, left there by a shoe when someone stood on the door frame to place the revolver on the top shelf. Your son, or anyone else taller than about five foot three, could have placed the Shugard Seuss on the top shelf without standing on the door frame."

"And how did you deduce that this short man was a burglar or housebreaker, and—how did you put it?—a confirmed scoundrel?" Moriarty demanded.

"There were tell-tale scratches on the front door lock, made by a lockpick or similar instrument. As to his having been in the apartment before: he brought a pry bar with him to pry up the strongbox under the bed, so he must have known of its existence."

"And his being a scoundrel? Do you mean something beyond the fact that he was a burglar?"

"Oh, yes," Holmes affirmed. "If there was a plot to implicate Paul Donzhof—let us continue to call him Paul Donzhof—this burglar didn't initiate it. It was a small piece of some larger scheme, and others told him what to do. His masters, whomever they might be, sent him up there to hide the gun, and so implicate Donzhof. They would not have wanted the apartment to look as though it had been burglarized, an act which might make the police less sure of Donzhof's guilt. Therefore the pry bar was his own idea. His greed was stronger than his instructions, and he had no particular qualms against going against the desires of those who were paying him."

"Was it not Horace who remarked that there is no honor among thieves?" Duke Albermar asked rhetorically.

"There you have the advantage of an extensive classical education, Your Grace," Moriarty said. "I never got much beyond Caesar and Quintilian."

The duke fastened his mild blue eyes on Sherlock Holmes. "And from this you were able to further deduce that the man was an anarchist, and could be found at a chocolate factory?"

"We should know shortly whether I was right," Holmes said, pulling out his pocket watch and glancing at it. "The police raid should take place any time now."

"Come, Holmes," Watson said, "how did you know about the chocolate factory?"

"I spent some hours hiding in a crate in the box cellar of the Werfel Chocolate Factory listening to anarchists prate their theories, while you were sitting in the Café Mozart drinking cold espresso," Holmes told his Boswell. "And the clot of dirt that I found in the wardrobe looked like the dirt that makes up the floor of the box cellar—a brownish-gray clay that I have seen nowhere else in Vienna. And when I brought it to my nose—I smelled chocolate!"

"I bow to the master," Moriarty said, inclining his head in Holmes's direction.

"If they catch this weasel, then the hand print on the wall should establish his guilt," Albermar said.

"Ferret," Holmes said. "Yes, it should."

"Fancy everyone's fingerprints being unique," the duke mused. "Who would have thought it?"

"It's a fascinating discovery, and should prove quite useful in criminal identification," Holmes said.

"You have come a long way toward relieving my anxiety," Duke Albermar said, "but the knot in my stomach won't fully dissolve until Charles—my son—is standing beside me. Preferably in the library at Albermar Hall, our ancestral home. I believe the library has always been his favorite room."

"Soon, Your Grace," Moriarty said.

"Now, as to this other business. What is it that has brought you all here?"

"A matter of the utmost moment," Moriarty told him. "It would not be an exaggeration to say that every country in Europe stands at this moment on the brink of disaster."

The duke of Albermar drew away from the table slightly, as though afraid that he might be contaminated by the madness he was hearing. "What's that you say?"

"I have discerned a dangerous pattern in a series of seemingly unrelated events, including your son's misfortune," Moriarty told the duke. "If I am right, we must act now to prevent a deed that might plunge the European continent into that general war that you once told me you feared."

"War? Yes, I do fear that there will be a general war. But not during what's left of this century. Not for at least two or three decades. It's the legacy that I fear our policies are leaving for the twentieth century, and they will not thank us for it."

"It may come sooner," Moriarty told him. "There are forces at work to make that so. I believe I have puzzled out the greatest part of one of their plans, although one essential piece remains hidden. I have brought my comrades along because each of them has discerned a piece of this puzzle, and you might wish to hear it in their own words."

The duke of Albermar's eyes slowly scanned the group assembled around the table. "If you believe such a thing, of course I will listen," he said. "But I am extremely hurried now. Will this not wait for three, or possibly four, days?"

"These days are crucial," Moriarty said. "The tale should not take long to tell."

The duke leaned back in his chair. "Speak on," he said.

"Perhaps we should begin with your son," Moriarty said. "He had the misfortune to pick up a message intended for another." Moriarty looked to his right. "Madame Verlaine?"

"When I visited him in prison he told me of this," Madeleine told the duke. "He obtained a written list, almost by accident, from a man named Hermann Loge, a clerk in the Austrian Foreign Ministry. Your son cleverly hid it in his rooms, and the police who searched didn't find it. The professor and I went to retrieve it."

"Damn!" Sherlock Holmes said, leaping to his feet. "You were in that apartment before!" He pointed an accusing finger at Moriarty. "That whole business at the apartment was a charade!"

"Not a bit of it," Moriarty said. "I disturbed nothing, I merely took the missive I had come for and departed. It was then, while I was removing the police lock and unlocking the door, that I noticed that the door lock had been picked; but I assure you that I left no additional marks on the face."

"And the clot of dirt?"

"It was there."

"And the revolver?"

"It had already been removed by the police."

"True." Holmes sat back down.

"What was on this written list?" Duke Albermar asked.

Moriarty turned to his adjutant. "Madeleine?"

Madeleine raised her eyes to the ceiling. "Seven numbered items:

ONE: TWENTY-FOUR AND TWENTY-FIVE APRIL;
TWO: THAT WEDNESDAY;
THREE: UNKNOWN;
FOUR: ENGLAND, FRANCE, GERMANY, AND RUSSIA;
FIVE: UNKNOWN;
SIX: THIRD AND FOURTH OUT OF SIX;
SEVEN: YES."

The duke's eyes widened. "And on this nonsense lies the fate of Europe?"

"Someone was prepared to pay a thousand kronen for that nonsense," Moriarty told him. "Herr Loge, the man who gave that nonsense to your son by mistake, was subsequently murdered. Your son was framed for an assassination, and his girlfriend was murdered, quite possibly because of that nonsense."

"I see. Go on," the duke of Albermar said.

"This is but one corner of the picture. Before I attempt to discover the meaning hidden in that list, let me show you a few of the other items that came to my attention. The next bit of information came from Jenny Vernet, this charming young lady to my right."

"Your Grace," Jenny Vernet said, doing her best to curtsey without getting out of the chair. "Mycroft Holmes sent me to make friends with Graf Sigfried von Linsz, whom he suspected of being highly placed in the organization Sherlock Holmes had come to Europe to investigate. He said it might represent a grave danger to the established order. Mycroft is Sherlock's brother."

"Yes, I know who he is," Albermar said. "He sent you—a mere slip of a girl—on a dangerous task like that?"

"If you thought that was the best way to get the information you needed, and you believed it was for the good of your country, wouldn't you?" Jenny asked innocently.

Holmes laughed. "Man, woman, boy, girl, it would make no difference to Mycroft. He would instinctively use the best tool for the job. He'd go himself if he wasn't too fat to move about easily. He'd prefer to go himself, as he never really trusts anyone else's intellect to be up to the task."

"And you were held prisoner?" Albermar asked, looking with sympathy at the lovely singer.

"Not at first. I was von Linsz's companion for several weeks, but for some reason he grew suspicious of me. Then, although I remained his companion, I was also his prisoner. He began to have me watched unobtrusively. Then the watching became more deliberate. I was actively discouraged from going anywhere away from him, and when I did there would be someone with me. At first I thought it was jealousy, but it was more than that, although that was certainly an element of it. I worked to convince him that I was not interested in anything he did, no matter how bizarre, unless it involved my career or our relationship; which was one of, let us say, very close friends."

The duke, a man of the world, knew better than to inquire as to the exact relationship implied by "very good friends." He went elsewhere. "What sort of things do you mean? What did he do that was bizarre?"

"Well, he ordered people around as if he owned them. One time he whipped one of his servants for not dressing properly. And yet most of the time he was quite a proper gentleman. Then there are his suspicions: he is always convinced that people are listening in on him and spying on him."

"Ah!" Moriarty said.

"But he's got a whole great mob of people out spying on everybody else. I overheard him giving some of them instructions on one or two occasions. And then, of course, he's the one who kidnaped Mr. and Mrs. Barnett. And he did it with this incredible air of élan—of privilege—as though he had the right to do anything he wanted to anyone he chose at any time. It was truly frightening. That was when I decided that the man was utterly mad. I did my best to act as though I thought that whatever he did was none of my business, that I was a mere woman who did not interest herself in the affairs of men; that I could accept his kidnaping an occasional stranger as of no more importance than his ordering champagne or changing his cravat. And he had no trouble accepting my supposed indifference; he wasn't in the least surprised. That was one thing he never cross-examined me about. Although he was dreadfully concerned with whom I wrote letters to, and what I said."

"Tell His Grace what you learned," Moriarty suggested.

"What I learned. Well, I learned that the graf has this insistent belief that Professor Moriarty is out to get him. He thinks the professor is the head of the British Secret Service, and has agents all over Europe, especially among the criminal classes. He almost killed a man whom he thought was a pickpocket—not because of his pocket picking, but because he assumed him to be an agent of Professor Moriarty."

"I am honored at the attention. What else?"

"I learned that the graf is one of the ringleaders of this weird medieval group. They call themselves the Knights of Wotan, and they're plotting to do something horrible sometime soon. And there's some man that even the rest of them don't know about who's giving von Linsz orders."

"How did you learn this?" the duke asked.

"I hid in the cupboard while they were having their meeting. I heard one of them, I'm not sure whom, say, 'England, France, Germany, and Russia—and of course, Austria. Everything's in place. The capture, the threat, the murders. It will have the desired effect.' Something like that. The real boss came in after the rest of them left and congratulated von Linsz. And they're going to blame Serbia. Some Serbian independence group will be held responsible. I don't know for what, but it is to result in a general war with Russia, Germany, France, and everybody!"

"You see, Your Grace," Moriarty said. " 'England, France, Germany, and Russia.' Item number four on our mysterious list."

"Yes, but what does it mean?"

"You are going to a meeting when you leave here?"

"So?"

"Indulge me, Your Grace."

"When I leave here I'm going to the opera. The Vienna Opera is putting on a special production of Wagner's opera *The Mastersingers of Nuremberg* for the kaiser, although officially they're not supposed to know that because officially His Highness is not here. After that I'm going to a three-day conference, as I told you."

"With whom?"

"The kaiser, Premier Joubert of France, Grand Duke Feodor of Russia, and Archduke Nicholas. We are leaving tonight after the opera on a special train. The conference itself will take place at Mariasberg, Archduke Nicholas's hunting lodge outside of Innsbruck, to insure our privacy and to keep the proceedings as secret as possible."

"I'm afraid the secret's out already, Your Grace. Consider: England, France, Germany, and Russia—yourself, Premier Joubert, the kaiser, and Grand Duke Feodor."

"That list! You think it refers to our meeting?"

"What's today's date?"

"April twenty-fourth. Oh. The first item on the list."

"It would be an unbelievable coincidence if the list referred to anything else."

"They plan to disrupt the meeting? But why?"

"My best guess would be that they plan to murder you all or hold you hostage."

"My god!" Albermar reflected for a second. "That would start a general war. It would indeed. The kaiser—the tsar's brother—the premier of France—the emperor's son! I'll be the least important person there, as popular importance is reckoned, and I'd like to think Her Majesty would hate to lose me, although I'm not sure she'd go to war over my demise."

Benjamin Barnett, who was sunk well back into his chair listening, suddenly sat up. "But why two dates? The twenty-fourth and the twenty-fifth? When does the conference actually start?"

"Tomorrow," the duke told him.

"And it goes on, you said, for three days. What's special about today—the day you go up to the hunting lodge—and tomorrow—the day the conference begins? Why not have mentioned the three days of the conference itself?"

"Because," Moriarty said, slapping his hand on the table, "they're going to strike on the trip *to* the conference." He leaned forward, his eyes fixed on the duke. "The trip is by train, yes? And it will go through the night, yes?"

"Yes. A special train has been arranged. We have a sleeping-car waiting for us at the station. The kaiser's private car will be attached on the way."

"Thus to the literal mind, traveling on both the twenty-fourth and twenty-fifth. And the cars, no doubt, will be the third and fourth cars in a six-car train," Moriarty said. "As item six on the list says."

Sherlock Holmes had jotted down a copy of the list, and now thumped his forefinger down on the notepad. "The man who gave the list," he said, "and got murdered for his troubles—he was responding to a list of questions. Question one: what date is the special train going to the archduke's hunting lodge? Question two—we don't know what that was yet. Question three: whoever made up the list didn't know the answer to that one. Question four: the leaders of what countries have been invited? Question five: again he didn't know the answer. Question six: if you're right, professor, and it is a logical assumption, what will be the position of the sleeping cars on the special train? Question seven: I would give a lot to know what question seven was."

"As would I," Moriarty agreed.

Madeleine Verlaine rose from her seat, her eyes closed. "A letter," she said, "I read a letter. It may help."

"A letter?" the duke asked.

"Yes. I read it in the cloakroom of Schloss Uhm. While the professor and I were doing our act I went through the pockets of the coats for material—mind-reading is much easier if accompanied by letter-reading first."

"What did it say?"

"I can't quite retrieve it."

Moriarty stood. "Madeleine," he said.

"Yes, professor."

"Keep your eyes closed and listen to my voice. You must relax. Sit down in your seat and lean back."

She did so, almost falling back into her chair.

"Now relax all your muscles, starting with your toes and working up. First tense the muscle and then relax it. Toes . . . feet . . . knees . . . thighs . . ." Moriarty slowly worked his way up the body, naming several parts of the body that were usually not mentioned in polite society. But nobody tittered, nobody smiled. All eyes were on Madeleine Verlaine, and they could see her body relax under the gentle pressure of the professor's words.

"Now cast your mind back to that day—to the minute you entered the cloakroom," Moriarty told her. "Where are the coats?"

"To the left, on a long bar along the wall."

"Now you go through the pockets of the first one."

"Yes. It is a man's black overcoat. There is nothing in the pockets save a silver cigarette case. The initials on the case are 'G. D. M.' "

"And the next one?"

"Gray with a black collar. A pearl-gray silk scarf in one pocket. The name Beske on a card case in one pocket. In the outer vest pocket an old crumpled and forgotten death announcement: 'Maximilian Beske. 17 August 1889.' "

"And the next."

"A woman's coat. Dark brown with fur edging. A letter from Bert to Olga Tartosky. Bert is in Australia, but hopes to make something of himself and come back. His English has gotten quite good."

"Enough about Bert. The next one?"

"Black. Stiff. With a belt. Wide lapels. Shoulder tabs. Very military in a Hungarian sort of way. A letter in the inside pocket. This is the letter—this is the letter I spoke of."

"Open it and read it."

For a long moment the room was silent, and then Madeleine intoned: "No salutation. It seems to be in the form of a telegram, although it's written by hand. It has, 'twenty-five April' in the upper right corner. And then, printed in capital letters:

'WE ARE FREE SERBIA **STOP** WE HAVE TAKEN OVER THE SPECIAL TRAIN TO MARIASBERG **STOP** ALL WITHIN ARE OUR CAPTIVES **STOP** WITHDRAW ALL IMPERIAL TROOPS **STOP** TOO LONG HAVE OUR RIGHTS AND LIBERTIES BEEN TRAMPLED **STOP** ALL OF EUROPE MUST RECOGNIZE OUR CAUSE **STOP** WE WILL HOLD THESE WORLD LEADERS HOSTAGE UNTIL

OUR DEMANDS ARE MET **STOP** IF YOU TRY TO RES-
CUE THEM ALL WILL DIE **STOP** WE FACE DEATH
FREELY FOR OUR COUNTRY **STOP** YOU WILL BE
NOTIFIED AS TO WHAT YOU MUST DO **STOP** WE ARE
FREE SERBIA'

"And then, written in longhand below this: 'The bodies of two Serbian nationalists will be found in the wreckage of the train.' "

"And that's all."

"And that's enough!" the duke said.

"There is something else. Something Paul—your son—told me," Madeleine said.

"Yes?"

"At a meeting of the anarchists Paul saw one of the members in a train conductor's uniform. And Paul didn't think he was a train conductor."

"Hah!" Moriarty said.

"What are we to do?" asked the duke of Albermar.

"I have a plan," Moriarty said.

"I thought you might," said Sherlock Holmes.

TWENTY-SIX

THE TRAIN

Die Tat ist alles, nicht der Ruhm.
[The deed is everything, not the glory.]
—JOHANN WOLFGANG VON GOETHE

The special train left Vienna almost two hours late because the kaiser so loved the production of the *Mastersingers of Nuremberg* that he stayed awake almost all the way through it, and insisted on going backstage afterward to congratulate the cast, especially the pretty young blonde who sang the part of Eva. The Kaiser's uncle, Crown Prince Sigismund, finally managed to pull his Imperial Highness away, and the train got underway just a shade before midnight with Kaiser Frederick Wilhelm Viktor Albert of Hohenzollern riding in his own private car and the other leaders occupying four of the five three-room suites that took up three-quarters of the wagons-lit deluxe car; the remaining quarter being reserved for triple-bunking servants. This was one of six such cars which the railroad reserved for those of the royalty or higher nobility who might choose to travel by rail.

In the fifth suite, Moriarty and Holmes were hunched over a table in the front room, making plans for the coming confrontation, while Benjamin Barnett slept in the bed in the adjoining bedroom and Watson slept on a couch in the sitting room.

The duke of Albermar came into the front room to find Holmes staring out the window and Moriarty leaning back in his chair with his eyes closed. "I couldn't sleep," he told them. "What have you determined?"

Moriarty opened his eyes. "While it is possible to assault a moving train," he told the duke, "we believe that it is unlikely. Therefore the train will be attacked when it stops. It is not stopping at any passenger stations along the way, but it must pause five times at coaling stations for the engine to fill up with coal and water."

"I see," said the duke.

"We have tentatively eliminated three of the stops," Holmes said, turning from the window, "the first, second, and fourth. The first and fourth are too close to major towns for any action to be unobserved, and the second is at a location without a telegraph office. We are assuming that the attackers will want to send their threatening telegram as soon as possible."

Albermar nodded. "I see."

Colonel-General Duke von Seligsmann, splendid in his full dress uniform, with his spurs clicking on the wooden floor and his saber clanking at his side, pulled the door to Moriarty's compartment open, braced himself against the swaying and rattling of the train, and came in. "Bah!" he said. "Men were meant to ride horses, not stumble about in trains. With a horse under you, you know where you are, but with the swaying and twisting and bouncing of a train, where in heaven's name are you?" He looked around the room. "Ah, Mr. Holmes, good to see you again. It looks as if you may have gotten the results we require after all."

"Your men are resting, General?" Moriarty asked.

"My men are polishing their boots and belts and sharpening their sabers," Seligsmann told him. "That is how they rest."

"If I am right, it will be some hours before they are needed," Moriarty told the general. "If I am mistaken, they might be needed in a hurry."

Seligsmann nodded. "They are used to doing things in a rush," he said. "Although usually they have horses under them at the time. But they are good men, well trained and orderly. We do, however, have one problem to which I should direct your attention."

"Ah!" Moriarty said.

"And that is?" asked Holmes.

"In coming to this compartment from the car in which my men

are waiting, it was necessary for me to pass through the kaiser's private car."

"Yes," Moriarty agreed. "It would be."

"Don't tell me that Kaiser Wilhelm objects to your passing through his car," Holmes said.

"No, no, it's not that. Rather the opposite. His Imperial Highness Frederick Wilhelm desires to be informed of just when the attack is planned for. He, also, is sharpening his sword. He wishes to lead the charge."

Albermar dropped into the nearest chair. "My . . . goodness," he said. "Considering that His Imperial Highness only has one good arm—his left arm, you know, is withered, a fact he manages to conceal very well—this is probably not a good idea."

"We'll have to think of a way to discourage His Highness," Moriarty said.

"I agree," said Seligsmann. "I will not go down in history as the general in charge of the action in which the kaiser was killed. I would have to fall on my sword as losing generals of old were expected to do. Which, come to think of it, would be preferable to explaining to Franz Joseph how I allowed harm to befall his imperial cousin."

"I think we will be able to dissuade the kaiser from joining in when we explain what will be required of the troops," Moriarty told Seligsmann.

"Good!" the duke said. "Now, just what is the plan you have devised?"

"Very simple," said Moriarty. "Holmes and I have agreed on the two most probable sites for the impending attack. What we must do is put some of your men out before we arrive at each of these locations to go forward of the train and form a screen. And then, when the enemy is located, attack them before they can attack the train."

"Simple enough," Seligsmann agreed. "And I approve for that reason. In my experience the more complex a plan is, the more it is likely to fall apart of its own weaknesses."

"There is a possibility," Holmes contributed, "that the attack will come at one of the places where the train has to slow down to a walking pace because of the uphill grade. It's not probable, because we don't believe that any such location will be within close proximity to a telegraph office. But we should be prepared in case our logic is wrong."

"I will post men between the cars to look out for any danger. I have forty-three men, do you think that will be enough?"

"There is no reason to assume that our opponents will attack in force," Holmes said. "They certainly believe the train to be unguarded, as the conference is supposed to be a great secret."

"When I was apprised of the situation, I tried to get the representatives to stay in Vienna until we could resolve this," Seligsmann said. "But not one of them would agree to remain behind. They all have the utmost faith in my—our—ability to protect them. Bah!"

The duke of Albermar smiled. "But I do have the utmost faith," he said. "I'll return to my compartment now, and pretend to sleep."

As the train bearing the leaders sped west through the night, heading into the Austrian Alps toward Innsbruck, twenty-two determined Knights of Wotan were waiting for it at a coaling stop just outside of the quaint little ski resort of Schladming. They wanted to bring back the glory of a Greater Germany that had never actually existed, but history was not their strong point. Their masters had told them all the truth that they needed to hear.

In a canvas bag by the water tower two members of the organization known as "Free Serbia" also waited. Each of them had been shot, artistically, several times, in various parts of the body. Whatever they might have wanted in their lifetimes, they would never want anything again.

The special train sped on through the moonlit countryside. In the rear car forty-three hussars sharpened their sabers; in the next car the kaiser slept fitfully, dreaming of glory; in the wagons-lit deluxe Moriarty was once again leaning back in his chair with his eyes closed, whether sleeping or contemplating the future it was impossible to tell. Holmes was staring out the window, watching the fir trees rush past and trying to remember something of importance. Something that had been overlooked. Something that had been said by someone in their meeting at the British embassy.

"The conductor's uniform!" Holmes suddenly announced. "Albermar's son saw someone in a conductor's uniform!"

"I have already contemplated that," Moriarty told him, without opening his eyes. "There are four conductors on this train. They do not know each other, as they were pulled from regular service to attend to the needs of their distinguished passengers and oversee the porters and other railroad menials on board, and have never worked together before."

"And," Holmes interrupted, his finger darting about the air for emphasis, "one of them might not be a conductor, but an agent of our adversary."

"Just so," Moriarty agreed.

"We must discover which is the imposter," Holmes declared.

Moriarty turned to him with a slight smile on his face. "How?" he asked.

"Investigate their documents."

"The imposter will have well-forged identity papers. We could not verify which is the forgery in so short a time."

"Have each of them in here and ask him some special railroad questions. Your brother was a station agent in the north of England, I believe, at one time. Surely you can come up with something!"

"Perhaps," Moriarty said.

"If not, toss the four of them off the train," Holmes said, making a tossing gesture. "We can survive without conductors for the next few hours."

"Unnecessarily cruel," Moriarty said. "I have already determined which is the imposter, and I've set the mummer to watching him. If we can discover what he is to do, it might give us some idea of what we are to face."

"You have? How?"

"Dirty fingernails," Moriarty told him.

"Ah!" Holmes nodded. "I must not have seen him. I'm sure I would have noticed. I pay special attention to the nails, and the elbows and knees."

"Even so," Moriarty agreed.

They sat in silence for the next half hour, each immersed in his own thoughts, and then Mummer Tolliver opened the door and slid in. "It's coming!" the mummer announced.

Moriarty opened his eyes. "How's that, Mummer?"

"The conductor what ain't a conductor was sitting in the galley drinking hot chocolate and checking his watch every few minutes—that's a great galley they's got on this train; they can give you four different kinds of coffee, as well as six or seven different kinds of tea and three different hot chocolates. And talk about pastries! Well, they has—"

"Mummer!" Moriarty interrupted. "To the point, please!"

"Sorry. Well, this gent gives one last check to his watch and then he ups and traverses to the rear of the train, all sneaky-like, and starts to undo the coupling between the kaiser's car and the last car, what holds all them troopers."

"What happened?" Moriarty asked.

"I bopped him on the noggin with my little peacemaker," the mummer explained, displaying his sand-filled sock. "And then I tied him up and gave him over to one of the kaiser's chaps."

"Excellent!" Moriarty commended the little man.

"If he'd succeeded, that would have done it," Holmes said. "Our opponents can't be expecting to face more than a dozen guards at most, but they're taking no chances."

"Very commendable on the part of their leader," Moriarty commented. "If I were he, I would have done the same. So—" he pulled out his pocket watch and clicked it open. "It's the watering station at Schladming, which we should reach in another ten minutes, that is to be our battleground. So be it." He closed the watch. "We must alert the troops."

"I took the liberty of doing so before I came up here," the mummer said.

Moriarty smiled and patted the mummer on the shoulder. "Good man." If he noticed at how the little man beamed at the praise, he said nothing.

Colonel-General Duke von Seligsmann pushed the door open and poked his head in the room. "The water tower we are approaching will be on the right side of the train," he announced.

"As we approach, the train will slow and my men will depart on the left side and go around. We should catch them by surprise."

"Unless, of course, they are awaiting us on the far side of the train," Moriarty said. "But I agree that is unlikely."

"If so, the battle will begin a minute or so earlier, that is all," said General Seligsmann, confidently.

Five minutes later the train slowed. For the past hour the train had been puffing its way up a fairly steep grade, but here the tracks were level, perhaps even slightly downhill. As they went around a slight bend the ghostly silhouette of the tower and coaling station came into sight ahead, a clear space in the forest of stunted pine trees they were passing through.

Holmes shook Watson awake. "Come along, old man," he said. "Make sure your revolver is loaded. The game's afoot!"

"Right with you, Holmes," Watson said, sitting up and shrugging on his jacket.

Barnett appeared in the doorway of the bedroom. "Action at last?" he asked.

"Come along," Moriarty told him, " 'He which hath no stomach to this fight, let him depart; his passport shall be made.' "

" 'We few, we happy few,' " Barnett quoted, "could do with a cup of coffee."

"After," Moriarty told him.

"All right. Let's go."

The four men went to the end of the car and unlatched the door on the side away from the coaling station. The water tower was now in clear sight, perhaps half a mile away. Colonel-General Duke von Seligsmann leaned out of the door in the last car, and his men dropped to the ground, one by one, and paced the train at a leisurely trot. As the last one hit the ground, the general came after him, and gradually made his way to the front of the running line.

Moriarty and his three companions lowered themselves from the car and trotted along at the break between the two cars, so they could watch the other side without being conspicuous.

Now the train was wheezing to a stop as it reached the water tower, and the band of Hussars double-timed to the front, ready to round the engine and attack from an unexpected direction, but there was still no sign of activity from within the coaling station. Even if they were somehow wrong about the attackers awaiting them here, there should have been a station attendant about, waving them on and making a note of how much coal they took. The hussars waited, gathered at the side of the engine, just barely out of sight.

The engineer and the fireman swung themselves off the engine to maneuver the water spout in position to fill the water tank.

This was the moment the Knights of Wotan were waiting for. Three men raced out from behind a shed to grapple with the trainmen.

With a shout of "Come on my brave boys," a man in a shining silver helmet and a tunic full of medals charged from the front of the engine, waving his sword high over his head. Behind him raced the platoon of hussars, cheering madly and waving their sabers.

"My god!" said Moriarty, "it's the kaiser!"

"I t-tried convincing hi-him n-not to g-g-go," said a man who had come up behind them in the dark, "b-but he n-never listens t-to m-me."

Moriarty turned to look at the stutterer. In the slight light spilling from the railroad car, he could that the man was, perhaps, in his early sixties, wearing the uniform of a colonel-general in the German Cuirassiers. "Well!" Moriarty said. "Your Highness Prince Sigismund, I believe?"

"Th-that is c-cor-rect," his highness said. "And you?"

"Professor James Moriarty, at your service."

"I s-see. P-perhaps we sh-shall speak later." And, with an abrupt nod, his highness walked stiff-legged away from them into the gloom.

"Professor," Barnett whispered. "That stammer—could the crown prince be the man Jenny Vernet overheard speaking to Graf von Linsz?"

"Perhaps," Moriarty said. "There are many stammerers in the world, and coincidences abound. But it seems likely. Since the kaiser is childless, Sigismund is next in line for the throne should anything happen to his nephew. He may be trying to arrange just that. We shall see."

A sudden volley of pistol shots drew their attention to the impending battle. "That can't be the enemy's main force," Barnett said, looking over the developing situation with a critical eye. "The hussars should have waited until the main force showed."

"General von Seligsmann would have waited," Holmes said. "The kaiser is impetuous."

A group of men emerged from inside the coaling station building and formed a rough line facing the hussars. Several more shots rang out.

"Revolvers only," Moriarty commented. "They were not expecting resistance."

The hussars immediately dropped to their knees and pulled their long-barreled 9-mm Mauser pistols from the stiff leather holsters. At the first irregular volley of shots from the hussars, their opponents broke and ran for the woods.

"They give up rather easily," Holmes said, "I had been expecting a fight."

"Should we give chase?" Watson asked.

"I think not," Moriarty said. "It was too easy. That may be a diversion. I don't believe the game is done here yet." Unsheathing the blade from inside his sword-cane, he crossed the tracks and stalked forward the coaling station building, Holmes, Watson, and Barnett following. A wave of hussars passed around them, in hot pursuit of the fleeing Wotans.

Moriarty reached the building ahead of his companions and tried the door. It was locked. He shattered the lock with one swift kick and darted inside, Holmes and Barnett following. The room was dark, with only the slightest spill of moonlight coming through the long, barred window that faced the railroad tracks. Two men were leaning against the window, motionless in the dark. Moriarty grabbed for one of them, feeling a rigid arm encased in a stiff leather jacket under his hand. It took him a second to realize that the man was dead, and had been so for some time.

A man appeared in an inner doorway, just a shadow in the darkness. He fired two shots at the intruders, without effect, and ran for a rear entrance. Holmes was on him in an instant, using a baritsu move to relieve the man of his weapon and another to pin him to the floor.

Moriarty followed a strange whirring sound through the inner doorway. The narrow inner room ran the length of the building, ending at an oversized window in the far wall. Moonlight flooded the far end of the room, revealing a man kneeling on the floor working over a small square box in front of him. When he saw Moriarty, he swore and grabbed for a pistol on the floor next to him. Moriarty threw his blade at the man with long-practiced skill, and dove forward. The man screamed and cursed, and then Moriarty was on him, his momentum throwing the man to the ground.

The man fought with an insane intensity, but Moriarty was almost as skilled at baritsu as Sherlock Holmes, and in a brief time he had him pinned to the floor.

Barnett was a few seconds behind Moriarty, and he tied the man's hands behind his back with wire from a roll found conveniently by the man's feet.

"Well," Barnett said, rolling the man over, "if it isn't Graf von Linsz."

The count squinted up. "Herr Barnett!" he exclaimed. "Then," he said, looking at his other captor, "you are—"

"Professor James Moriarty, at your service," Moriarty answered.

"Goddamn!" the count cried, "you must be the very devil!"

"I wouldn't speak of devils, if I were you," Moriarty said, looking over the device von Linsz had been working with when he was interrupted. "That's an electric dynamite igniter. You weren't attempting to capture the train; you were going to blow it up!"

Barnett squatted down and examined the apparatus. "It's all hooked up," he said, "and the handle's been pushed. Why didn't it go off?"

"Perhaps a general war in Europe was not meant to start quite yet," Moriarty said. "Perhaps there is some sort of higher force that watches over we foolish mortals."

Watson came through the door, brushing himself off. "Holmes seems to have everything in hand out there," he said. "Sorry I'm late. I stumbled over some wires outside and got all tangled up. Had to break them to get my foot loose, and it took a few moments. Hope you'll forgive me."

"Forgive you!" Moriarty clapped Watson on the back. "Why man, you've just saved the lives of everyone aboard the train. You may have just prevented a general war!"

"No need to be humorous about it," Watson said. "I said I was sorry."

TWENTY-SEVEN

OF CABBAGES AND KINGS

We can easily forgive a child who is afraid of the dark;
the real tragedy of life is when men are afraid of the light.
—PLATO

It was Saturday evening and the British Embassy in Vienna was giving a reception for His Grace Peter George Albon Summerdane, the seventh duke of Albermar, Her Britannic Majesty's secretary of state for foreign affairs, who, the guests were informed, just happened to be passing through Vienna on private business; and His Grace's younger son, Charles Dupresque Murray Bredlon Summerdane, who was returning to public life, or at least public view, after a long seclusion.

In a small side room off the reception room, His Grace the duke had gathered a small group of people who, in the past few days, had become his special friends.

"A few words," he said, standing before the group. When they had all turned to look at him, he raised his glass. "A toast," he said. "To all of you who have helped save two of the things most precious to me in all the world; my son Charles, and this fragile amity between nations that is preventing—or at least delaying—a war that will be as horrible as any the world has yet seen."

They drank the toast in silence, as any reply seemed too artificial or too trite.

"I will not go on about how gratified I feel to have my son back, as I would not embarrass him," the duke continued. "But let me say that anything any of you ever need—anything at all—you have but to come to me, and if it is in my power, you shall have it."

Holmes turned to Moriarty and murmured, "Well, Moriarty, how does it feel to have been of some service to your country?"

"It has not been without its points of interest," Moriarty replied, "and the duke's remuneration will go a long way toward paying for some equipment I need for my laboratory and observatory on the Great Moor."

"Jenny identified His Highness the Crown Prince Sigismund as the man she overheard that night," Holmes said. "We told von Seligsmann and he's pondering what to do about it. He doesn't think telling the kaiser directly is wise, but perhaps one of the kaiser's aides—"

"I'm sure the Prussian bureaucracy will manage to render him harmless," Moriarty said. "Nothing enfeebles a man quite as effectively as being caught in the roils of a vast bureaucracy."

Charles Summerdane took the hand of Madeleine Verlaine as though undecided whether he should shake it or kiss it. Madeleine solved the problem by shaking his hand firmly. "It has been a pleasure being your sister, 'Paul,' " she said. "I never had a brother of my own before. Come to think of it, if I had such, he probably would have ended up in jail, what with this and that."

"I understand that I have to thank Professor Moriarty for saving my life," Charles said, "but I thank you for saving my sanity. Were it not for your occasional visits, life in that dank little cell would have been even more intolerable than it was."

Madeleine ran her hand across his chin. "You look quite different without your beard and mustache," she said. "I could hardly recognize you."

"A good thing," Charles said. "If any of my old compatriots, or any of the Austrian police, recognize Paul Donzhof in the son of the British foreign secretary, words would be exchanged."

"I can see that," she said.

Charles squeezed her hand. "Madeleine Verlaine," he said, "I hereby appoint you my honorary sister, from this moment forth, in good weather and in bad, my house shall be your house."

"Thank you, sir," she said, curtseying to him. "I'll remember."

"I mean it," he told her.

"So do I," she said.

Sherlock Holmes walked over to where Watson was sitting by the window, watching the four-wheelers pass by in the street below. "Come, Watson, old man," he said. "It's time we started back to London."

"I agree," Watson said. "Perhaps there'll be some fascinating crime for you to work on."

"And for you to write up, eh Watson? Well, perhaps. And if not, there's always . . ."

Across the room, Moriarty walked over to where the Barnetts were standing. "I hope you're recovering from your ordeal," he said to Cecily.

"You know," she said, "I believe I've quite recovered. Unhappiness recedes into the past when it is replaced by joy, and I've been quite joyful for the past week, reveling in all those thing that I once took for granted, like walking down the street, and doors without locks."

"I feel responsible for what happened to you," Moriarty told them. "I don't know how to make it up to you."

"Being your friend is certainly what got us in the clutches of that madman in the first place," Benjamin said, "but very few people could have gotten us out of that castle so neatly, or would have gone to so much effort. A man-carrying kite! Who would have imagined such a thing?"

"Where are you going from here?" Moriarty asked.

"Prince Ariste and his wife have asked us to spend a few weeks with them," Cecily said. "Playing bridge and shopping."

"Ah!" Moriarty said. "Give them my best."

"We shall," Cecily said. "Tell me, what will happen to that vile creature—Graf von Linsz?"

"He seems to have lost his mind," Moriarty told her. "He sees henchmen of his mythical Professor Moriarty everywhere, and is cowering in a corner of his cell afraid to let anyone touch him and refusing to eat. He may be faking, but it is a debatable question as to whether a lifetime in a hospital for the criminally insane is better than a lifetime in an Austrian prison."

"Poor man," Cecily said.

"Poor man!" Benjamin looked shocked. "After what he did to us?"

"Poor man," Cecily repeated. "What a wonderful life he could have lived, with his money and position, if he didn't set out to— what did he set out to do?"

"Overthrow the existing order," Moriarty suggested.

"Just so. And whatever for?"

"There are many injustices in the world," said the Duke of Albermar, who had come up behind them. "The poor are scrabbling for livelihood, for life itself, while the rich arrogantly indulge themselves in unseemly displays of wealth. But I'm afraid that von Linsz and the others like him are not trying to improve the lot of anyone but themselves; they wish to replace the existing world order with one to their liking—one with them at the top."

"Well," Barnett said, "maybe we've slowed them down."

"We have cut off one tentacle of the beast," the duke said, "but the creature still lives, and it will grow another and another—it will not be stilled until governments cease trying to establish their legitimacy by stirring up ancient hatreds and false rivalries, and join in a commonwealth of nations."

" 'Till the war-drum throbb'd no longer, and the battle-flags were furl'd / In the Parliament of man, the Federation of the world.' " recited Cecily.

Moriarty nodded. "Tennyson."

"That will not happen in our lifetimes," Benjamin said.

"Nor our sons, nor their sons," said the duke, "but it must happen if we are to survive without blasting ourselves back to savagery or oblivion. For the weapons are getting more powerful and the wars are getting more absolute."

"Tennyson goes on: 'Yet I doubt not thro' the ages one increasing purpose runs, / And the thoughts of men are widen'd with the process of the suns.' "

"It's always good to end on a hopeful note," the duke said. He looked at Moriarty. "Where do you go from here?" he asked.

"Norway, I think," said Moriarty. "There's a man in Trondheim who has published some interesting work on the corona of the sun, and I'd like to speak with him. After that, there are some interesting ruins in Algiers that I'd like to take a look at."

"Godspeed," the duke said. "You'll find a sizable check deposited to your account in London when you get back."

"Always welcome," said Professor James Moriarty.